About the Author

Jason J. Joyce is a software security program manager and aspiring American author. He spends most of his time with his wife and two daughters at his home near Phoenix, Arizona. He enjoys camping, hiking, golfing, fishing, and pretty much all things involving water.

Tranquility Base

Jason J. Joyce

Tranquility Base

Olympia Publishers
London

www.olympiapublishers.com
OLYMPIA PAPERBACK EDITION

A CIP catalogue record for this title is
available from the British Library.

ISBN:978-1-80439-149-5

This is a work of fiction.
Names, characters, places and incidents originate from the writer's
imagination. Any resemblance to actual persons, living or dead, is
purely coincidental.

First Published in 2023

Olympia Publishers
Tallis House
2 Tallis Street
London
EC4Y 0AB

Printed in Great Britain

Dedication and Acknowledgement

I dedicate this book to my daughters, Jacqueline and Charlotte. I love you both very much and want only that you live a life full of wonder, hope, health, and happiness.

To my beautiful wife, Tamara, who is always at my side, my best friend, confidante, co-conspirator, and a wonderful mother, I want to say thanks for the push. One cold October morning, she simply said to me, "You should write a book." And so I did, and here it is. Tamara has always been a huge supporter, and she endured countless discussions on plot points, character names, and so much more, and really helped make this vision a reality. She has truly been there for better or worse; helps me celebrate the best and lovingly gets me through the times when I am at my worst. Tamara, I love you more than words can ever express.

I would also like to thank my mom, Judy Joyce, who, of course, was the first to read Tranquility Base. She loved it and thinks you all should buy at least two copies, but maybe she is a little biased. She was a great first reader and helped me think through some of the finer plot points. I want also to thank my good friend, Chris Lodwig, for all his support as I went through this process. Chris and I have worked together for years, and I was inspired by his own journey as an aspiring author when I set out to write this book. If you're in for another great read, you should check out his book, *Systemic*. I would also like to thank my mother-in-law, Anna Evans. Her own adventures as a new writer helped shape how I approached this. Thanks to my colleague and friend, Balbir Singh, who provided some good suggestions about introducing characters earlier on. To my dear friend, the professor Dr. Adam Jabbur, whose meticulous editing and insightful feedback make this book all the more readable, thank you, Adam. I want to thank my twin brother, Dr. Justin A. Joyce, for his help and wisdom. Justin is definitely the scholar and author in the family, and it was great to be able to chat through some of the logistics of publishing with him. To my longtime buddy, Randall Myers, I want to say thanks for being a great beta reader and for all the comments. Thank you to all the great people at Olympia Publishing for taking a chance on me and this book. Marty Salinas, a family friend and author, also helped with feedback on an early draft, and for that, I want to thank him. I also want to extend my appreciation to the songwriter, Frank Turner, for allowing me to include an excerpt from his lyrics in the book. I know that the themes and emotions explored in his songs are universal and have touched the hearts of many people, including mine. And a special thanks to Chris Cohen, Courtney Cohen, Ryan Kivett, and Katie Kivett for all the fun we had brainstorming character names. It is with the support of such great people that I was able to make this dream come true.

In addition, I want to thank you, dear reader; for whatever reason, you chose to take this journey with me, and for that, I am eternally grateful.

Finally, I would like to take a page from a pioneer in Computer Science, Dr. Donald Knuth. If you notice any issues, character, or plot flaws or have any questions, please do reach out. I would so much like to engage with my audience.

JJJAuthor@Outlook.com

Chapter 1

DZ: 23N 08035344: Population 1.43M

He heard the drones calculating their attack outside the bedroom door. Their hovering propellers gave them away. Just as sure as he knew who he would marry, what his job would be, and that their baby was coming today, Kitteridge knew that the Collective was coming. He just wouldn't know when they would arrive until it was too late.

Neither of them had slept in weeks. They had been preparing for the Interval, but it had become real weeks ago, when Kitteridge heard about the roundup at the community center. Marianna and Kitteridge had sworn they wouldn't go out like that. They were destined for a seat together on the trip; they would go as a couple, or take the Romeo and Juliet exit. Constant thoughts of how close Tranquility Base was remained a source of hope ever-present but elusive. Everyone's the hero of their own story; they were so sure they would all make the trip. If their baby could survive the Interval. But for most of the 1.43 million babies tonight, there would be no Interval, only death.

The buzz became deafening as the drones used their propellers to cut a hole in the door. They make quick work of it, seconds really, and then they enter the room. Light-sword under his pillow, Kitteridge silently slips out of bed under the cover of darkness. A quick sling over the shoulder and he bounds for the door with his ROPU safe at his side heading straight toward drones 64 and 63.

Sensing heat and movement, 64 fakes left, and drone 63 swoops in for the kill. It isn't programmed to kill men; they are tech support agents, after all. But if they get in the way tonight, they will be agents no more. Drone 63 latches onto Kitteridge's head, and its dilithium-powered laser saw begins slashing at his face. The long-spiked tail is released in a flash as it pokes and tries to puncture his ROPU. Wriggling and writhing around, the drone tries to take care of this unwelcome guest. He will be counted as collateral damage, but that was considered acceptable in a roundup mission. Despite the coordinated juke, Kitteridge is ready for the attack and manages to grab the drone around his head and hold it away. Unsuccessful at dispatching this unwanted attention, 63 rotates its saw blades and begins to press them up against Kitteridge's cheek. The air wooshes around him as the blades nick the stubble on his jaw line.

In one quick and efficient motion he brings the light-sword up between his eyes to fend off the attack. The blade goes astray and hits the drone's laser-saw right in the middle. An explosion of lights and sparks shoot off from the collision of laser blades. Without knowing it, or without knowing how he did it, Kitteridge introduced light-dancing tonight at DZ: 23N. Drone 63 was hit with the light show and immediately began a show of its own display. It hovers briefly and then slowly descends in a flashing burst inside its metallic body. As the drone hits the house floor, its signature airlock releases, and the cargo hold opens. Kitteridge didn't know exactly what happened but knew that it was special and something he needed to know more about. Seeing the precious crystals inside the now-opened cargo hold, and how much it means to his own survival, Kitteridge quickly bends down and begins stuffing the crystals in a messenger bag.

In all the commotion to dispatch the drone, he had forgotten all about his wife and the unborn baby he had sworn to protect. He had left Marianna in bed! He wheeled around to see drone 64 swoop in for the kill.

*

WHOOSH! The buzz of 1,024 compact drones from the Collective swoop down in perfect binary formation. The designated drop-off day has come, and the drones arrive right on schedule. However, this drop-off would be unlike any other. No one was ever sure what happened or why the cable didn't take, but, as a result, scores would die over the next millions of seconds. It couldn't have been sabotage? Normally, it would be fourteen years before the slaves on this remote planet would be put to their ultimate test. Cargo rockets regularly made the long journey and unloaded the precious cache without incident. These ventilators were designed to protect the people from dilithium crystal poisoning, but only for fourteen years. The Interval would then decide your fate and determine your eligibility for a trip to Tranquility Base. It is this hope that keeps the population under control.

ZIPP. The latching cables lower out of the crate on all four sides and dangle above the Platform below. The air from the drones' circular blades ensures the containers stay aligned for docking as it lowers down. ZOOM! The drones break formation in a flash and create a new hollow cube pattern that surrounds the container as it continues its gradual, but precise, descent. There is no wind on this planet any more to interfere with its trajectory. Gravity seems to be the only universal source of power here. That and the Puff. Four equal size swarms of 256 little metallic bodies make a square around the storage box. Lights go on in unison with the slightest CLICK as the drones in front all turn on their headlamps. TICK TACK TICK the drones land, scramble up and surround the container, their tiny legs clicking along the metal sides.

*

The only thing surer than drones going about their work was the human need for smell and the desire it drove within them. The relief from their constant need was contained within the dilithium crystals all around them. No one knows when and why dilithium crystals started growing. Some believe they are a long-dormant resource. Some believe it is an ancient precious material from the Earth, to be mined and harvested. Something that grows quietly away in the depths of the Amazon rain forest. It was quickly discovered across the galaxy, as if it had bloomed overnight. The leading experts in the scientific community believe, however, that dilithium crystal growth is a result of the COVID wave of pandemics that ravaged the planet Earth during the first half of twenty-first century. It killed billions and disabled most of the population left behind. People took to the stars and left Earth to explore the galaxy and find a place to get away from COVID. But Earth was not enough to satisfy the killer. The sneaky virus even managed to mutate and survive the harsh conditions of outer space. Galactic domination appeared to be its goal; it mutated and expanded again and again. Planets across the charted system fell victim to wave after wave of COVID mutations. Those who somehow miraculously survived passed on all inherited immunities to the various strains over time as immune parents bred. COVID was no longer the universal killer, and only one side effect remained. Everyone, no matter where they were in this galaxy, lived out their days in a constant quest for smell.

The brain could not sever its evolutionary need for smell. While the sense was originally necessary for survival, nowadays there was no risk of consuming rotten food. The always available Life[x] tubes were good for decades, but the quest for smell consumed the people's thoughts. The DNA sequence had been set too deep. Without smell, people couldn't enjoy their food because it became dry and sandpapery in their mouths as they could not taste without smell. But with Puff, even the regulated rations of Life[x] seemed like an entire seven-course feast. The feeling was intense and all-consuming even. However, it didn't last long, just a briefly fleeting time. It was enough to create an addiction and make you a Puffer. The Puff heads had long ago decided they did not care about the side effects.

It was an accidental chemistry experiment that discovered how to make Puff and restore one's sense of smell. Dissolve dilithium crystal by boiling it in vinegar until it releases an odorless steam. When inhaled, the vapor temporarily restored one's ability to smell and Puff was born! The effect didn't last long, maybe a few hours, even just minutes, or a few precious seconds for a lifetime user, one who had developed an immunity from overuse. But the euphoria and memory of taste and smell kept the population in constant hunger. Even those who could hold out for the agonizing fourteen years fought back every day to keep the wolves away. The yearning for smells was built into their DNA.

The Waster Kings ruthlessly controlled the manufacturing and distribution of Puff. Making it was dangerous business and best left to the experts. Done too carelessly and it could result in accidents leading to death. Hallucinations, visions of grandeur, and self-mutilation were common side effects. You knew you had a bad Puff if the itching started, and makers were constantly itching just from the exposure to the vapors on their skin. Makers wore head-to-toe white linen cloths and covered their bodies in talcum powder to deal with the itching. The makers guild would gather at large Greek-style bathhouses and soak in Epsom salts as they formulated new and unique Puffs. But the sores and open wounds, and the constant scratching, made it hard to hide your role as a maker for the Waster Kings. Making Puff had to be a mobile business, too; units were now turnkey operations that were constantly on the move to avoid detection. If you made it too often or in too much quantity, the Collective would notice something was off. The Waster Kings not only mastered the science of Puff making but also the dark art forms of extortion, prostitution, robbery, extortion, and enslavement. They held the population of this small planet in their grips. Capone could only have dreamed of such loyalty and submission.

*

CRACKLE fills the air as dilithium crystal powered laser-saws begin to slice the container lock. SNAP the lock gives way just as THUD the container settles down into place. SWOOSH. The airlocks on the container open and another 1.43 million respirators begin their journey across the planetary zones. A new story unfolds with the voyage of this container and its lifesaving cargo.

BOOM! The container destined for DZ: 23N hits the ground and starts to slide toward the edge; the latching cables haven't attached the crate to the Platform. The crate is immediately encased in the dust surrounding the floor and appears to melt into the Platform as it disappears into the dust. The lifesaving respirators carefully packed inside will not be delivered to DZ: 23N, and the collateral damage must now be dealt with. The drones quickly set forth on their new objective. They are now predators of the Collective seeking to eliminate the unborn babies of DZ: 23N. TICK TACK TICK they make their way off the Platform.

A silent alarm sounded forth as the container hit the Platform. 512 drones split off and begin their new mission to collect and process the scattered respirators. That's okay. Better they go back to The Collective than be picked up by the Waster Kings and their content made into Puff. Only the Collective had mastered the refinery of dilithium into power cells. The Waster Kings knew only one thing, and that is how to make dilithium into Puff. Well, that and the Waster Kings knew all too well how to use fear and careful management of supply to control a population. They didn't have to do anything to encourage demand; the need for smell was as natural as anything.

The remaining 512 drones unlock all eight propellers, and the sound cloud dissipates in a rush of air as they head off to DZ: 23N. The drones will track down and eliminate the children who will be born without ventilators and unprotected from the side effects of the thick cloud of lung-choking smog that permeates the air. This entire planet has been locked in under a giant and smothering blanket of fog. The thick cloud-like stuff hung in the air and remains the only visible thing above the frozen Platform. The drones will be successful, and the prey will be found. The Collective knows that these fragile humans will die without a ROPU respirator. Having all been scattered, lost, or recycled, there were no respirators to give them. Better to kill these fragile babes now and put them out of their future misery. Even if they survive their Interval, they would be relegated to a life of looting and vandalism as a member of the Waster Kings' gangs. "Save them from a life as a Puff head" is how the algorithm was coded. And because these drones were just early enough, they could make quick work of the job. The Collective secured a constant efficiency in all things.

*

By this time in history, the Platform had covered and encompassed everything on this planet. There was no ground, just sky and Platform. The landscape compressed from years of decay and slow decline as the atmosphere pressed in and choked the planet to death, leveling everything like a giant earthmover crushing mountains and filling in valleys. It was a flat and endless plane. It is a barren wasteland populated by The Collective and its enslaved tech support staff and the discarded Puff heads.

The planet's surface is the Platform. It is an endless and continuous hexagon-like pattern with large 150-meter sections connected by the vast dust clouds below. A collection of these made a honeycomb-like foundation for settlements. Gaps between the shapes were filled with a rippling and swirling dust cloud of dilithium crystals. One misstep and it was clear these gaps were deadly. Nothing ever came back if it fell over the Platform.

There are no more trees, no hills, and no valleys here. The rivers, oceans, and lakes have all gone dry, parched from the dilithium crystals. The sky stretches out flat and cold as far as the eye can see. It is dark as night with no stars to pierce through the smog. The sun is gone, and none of the huge planet's sixteen moons can be seen. There is no wind, no water, no weather, and no tides. The sterile Platform appeared dead to the naked eye but teemed with the power potential stored in the dilithium crystals encasing it. The Platform had become one giant crystal. It is cold and almost frozen with a slippery surface that must be traversed carefully and with intent. Drones have no issue navigating the surface because their magnetic levitation booster allows them to hover a few meters above it, a trick the human population quickly adopted, and slide racing became a thing.

How high the Platform really was remained an elusive question. No one spent much time pondering it, though. The Platform just was. It was rooted with deep structures into solid ground somewhere, somehow, or so everyone said. Built over time, it separated the planet like a heavily cinched belt around a rotund waist. It isn't clear if the surface rose or if the hills and mountains were ground down. What really made the Platform special and useful to the Collective was its interconnectedness that kept the continuous communication loop going all the time. The entire Collective knew every movement across the entire Platform and the moment it happened. The Collective regularly sends its sweeper drones to perform their ultimate recycling project. A mission that never ends.

Drones of the Collective are so omnipresent and so quick to show up on scene that many believe the Platform is simply made up of drones. Perhaps they all work as a group to hold the structure together and in place. Perfect union of connected electronics all beeping and blooping back and forth at each other. There are those who say that the Platform isn't more than five miles across but that the drones keep moving it around to the different drop zones scattered across the planet. No one hazards a guess as to how they move it, how often, or why. It doesn't matter.

Looking up from your feet and you can't even see your boots really. The surface was lousy with dilithium dust. It clung to everything. Big mounds making small little hills scattered across the Platform as the base. Moving up from this crystalline foundation you had the dust, then that choking wall of smog cutting everything into thirds. Dark sky, which will never again know the warmth of this galaxy's sun, hung above the smog. The cold and foreboding sky above, the chocking smog that hung from about head high on up, and the layers of dust on the Platform below smog. That was it, and it was all expansive swirling clouds of darkness as far as the eye could see, or the mind could imagine.

The dilithium crystals built up in the atmosphere and hung around in the air in a thick visible cage. Without air currents or pressure, most of it settled down onto and around the Platform. These ever-present dilithium crystal spores clogged respirators, leaving the wearer to quickly succumb to their dusty fate if stranded outside for too long. And you didn't have long at all. Suffocation from dilithium poisoning was the most painful three minutes anyone could endure. It wasn't clear if you stopped breathing first or if the power of the dilithium spores melting your lungs got to you quicker. But the choking, wailing, twitching, and black chunks of vile vomit that burst forth are assured. No fooling, an absolutely terrible way to go. So, no playing outside, kiddos, back inside with you right away!

*

Though it appeared to have fully melted and dissolved into the crystal dust, the container burst open upon hitting the Platform. The gentle undulations of the somehow still stable ground tipped the container over on its side, and the 1.43 million respirators littered the surface. These respirators would be picked up and refabricated by the sweeper drones of the Collective. They make sure nothing goes to waste on this barren land, or at least nothing remains behind that could be useful. Repair and refurbish appeared to be the Collective's mission. They are nothing if not efficient, the ultimate recyclers.

Once the target is found, the drones make quick work of the gruesome task. Under the darkness of the ever-present night, the pregnant women will be hunted down and destroyed before they can give birth, before the hope of their child's future on Tranquility Base could dissipate when they learn about the lost ROPUs. "Put them out of their future heartbreak while they are in a good place," the programming went. The citizens of DZ: 23N were helpless to protect their families. Light-guns were expensive and hard to make out here. People armed with makeshift spears and broom weapons fruitlessly swing at the impending doom of the hunter drones.

Sadly, it was the men who saw to the efficiency of the entire operation. Everyone knew that seats were limited on the trip to Tranquility Base. Wrongly thinking that they would secure their own seat on the trip caused most of the husbands to resort to their baser survival instincts. The gathering at work was a secret meeting where they voted on the best course of action. Not everyone agreed, and some even pledged to try to escape, but many breathed a sigh of relief. This early arrival and early extermination meant that the children would never be born. Families would continue to receive their credit allowance as long as they maintained their empty nest. The credits were necessary for survival. They could be exchanged for Life[x] or most likely for more Puff. Those who remained behind and didn't go to

Tranquility Base knew that they didn't have long and often gave in and took to the Puff. Stay here long enough and everyone turns to Puff. The side effects of the dilithium crystals will eventually kill them off anyway once their fourteen years on this planet are up and their own respirators are worthless; refined dilithium power cells dried up. Stay here long enough and everyone turns to Puff. When you're going to hell in a hand basket, you might as well enjoy the ride. Preach on, Jerry.

Of the 1.43 million pregnant women, almost all had been rounded up by their husbands and gathered together in the community center at DZ: 23N where they patiently and obediently awaited their fate. The drones would swarm the community center and quickly dispatch its inhabitants. Knowing it was going to be quick and painless gave them all confidence in their subservient choice. The men had pushed them there in consistency with the protocols of collection they had agreed to at their secret meeting at work. The husbands would be rewarded for their participation and proactivity. Having everyone huddled together made it more efficient; the killing that is. Like proverbial lambs to the slaughter these women shuffled into the center. They knew their destiny and were accepting of their sacrifice, even if they didn't go to Tranquility Base and their men had just spent the extra credits on Puff. Knowing their husbands could die happy with the smell of cinnamon buns in their nose would be worth it. Oh! to smell and taste a cinnamon bun.

Chapter 2

00:00 Seconds: 14 Years till Tranquility Base

There was no other way of saying it; Blavos was down on his luck with no end in sight. He used to be the envy of the Credit Dealers and Collection Guild, and he had built up his own cadre of star tech support agents over the years. His work had caused him to make lots of friends, and there were people who had trusted Blavos and took his bets at face value. When Blavos won, you won. But Blavos had been losing, and the people of this DZ are losing faith in him, about ready to write him off as just another washed up old-timer.

Blavos was a good handler all right. A handler is supposed to have all their ducks in a row, someone who has figured out the right balance of work and fun, can still get up and do a great tech support shift, but who also appreciates a good dining experience and is sure to know just the guy to hook you up for that special occasion, with the right Puff of course. And for many that handler was Blavos. Only these days he was running out of special favors he could still deliver on; his usual coworkers and helpers having turned sour on doing business with Blavos, ever since his latest StatStar was found taking a bribe and fixing the last race. The long-extended battle, neck-and-neck right over the finish line, made for quite the spectacle. All eyes were transfixed. The viewing audience broke records for that race, but the excitement palled in comparison to the chaos at the payout booths when the race was over, and Blavos' guy had finished second. He was supposed to be the hands-down winner. No one even bought the trifecta to cover a possible win, place, show. The only guys laughing and smiling, high fives and hugs all around, were the ones who had bet against Blavos. And nobody does that. So, when Blavos' racer and a few happy gamblers came around from the back of the betting booths, everyone knew the fix was in. Blavos had nothing to do with it of course, but everyone blamed him for their losses.

But that age-old rule, bet on whatever Blavos is betting on, is fading, and Blavos and his team of StatStars are now considered tarnished goods by many. People trusted their hard-earned credits to guys like Blavos, and if they didn't believe in him, Blavos couldn't stay in business. Handlers were the only ones supposed to have a fix on the lines for the slide races, and they all openly discussed the take, who was set on a streak and who was a long shot who deserved her chance at the limelight. Fortunes in credits changed hands in every race and the handlers got a piece of it all. But now Blavos was drying up on both ends. His current team of StatStars calling into question their business relationship and wondering if they are still with the right handler in Blavos. Other handlers didn't want to work to fix races and set odds with him any more. But, worse, he now had his own credit dealer assigned to him from the CDCG. While it sounds good, elite, and expensive, to say you had your own dealer, it was no honor or privilege. A dealer was just a guy hanging about watching your every move and seeing if he should either beat you up and steal your credits, or just beat you up. Usually both in Blavos' case. He had always lived a fast-and-loose lifestyle and relished living hand-to-mouth and racing payout-to-payout. Blavos liked to fully leverage himself on every race by always doubling his stake with every bet and betting it all. It was a stressful and reckless spending lifestyle that ensured it was always a life of famine or feast for Blavos. He actually preferred it that way and felt it kept him on his toes to always be one move away from destitution.

Most people got a credit dealer after their first big score because the Collective knew people couldn't handle even a small amount of extra credits and would soon be in debt. They would outspend their recent good fortune, for Lady Luck never shines her light on a soul forever, and when she turns her beam off, it is cold and dark in the night. Sure, most people took their winnings and immediately cashed in. They threw a lavish party with their friends and no doubt tried to smell something. Credits couldn't buy happiness, but they could buy Puff, and that was a close second. Even if just for seconds.

Blavos had followed his usual style and bet everything on his last race. Whatever his StatStar wanted to do, he was in. Blavos had used this system for so long that he didn't even take the time to check his bet receipt that day. He would have known immediately something was off – no StatStar bet against himself. No one bats an eye when a StatStar and his dealer all win big from the race, but when it turns out the fix was in and betting against Blavos was the smart money, things go south for Blavos in a hurry. "Who knew?" they said. "Who could have guessed?" But when they saw Blavos' name on the payout board, people knew that Blavos had bet against Blavos. Which just didn't happen. And no one was shocked more than Blavos himself when his racer double-crossed him and bet to lose his own race. No doubt he took a bribe or got a promise for a Puff 'first timer'. No one could know the depths of danger it would put them in, but there was Blavos' name, top of the winner's board. But it had happened and Blavos was ruined in a single night. All the friends he had made and the relationships he had built over countless nights were gone. They all joined forces and now all sit in the same column in the register as all the enemies Blavos had made over the years. He needed to make a little room between himself and the heat, take some time away, maybe even scout some new agents in DZ: 23P. Blavos had made quite the name for himself and had built a reputation that would secure his seat to Tranquility Base. But now that was in question. He didn't have much time, just a few million seconds really; he set out to find his next StatStar.

*

Half the original 1,024 drones that showed up went off to collect the ventilators. They had become sweeper drones the moment the Platform spilled out the respirators. That left the remaining 512 drones to transform into hunter drones and speed off to carry out their horrible mission.

The squadron of 512 was whittled down to 256 in a matter of seconds. Anyone looking up from the Platform would have noticed the giant swarming cloud of dark drones quickly bank sharper and sharper to the port side. Drone 512 had hit a cluster of dilithium spores in the air, big and sticky enough to slow down one of the main propeller blades. It reels violently back and forth, spinning in circles and making a slow corkscrew loop as it attempts to dislodge the spore. Drone 511 immediately noticed its KNN was off course and went into pairing and maintenance mode. Its propellers rotated and the drone hovered down and landed safely. The last few feet are a silent hovering and gentle lowering as the magnetic-lev boosters connect with the force of the Platform. Always trying to keep binary uniformity, drone 512 joins its known-nearest-neighbor and slowly descends onto the Platform, ready for pairing and maintenance by tech support. The two drones sit side-by-side and wait for the sweepers to arrive. 510 notices its pack is off, and the calamity ensues. Drones now begin a big slow circling funnel cloud of propeller blades. The dust clouds circle up and a rather large twister-like phenomenon hovers above the Platform. The drones are all signaling each other back and forth trying to direct each other back into order. Something has interfered with their binary uniformity; with 512, 511, and 510 all down, the remaining drones know what to do. They would drop off until things were right again. One by one, the formation would self-correct until they reached binary unity again.

Once safely on the Platform, drone 512 doesn't wait for the signal from tech support to open for maintenance and unloading. Its cargo hold and access panels all open in unison as the airlocks unleash, ready for the sweepers in their endless scavenging to pick it up along with its precious cargo. The ultimate recyclers. Drones 511 and 510, along with the others that get the signal and drop out of formation, all gently maglev down to the Platform and then release their cargo holds.

With 512 down for maintenance, the remaining drones all turn on their neighbors and send the pairing sequence code. Each corresponding pair drops down for maintenance and waits to be returned to the Collective. Hundreds of drones drop from the sky and wait. Once the swarm is back to a stable binary base, the remaining 256 drones continue their journey to DZ: 23N. There are souls to fetch early.

Drones needed maintenance regularly here in the harsh environment of the outer layers of the galaxy. If the drones weren't cared for, the population would suffer. Rations and credits were lowered, and people went hungry. Hungry people rebelled, and that was bad for business. To keep everything, everyone, and every drone in order, the Waster Kings ran the tech support staff of DZ: 23N. They saw to it that schedules were kept and everything was done correctly. The Collective didn't seem to mind, or even care, so long as some agent, any agent, showed up for tech support duty. The Waster Kings banded together to organize the tribes and clans of the DZ and establish an efficient tech support staff that serves the Collective. True to form, the Waster Kings found a way to make money off this, too. You could bribe your way into a better shift schedule with the right credits and contacts. And everyone knew that you could bet on the outcome of an agent, a good way to earn some new credits. But really those credits were for Puff. And the real betting was on the elite tech support agents that competed in the Derby Days events, those StatStars, as they were lovingly called by their fan base. The Waster Kings ran the massive underground sportsbook that powered and paid the StatStars. They tracked individual agent stats, and those with high stats or potential were assigned 'handlers' by the Waster Kings themselves. The handlers saw to it that their high rollers had the inside scoop and lots of free credits. And Puff of course. But not everyone won their bets, truthfully, most didn't. Anyone on the downside of a bookie could be met at their next job by a 'credit dealer'. These unsavory characters never did any dealing, though; they just penalize you for your lost bet and took your credits or rations. Or, depending on the dealer, they take both. If they leave you without a beating or a broken bone, consider yourself lucky. True to the code of the CDCG, anyone who suffered a beating got to indicate which body part they wanted beaten, stretched, broken, or even outright removed. As they say, it is the little choices in life that count. So long as a credit dealer came back to the guild with a trophy, some body part, to prove she had done the job, it didn't matter which body part. So, the choice was often left to the one being beaten up.

The Collective drones were not dangerous by nature, and, in fact, caring for the humans of DZ: 23N was a core part of their mission. Drones don't usually go after the human slaves. But go against a drone and try to pry open its cargo hold, for example, or prevent it from murdering your wife and unborn child, doing these things was almost impossible without incurring a drone retaliation. Their dilithium-powered laser saws were enough to deal with for even the most accomplished warrior. Dealing with that while also dodging and fending off the drone's deadly tail as it tries to pierce your ROPU is usually more than enough. If you can handle all that, eight spinning propeller blades coming at your face definitely did you in. The best Waster King soldiers, those dedicated few who spent countless hours in combat training, could barely hold them off. But the swarms of the Collective's drones that would amass as the battle raged on would easily overcome all the Waster Kings. Drones were generally regarded as dangerous. They were to be respected and not messed with.

That was before light-dancing; it hadn't spread its way across all the DZs yet. Once the signal, and its fortunate side effect, was accidentally triggered and discovered, it was quickly miniaturized and weaponized for use by the Waster Kings. The key was hitting the drone with a beam of light; the dancing was just a side effect from most jubilant warriors upon seeing their downed drone. The drones hate the idea of anything touching them; it messes up their sensors and calibrations. In order to

29

avoid massive sensory overload, they shut down into maintenance mode when touched by a concentrated beam of light. They wait patiently in a blissful and restful state. Silently awaiting tech support for repair or the sweepers for collection. The ultimate recyclers.

All you had to do was hit a drone with a concentrated beam of light to send it into maintenance mode. Think a laser-pointer from the mid-90s corporate American boardrooms. The kind that a sweaty overweight intern in the back would click to try and highlight points in yet another all-too-boring slideshow. Even though the drones were stunned by the laser beam, the celebratory dance after downing one was up to you. Everyone had their own signature dance, like a touchdown shuffle. It wasn't much to brag about, though really. And you didn't have to be particularly precise, either. Tag 'em on any surface and BOOM send them into maintenance mode. The light immediately resonates, glows, and bounces continuously inside the shiny metallic surface of the drones. It is too much for their sensors to process at once, so they assume a system fault and switch over to maintenance mode. In this state, all sensors and propellers remain off and the cargo hold airlocks are released, leaving the drones and their precious cache vulnerable to looting. Like all things in The Collective, the drones are in continuous communication with each other. Sensors on a single drone can broadcast to all drones within a five DZ radius. With the seemingly endless population of drones covering the Platform, the Collective knew what was happening everywhere on the planet's surface almost as soon as it happened. Responding to an event with a swarm of drones wasn't a question. It was just a matter of time and physics to get there. And they were getting faster all the time. A drone downed by light would sit patiently and wait for the swarm of sweeper drones to get it. So, while light-dancing was popular and effective, it wasn't a panacea. You still had to get out of there fast and back into the shelters before the swarm came, or the dilithium crystals ravaged your body from the inside out.

Once you hit a drone, the light remains inside and bounces and zooms around. A dazzling array of light and colors bursts forth from the drones. The light finally settles into a deep and soothing glow that emanates from within the droid. One simple zap to a drone with a light-gun or light-sword and they stop in their tracks. Sort of like Laser Tag but with higher stakes.

Every soldier has their own style of light-gun. It is a testament to their individual skills and training. Like the legendary lightsabers of a galaxy far, far away, successfully wielding one demonstrates a mastery few ever achieve. Some use a traditional pistol form with its trusty grip and wide assortment of carrying cases across the shoulder and hip. Sadly, because they are dilithium powered like everything else, one had no need for a bandolier to carry spare bullets. But capes are a thing again, even for men. While the pistol-grip is prevalent, others prefer the up-close combat style of the martial arts masters of yore and wield light-swords and blades. Plenty of cool gear still available to stash a sharp knife or stick. And nothing hides a sword at your hip like a cape. Did I mention almost everyone wears a cape here?

*

Climbing up the walls like a swarm of spiders, the Waster Kings begin their attack. Just like their advisories, they splinter off into groups all the way down to pairs. They have each other's back, and a small phalanx of the Waster Kings' soldiers, equipped with their trusty light-guns and swords, can handle a battalion of Collective drones.

Eight soldiers reach the top of the Platform and swing wide their capes. The goal is to eliminate the drones before they reach DZ: 23N and carry out their gruesome mission. They all unleash the fury of their light-guns on the hunter drones flying away to carry out the deadly mission. Eight other brave soldiers scatter off to loot the drones now hovering down into maintenance mode by the Waster Kings' soldiers' first volley of light beam blasts. The ultimate prize is the ventilators now scattered across the Platform and making their way to everywhere but DZ: 23N. Everything gathered by the Waster Kings is repurposed and reused; they share that with the ultimate recyclers. The Waster Kings are here to battle it out with the drones and claim as many ROPUs as they can.

Light bursts forth from the eight light-guns on the Platform and targets the starboard formation of the drones zooming toward DZ: 23N. Volley after volley, they hit the drones in a sweeping wave with eight soldiers across all firing in unison. Eight, then sixteen, thirty-two, sixty-four, and 128 drones hit in waves by the Waster Kings. The entire series of volleys lasts mere seconds. The light scatters across the sky and within the drones. Against the dark backdrop of smog, it shines out glowing lights that penetrate the perpetual night like the Fourth of July or some cheap roadside attraction with spotlights. They don't have holidays or festivals like that any more and never really did way out here on this planet. But younglings often hear the stories. Those dreams and collective memories fill them with hope of what life will be like once on Tranquility Base.

Expert sharpshooters in their own right, all the soldiers' light beams hit their targets. As expected, after half the drones are down, the formation bounces away, the rest give up and begin making their way to DZ: 23N. The Waster Kings let them go and know the drones will be stopped at the compound gates. Those who missed even slightly could count on the beams of light echoing off any nearby already hit drones, sort of like a shotgun scatter to take down a few birds with one shot. But they don't have sports any more, either. They were outlawed here by the Waster Kings for fear of inciting violence. The only sports that remain are the Derby Days events and all their qualifiers over the years.

The hit drones drop down into maintenance mode. The eight militia men and women go about dismantling and unloading the downed drones. They must hurry because at this point they have only about twenty to thirty minutes before the sweeper drones show up to recycle. The sweepers were getting faster at showing up on the scene. Can't leave any ROPUs, not with their oh-so-valuable dilithium crystals inside.

Hit in waves and the drones drop in waves. The remaining drones still hovered around the Platform in their slow-moving twister cloud. As each one drops down into maintenance, the remaining drones turn on each other. They send their partners into maintenance mode and follow suit on their KNN. This continues as they turn each other off until they get back into binary balance. This attack happens in a matter of minutes. The Waster Kings make quick work of the area. They leave behind looted drones waiting in pairing mode with their metallic bodies scattered across the Platform glowing in the night like a set of runway lights at an airport. The split-off squadron gets back into binary unison, and all 128 remaining active drones continue their relentless pursuit of the unborn children in DZ: 23N.

Floating ever so slightly, the entire field of dust appears to be constantly moving. The Platform is stable but in constant motion and flux. It makes for tricky recovery, but the Waster Kings quickly gather as many ROPUs as they can before they disappear below the Platform just as quickly as they had come. The Platform was always flowing in random haphazard directions with the slow ooze of molten hot magma. But this viscosity was patient and deliberate. The Platform seems to ebb and flow like the tides of old. There is no rise and fall of the ocean, but the surface of the Platform moved in giant sweeping waves. Small but just ever-so-noticeable and just as unpredictable. Settlements had to be built to withstand the flex and pressure, sort of like earthquake-proofing on steroids. But it was tricky business to navigate for sure. There were places where the Platform seemed to reach up, snatch you under, and swallow you whole. Stumble and POOF you were gone. No one is sure what happens below the Platform.

There were no milestones or landmarks. Destinations were indicated by distance travelled or the towering signs to indicate the hundreds of thousands of landing and pickup zones for Tranquility Base. Hills there today could be swallowed by the Platform just a few hours later by its constant motion. Or that hill moves twenty-five meters starboard. A wave might flow in a large whirlpool and can't be relied on for navigation. Navigation across the Platform was possible if you followed the signs demarcating each DZ, but these signs were spread out far and wide. And often unreliable as if someone kept moving them. How could DZ: 23N intersect with DZ: 23A?

The sky was one thing, and probably the biggest killer to the planet. While the perpetual night had won the war long ago, from where you could stand on the Platform it was the smog that didn't get the memo and kept up a constant barrage that rages on still to this day. The smog had become a blanket that hovered around five to ten feet in the air. Just enough to make seeing difficult outside. Not like you had a reason to go outside any more. Life inside the settlement was just fine. It could be endured for fourteen years, and then life would be better once you got to Tranquility Base. You would be free to roam the hills and mountainsides all around you. Feel the water flowing over your hand and the rush of wind in your sails as you join your ancestors and take to the mighty seas once again.

The combination of fog and always-dark night had managed to cover and subsequently kill all life below and inside it. No one knows exactly how long it took, but the grass died first. The long slow death of the remaining flora occurred over hundreds of years, they say. But with night always present, it became impossible to tell time. It was measured in seconds, each one held dearly.

The animals died off as their source of food and shelter was consumed by the dust cloud. As biology tried to take over animals mutated into forms no longer recognizable or previously recorded. DNA lines were merged as population control was left unchecked without predators around. Many animals turned on themselves, eating their own young to survive, and then dying out as the old became infertile and couldn't produce offspring. The entire planet's population, millions of years in the making, didn't last long. About fourteen years was as long as any animal could survive with the dilithium slowly eating away at their lungs. Fierce creatures once roamed the ever-expanding Platform, but not any more. As they fell, the dust kept them preserved and in place. Like items in a mausoleum, these skeletons litter the surface of the Platform, but these days they are few and far between. They are the only fleeting landscapes visible until they are covered by dilithium dust or recycled by the sweepers. It is said that new initiates to the Waster Kings hold secret ceremonies at these petrified fossils. Worshiping and taking on ancestral forms from long ago. The Waster Kings were split into different houses, each with a fearsome predator as its avatar.

The flora on this planet held on longer, its lifespan measured in decades and millennia, but it slowly faded away too. Without roots holding the ground together, massive landslides gave way and rivers broke free. The planet became a huge swamp: a pool of dead animals and trees, roots, leaves, and branches all decaying like the bottom of an Amazon rain forest. The death and destruction of a lifetime ago, before dilithium crystals started appearing, is all that lies below the Platform, some say. But most don't say anything about what might be below the Platform.

*

128 drones arrived at DZ: 23N all at once. Once over the dust shield and into the compound, the drones split off into pairs. Units formed up and sped off into action. But the accident with the container had set everything in motion early, and the drones arrived ahead of schedule. Turns out they have arrived a day early, and the 1.43 million babies born tomorrow will be hunted down and put to an early test, one that they can't prepare for but that will determine how they live out each second of their lives after birth. The question wasn't if the drones would find and dispatch all the children, for that was a certainty. But how many would be able to do it and could breathe without respirators was the question that only time would answer. Three minutes and thirty-one seconds of time to be exact. It was the ultimate test

because surviving your Interval meant you were destined for Tranquility Base.

The prey had been found. The Collective knows these fragile humans will die without a ROPU respirator. There were no respirators to give them, having all been scattered, lost, or recycled. Better to kill these fragile babes now. Put them out of their misery, even if they survived their Interval, and don't relegate them to a life of looting and vandalism as a member of the Waster Kings gangs. "Save them from a life as a Puff head" is how the algorithm was coded. And because these drones were just early enough, they could make quick work of the job. The extra credits they gave out would ensure an efficient collection and dispatch. The Collective practiced a constant efficiency in all things.

The first round of killing was quick, and as promised, efficient. More than 900,000 bodies drop to the ground in a hump as waves of death pass over the crowds gathered inside the community center at DZ: 23N. The remaining women trample over each other as they try to escape, now no longer certain of their chosen sacrifice. After just a few short minutes, the violence stopped, and the drones raced out of the community center headed off to dispatch the fleeing horde of remaining lives at DZ: 23N.

Chapter 3

00:00 to 31,536,000 Seconds: 13 Years till Tranquility Base

These days the combined ventilator/respirators were small and very portable. The nose piece is actually really comfortable and you forget it is there. Now that the ROPU 6000 models were standard issue, everyone got a good, lifesaving, helpful appliance to carry around and keep them alive. No one went around without their Recycled Oxygen Portable Units. It just couldn't be done.

All ROPU units come with a sealed compartment to house their dilithium crystals. This storage bay cannot be opened by design. Everyone was given the same amount of time. Each ROPU was loaded with sufficient quantities of dilithium crystals to power them for a set time. They had been set that way at Tranquility Base. Exactly fourteen years from initial touchdown the respirators would stop working. Your Interval was the final test and one that you had no way of avoiding. Could you breathe without your trusty ROPU?

Each soul, from the moment of birth, has exactly 441,504,000 seconds until the dilithium crystals inside fully evaporate and lose power. Without power the ROPUs were just metal contraptions with a dangling hose. Useless to anyone but The Collective now. Once drained of their life-giving purpose, the ROPUs are discarded and sit and wait until the sweepers come, the ultimate recyclers.

The ROPU's six-foot ventilator hose and nose piece are attached on the left side and are usually roped up and held in place around the wearer. Slung across the body like a bandolier and tucked in place under the now ubiquitous capes. Yeah for capes. The new 6000 model units weighed under two pounds, unnoticeable really. They are fully sealed, waterproof, and act as a floatation device in the event of an emergency landing. Everyone had them, protected and safeguarded them as if their life depended on it – because it did. Even the Puff heads kept their ROPU with them at all times. ROPU had become such a critical part of life that even those who stuck around post Tranquility Base still kept theirs, hose and all. It was sort of like a pacifier, a habitual thumb sucking that lasted a lifetime, however long that was.

The 6000 Models seemed to be designed with one thing In mind, other than keeping you alive, of course. Do you think its coincidence that these days Puff had become easier and easier to consume now that they have perfected the delivery device? That can't be an accident. Trust me, been doing this for a long time. For just five credits, exchanged with the nearest dealer for the modification, and they would tweak your respirator hose with an extension piece. And wouldn't you know it? The little, recyclable, Puff tubes fit right inside. Easy to load and quick to unload for your next hit. Everyone knows how important it was not to re-hit the same tube. Most importantly, the modified extension made sure there was little lost vapor, thus ensuring the hardest hitting high. The cost was widely considered worth it, and most people saved for months to afford one. Hours toiling away at work exchanged for a few minutes of smell. Maybe even just mere seconds. But it was always worth it.

The Puff experience was uniquely designed to relive, ever so briefly, the smell of the world that used to be. Puff heads could easily be found by their modified ROPUs. The hit is quick and the sensation starts as it tingles in the nose. Ones senses are immediately flooded as the nose becomes more than a decoration for hoops and dangles. From the moment the Puff vapor hits you it is nirvana at its finest, the very definition of euphoric bliss. The nostrils flare uncontrollably, your pupils dilate, and your breathing becomes strained and shallow. The muscles in your neck and arms go limp as you feel each hair along your arms stand up and tingle as the sensation courses through you. Vertigo and flashes of light are common. Along with the nose bleeds. If you didn't spot a Puffer by their modified ROPU, the ever-present blood stains on their scarf or bandana would be a telltale sign. Everyone had a long shawl that they used to keep away the constant dilithium dust. Those scarves could be easily washed and reused, which made them ideal as blood rags. No one wiped their nose on their capes, after all; that is just bad form.

*

Back at the house, drone 64 swooped in for the kill. Marianna was sleeping and never saw it coming. The drone simultaneously split her respirator and her skull in half. Her lifeless body lay twitching on the bed as he screamed out and rushed to her side. Before he can get there, 64 deploys its dilithium-powered laser-saw and births the baby like a C-section.

She is healthy and screaming, the newborn baby girl that was. Mom was dead instantly and mercifully felt no pain. A screaming baby is a foreign sound these days because they are normally soothed and calmed by their ROPUs, the little devices strapped on from the moment of birth. Screaming meant air and that meant breathing. Breathing without a ROPU lasts only minutes.

Drone 64 lifts the baby from her mother's abdomen and sets to cleaning and wrapping the child. Before wrapping it like a burrito in the Collective supplied blankets, 64's tail punctures the baby's stomach and embeds her personal tracker; all drones in the area will be tracking her movements as she makes her way back to the Collective. 64 then fits her neatly with her very own ROPU, but doesn't put it in her nose just yet. Even though she may breathe without it, her three minutes and thirty-one second Interval would decide that, the crippling crystal spores will clog her lungs without the lifesaving filtration of the ROPU. She will need to be protected from the harsh environment on the Platform if she is going to survive her journey back to the Collective. If she survives her Interval, that is.

Kitteridge is stunned by the horrific sight before him and crouches on the floor. He watches with anticipation as the seconds tick bye. Knowing the birth was near, he had programmed his and Marianna's wristwatches to track exactly how long the world had to stand still and wait. Three minutes and thirty-one seconds will be all she needs to prove she is a miracle baby, and one destined for Tranquility Base. A human mammal that can survive on this desolate wasteland without requiring an ROPU is rare. It is customary to remove your ROPU hose only after your power crystals have stopped working. After your fourteen years here as a slave are up. If you can survive the three minute and thirty-one second Interval, then you got your seat on the trip to Tranquility Base. As the baby wailed away, Kitteridge started the most important timer of his daughter's life. Three minutes and thirty-one seconds for her Interval.

Two more drones enter the room and take over the duty of

transporting the babe. They are effortless and oh so gentle as they begin to slowly carry her away. Three minutes left before judgement day for her.

Her heavy head lolls to the side and Kitteridge can swear he sees wisdom and recognition in her eyes when they blink and flutter open for the first time. It is then that he notices the thin line of blood running in a line across her left cheek. Somehow the drones hadn't been careful enough with her. He could tell that it was deep enough to leave a helpful scar. Something that would set her apart from the other children, however many survived tonight and made it past their own Intervals. Kitteridge needed a way to recognize his daughter if he was going to save her. Their eyes lock and he makes a silent promise – he will search to the edges of the Platform and beyond to find her; he vows to never stop looking. He knows he can't save her now; it would just mean suicide. He is her only chance to escape the life of tech support. If she makes it.

Two minutes and seven seconds left to her premature reveal. The drones hover awaiting the Interval to pass. If she doesn't make it, there is no sense in bringing her back to the Collective. She won't be valuable or studied. Just another thing left for the sweepers, the ultimate recyclers apparently had a use for dead people too.

Drone 64's battlefield programming kicks in and it wheels around to attack while it waits to see if Kitteridge's daughter will pass her Interval. It doesn't hesitate so much as calculates. It zooms forward silently powered by the maglev underneath as its propellers flip and begin to spin in attack mode, the guards down now. It lunges at Kitteridge, still crouching nearby watching and counting down the seconds. He quickly dodges the first volley from drone 64's tail and he smoothly rolls under the bed for protection. 64 drops to the ground and begins rolling toward the bed chasing after Kitteridge.

One minute and forty-five seconds. As 64 rushes underneath the dangling covers of the bed, Kitteridge nails it right in the middle of the optical unit with his pocketknife. The five-inch blade cracks one of the drone's sensors and goes right through and severs the main power cord. The drone slumps down in a compact metallic heap under the bed. Kitteridge doesn't know how long till the swarm of sweeper drones come to pick this one up, but he is counting down to something much more important right now.

The brief encounter with 64 takes forty-three seconds. One minute and two seconds till we know. Exhausted from the brief but intense fight, Kitteridge makes his way around the home. Packing only what he needs to survive, being sure not to leave the precious dilithium behind. Sadly, there is nothing more he can do for his wife. What is left of Marianna's body will remain here until the rest of DZ: 23N becomes engulfed in dust and smog; her soul has already made its way to Tranquility Base. He looks around with a sudden longing, wishing he could use her ROPU. He doesn't know why or when he will need it, but it had been destroyed in the attack. A 'spare' ROPU was unheard of; at a minimum it would score him some credits or sway with the Waster Kings. Kitteridge must leave because he knows they will come looking for him. Thirty-seven seconds whizz bye as he grabs his compass and a few remaining essentials. A quick check under his base layer, and yes, he has his fire steel on the chain around his neck still; Kitteridge knows he needs it to keep back the constant thirty-four degree cold. It wasn't extreme enough to be dangerous but just cold enough to make a night of terrible sleep with frozen toes and aching fingers no matter how much you wiggle them inside your boots and gloves.

A quarter of a minute and the child is still wailing but is quickly turning blue. Its lips pressed together in a thin white line, gasping for air between cries. Eyes jammed shut. Ten, nine, eight seconds left until her destiny is revealed.

It seems as if the whole world has gone silent as he waits for the sound. He longs for the screaming and wailing to stop, only hopes and prays for a gentler sound. That of his newborn daughter breathing on her own, as miraculous as that might be. He knows and he waits in fear of another sound. The sound of her lungs collapsing under the heat of the crystal spores hanging even in the inside air. The dust shields could only do so much these days. Seven, six, five.

Cries and screams pierce the air. Uneven tones and intervals make it sound like a constant wall of sound. It presses against the house threatening to burst from the inside out. Four, three. It is only then that his epiphany occurs. The sounds of pain and suffering are not just the wails of his namesake. He hears them coming from all around, inside the house and from outside. All of DZ: 23N is in total chaos. The drones, having made quick work of the gathering at the community center, are weaving all about tracking down the remaining women, those who fled hoping for a better life for their kids. They will be found and dealt with. The drones are programmed to be empathetic and dispatch them quickly before the dilithium ravages their young bodies. Those kids who aren't found will die anyway but it will be a more painful one. Three minutes and thirty-one seconds is a long time to writhe in your own agony. The bloodshed continues outside and across the DZ as the painful anticipation inside is about to come to an end.

As he listens to his neighbors and friends being slaughtered,

44

the time ticks away. Two, one second left and then gone. The Interval, as it's called, had passed. The waiting was over. Either she would make it, or her first few minutes would be the last of her preciously short life. All she would know is the buzzing sound of drones. That would be her first and final lullaby.

There is nothing more he can do for her. If she can't breathe without the ROPU, she will suffocate and die. Or that is the nicest way to think about it. The reality is much worse. If he gives her his ROPU then he will die. And they can't share; it isn't like the scuba tanks from before where you could buddy breathe with someone. Without your own ROPU, you die; they are called Personal Units for a reason. That simple.

If she makes it, she will live out her days performing tech support for the Collective. Counting the remaining seconds until her own ROPU shuts off. If you survived the test, the one you had been preparing your whole life for, once your Interval was over you made your long journey to Tranquility Base. There life was counted in years and decades even and no longer constrained to short, predetermined seconds like here.

At exactly three minutes and thirty-one seconds, her cries stop abruptly. Even from across the room he can hear the gentle sound of her chest rising and falling. She had done it, survived the Interval. Satisfied that she passed her most important exam, the two drones quickly and efficiently slip her ROPU hose into her nose and carry her away from the house in a fast zoom. They carry her off toward the Collective. Kitteridge knows that his new purpose now is to find his daughter and hijack their way to Tranquility Base.

As he turns toward the entry way to leave, he pauses to notice drone 63 just sitting patiently, waiting for maintenance to begin. Its steady calming glow is a beacon in the otherwise dark night. Kitteridge cautiously walks toward it to get a closer look and his communicator beeps to life, vibrating incessantly to get his attention. He notices a message asking if he wants to pair with and troubleshoot a nearby drone? Ever since Kitteridge destroyed 64 under the bed, 63 has been broadcasting out a legacy message over the ancient Bluetooth protocol. Not knowing what would happen, or how it would change the course of his life, he accepts the prompt and drone 63 springs to life. The drone scans around the room and then immediately runs up his pant leg, circles his waist, and then settles right on the middle of his ROPU. You hear the air locks release as 63 takes hold. It has found its required power source apparently.

He is left wondering if this is some sort of trick by the Collective to track him (and his child). But instead, he bears down and focuses, steeling himself for his journey and the trials ahead. He tries a little bit to shake the drone off, after seeing its buddy murder his lifelong wife and then two more take away his baby girl, Kitteridge wasn't feeling too fond of drones at that very moment. But the thing held on tight, and he began to wonder… this drone might prove useful after all. If for nothing else than to study and see what happened with the lights and if all drones can be stunned like that. What a game changer. And what the heck was pairing mode? What did it even mean to have your own drone on this planet? What was the deal with the lights? Could he train this drone? Make it open its precious cargo hold on command? That would be a neat trick. He wondered what else he could make it do and if he could pair others. He would need all the help he can get to search out and find his baby girl.

Kitteridge opens and closes what is left of the door to his home for the last time. Fourteen years he has lived here and had managed to outlast most of his peers at DZ: 23N. As his footsteps

46

scatter the dust, you can't help notice that there is death everywhere. Not all of them were clean kills unfortunately. The men, left behind to wait out their own Tranquility Base trip, go about cleaning and organizing the carnage. An efficient dispatch and removal, which was the deal after all. Bodies pile up across the Platform. Mostly the lifeless bodies of women with their unborn children still inside of their wombs. Some babies, their little hands and feet protruding out of the piles like pudgy little hot dogs made their own gruesome appearance, scattered about in the massive death heaps on the Platform.

With drones 63 and 64 out of commission, the platoon was unbalanced. It was quick and very colorful, but as predicted just thirty-two drones continue their mission. The remaining downed squadron now scattered like little glowing streetlights on the Platform, patiently awaiting tech support.

*

Kitteridge's electronic owl, a gift at birth, had watched over them faithfully all their life. The owl was a birthright in this family, having been passed down for generations untold. And now he belonged to Kitteridge and was forever a loyal servant to his master. Fully recharged, the owl now awakens with a small but barely audible hoot and opens his massive eyes. His ears have been perked the entire recharging period, taking in all the sounds around, including those of the horrible ambush and massacre. But this electronic owl is programmed to awake from electronic slumber only if there is a threat to its own life during recharge mode. It is supposed to be able to dream of electric sheep in peace. Recharge time was sacred.

This owl knew the instant it turned back on that something

was wrong. The entire room was in disarray and what was left of Marianna lay open on the bloody mattress, splayed out like some amateur dissection. Kitteridge's owl scanned the room quickly, but already knew from the carnage what had happened and why the drones were here. The fact that they arrived early, before the birth, remained a mystery. He would have to calculate that later on, for now it was time to take wing and find his owner. He knew he had to get moving before his master was too far ahead. There is nothing the owl can do here but stay close to his owner and carry out his new mission. The family protector would become Kitteridge's eyes and ears in the quest to find his daughter.

The evening started with 1.43 million babies waiting to be born. The population of DZ: 23N had literally waited their entire lives for this moment. Their babies would be born, equipped with a new ROPU, and carry out the tradition. They would be trained as tech support agents. While technically slaves, they would have been well cared for by the Collective. This milestone was meant to be a joyous celebration of life everlasting. The waiting had become tangible here years ago. Gestation takes longer here; all these women have been carrying their child for over two years. Ever since their twelfth birthday when they were married to their pre-assigned partner at the arranged marriage ceremony. But at DZ: 23N, as dawn turned to morning, only thirty-two babies had survived. They were scattered across the Platform. Held in the loving arms of their now fleeing mothers, these refugees were trying to make their way to the Waster Kings. Other than the Collective, the Waster Kings are the only other inhabitants, and the only ones that could help them survive now. Their only hope for Tranquility Base.

Kitteridge was seeking the same thing as he stepped out into the morning. He knew he needed to find the Waster Kings himself and tell them what happened at DZ: 23N tonight. This massacre could not go unpunished. The Waster Kings were ruthless in their fight against the Collective and its drones. Ultimately, he knew that the Waster Kings would rally a posse to go and get his daughter back. Kitteridge just needed to find her.

After the assault at the community center, or the culling if you want to think of it that way, the thirty-two drones had already fanned out to take care of the remaining inhabitants of this DZ. A few self-appointed leaders stepped up and began barking orders, pointing and directing the countless other men collected outside the doors of the community center. They were waiting to collect their extra credits for betraying their wives and children, rounding them up like cattle. These traitors would be rewarded, and all quickly shuffled and waited around to get what was coming to them. The drones were waiting for them. Their constantly whirring propeller blades made a little dust cloud that gave their location away for all to see. Kitteridge doesn't stick around to see what happens. He won't be going to Tranquility Base so didn't care what happened. He only cared about finding his daughter; then he would worry about getting them both seats for the next trip.

Whatever happened at the back of the community center, it was very loud and very quick. A little mushroom cloud boomed over the building, whooshed out, and blew dust everywhere. The mist clouded over everything nearby. It was loud, that was for sure, and there was a big flash of light. I guess with all that noise it could have been the rocket to Tranquility Base! No one had ever seen one, so Kitteridge couldn't tell. All he knew was a bunch of men who were supposed to have been selected for the trip made their way around the community center but never came back out. Wherever they went, they were gone now, and he did

49

hope that his friends and neighbors were on their way to Tranquility Base. But for the first time in his life, he began to doubt the hope of Tranquility Base. As the dark seconds of the early morning ticked on, thirty-two drones floated up, deadly task now done here, and spread out again to continue the hunt for the remaining survivors fleeing across the Platform.

He didn't have much time; the Collective was efficient. No telling what they had planned for his daughter or how long he had to save her. But another timer had started for both of them. She had fewer than 441,504,000 seconds left before her ROPU shut down. And tomorrow morning his own reveal would begin. Right on time. His dilithium crystals now drained, Kitteridge's Interval will begin. Three minutes and thirty-one seconds till the end or the rest of your life. Only this time he won't be going to Tranquility Base. At least not without his daughter. His 441 million seconds had been somehow extended, he hoped, but only tomorrow would tell.

The remaining citizens of DZ: 23N do not go down without a fight. And a few more drones are downed. A group of women lure a small squad into a booby-trapped alley. Two more are killed by suicide bombers, having long ago sworn an oath that they would sacrifice themselves, become martyrs to make room for others on the trip to Tranquility Base. More drones are downed in the process, but the total lives lost are too many to tally. The remaining drones speed off and go back to binary unison. Sixteen drones make their way to oversee the distribution of the babies who survived their Interval.

Partly from the battle, partly from the heartbreak and loss of Marianna, but mostly due to the momentous task ahead of him, Kitteridge was exhausted. Once outside DZ: 23N he knew he was close, and the Waster Kings would find him soon. He just had to wait out the night, however long that was. It was always night here. He curled up on his back with his cape drawn around him for protection. The drone, now paired on his ROPU, glowed with a pleasant warmth. Kitteridge was completely spent from his ordeal today, and not even the worry and anticipation about his daughter could keep slumber away. He drifted off to sleep, completely forgetting that his own Interval was scheduled for tomorrow. And unlike a dental cleaning, nothing he could do would reschedule it. He drifted off to sleep through the long dark night.

His slumber was a fitful one. He forced his eyes closed but kept seeing the image of Marianna lying dead and splayed out across their marriage bed. Flashes of the screams from his daughter, and the all-knowing look in her eyes as the drones carried her away. He tossed and turned, rolling inside the warmth of his cape. He would see a drone light-saw piercing down on his wife's ROPU. Then he would roll over on his side and stick his arm under his head, with the ROPU-as-a-pillow smooshed between. And then stick his legs outside the cape. But that wouldn't do as a fresh image of the hell he just witnessed came rushing in. Roll over, shuffle the cape, fluff the ROPU-now-pillow. Squeeze it like a teddy bear to keep out the cold and the monster drones. He knew he would either pass the ultimate test tomorrow, one that he can do nothing to prepare for, or die a horrible writhing death. His fourteen years have passed. He has done his duty, served his time, loved his wife, and watched over his unborn child, preparing his family for the trip to Tranquility Base. His Interval would be here soon enough.

His ROPU alarm and his wristwatch go off at the same time. Ready or not, his Interval has started. He wasn't sure how long he had dozed off for, but time before now didn't matter any more to Kitteridge. 441 million seconds had passed. His Interval had started. The last breath of purified air goes into his lungs as the ROPU shuts down. Three minutes and thirty-one seconds left to the reveal. He was wide awake now; that was for sure.

Awakened by the sound of Kitteridge's alarm, 63 beeps to life as well. Kitteridge expertly shoulders his ROPU while he paces around, transfixed by the remaining seconds ticking away. 63 unlocks from his ROPU and maglev floats down and begins to scan the Platform. An antennae and infrared scanner, parts of a drone Kitteridge had never seen, pops out of 63 and the scan continues. Kitteridge knows he has nothing to do but wait. It is then that he sees 63 off in the distance a little bit and watches. Better to watch what his new little friend is up to than stare at his watch waiting for death.

63 goes off a few more feet and scans the Platform for a few additional seconds. Apparently happy with its chosen location, the drone brings its laser-saw to life. Just as it lowers down to make contact with the crystal-coated Platform, 63 makes a last-minute shift and zooms portside 45 feet in an instant. There, that's the spot. Maglev down, rotators back and eight multi-jointed arms appear out of the cargo hold of drone 63. It uses the laser saw and mines a few crystals from the Platform, holding them aloft in its pinchers, a protective crab-like stance. Once satisfied with the weight and distribution of the load across its eight arms, 63 scampers back up to him and floats back onto Kitteridge's ROPU.

It doesn't take long, about three minutes in total, to mine the crystals. It is a curious sight and one that helps distract him just a little bit. Just twenty-three seconds left before his recycled oxygen is no longer purified in his ROPU. His Interval was upon him. His ROPU must have been programmed at birth. Of course it was. Very efficient.

Drone 63 floats back to him and quickly secures itself onto his ROPU. The airlocks close and the ROPU whirrs back to life. The regulator surges lifesaving oxygen and he breathes in a deep sigh. But he doesn't feel the relief of a lifetime. His three minutes and thirty-one seconds had passed. But he knows he hasn't survived. Drone 63 had just topped off his ROPU with more dilithium crystals. He doesn't know how long these new crystals will last. But he is filled with a new sense of anxiety. He hasn't really passed the test and he doesn't know if he ever will. Will all his searching be in vain if he can't make it to Tranquility Base? No, for his daughter's future he must carry on. He saw her breath without a ROPU all on her own, or at least he thinks he did. His memory of the nights and months before this have already started to become hazy.

He might not have survived, but he was alive, as paradoxical as that was. No longer anxious or afraid of his own Interval, he was now only filled with the focus on finding his daughter. Well, that, and the hunger for smell of course. No one could resist that.

How long would drone 63 keep watch over Kitteridge and fill his ROPU? How long would each fill last? And why was it doing that? Could he figure out a way to unlock it himself? If he could pair more drones, could they help others? He had no idea how much time he had left but he knew exactly how much time she had. Down to the second. Kitteridge, his new drone pal, and his constant companion, the family electronic owl, all make their way down the streets of this DZ and begin their search for his girl.

*

Back at what is left of Kitteridge's home, another survivor has been stalking the drones carrying away his daughter. Somehow hidden amongst the shadows of the dust she creeps up on the hovering drones. A quick TAP, TAP with her light-sword from under her cape and both drones smoothly lower down, ready for maintenance. The woman gently lifts the little babe and wraps her in her coat. She will take this baby back to the Waster Kings, but she knows she must be careful. An extra child would be noticed, and binary unity would call for her elimination. The woman lovingly wraps the baby in her shawl and the newborn disappears from sight. They make their way out into the night. She will watch over and care for the baby; this woman had nothing else to do living here past Tranquility Base. Recently, she felt that her grip, her wall of mental and physical resistance that had kept her from Puff all these years, was slipping away from her. If she didn't have anything else to do, she knew she would turn to the Puff. But this gave her a new purpose, life's ultimate purpose: to raise and care for another.

Chapter 4

2 Years before the Container Accident at DZ: 23N

The dilithium crystals weren't supposed to explode like that. But the vapor that burst in his face two years ago in many ways saved his life and his marriage.

It only happens once in a while. Sometimes you get a 'popper'. They are rare but do happen. That it was Kitteridge's first time trying Puff, well that was just bad luck. But like most Puff heads, his first hit was the best, accident aside. He would spend the rest of his days chasing that dragon. He was addicted instantly and didn't care about the side effects or what it did to his health or family. Kitteridge wanted, no, now knew that he needed more smells. But in this case the sticky dilithium crystals congealed inside his Puff tube. And they exploded violently when heated through his ROPU hose, hence the colloquial but universally hated 'popper'.

It wasn't cheap but he had saved up for months. Not to mention the fact that he had sprung for the ROPU hose modification upfront; he wanted his first time to be the best. He had done his research and knew just what to ask for. Kitteridge wasn't going to be taken advantage of by someone thinking, knowing, it was his first time and trying to sell him some newbie special. He had it all planned out and was all set on getting the best, damn sure he was ready for the experience. He had been waiting for that complex blend of smells and tastes to awaken his senses that had been dead, but ever yearning, since birth. The lights were about to go on and he had his finger on the proverbial switch. He wouldn't go for anything lame, like some newbie special 'first timer'. Nope, only the best. This new dealer was supposed to have access to way more interesting stuff than most. Kitteridge had arranged everything down to the second, and he was going to be sure to get something unique, something truly special, and something worthy of his best and first time. He wouldn't be pushed around. Only the best, most complex experience would do for Kitteridge.

Best to start him with something simple they 'agreed' – not so much agreed but it was to be the 'first timer' for him, the dealer insisted; hit the savory taste buds and watch them explode, it would be more than enough. Slow roasted, hickory-smoked, prime rib French Dip, with a fresh sandwich roll, and plenty of au jus for dipping. That it cost extra credits for the favor of melting down the Life[x] into au jus didn't matter to him. Nothing mattered to him more than chasing that first smell. Arby's was now his paradise, an oasis that could never be found again.

Back at his home now, he knew he had to get started because there were lots of little things to arrange just so, they said. For Kitteridge, the ritual was foreign, what with him being a virgin to Puff and all. He had heard about it and knew that preparation was key to the experience. I mean, sure, you could do it in the back alley behind the dealer's place, but that was desperate. Your first time was supposed to be special. He did his research, talked to the guys around the office, even wrote some notes down from the dealer who gave him the Puff. Well, no one gave Kitteridge anything. The dealer didn't so much as give it to him as

Kitteridge had worked his ass off to save credits, even stretched out his rations to trade-in, so he could buy it. He even convinced Marianna to stretch her rations more; he's still not sure how he managed to convince her that was a good idea, but she pitched in as well with no complaints. He thought he saw her getting skinnier due to the smaller portions, but that was probably just the long gestating baby inside her. Kitteridge was excited to be a father; it was something he always knew he would be good at and looked forward to. And he knew Marianna was going to be a good mother; he was sure of that. But right now, he had more pressing things ahead of him. He wasn't sure how long the experience would be, or what state he would be left in when it was over; the high could last minutes or hours. Would he be able to hold himself together if she came home and he was still high on Puff? Thankfully, he had waited until she went to one of her electorate rallies. Those always ran long.

Studying his notes all the way home, he attended to his inner sanctuary and prepared himself for the life-changing experience. Okay, his 'sanctum' was just a tiny bathroom in the hovel of a home he was forced by marriage and the Collective to share with Marianna these last hundred million or so seconds. It was packed on one side with the maglev evacuator booth, and other than the door swinging inward, the bathroom was roomy enough to sit down, even lay down if things got too much for him. Plus, it had a dimmer switch that controlled the lights, and the floor was heated to a cozy eighty-one degrees. This room was one of the few domestic wins Kitteridge ever got in the constant parlay of a married couple, the self-sacrifices of a back and forth that they knew they had to make work in order for life to go on here. There simply wasn't another option, no one went against the marriage assignments. Don't get me wrong, though. Kitteridge and his wife were among the lucky ones. They found their conventionally arranged marriage pleasant and convenient. They enjoyed each other's company in every way a husband and wife must if their relationship was meant to endure; physically, romantically, emotionally, and mentally they were better together. Sexual attraction was never an issue because everyone always looked so polished and fashionable. Plus, playing sexy time with your wife was an excellent form of entertainment while you waited for your next tech support call. They were a good complement; some would say a perfect match. He liked to work and was good at it. She enjoyed not working. She had found other things to keep her mind occupied and stave off the hunger for smell. They truly loved each other, Kitteridge and Marianna of DZ: 23N. But the one thing he loved most, even before ever experiencing it for himself, the one thing above Marianna, was smell.

He had been preparing for this for months and had been dreaming of it for years. Kitteridge came into the home and took off his cape and jacket and hung them up on the hooks that she had him install on the door. Marianna didn't like a messy house and jackets lying around covered in dilithium dust just wouldn't do, thank you very much. The hooks and organizing procedures and preferences were her domestic wins. She never lorded it over him, but, then again, he was quick to react when she asked. That seemed enough to satisfy her nesting instincts. He kept his dusty boots off the furniture, and she made sure to keep a bare minimum of pillows on their marriage bed. Ever since she became pregnant, there has been an ever-growing wall between them. An impenetrable and constantly growing wall of pillows. Lately Marianna has even taken to balancing her ROPU on the top and he can only see the very top of her head now when he looks over on her side. In fact, Kitteridge had taken the time to make a detour and pick up another pillow on his way home. Happy wife, happy life, and all.

Safely back at home, Kitteridge shuffled around and slung out the trademark brown and green pouch from under his cape and searched for the Puff tube. He couldn't find it in his pouch. Where was it? Not in his coat pockets or in his vest. His pants and their various cargo compartments, with zippers and snaps, are full of useful stuff for everyday living here, but no Puff tube. Even his secret boot storage, the one where he keeps the knife his father gave him, has no Puff tube. He reaches back into his pouch and pushed everything aside, frantic for now he couldn't find the tube in there either. In a panic he ripped the bag off and emptied it out on the floor and scattered everything about looking for the tube. Not until he put his hands up and into his hair, ready to pull it out in frustration, did he feel the tube in his left hand. It was warm and squishy from him squeezing it so tight in his grubby mitts. He had been waiting so long that he didn't want to lose it. He must have carried it with him all the way home just to keep it safe.

Even though Marianna was gone, he saw sure to schedule this for when she was away at one of her electorate rallies that always ran long, he creeps down the hallway just the same. He stops halfway and turns back to the front door. He was pretty sure he had locked it but better to be safe. Kitteridge didn't know how he would react to his first Puff, so he wanted to be safely inside his modest but respectable home. Home alone for hours was how he had planned it. Dedicated time just to focus on the smells of roast beef and fresh sourdough rolls. He didn't know what au jus smelled or tasted like, but safely alone in his home, Kitteridge's mouth started to water all the same. Pavlov and his dogs couldn't be more predictable.

This would be the third time Kitteridge had tried to Puff, and he had his fingers crossed that it was the charm. The anticipation, years of waiting, months of savings, and then to have it scrubbed, was agony. Worse than even the constant search and thirst for smells. The first go round she came back two hours early but thankfully he hadn't started yet. It just looked like he spent a long time in the bathroom, having trouble with the maglev evacuator again, she probably assumed. The second time, once it had all been arranged, she was going to meet a friend, and he travelled across the compound for the meet-up, but the dealer was a no show. He waited well past the allotted time and had to head back home empty-handed; Marianna was suspicious that he returned so quickly that night but didn't say anything to Kitteridge when he handed her a surprise pillow. This third time the dealer was there all right; it had cost him an extra two credits just to make sure the guy showed up on time. You could trust this guy, they said; he had been doing this a long time now. But the dealer could also modify his hose right then and there, fit it with the extension for Puff. Lord knows he couldn't wait the standard two weeks to have his ROPU hose modified to take Puff tubes.

Down the hallway and into the bedroom he takes his boots off and then his pants and then his boxer briefs. The waves of heat cause your legs to sweat, they say. Better to just let them be free, they say. His vest and shirt come off next, but he leaves his socks on. They say you need them for traction when you finally do get up. Kitteridge slings his ROPU over his now naked body and grabs hold of the modified hose, ready to insert the tube. Nude as his wedding night, except for his socks, the special ones with little traction nubs on the bottom, he shuffles out of the little bedroom and into the third door on the left. He does all this with the Puff tube still clutched in his hand. He had waited so long for this that he couldn't just let it go.

Safely in the bathroom now, he closes the door and lowers the lights. Lights were key to the ritual: too dark and the demons set in; too light and then the gorilla panic gets you. Glad he sprung for the dimmer switch when they upgraded the bathroom a few million seconds back. She had argued against it, and he knew it was because she wanted the whole house to be as bright as an operating room. But he had insisted and prevailed. Lights low, nice and dim, please. Too bright and the dances of light and sparkles that explode in the back of your eyes were blinding. It took a little futzing with the dimmer switch; it was a cheap and finicky one – too low and it just turned the lights off, up a little was a nice pleasing tone but there was a noticeable flicker. Just a hair lower than mid-point is what everyone recommended when he researched the dimmer. There is even a thin line, ever so slightly raised like thin brail marks for the blind, to mark the ideal position for the dimmer. Seems the people who make and sell these things had Puff in mind when they made them. Kitteridge complies, no flicker, nice glow; that will do just fine, thank you very much.

Kitteridge put the fuzzy bathmat under the gap in the door to prevent any residual vapors from escaping. He paid the extra credit for the leakproof tube and hose-mod, but you couldn't be too sure. Kitteridge had read about a woman who didn't do this, and the vapor escaped, just enough to addict her daughter outside in the simple hovel. The dealer who sold it to him had confirmed it too; true story, he said. Trust me, the dealer said, been doing this a long time. A thick bathmat was essential. Safely tucked under, double folded, and the bathmat is pressed in place. He is satisfied that even if she comes home, she will just think he is screwing around to get the right suction on the maglev evacuator. Marianna likes it softer than he does. It was a delicate balance of external air pressure, and the maglev suction settings were known to be tricky.

Kitteridge placed his headphones in and turned on the white noise. Anything other than soothing static would be too much during his altered state. The hallucinations alone were going to be enough. He slid down the wall and took a seat against the door. The bathroom floor, set to a balmy Bermuda 81, had already started to make his legs sweat. Thin beads of moisture form cold drops on his legs, so he pulled them up and sat crisscross like a schoolboy again.

He originally had pushed for the cinnamon bun experience. The news was always talking about upcoming and recent Puff breakthroughs, and rumor had it that this last batch 'was it'. The code had been cracked, the last elusive smell and taste experience had been recreated, and it was worth every credit. Be the first to try it and you will be the envy of the compound, they said. He knew it would be expensive, and even harder to get; you had to find someone willing and able to bring it all the way from DZ: 23A. Even though they intersect it is a long and treacherous journey, what with the Platform constantly shifting about. But Kitteridge saved up, both credits and time. He had passed judgement for himself and his actions and was ready. Kitteridge knew he might have to try a dealer or two to find the right one, but he was willing to wait. He wanted his first time, the time that he knew the hit would be the longest and strongest, to be the best it could be. And what could be better than the cinnamon bun experience? Rumor is they used to have dedicated stores just for vending out delicious freshly baked single serve cinnamon bun treats. It was a unifying gathering of the masses. But now everyone just hungered for the smell of a cinnamon bun. Especially Kitteridge.

But the dealer told him he wasn't ready for that. Too much, too soon, and trust me, I been doing this a long time, helped many through their first time. The vertigo and vomiting of a noob would be sure to ruin the experience. Plus, it was way too expensive for him to afford. This particular dealer was recommended by many like a sommelier at a fine five-star Michelin restaurant, one who has been doing this for a long time now, you can trust him, long time now. Well, he simply couldn't, just shouldn't, wouldn't even select that flavor for himself. It wasn't right, still not the perfect mix. The cinnamon bun reward credits, all 250 of them, would go outstanding. The Pufflier's recommendation, or rather condemnation at him for even suggesting something so outlandish as the cinnamon bun experience, well that weighed heavily on Kitteridge's mind too. This guy knew his stuff, and Kitteridge trusted him. Been doing this a long time, they say. And from the dark, crimson-stained scarf around his neck, Kitteridge could tell the dealer was no newbie when it came to different Puff experiences. Prime rib cooked to a medium-rare perfection, center cut, please. What's that, the dealer said? "Oh, yeah, the 'first timer' we call it. Perfect for you. You can trust me you know. And for you, one credit off. I like you for some reason, must be the face. Remind me of a kid I used to roll with back on DZ: 23A. Weird how they intersect sometimes, huh?"

There was no doubt about it; the popper Kitteridge got was a raw deal. Some say it is just a bad batch by a lazy or novice maker that results in a popper. Some say the maker's signature anti-itch powder causes a bad reaction when accidentally intermixed with the crystals. When heated through the ROPU hose, the Puff-enhanced vapor was released. Euphoria and nose bleeds were sure to come. Unless you got a popper – then your experience will be impactful indeed. Nose bleeds will be the least of your problems when that thing explodes in your face. The high was very, very short but life-changing for Kitteridge.

He swore off the Puff after that initial batch and first experience. He vowed to Marianna that he would never touch the stuff again. But the pain and the hunger would always remain. The explosion from the bad Puff popper had sent the vapor straight into his eyes. Unprotected, his eyes immediately cast over a deep black pale. It was a mutation that humans developed eons ago to protect them from the dilithium dust. Kitteridge's eyes would never be the same again, but, most importantly, he would still be able to see. No more pupils or whites in his eyes. Just big dark opals shining back. They had a milky haze to them, just a slight sadness peeking out that gave them an almost gunmetal-black quality. The color and pale of the extra eyelids that protected his sight made for a hardened look, little solid diamond shapes of darkness that protruded out slightly. Kitteridge wasn't left looking 'bug-eyed' so much. But his eyes were big, and very black. As Kitteridge struggled back to his feet and saw his altered image for the first time, he knew there was no way Marianna wouldn't notice. It was the last thought that passed through his mind before he blacked out.

The explosion in the sanctuary – well, shared bathroom – stirred no one. That was the idea, after all, and at least some of his plan was working out. He would lie on the bathroom floor for many thousands of seconds, Marianna was of course gone at one of her electorate rallies, and those always ran long. When she did return, she found him lying on the tile floor naked, sprawled out over his ROPU, in the dim dark. Man, she hated that stupid dimmer switch! She had to really press the door open because for some reason the bathmat had been jammed under the door. He was lying face down, naked, and appeared to be breathing. She did notice his socks were still on. Marianna knew at once what had happened and breathed a sigh of relief. She was prepared for this, knowing he would lose the battle and turn to the Puff eventually – had been waiting for millions of seconds. And in many ways encouraging him as of late; he didn't need a new scarf, but she bought him one as a surprise a few months back. It was a little darker color than his current one. The luxurious velvet scarf was a deep crimson red just in case he needed it to wipe away any blood before she came home. And the special socks with the little nubs on them was a sure sign of the secret pact they had made without saying a word. She didn't know the details of what happened, but it was clear it most definitely had not gone according to script. Kitteridge was a planner by nature; no way had this been part of his grand plan. Most people's first time they are found sitting down just simply recalling over and over the smell and taste that they will now chase forever. She rolled him over gently, preparing herself, not knowing what to expect. His eyes appeared closed forever and were no longer shining back the hope of Tranquility Base. She was prepared for his Puff addiction and had even been secretly saving her Life[x] rations so that they would have extra to exchange for credits and more Puff. Her life to come would support them both until they made their return; in many ways they had been preparing for that too by agreeing to stretch their rations together. She confirmed with her nurse drone that she could stretch further, lose a little more weight, and still not hurt her unborn daughter. Marianna didn't say anything at the time, but she knew and kind of actually wanted him to spring for the ROPU hose modification. If he was going to Puff, might as well go all out and be as safe as possible. Though she hated the stuff, even Marianna knew the ROPU hose mods would make sure you didn't re-hit a hot tube. She had agreed to just half a ration of Life[x] a month when he suggested it. But Marianna was sure that life would be better there on Tranquility Base. She knew it. And surely, they would see the suffering he had gone through, the suffering they had both gone through; maybe his new eye color and look might actually work in their favor when it came time to seat assignments, she thought.

His pre-selected wife Marianna, assigned by simple marks on some ROPUs, had been on Kitteridge about the stuff for years. She could tell he was losing his grip on this inner demon. When the nightmares and pre-withdrawal symptoms set in, it changed him. She got him out of the bathroom and into the bed; it took a little bit as she had to move off all her precious pillows. But he rested for many thousands of seconds before awakening with a bed shaking nightmare. This time he wasn't yelling or moaning. Kitteridge just needed to curl up and cry even though he could no longer produce tears. He knew the next million or so seconds would be painful, and he wouldn't sleep much. Neither of them would as Marianna attended to him and brought Kitteridge through his recovery. Withdrawal from just one hit; Puff was that powerful. Kitteridge couldn't sleep or even enjoy his daytime naps. His dreams were haunted. He would wake up screaming, punching, and kicking the bed. Marianna feared for her life when he was overcome by the night terrors. She began to lose track of the times she found him sleep walking, mumbling and wandering around, with his dark cloudy eyes staring out at nothing. Sometimes his moaning was enough to wake her up. And if that didn't, the fact that he was practically attacking anything nearby was definitely enough to wake even the dead. But she eventually had enough and knew he was near to his breaking point. She knew that one day soon Kitteridge would give in to his overwhelming desire for smell. His baser instincts, the addictive qualities of his personality, would take over and win the long fight.

She knew Kitteridge was close to his breaking point because he would talk food, taste, texture, and above all smell. He babbled about it constantly. Sure, most people talked about smelling again; parties where you went around the room and shared your artisanal cuisine fantasies happened all the time. But few people got into yelling matches, arguing with themselves in a constant low chatter. He was always talking about food. His desire for cinnamon buns was absolutely consuming his thoughts and mind. He began to wax philosophically about food, especially at night.

The nightmares made it worse for Marianna and made his desire even stronger; lack of sleep was known to bring on the hunger for smell. There is nothing like being awoken to the sound of someone yelling over and over "BLUEBERRY PIE" or worse yet, "GET OFF OF HER!" The worst was a grippingly real nightmare, an image of the house buckling under the flood. Huge streams of water cracking the foundation of the Platform and crushing everyone inside as it sunk down. His screams for her to "GRAB THE GIRLS, GRAB THE GIRLS" had brought her to the breaking point. Marianna would no longer fight against it; she would just help him through it. Enough with the nagging, veiled hints, and suggestions. Now was the time to just be with him, Kitteridge needed her almost as much as the baby growing inside her. She was his umbilical cord, keeping him grounded as much as she could. At just age twelve she considered their marriage a failure even though she had confirmed her pregnancy and been with child for the last year. She was willing to fight for her daughter to have a better life. It was Tranquility Base for the both of them. She would secure her seat and make sure her Puff head loser of a husband came even if Marianna had to drag his ass along too. She just knew that Tranquility Base had room for all three of them and for Kitteridge, especially, life would be better there.

*

But those days of stained scarves and dirty bandannas were over. He had been sober and without the drug for thirty-one million seconds. His year without Puff was to be his gift to the newborn baby. It was a promise he made partly from the catalyst of his Puff mistake and partly because once 'it' had a name it hit home and really became real for Kitteridge. He reminds himself of his sobriety every morning when he awakes with a "Good morning, Rachel" and says goodnight to her as he settles into the dark sky. After all this searching, the countless homes rummaged through, the nights spent looking for a girl with a scar, Kitteridge didn't know if he would be around for her much longer unless he finds her soon. Before the dilithium side effects ate him alive from the inside out.

Even with the thin scar on her cheek, his chances of finding her were not good, and they lessened every day. If… no, he was sure that he would, so once he finds her, he doesn't know what he will need to do to save her and get out of there alive together. If he found them, or rather when they found him, the Waster Kings would be by his side during the rescue mission. But what happens after that? And how will Kitteridge make it until the next trip to Tranquility Base?

Chapter 5

00:00 to 31,536,000: 13 Years until Tranquility Base

Back at DZ: 23N and the houses gathered to distribute the surviving orphans amongst them, those who had been picked up by the Waster King scouts as they fled the scene at the community center. No hope for Tranquility Base for them. But they had their children now. They were still alive and breathing through their little ROPUs' hoses. Those who had survived the drone attack and passed their Interval had been rounded up. The remaining hunter drones, all sixteen of them, left in unison when the nursemaid drones arrived the next morning to begin the new mission of protecting and caring for their new workforce. There were thirty-two left to watch over, which meant that each house would get eight babies to care for. The sixteen nursemaid drones would remain with the children all their lives and care for them at each clan house.

Each house had grouped themselves by allegiance to the flora and fauna of old as a way to live out their legacy. There were the animal clans, named after the fierce predators that once stalked this land, and the flora tribes. Hundreds of years of stories, passed down through generations, had kept the image and spirit of their ancestors alive. There was the Lion Clan, the Bear Clan, Clan Eagle, and the mysterious Spider Clan. Each gathering and performing rituals and rites of passage ceremonies at the crystal-preserved statues that littered the landscape. For protection from the flora tribes, and the drones they knew were coming, and the ever-present dust, they built massive, electrified shield walls around their village compounds. These surround their hexagonal dome-shaped houses and other various indoor compounds where they lived safely protected from the deadly outside environment. Huge sprawling settlements were protected from the drones inside the shield walls. These tribal villages united under different banners based on location and considered these settlements their home base of operations and housing. There was Lion's Den, Bear Cave, Eagle's Nest, and Spider's Web all scattered across the landscape of the Platform. But the Collective navigation marking signs just referred to them by their DZ designation, DZ: 23N, 23S, 23B, and of course DZ: 23X.

The thirty-two orphans were distributed and assigned their new allegiances in a quick round-robin fashion. Each house gets their eight babies and their eight nursemaid drones. The remaining Collective drones scatter away from DZ: 23N. Their mission complete, they now go back, presumably more recycling to do. Where they go no one is certain. Some believe they become part of the Platform again and go back to constantly moving it around the planet. No one knows why. Or cares that much. After fourteen years, these people will go to Tranquility Base and live out their days not worrying or caring about drones any more. In the meantime, now that the orphans have been assigned, the monthly rations of Life[x] will begin arriving and the population will be well taken care of. These individuals are needed as tech support superstars. Those propeller blades aren't going to change themselves.

The accident at DZ: 23N is deemed sabotage by the Collective. A deliberate attack by the Waster Kings always after their precious cargo, it was declared. To punish the children of DZ: 23N, the Collective cut the Life[x] rations in half. They know this is what the Waster Kings are after, anyway. Fewer rations means fewer attacks, and fewer attacks leads to better tech support. After about six months, the emergency rations are gone. DZ: 23N has thirty-two reasonably healthy and growing happy kids. But they are hungry and no amount of Life[x] can satiate them. Simply put, they eat too much for their current supply line to keep up.

The nursemaid drones know this is coming. They have communicated amongst themselves and decided the day and night to rectify the situation: half the rations naturally meant half the mouths to feed. The extras would have to be eliminated; the logic went. Simple supply and demand, it goes; not cruel, just economics. You couldn't argue with the numbers, right? The fact that they could probably stretch the rations and keep more than half alive forever wasn't in their programming. Their relentless drive for binary unity caused them to agree. Half the rations equals half the population. Plus, the seats were limited on the trip to Tranquility Base. It is better to terminate some of the helpless souls now than to have their hopes dashed and die of a broken heart if they can't survive their Interval and aren't selected for the trip. It was empathy, or so the programming went. The nursemaids all act together and the Platform keeps them in synch. A quick swipe of their tail and the laser-saw split the kids down the middle. It was over in an instant. The sweeper drones knew what was about to go down and were at the ready, even had tarps out underneath the split apart babies to make sure the blood didn't hit the Platform. The drones had learned it tended to leave a slippery mess.

Six months after the attack on DZ: 23N and the night started with thirty-two children. After the sweeper and nursemaid drones leave, there are signs of only sixteen. These are the sixteen children of DZ: 23N. They will grow up here on this desolate planet, and for now they will be well fed with their full rations. The ever-present danger of dilithium poisoning would keep them bound to live indoors. Sure, the bold, or some would say stupid, could be convinced or cajoled into a skip outside for a dare in their teens. Everyone did a 'dust dip', it was a rite of passage. Fun, but done with a seriousness of purpose because most of all dust dips had to be done quickly. Back inside in exactly three minutes. Anything less and you were considered a wuss, someone who didn't pass whatever stupid initiation it was. Besides, it was foolish to try to return before three minutes. Your buddies would be holding the door closed until just the last second. BURST! the door would pop open right at one hundred and eighty seconds and you all would spill in laughing. But anything more than three minutes was just suicide. Everyone knew that and everyone followed that rule.

Sixteen children would grow up here in this compound. Their life had meaning and purpose, pre-assigned and determined down to the second. They would live out their days and have many of the same milestones and experiences as you and me. They would marry, get a steady job, work hard most of their lives until retirement, and all worked toward the same goal. But the life experience here was unlike what you and I think of today as growing up. They did go to school; that is the same. But there was no school dance and no pep-rally for the home team. There were no advanced degrees or further fields of study, no music and no poetry. It was a vocational world when it came right down to it. These people were here for a purpose and were sent here to do a job. And the Collective would see to it that they did their job or would impose more rationing shortages until they do. Just like the Waster Kings these drones know how to control a population. Seems hunger is another proper motivator.

Brides were matched with their husbands at birth. More accurately, respirators/ventilators were distributed in pairs. The carnage and binary unity achieved by the drones over the last year has culled this Interval's population of DZ: 23N to just the sixteen babies, their nursemaid drones, and the elders living and working Past Tranquility Base. From the moment the cargo container hit the Platform, each ROPU had been marked with an associated pair during the original housing assignment. The couple would grow old together, always knowing they would marry, have a child, and retire together on Tranquility Base. The only thing standing between them and their future was their Interval when their ROPU ran dry. They would grow up side-by-side with their future spouses. The Waster Kings saw to it that the betrothed were housed close to each other. The children were raised like siblings, or close cousins, in many respects. But Waster Kings, and the nursemaid drones from the Collective, would weave elaborate stories and encourage any budding feelings or romance between the pair. These children grew up knowing they were destined for three things: 1) tech support; 2) whom and when they would marry and expect to birth a child; and 3) that they would be among the ones chosen to go to Tranquility Base. Surely, I was unique. Just like everyone else was so sure of their own individuality and supreme worth. The Collective saw to this desire and 'bred' it into everyone. It was the lifeblood of hope that you would be among those saved and return to Tranquility Base. The chosen few who could survive their Interval. The rest left to rot out their life PTB.

At age four, after 126,144,000 seconds, the pair selected at birth and raised together as close as siblings would be married. It would be a large ceremony and gathering of all the houses. Everyone had the same amount of time on this planet, so might as well get married at the same time. They would live for their remaining years here, working as tech support agents, teaching others the skills, or running Derby Days events trying to be a StatStar. Or rather the husbands would go to work. Most women left the workforce after they got pregnant. The husbands still worked tech support shifts while their wives were busy gestating their young. It was a long and tiring process growing a baby here on the Platform; women would endure approximately two years until their babies big day arrived. Twenty-six months was a standard development period for human babies here. And it was exhausting for the mothers; most were just too tired for the rough and tumble life of tech support. The dilithium crystals seemed to slow down the formation of the baby prior to birth, it was thought to harden and prepare them for a life of dilithium exposure. Then, post-partum, things sped up; actually, accelerated growth outside the womb was expected and considered normal. What you and I think a child of five years-old looks like is nothing next to a child living five years here on the Platform. On the Platform, at age five people looked more like what you would think a later teenager does. No one knows the full progression of growth in humans on this planet because most are killed off by the side effects of dilithium poisoning. If they survive their own Intervals.

The children of DZ: 23N are moved out of their collective orphanage after marriage. Each couple is sent away in shifts; someone still has to cover the Platform and drones, so each couple is sent away on a three-week and three days honeymoon 'shift'. Everyone knows they are to spend this time producing a baby at DZ: 23A (so weird how they seem to intersect at just the right time). Each new family is then given their own hexagonal-dome shaped house upon their return to their home DZ. Ensuring their safety, health, and happiness, the Collective would make sure each occupant was protected. At least until their reveal at the Interval. Once their ROPUs had dried out there was nothing even the Collective drones could do to protect these people. The clans and tribes, the remaining inhabitants of the community, would ensure the gift of the watch owls to each baby. Mechanical watchers that will protect each child from birth, until it is passed on to their own offspring. The owl was universal protector amongst all tribes and clans even the Spiders. The owl is an ancient wisdom revered by all.

Just like caring for a newborn baby, the Collective supplied nursemaid drones watched over the remaining sixteen babies who couldn't escape DZ: 23N. These orphans would be raised together but put to work as slaves. They would become the lost children but not discarded orphans as they would be raised under great care. Each child was granted a nursemaid drone to watch over them and provide for their every need. The family owl watches the drones, ever mindful of their presence, suspicious as the most gifted watcher of watchers.

The nursemaid drones changed, bathed, clothed, and fed the children. Life[x] was abundant but difficult to make into any texture other than that of day-old oatmeal. But the Collective was ever careful of their tech support staff and made sure to send just enough Life[x] rations to the population of each DZ. Every ration, encased in their disposable and, of course, recyclable tubes came on time. A single ration could last a fourteen-year-old man about thirty days. One Life[x] ration per month kept you nourished and hydrated, and it was good for your thinning hair and nails. They came monthly, just often enough to keep you working hard till the next package of goodness arrived. Hopefully, this time it will taste like the cinnamon buns, when paired with the latest and greatest Puff. Everyone always hoped and was always disappointed. The goo of the pasty Life[x] actually enhanced the experience of warm dripping cream cheese frosting in your mouth, they say. Better than the real thing, even! Your taste buds almost explode with the bulging rush of sugar in the frosting. But even the most expensive Puff experiences never lived up to the hype. There was a credit reward promised for whichever Puff maker could perfect and package the proper cinnamon bun experience. Guaranteed exclusive distribution rights would mean not just the inventor's cash and riches but true wealth. Every month was like the Mega Millions and Powerball lottery combined all together with the last pitch of a double header, the free throw for the penalty shot, the slapshot for the overtime win. The anticipation of the glory was an experience itself. You never won the lottery, but it was still fun to play. You never would get cinnamon buns, but the smell would still wake you up in the middle of the night. Or was it day? The constant darkness didn't matter, for everyone was trying to smell all the time. Sniffing or even snorting was common as noses search desperately for something besides dilithium dust and spores to fill it. For many, sniffing and snorting became like an unconscious tick – something to fill the gaps between words like 'um' or 'like'. Complex dialogues of only snorts, sniffs, and nasal grunts and whistles had developed to take advantage of this. And everyone liked and searched for smells, especially the desirable but elusive cinnamon bun.

The population of this area would never go wanting, except for smells and taste. The Collective knew this was on the edge of good form but did use this human need for olfactory satisfaction against them. The fact that the nose was actually intended for something had become a sort of population control. An underground market existed for strong Puff that would bring out and enhance the experience of choking down Life[x]. The thick chalky paste would crumble like cardboard in your mouth without some good Puff. But mod your reg hose, man! Spend the credit and grab that Puff tube by the horns and get you some! Then great mouth-filling bites would lump out of the tube in a goop, but you wouldn't care that you were cheap and didn't spring for the texture upgrade. The loopy goo smelled so good you didn't care. In fact, you didn't care about anything. Other than smell. Even the 'first timer' Puff was still a solid choice.

These monthly packages would keep the slaves tied to their hovels waiting for their next meal. But it never felt like you were hungry. The Life[x] sort of stuck to your bones that way. Something had to make it take thirty days to digest and absorb. And there was very little byproduct or waste. The maglev evacuators made quick work of that but only when they were in working order themselves that is. Seldom did the evacuators around DZ: 23N seem to work.

Maybe because it was so bland, and just frankly not good, people never hoarded their Life[x] rations. Those who did could command a high price from the Waster Kings. If they were nice. They could also just send a representative from the Credit Dealer and Collection Guild to bend your ROPU hose until you gave up your rations. That was the hard way. Most people chose the easy way and just gave up their rations without a fuss.

The Life[x] was good enough for you all right. But the actual eating experience, even when lacking smell or taste, well, it left a lot to be desired. It had to have been designed that way on purpose to ensure that the underlying drive for smell was never satiated. To try and combat this, and make more money as add-ons to Puff, the Waster Kings were always coming out with new flavor and texture combinations. But they weren't cheap. New food-based experiences went anywhere from one to fifteen credits. The long-standing bounty of two hundred and fifty credits for the perfect cinnamon bun remained unbroken for hundreds of years. That was a lifetime of earnings, one that could be collected and saved only by crooked politicians and hip-hop superstars of old, the kind that could build generational wealth. Most Puff makers at least dabbled in a side hobby of cinnamon bun bakery; they all agreed the itching was worth it.

The one thing the Waster Kings needed was new mixes and textures. The abundance of Life[x], and the desire for making new and interesting mealtime flavors, meant another constant source of demand from the population. Something that paired with the Puff and would turn eating into a dining experience. This was carefully measured and rationed out to people by Waster Kings. Even the most hardened Puff users had to wait between hits, by design. Choke the supply and reap the demand. Because of course the expertly paired texture and Puff combination didn't come in your regular monthly package. That was just bland tubes of goo. But different textures were readily available and sold at underground markets where the currency was credits bartered back and forth. The Collective knew and even encouraged this process and exchange. It ensured a motivated and efficient workforce. They didn't care about the hunger and greed it created in the human mammal. Everyone dreams of cinnamon buns, and no one can eat just one. If a Puff maker could just perfect the cinnamon bun and win the reward, that would be huge. But the long-term royalties... just think of the passive revenue stream... even better than writing a dystopian sci-fi novel as a side hustle while you worked full-time. Trust me, been doing this for a long time.

Life[x] in its purest form was just a lump of sticky dilithium crystals, but the Collective had figured out how to collect and process it and created a vitamin-rich mix that ensured not only nutrition but also hydration. Knowing you could go a month without food or water made for a different life experience. Different forces of hunger drive you and they always would. Mild psychotropics and hallucinogens were baked right into Life[X]. It helped solidify the stories of Tranquility Base and locked in the hope that drove them all. That, and at around twelve years-old your rations started containing just enough MDMA to make that honeymoon experience one of legend.

Life[x] was hard as a rock, but, once refined, it became that sticky, odorless, and colorless goo everyone knows, loves, and dreads. A slime that was stuffed and crammed into little tubes and sent out to each DZ monthly. The standard textures, soft and chewy, or hard and crispy, were in your regular ration. But the Waster Kings had learned to make so much more. They couldn't make everything, and the cinnamon bun remained elusive. Recipe hunters were always on the lookout. Breakfast had been conquered long ago. There was nothing like fresh orange juice and bacon with eggs and toast in the morning. Spread some homemade marmalade preserves on there and you can't ask for a better start to your day... or night, as it were. Life[x]'s ability to suppress hunger meant lunch was an extinct and foreign concept. But dinner was an affair to remember if you had the right Puff and Life[x] texture mix. Want some you say? I got the perfect dealer, been doing this a long time; you can trust him.

All of your standard cuisines were available. For the low price of just a few credits you could get savory Szechuan noodles or sweet pineapple fresh from Hawaii. French dip was great, of course, the perfect starter to Puff, your classic 'first timer'. Chicken fried steak was awesome and BBQ ribs just fell off the bone. Filet mignon and chicken were especially good but unique in their own right. Because the Life[x] was chemically mixed and balanced to perfection, nothing tasted like chicken. Chicken tasted (and most importantly smelled) like the best fried bird ever to roam the earth. Chicken was a premium white meat, not like pork. And we are not talking about some bland and dried out bird that has been baked to a crumbling crisp over 21,600 seconds. I deep-fry my birds in peanut oil. You and I are not the same. Chicken was considered gourmet, as was ice cream. The bacon ice cream, a concoction by some evil genius maker, was especially good. Only the elite tech support agents who knew kernel code enjoyed bacon ice cream. The rest just ate the bacon plain. But it was the best crispy crunchy bacon you could imagine. Definitely worth the nosebleed.

The crowd favorite texture was a tie between the perfect little blue circle ring ones that were sold in little packages, or the red bags with their stringy cheese-like texture. People called them blue ringers or red stringers because branding was never a strong suit for the Waster Kings. The two 'artisanal' Life[x] textures melded into that right juicy mix and slowly dissolved in your mouth when paired with the right Puff. Interestingly enough, though, they hardened into small sticks when baked. Just a bite or two in size meant you could get a number of sticks from each batch. Perfect for carrying around and complementing your crunchy circle ones. They could be mixed together to create almost any sensation. The balance of sweet and crunchy with soft and savory was perfect. All a hard-working slave, er, tech support agent, needed.

The dilithium crystal is a vast and wondrous thing. Its full potential likely still untapped. It grew in unlimited quantities, and the entire planet's surface appeared to be made from it; the Platform and its crystals were ubiquitous. One of the rather interesting and more useful side effects of the crystal was the increase in growth rate of the human mammal. DZ: 23N had its sixteen babies all well cared for by the nursemaids. After just one year of life, thirty-one million seconds passed on their ROPUs, the babies are all running and playing at recess. They are fully grown, walking, and talking. Carrying on rich conversations and studying hard for their next tech support exam. The crystal dust accelerates growth rates so that they just keep on going, starting at birth, but then seem to slow to a crawl around what we think of as mid-thirties. That would be just a few short years out here on the Platform.

Chapter 6

31,536,001 to 63,072,000: 12 Years until Tranquility Base

Every new inhabitant of DZ: 23N, all sixteen remaining babies, were born just two years ago. They are like every child on this planet – a perfect specimen and an outstanding example of the most iconic human physical traits. Countless blood lines have mixed over the centuries and the resulting people were just beautiful. Strong and virile they possessed everything needed for thriving here. They are solid as a rock, the three hours of physical fitness, gymnastics, weightlifting, and swimming ensure their sculpted bodies were always ready, but flexible and extremely agile from the daily one-hour yoga sessions. Long flowing hair like something out of an old shampoo commercial on TV. Polished nails were always the right length and shape. Just a slight feminine extension and curve for the ladies starting from birth. There was no need for nail color or manicures really. Haircuts were a thing of the past as their locks shifted and took on a color and shape of their own.

Despite the shifting appearance and similarities, people looked different enough that you could still them apart, even through all the constant appearance and outfit changes. It was easy enough as there were no siblings amongst the population. All were single orphaned kids to be raised by the Collective, although no one felt alone. These fine individuals had been selected literally from birth to serve. They had been judged and deemed worthy of raising, fitted with a ROPU, and sent to their new domiciles where their nursemaid pairs would be waiting. They will raise them with care. Not so much raise them with love, like from a parent to a child per se, but the kids of DZ: 23N would never go wanting or in need of anything. The Collective would see to that. If left wanting it had proven to lead people to immoral behavior like hoarding, looting, prostitution, fighting, or wars. That always ended in a massive uprising of the people against the Collective. Give them too much choice and they uprise, sometimes they turn on each other but most of the time they just stop fixing the drones. Give the people not enough choice and they rebel. Tell them they are destined to live out their days here stuck inside their hexagonal hovels waiting to be called out for tech support duty; yes, you really need to spend two hours of your precious lifetime, to now go out in the cold dark night and fix it, and soon. Before it hits your stats. Probably just a slipped rotator or fan blade, hopefully something easy. The Collective also learned the power of hope and a good narrative. People could be easily kept docile and under control by promising them something as a reward with some vague notion of proving their worth was enough.

But no matter the age, situation, or even time of day she would arrive on scene to fix the paired drone looking as polished as if she just stepped from the shower. Her face's own glow would radiate in the metal frame of the drone casting a pleasing glow which just highlighted her perfect features even more. Her lustrous hair was trimmed close to her head but still looking fashionable and attractive. She went to bed a blonde with curly curls and woke up at dawn, or was it civil dawn? Even earlier than that it must be, probably nautical dawn. That brief and fleeting moment where the sun is just far enough below the horizon as to not be visible, but its light and rays are enough to light the way for ships at sea navigating a tricky and shallow channel. But whatever the scene or time, whenever she arrived, she looked like a runway model strutting in and ready to get that drone up and moving again. Her now long flowing red locks, straight and perfect with no bangs, announced her arrival. She was a redhead for the day? Cool. Wonder what it will be like tomorrow? Features, hair, nail color, eye color, even skin tone all changed day to day. You woke up one day a smooth, fierce looking African warrior and by the next day you were a chubby faced kid from New Jersey. No matter what the look, you were always red carpet ready. Somehow, even with all this shifting, the humans could tell each other apart, including through changes in appearance and clothing.

Sadly, the one thing that did remain the same, year after punishing year, was the almost overwhelming need to smell something. Anything, just something to make your nose tingle again and your mouth water. Fourteen years of hunger that cannot be staved and a thirst that cannot be quenched was too much for most people, even the steeliest. COVID had ensured there was no serious long term physical withdrawal, no stomach pain, no hydration sickness. But the mental need and the desire was always there. Not all bad considering Life[x] was rumored to smell terrible. COVID had ravaged the population of Earth and many more planets including this one. Those who it didn't kill… and it killed a lot, a whole lot. Billions lost forever. A lot of people across the galaxy died from COVID. The survivors were left without their sense of smell. But there were no sicknesses to speak of. Ever. One was always healthy of mind, body, and soul. Complete with the desire and guilt of an unmet, almost primordial, need to smell. There was just no way to keep the wolves away.

There was no more cancer, in fact with the exposure to dilithium, massive and rapid mutation was expected. A pleasant side effect of the ROPU hose always in your nose meant there was no more sleep apnea either. Nothing ever killed or even struck you down for a day here. Even mental health was great and the Collective saw to that with their epic tales of a better future ahead. Provided you were good enough and selected for Tranquility Base. Turns out some Life[x] and the hope of Tranquility Base was enough. No more colds, no depression, no suicide, not even the common flu. Sure, you had the COVID flu, but so did everyone else and there were no symptoms. Other than a constant need for smell, everyone had been struck with that, born with that inherited sickness. Living here it was very much what you would expect if you lived on a remote, barren planet, devoid of sunlight, plants or animals, a constant thirty-four degrees, with no visible sky, moons, stars, or even weather, with a perfect looking and stylish workforce kept happy with stories and a single serving of goo every month.

The Platform was no place for people to stay out on for extended periods of time. Get out, fix your drone, get back. At age five, after spending their lives focused on education, well trade skills really would be more accurate, they would go to work as tech support agents because after five the children of DZ: 23N are now of working age. Their primary mission is no longer education, but hands on, in the real world, life on the Platform doing tech support day in, day out, until you retire. And then, if you were good at your job, kept up your stats, and didn't owe anything to the Credit Dealers and Collection Guild, then you get to go to Tranquility Base.

*

Another top off by drone 63 of his ROPU and Kitteridge is on the move. On the ground Kitteridge is almost invisible. His maglev boots allow him to hover across the surface of the Platform. He zooms along making a tight little dust cloud around him. His rolling whir is easily spotted from above by his faithful owl. Eager to make its way back to his owner, the owl swoops down to reunite with Kitteridge Oak. This family heirloom and protector has been his helpful eyes and wings in the search for his lost, no stolen, daughter.

His daughter has been his singular driving mission that has been pushing him on for the last two years. He no longer really notices the hunger for smell. Not really. Maybe just a little bit. But he has been suppressing it for months now, doing it for his daughter. Rachel needed him to remain strong now more than ever. Kitteridge knows that his daughter will be well taken care of by the Collective. But she needs to know of her heritage. What happened here at DZ: 23N. And together they would figure out a way to Tranquility Base.

Able to support a population of 1.43 million, DZ: 23N was massive. The surface is lousy with large domestic bubbles, scattered as far as the eye could see, stretched across the Platform in perfect little geometric shapes. Pleasing actually, like a jigsaw puzzle carefully put together, the Collective was efficient like that. These domes littered the surface and made up the compound of this DZ. The little houses all glowed inside, constant darkness outside meant constant artificial lighting inside. The lights helped shine the way making easy navigation beacons in the ever-present darkness and smog.

If he really hustled, he could make it through a home in about an hour if he did a really thorough search. Which he did initially, it was possible that people were still alive under the rubble of what used to be their home. But as the seconds wore on, he became less and less thorough. He would poke his boot, kick some stuff around, holler out a cry or two. Then he would mark his notebook with another house recon done. He started counting the number of houses he searched. It became Kitteridge's sort of mark of the day, a show of progress that helped keep him moving. "Good morning, Rachel", search, mark, "Goodnight, Rachel", rinse and repeat for over two years now. By this point he could cover a series of homes in a day, at a good clip he could make it through a dozen or more hovels in a shift. Kitteridge worked in shifts. He would search for eight hours, and then try to sleep for four hours. He lost count of how many times he did that, and his little notebook quickly ran out of room from all the tallying.

The only thing Kitteridge had to measure the time by was his Life[x] consumption and he had long ago finished the ones he quickly swiped from his home before he left. That meant he had been searching for his daughter for over two years now with sadly still no sign of her. But that didn't matter to him because it was just the simple act of the search that kept him going. He knew somehow that she was still alive and that he would find her. He still wasn't sure if he was destined to make it to Tranquility Base or not. But she for damn sure was! He saw her breathe without an ROPU for god's sakes. "Good morning, Rachel", search, mark, "Goodnight, Rachel."

*

For the last two years the family owl and drone 63 have kept their distance. Clearly the owl is suspicious but 63 seems to just ignore it. Except when the owl is recharging and then drone 63 gets uncomfortably close to the back of the bird's head. Today, tonight, whatever it was, as the owl makes its way through the sky, the smog, and down to land on Kitteridge's shoulder it brings its wings back into a defensive position. It halts mid-air while flapping and hovering just a foot or so off his back. Drone 63 has come alive, unleashed from the ROPU, and appears to be in some defensive/protective mode. Oh, it is so on, bring it says the owl! Get some, I've been waiting for this responds 63. Let's dance! Its laser-saws are buzzing with electricity arcing and dancing around. All eight propeller blades are spinning, pushing upward toward the owl. The blade guards come down as the owl screeches. It beats its mighty wings and raises its talons coming in quickly for the kill. Drone and owl collide mid-air and smash into Kitteridge's ROPU, safely tucked away behind him. Kitteridge isn't sure what is going on behind him, but he throws the ROPU off his shoulder without thinking and the quick motion rips the regulator hose from his nose as the ROPU flies across the room.

Another Interval for Kitteridge has started. How many more of these must he endure before he knows? For over two years now he has been awakened by 63 refilling his dilithium crystal supply. It happens seldom enough that he notices when it does happen but often enough that you no longer notice it happening. Usually there is just a quick hiss, airlock release, hiss, lock and then ROPU whirring up. Drone 63 has gotten good and does it now before the ROPU alarm even beeps. Just unlocks and crawls down his back then reaches into the messenger pouch Kitteridge carries now packed with mined crystals. But now, with his ROPU on the ground meters away, he must see if he really can survive his Interval. Three minutes and thirty-one seconds tick off. Only this time he doesn't even have his watch to help distract or focus him, that thing stopped working the moment his first 441 million seconds were up. No wonder people can't tell you how long they live PTB out here, the only measure of time here was your tech support shifts, your stats hopefully increasing, and the various Derby Days qualifiers. Rinse and repeat until you try and survive your Interval.

The ROPU continues its gentle slide across the floor of this abandoned house Kitteridge had chosen this 'night'. It tumbles down with the bird and bleeping robot still now attached. The owl and drone stop fighting and immediately make their way back to Kitteridge. Well, that was somewhat encouraging, or discouraging. Both were either trying to protect him or kill him. Neither cared about his ROPU nor the crystals inside as he originally thought. But with forty-three seconds gone he definitely cares about his ROPU and its lifesaving crystals.

Two minutes and twenty-eight seconds left until he finally knows his Interval truth. The waiting for fourteen years was hard. But everyone did that. The extra two years of searching, hoping, and frustration had been an extra special painful and anxiety inducing experience reserved just for him it seems. He knew that his Interval would be quick, but the mental anguish and the anxiety was hellishly hard to get through. He had done that. Many times over now. It wasn't right that he had to keep reliving that. He did like the fact that he was still living. He wanted to keep it that way, but he had to make his way back to the ROPU. He gets on his hands, knees, and begins to crawl over to his ROPU on the ground. He hopes to make his way under or around the chaos of robots duking it out like some MMA bout. It is sort of a fitting location for the battle in this actual octagon like structure, no fence or cages, but the same thing. Let's have a clean fight gentleman, no biting, and no rabbit punches – now get back to your corners but remember there is no bell. And I won't stop the fight tonight until only one of you is left standing, floating, ticking, whatever. FIGHT!

Drone 63 turns on the owl and grips it in its own mechanical talons, capturing its prey in a giant bearhug. The drone zooms up to the ceiling with its prey package in an instant, knocking the owl on the head, slightly crushing its bird like beak against the inside rafters. As quickly as it went up drone 63 comes down with the owl. It has flipped the bird over and now rides on its back, pressing down the bird's head as it smashes it to the floor. But the bird fights back and frantically beats its wings and takes its turn smashing the drone on the ceiling and then subsequently on the floor for good measure. This parade, up and down, drone and bird, robot and android, propeller blades and wings, smash, boom. Smash, boom. Sort of fun to watch, like a tennis match of the years past. It was hard to endure when it happened right between you and your next breath. Sure, he had ringside seats for the fight, but he was fighting for his own life with every fleeting next second.

One minute and twenty-seven seconds remain, and Kitteridge makes his way to his feet, this crawling business is too slow going. He decides to take a step forward into the chaos and clutter going on in front of him. He takes a step, and the cloud of robotic motion and violence moves back a step. Forward step, backward cloud of metallic screeching, buzzing, death. He walks the fighting whirlwind, a Yosemite Sam of bleeping and screeching, walks it backward away from his ROPU. The entire process takes an agonizing eighty-three seconds before he has shouldered his ROPU. He puts the hose back into his nose with four seconds to spare. Another Interval gone and he was still alive. He hadn't passed so much but was still alive and ready to fight. He was getting good at this passing but not knowing if he passed thing. Kitteridge was starting to accept it now and getting all Zen about it actually.

Kitteridge didn't know if he would have to take them both on and if he even could. But as soon as he began breathing from his ROPU again both his protective owl and what appeared to be his protective drone stopped fighting. They both hovered close by with the owl at shoulder height and drone about knee high floating on maglev. They were definitely not friends and clearly not getting along. But now that he was breathing again the two electronic companions had stopped fighting and a sort of working truce had formed. 63 settles and locks back onto Kitteridge's ROPU. The owl flies down and begins to recharge after its fierce battle, satisfied that imminent danger had been averted, it had done its job and not failed its master like last time.

Drone 63 appears to have been waiting for the recharge cycle. As soon as the owl's eyes closed over 63 unlocked from Kitteridge. Floats out of his cape really and miraculously begins to repair the damage it did to the owl's beak, 63's nursemaid programming had kicked in. Apparently, it would protect them both now that it was paired. Awesome, that should surely come in handy. And even more awesome neither electronic menace was trying to kill him. Hopefully, they will extend the same welcome wagon to Rachel, when he finds her.

*

Three more tubes of Life[x] down and still no sight or sign of his daughter. He had managed to find a few survivors and almost all agreed that any remaining surviving babies had been taken south toward DZ: 23S and so he would try to make his way there. No one had seen a baby with a scar, at least one woman said she did, but then again, she complained of pain in her left wing, so not sure how much to trust her observations. She had no wings of course, but the left one hurt something awful, it burns and itches especially in the morning she lamented. In retrospect when he asked her if she had seen a baby with a scar he shouldn't have been surprised when he had led her to the answer he wanted to hear. Kitteridge gave her the promised Life[x], he had been rationing knowing he would need something to barter with, so he had plenty, plus by now he knew where to find more because everyone seemed to keep their rations in the same place. Emaciated and clearly hungry the woman decides that the best thing to do is rub the Life[x] all over her left wing. Kitteridge walks away, turns around only to see her squeezing the Life[x] tube out all over the ground, but at least it was on her left side. He hoped that made her feel better.

In spite of the constant disappointment, he managed to carry on. He worked in his usual shifts and counted the houses because it was so hard to measure the passage of time or progress. Twelve houses searched tonight and now it was time to rest. He usually picked another house, a lucky thirteenth if you will, to camp in. Rest for four hours and then Kitteridge and his small search party would continue their hunt.

*

Life[x] rations were abundant and left in homes all over DZ: 23N. No one was sure how long a tube lasted until it went bad. Or did they ever go bad? He had heard rumors that they could even outlast the legendary Twinkie for shelf life. The Twinkie experience, regular or deep fried, had been a crowd favorite Puff for a while now. Another one where the Life[x] texture actually enhanced the creamy filling. Still not as good as a massive cathead-sized cinnamon bun, but a common after-dinner treat served at almost every party. You find them more at DZ: 23A and you would think that because they intersect sometimes it would be easier to score.

Months more of searching had passed. The owl could easily see their progress through the compound; drone 63 had the clever idea of turning off the lights when they were done searching a place. Always efficient, 63 even saved power when no one was using it. It made for a nice wall of progress and something he could use to navigate. It was good Kitteridge couldn't see it from the air the way his owl could. His house by house, line by line, approach was depressingly slow. Hardly a blip of progress on the sea of light across the Platform. He knew he had to figure out a way to hurry things up. She had millions of seconds before Tranquility Base, but his time was questionable.

Four more tubes squished, squeezed, rolled, and pressed – eight or nine months, probably more had passed. He couldn't tell if the constant movement made him eat more Life[x] or less. The stretching of rations didn't help either and he was getting thin. Kitteridge wasn't even sure why he was rationing when he should just be collecting and consuming the abandoned tubes. Next time he found another bag he would start eating, and carrying, more. He knew he had been searching for a long time now and more time yet to come. Try as he might he would never know the pleasure of holding his baby daughter as an infant in his arms. At her accelerated growth rate, she would be running around and speaking her first words millions of seconds ago by now. He wondered what the Collective nurse maids taught them to say first… probably something to do with tech support no doubt. He loved her the instant he saw her and loved her more each passing second since she was taken away. Kitteridge still had the hole in his heart, and it constantly ached for his dearly departed Marianna. His desire to find his daughter, protect her, was filling a different void in his heart. The two could exist side-by-side, sort of a sweet and sour. That was the way of things, love and loss, victory and defeat. Kitteridge, 63, and the family owl could use some more wins right about now.

He had decided the moment she was born that Marianna had been right. She had selected the perfect name for their new baby girl. Marianna knew somehow it would be a girl. Rachel she would be. Every night since the pregnancy was confirmed he went to bed thinking about Rachel. He would whisper out loud the only three words he said all day now, "Goodnight, Rachel." He would stir awake, ready to start a new shift, and say to himself and those around "Good morning, Rachel." Marianna had known her as Rachel, and so did he. She wouldn't know her real name, but he would find her with the thin scar on her left cheek. He would tell her all about his travels, and her mother, on their way to Tranquility Base.

The owl still doesn't trust the drone and 63 doesn't seem to acknowledge another sentient lifeform. Screeches go off to signal the drone has moved away to fetch more dilithium. Beep, screech, hoot, then back to gentle metallic whirs, the 'breathing' of each robot. The drone keeps getting crystals to keep Kitteridge alive. The owl knows that Kitteridge's Interval has long ago passed and yet he is still alive. And that is thanks to drone 63.

The drone keeps trying to land on the owl. Mid-air flights and battles ensue. Whenever the drone is not locked onto

Kitteridge's ROPU or mining crystals it is always hovering six-inches off the back of the owl. The owl finally goes into another recharge cycle after weeks of extended battery. All the searching and flying have left it drained. Once fully asleep, ears still extended and listening, the drone maglevs its way over to the owl's back. It gracefully touches down with its legs extended straight out and hovering over the sides of the bird as it perches. The drone has made contact with the back of the owl, ever so gentle so as not to set off the bird's motion sensors, drone 63 was that good. The arms had not closed around the owl. Yet.

His ROPU is on the ground next to him as he watches this all happening. 63 lifts its long tail in slow motion making its curved arch high overhead and over the top of its propeller blades. A small needle like probe extends from the tip and waits, floating inches off of the owl's head, mimicking a desert scorpion poised for the kill. The drone hovers there waiting. Kitteridge is not sure for what, but he is transfixed and waiting as well. The owl, now fully charged, gently awakens and his ears twirl around and takes in the sounds as it finishes processing the audio recordings from its slumber. Nothing made a tick while he was recharging it seems and so the owl slowly raises the lids on its large metallic eyes.

As soon as its eyes are fully opened the lights start to flicker on. Slowly at first and then all at once. Open, closed, flicker on, flicker off. Flash, Flash. Open, flutter, close, and then the instant the eyelids open for good, STAB! 63's scorpion like tail quickly pierces the back of the owl's head. Well, it doesn't so much pierce or damage the bird as it seems to find a mechanical maintenance port of sorts and has jabbed into that with the scorpion tail. The owl doesn't make a sound, but it instantly freezes all motion including the gentle sound of its whirring mechanical breath. It is clear to Kitteridge now that drone 63 has taken control of the owl. It has its eyes, ears, and wings. The enhanced optical and audio sensors will be a substantial boost to the drone. And the wings can take him much higher than his maglev or even propellers can go. They are paired together now, or at least until 63 decides otherwise it appears. A piercing electronic screech emerges as the pair float off together and make their way out until they are swallowed up by the smog and dark sky. He can make out the twinkling of their lights and bleeping sounds is all.

After many thousands of seconds have passed the owl and drone 63 return. The drone safely airlocks in place and begins refilling Kitteridge's ROPU while the owl lands softly on his shoulder. He has been busy while they were away as well. He found a satchel that he can use to store more Life[x] and dilithium crystals. Kitteridge slings it around his shoulder, under his cape, and grabs four more tubes of Life[x] before the trio head out to continue searching for Rachel. Other than mine some crystals, which are quickly stashed in his new messenger bag, it isn't clear what the pair did out there. Or if they would be doing it again. It is clear that the owl has no idea what happened either, just simply waking up from a restful recharge is all.

Tonight, this night, this shift, some seconds, whatever you want to call it, was a quiet one. No more drones to speak of, except 63. Kitteridge is startled awake by a nightmare all the same. A scene from many million seconds back. He remembers early on the hunter drones had circled back onto the streets of DZ: 23N. The Collective knew that any survivors would be looting around the rubble and so sent the hunter drones to finish the job because some had escaped. Hunt down and kill the remaining fleeing mothers. He did his best to save them, but none escaped the drones and their deadly round up. He usually arrived too late or had to watch in horror if he arrived too early. He would slink away because there was nothing more to see there anyways.

After twenty-four months of traveling together he had become rather found of drone 63. He needed to think of a name for it but figured that time would sort that out as well. The only name he could think of any more was Rachel. Twelve houses a day was better progress, but he still needed a way to scale to search faster. He needed to figure out a way for his process to continue without him.

*

People celebrated ceremonies at Derby Days qualifiers with massive Puff parties. They always had a Hawaiian theme and the sought after party special was called the Dohl-Whip. The makers had managed to combine the sweetness of pineapple with the creamiest of Life[x] ice creams. Some say it was the cleverly dyed yellow rings that gave it that pineapple bite. Some say without a clearly disguised string cheese baked in there you wouldn't get that slight sour taste in the back of your mouth. The taste is not enough to bite the inside of your cheeks, but a pucker is not uncommon, and very sought after. Without smell the taste buds have nothing to do, and so every bit lingered around on the tongue. The Dohl-Whip was the perfect treat to let linger as it dissolved in your mouth. The right Puff and Life[x] created a delicious Polynesian dreamsicle and people waited in line for these at the party. And the Collective made sure there was more than enough Life[x] on hand. And Puff. They turned off a sensor or two and allowed these ceremonies to continue. And the Waster Kings made sure they were an affair to remember, usually lasting up to three days. These get togethers were the only thing the people of DZ: 23N had to look forward to and life became a predictable rhythm for most people. Sleep, tech support, party at the Derby Days qualifiers, rest, rinse, and repeat. The population measured time second by second, always looking forward to the next slide race. That and the trip to Tranquility Base. People also measured time second by second as they dreaded their Interval, the final test that they had to pass but could do nothing to study for. The Interval gets most everyone in the end. Trust me, been doing this a long time.

The nursemaids, assigned to each child from birth, go about their mission with great care and precision. Graceful even. Their mix of sounds of propellers and hands and wheels spinning make for an infinite array of things to look at and hear, like the ultimate kaleidoscope and bright mobile. The children's every physical need will be met by Life[x] of course. And they will focus on their primary mission of learning tech support trade skills. And along the way they will all try to figure out the maglev evacuators. There are debates that rage about the right technique for it, it can be tricky.

They had a long way to go these lost children of DZ: 23N and still much to learn. There was no doubt that they learned things for a reason. Every movement and every motion had purpose. Not long after you naturally closed your fist, the Collective drones put a wrench in it. These children will go without needs or wants. Well, the smell. There is always that these days. At this age, they don't know what it is. But they need it. Wake up in the middle of the night, to go pee but wind up searching the house for something, anything to smell. They have a long way to go, a lot to learn, and a lot of smells and hunger to overcome as they don't go to work until age five.

By then all are indoctrinated into the legend, myth, and hope of Tranquility Base. It drives them, just like the desire to taste and smell, the hope of a better life on Tranquility Base keeps them in motion. The lost children of the accidental crash on DZ: 23N will have no physical, mental, or emotional wants. They had hope. And yet, even hope was not enough for some. There were some that seemed destined for the Puff at birth.

Chapter 7

63,072,001 to 94,608,000: 11 Years until Tranquility Base

Four hours till the attack; he wakes up – tonight will be different, special with months of planning coming to a close in one battle. But he knows tonight isn't any different really, just life on the Platform trying your best to keep the wolves away. He got up early in the night, what you think of as four a.m., he couldn't sleep these days. Not since the trip to Tranquility Base had left without him and he hadn't been chosen. Neither of them had and the memory of that haunted him. Because he didn't make the cut, she wouldn't be going on that trip either. Even if she could find a way to sneak on without her spouse, Hasboro would be culled before they could even hold hands, binary unity and conformity after all.

He is glad he is up early because even though his ritual won't take long, he wants to be sure he won't be interrupted. The rest of the tribes have all gathered on the outskirts of the community center that now served as the orphanage housing all sixteen children. Each child is the size of a young adult now and they all had their own rooms occupying the first floor of the center.

Hasboro is alone now as he is every 'morning'. Just him and his thoughts as he prepares for the battle ahead. He quickly and gracefully moves his giant body off the huge bed. He has slept for years fully clothed, cape and all, always at the ready. His ritual meditation, stretching, and yoga complete, he moves on to his required medication. It is Hasboro's own homegrown concoction, and he unveils a sling bag from under his shoulder and empties the prepared mix out onto the formal silver platter he uses for the occasion. Every day like clockwork he ingests the dandelion infused dilithium dust – its unique mix of properties and qualities have somehow managed to keep him alive all these seconds without an ROPU. Hasboro is one of the few people living PTB without a ventilator in their nose all the time. In fact, Hasboro has been living on the Platform for years without his ROPU. Ever since he found the dandelions and hijacked his own Interval, years before it was due. He has lived, taken his daily medication ritual, and thrived here on the Platform, without an ROPU, for many millions of seconds.

He carries on as best he can. At least until he can be reunited with his beloved Rosalia. He saw her from time to time at ceremonies and parties. That was good and he always looked forward to those days. In fact, they were a reason to keep going. Just to see her pretty face again he missed her that much. What he wasn't sure of was how she felt about him still. He knew she loved him dearly once, but he feared she blamed him for their non-selection all those years ago. She still talked to him and acknowledged him, Hasboro could always detect and wait for that sweet, sly, side grin of hers when he winked at her across the room. No one called him Lucius any more, it was just Hasboro. She used to call him Lucius and he missed the precious whisper of her voice.

Light sparkles and crackles burst and fizzle in the air around him as he lifts the dust into his big meaty palms. He slowly lowers his massive head, and his dreadlocked hair drops down across his face and in front of his shoulders in great big locks. He lifts his great palms up to meet his face and they are outstretched and filled with a rich dark yellow like powder of specially infused dandelion pollen. The cloud is overflowing out of his hands and spilling down his arms as he plunges his face into the fine dust. He takes a large inhale through his nose and cocks his head back. He quickly stands upright and shakes his head from side to side. His great colorful mane, filled with lockets, ringlets, ribbons, and barrettes waves back and forth. A massive cloud of yellow dust fills the air with a snap and crackle as it dissolves.

The dandelion-enhanced dust coats Hasboro's nasal passageways and lungs, protecting him from the dilithium dust and side effects of long-term exposure. Regular application appears to be working well because he is still kicking after all these seconds. He could probably go longer; he isn't sure how often he really needs to inhale the dandelion infused powder. He has been making it part of his every day since as long as anyone can remember. It is sort of his morning pick-me-up, not that he needed it with all the caffeine they put into Life[x] these days. He carefully grinds the dandelions into a pulp and mixes it into the powder. He gathers up his grindings and gently nudges them into his sling bag. The remaining sludge he whips across his cheeks and brow, makes a long messy line from forehead to chin with it. Hasboro's face is stained a deep yellow, like troughs of liver spots from constant application, it gives his face a distinctive look. Not so much like scars but like tribal tattoos or a tiger's stripes stained across his face in rich yellow streaks. Combined with his dark opal over-eyelids it gave him a mix of looks conveying just two emotions: gentle and kind with a loving word and caring arm or fierce and ready to deliver a bloody death blow. He had the latter face on today.

His daily ritual now complete, Hasboro quickly grabs his

famous light-sword, the one with his trademark insignia, and strides out of the tent. He must meet the captains of the other clans; they have surely gathered by now. He knows they will all wait patiently, and no one will question his tardiness. They all know of his ritual. No one has ever seen it, but they know it has something to do with the sling bag under his cape. It must, otherwise, why does he carry that thing around? By now everyone suspected that his rituals gave him that distinctive look. Others say that the magic mix is what contributes to his large stature. Hasboro seems to have never stopped his accelerated growth. At this point, his fighting stance is pretty impressive and actually quite menacing. Hasboro's face hasn't aged so much, still appears to have the face of a thirty-six-year-old, but he has grown massive in size. He towers over the population and casts a long shadow that clearly indicates he can stay here long past Tranquility Base.

He likes to run a tight ship and so confidently slings his cape over one shoulder and joins the small gathering at the circle fire in the camp. He makes sure his light-sword is jutting out just enough for the hilt and its lighted spinning disco ball on top. No one says anything when he arrives, but they all nod, and the voices come to a halt when they see the dances of light reflect off the campfires all around the Platform and tents. The light show announces his arrival on every occasion. Glowing and flashing means he is near, faint and flickering means he is gone. Gandalf himself couldn't make much grander an entrance. At seven-feet, nine-inches Hasboro towers over everyone. His muscles ripple under his vest and no amount of cape can hide them. He is an impressive specimen, and his trim four hundred and fifteen pounds allows him to put some real power behind his punches – all in the rotation of the hips, they say, but a little muscle never hurts. Just like golf if you can remember the stories of that old game. No one says anything out loud that is; the men of Bear and Lion clan had long ago learned to communicate telepathically with each other. It created a unique bond, sort of like the Spiders and their precious Apple trees. But this brotherhood could be extended, and the Oak clan was catching on and could make out bits and pieces. Hasboro understood it all, the spoken and unspoken. He had gathered the clans and tribes and driven them out here together for this battle. The orphans had been raised by the Collective long enough and the time was ripe for the rescue. He gave the formal sniff and started with a snort.

After a brief and silent review of the plan the tribe elders disperse to distribute orders and prepare for the raid. The mission is clear, storm the community center and take the children out, alive. There are expected to be only a dozen or so drones onsite but be on the lookout all the same. The group has a little over three hours left before they begin the assault.

Two hours before the attack a small battalion is sent out as an advance squad. Eagle clan runs the show, sending out their scouts. They will recon up ahead and report back any changes prior to the attack. Four soldiers quietly shuffle out, and after some thousands of seconds, all report back. Location confirmed, heat and motion sensors confirm sixteen children and sixteen drones. With a crew this size it should be an easy in and out mission.

Thirty minutes before the attack and the alarms on each of the tribe leader's wrist comm units go off. Hasboro has dispatched an 'all-hands' and everyone quickly dons their ROPUs and heads to the campfire for rally and review. They will buddy up, assign cars, and get their light-guns ready.

They quickly gather by the fire to confirm the attack plan

and role assignments. But Hasboro informs the group of a change in the plans, something has come up. He has been reviewing the motion sensors and has identified a seventeenth person in the community center. Its size and speed indicate a person and not a drone. But why they didn't show up on the heat sensor he couldn't say for sure. And where was its nursemaid drone? And how could they have let such binary abomination go unchecked? Seventeen wasn't evenly divisible by two even once.

Seventeen was special, Hasboro knew that much, and not just because it was a prime number. Everyone agreed it deserved special care and attention during the rescue. Bear and Lion clan already had their mission orders and were off to storm the community center. Eagle clan scouts stood safely outside the front and back of the building to fend off any escape attempts. The Spiders were busy finishing breaking down the various camps getting ready for a quick departure after the rescue and when they are finished, they will join the raid and make a large surrounding perimeter just in case the Collective sends in any reinforcements. Hasboro had already made his way into the compound many seconds ago. He crept in from the ventilation shaft and would see to child seventeen himself. How could this have gone undetected for so long, he wondered?

By now the camps will have all been broken back down and ready to make way after the rescue. The houses had already been given numbers and knew the children that would be coming home with them. Thankfully, there were enough people PTB that all four houses had a mentor for the quad to share. These treasured souls would teach the children all about Tranquility Base, and what they needed to do; to survive until then and to earn their seat on the trip. Spots were limited, everyone knew this, none more uniquely than those living here still past their trip to Tranquility Base. They were not among the chosen. Perhaps they knew why and could pass on some wisdom. Or they served as a warning sign of a life to come if you weren't good and didn't earn your seat. Most PTBers were Puff addled anyway and served as an alarming beacon of their own. DZ: 23N was lucky, most of their elders were capable and led the charge.

The battalion storms the community center in waves. Think Mad Max meets Priscilla Queen of the Desert, Freddie Mercury had a love child with Elvis, born with the soul of Aretha Franklin and the hip moves of James Brown. Sixty-four cars from the 1960s era burst onto the Platform and storm off toward DZ: 23N community center. They are painted in a rainbow of garish colors with big broad stripes and swashes across the hoods and sides of the vehicles. Every curved surface, fender, bumper, and mirror had been chromed out and shined out in the dark sky. Lights and sirens mount the top of each car and large flowing ribbons of glittering canvas spread out in wide swaths behind them, anything to catch the light and possibly put some drones in maintenance mode was the inspiration behind tonight's camouflage. The cars pushed through the gates of the compound in a 'flying V' formation. The squads all converge and crash through the front wall of the community center. The children are all quickly collected and never once question what is happening. It all happens so quickly and efficiently that it must be the work of the Collective, they think. These children are too young to understand Collective and the Waster Kings. But the nursemaid drones have taught them a few things according to the protocol. They all knew how important it was to protect their ROPUs, and that they were destined for Tranquility Base. It was that TB certainty and hope that he relied on. Hasboro had passed word amongst all the forward squadron leaders to simply scream,

"Follow me to Tranquility Base!" and sure enough the kids came running. They didn't know why or by whom but the sixteen children of DZ: 23N were no longer lost.

Hasboro snuck through the ventilation shaft and jumped down onto level two. All the children, Waster King soldiers, and drones were fighting down on level one. There should be only silence and stillness on level two. But just as Hasboro had suspected there was someone moving around up there. Hasboro simply landed, circled himself in his cape, and took a seat on the floor of level two. He sensed the motion stop and freeze, just over his left shoulder. He let the motion sensor gently fall to the floor because he no longer needed it. He could hear the breathing behind him. It came in slow measured breaths.

Hasboro waits and is rewarded. Curious and social creatures by nature, the human animal behind him gives in to her protective instinct and simply says, "Hello."

He is not surprised and simply answers back a warm, "Hello yourself." He slowly rises, hands outstretched in a sign of peace. As he reaches full height, he informs his visitor that he can't see anyone. A gentle hand stretches out and grabs his.

She doesn't know why but she trusts him the moment he landed on her level. She knew he was coming and could hear him shuffling and making his way through the vent shafts. And by now, her well-trained ear, the one that kept her hidden all these years, could tell that big slow-moving snorting and sniffing thing in the air recycling vents wasn't another drone trying to seek her out. Curiosity had gotten the better of her and she holds his hand as she removes her protective shawl. It has kept her hidden safely away from the other children and nursemaid drones. She has been living here for the last three years. Living off the storage closet of Life[x] rations kept at the community center for an emergency.

Surviving was an emergency for her, she reasoned. She didn't know how she came to own the invisibility cloak, had she found it or had someone given it to her? It wasn't so much magic as it was science; the cloth was woven from dilithium crystals that had been stretched out to become fibrous and yet breathable and porous and it made great clothing material. The fabric was then coated with more dilithium crystals, this time little black spores that didn't so much catch the light as swallow it up, leaving the nearby area somehow even darker than before. The effect was nothing short of miraculous, as long as seventeen stayed under the shawl, she was invisible to the eye and heat sensors. She was able to move around and even make sounds underneath the protective blanket and not be seen or heard. Without it she would have been dead long ago, she knows that much because she had seen what the drones could do and how merciless and deadly they can be. Stay hidden and stay safe. It had kept her alive so far.

Seventeen had snuck around and hidden amongst the shadows, watching and learning, imitating the other children for as long as she can remember. She knew what they knew and had heard the same stories of Tranquility Base. She had learned the tech support skills just like the others. The other thing she shared in common with all the others though was the longing for smell. She was born with a grand hunger and primal desire for cinnamon buns just like everyone else. And she had heard the warnings, but still felt the allure of Puff.

The drones did not go down without a fight. Cars erupted with soldiers with about half running into the community center yelling about Tranquility Base and the others each taking aim at a drone with their light-guns. These nursemaid drones were in full protective mode, and they were fast. Most of them dodged the first attack and quickly rushed the soldiers. Another volley of light and about half the drones downed into maintenance mode. The remaining robotic assailants are taken out quickly, one by one, and the children are all loaded back into the cars for departure. No Waster King soldiers even suffer a scratch.

Up above, on level two, Hasboro spoke to seventeen for just a few seconds. He didn't want to resort to it, but he knew there wasn't much time before the sweepers showed up. All he had to say was five simple words and she would follow him anywhere, just like the others. Except Hasboro knew she wasn't like the others. He could tell by the thin scar on her left check. It stood out, just like she did. With the shawl, and Rosalia's help, he would ensure she was safe. He didn't know how she was going to make it to Tranquility Base, surely, they don't keep a seat for runaways. But he had some million seconds to figure that out. All he knew for certain was that he recognized that shawl. Not so much the actual thing, not really, but he had heard about it. He always saw this huddled old woman at the Transportation Center. One minute she would be there staring, her little eyes piercing into your soul it seemed like she could see right through you and read your deepest secrets, blink and then she would be gone. Even if she could read minds and uncover buried secrets all she would find is a planet full of people wandering around dreaming and hoping for cinnamon buns. That was no secret.

After the raid, the drones are all left in maintenance mode, and they are cleaned up by the sweepers just minutes after the rescue mission leaves DZ: 23N. The Collective has sent a small battalion, thirty-two drones, to collect the remaining sixteen children, now on the run again. Even though these new drones know nothing about the kids, haven't been with them every second for the last three years, they can easily find them. They will home in on the trackers in their bellies that have been active

109

and signaling away since birth. The drones quickly zoom past the community center as the small horde of children's signals goes beeping off into the distance and the drones make pursuit.

Thirty-two drones break off and chase the sixty-four cars as they speed across the Platform. It quickly becomes apparent that protecting the children is now no longer the drones' primary programming. This is obvious after two drones quickly dive bomb the nearest cars. A small collision and resulting explosion that downs the surrounding five drones and engulfs eight cars, all passengers inside are sure to die a fiery death. Twenty-seven drones speed off toward the cars as they break away into two groups, now three, now four. The cars keep dividing into smaller groups and then begin to zigzag and crisscross their way between them. The drones swoop down, highly effective little missiles making loud and deadly little booms as they bomb the surface of another classic car and kill everyone inside. Twelve drones down, fifty-four cars left. DZ: 23N becomes a chaos of cars and drones, zooming and swooping across the Platform, leaving gaps of smoke and dust. Thick billowing clouds of it are coming up from the dilithium dust and from the fiery remains of the cars below.

The Waster Kings have long ago figured that a quick sub-exfoliant electric shock to the stomach would disable the Collective tracker implanted by the nursemaid drones. If you passed your Interval, then everyone got a tracker. The electronic devices were quickly disabled one by one amongst the cars and a subsequent decoy tracker placed in the runaway cars. These brave souls driving the dummy vehicles would sacrifice themselves to save the lost children during the rescue; it was these cars that the drones bombed in their kamikaze style attacks. The cars containing soldiers and children had long split off to safety. The drones broke and redoubled, broke and redoubled repeatedly, car after car, all chasing the remaining beacons. Once all trackers had been destroyed the remaining twenty drones just sort of stopped and hovered mid-air just above the line of smog above the Platform. Of course, a few drop down into maintenance mode as they achieve binary unity again at sixteen drones.

The rescue-raid had been a success; more so than any had hoped. Sixteen children were sought after and seventeen returned home. It was a cause for celebration and one that went for many long nights, or on this world was it more appropriate to say the party raged on into the long night? Or in spite of the darkness? But the time for rescuing the children had come and gone, and now the time for celebration had come as well. All the clans and tribes put down their petty disputes, the Bear and Lion clans agreed to speak out loud for everyone's benefit, and even the elusive Spiders joined in once the camps had been reestablished.

The Waster Kings had been watching over the children since that fateful accident at DZ: 23N those many seconds back. They knew they could save the regulators that night and given time they would save the kids. But they also knew the Collective would do a better job of raising and training them, at least for their first three years of life. Over trial and error, the Waster Kings learned that if you took them too young, they tended to rebel having not established a firm enough hold on the promise of Tranquility Base. Wait too long and they fight you, convinced they are living the way, well indoctrinated by then. But three years-old, just over 93 million seconds living sucking on a ROPU, and the lost kids were old enough that they had mastered how to use a maglev evacuator on their own, when they worked that is. The seventeen kids will walk, talk, run, bike, balance, throw, learn and practice all the fine motor skills needed for tech support, well before they are needed. Which turned out to be the same muscles and mechanics needed for a mid-level Judo belt, they did a lot of martial arts at DZ: 23A apparently. Who knew?

*

Before the rescue mission Hasboro had been reliving over and over his own fateful Interval and selection for Tranquility Base all those years ago. His Rosalia had always been a dreamer and the idealist more than anyone Hasboro had ever met. She was sure she was going to Tranquility Base she just knew it. Rosalia also carried a more altruistic bone in her slight but athletic frame. Her chest was light but still big enough for her heart and she was always looking for ways to make the world here on DZ: 23N better for those around her. She would sacrifice herself and sometimes her own rations. Anything to help out even the most hard-up of Puff cases. Anything she could do to relieve the human condition, that constant existential crisis, Rosalia was always the first to raise her hand. She couldn't do anything about the Puff and need for smell though. But she was strong and didn't want to chance her seat assignment to a fleeting moment of spurned happiness. She would be happy enough on Tranquility Base there with no more constant yearning for smells. She remained strong against the Puff. Just the stories and dreams of cinnamon buns alone would be enough for Rosalia. Although on special occasions she was known to dabble in different textures for her Life[x], she figured that was harmless fun.

Rosalia's single biggest driving hope, the one she dreams about most is Hasboro, her one true love. Their love was a force driven by nature and just as strong for them both. They knew their relationship would be complicated from the moment they met. Exciting, thrilling, and adventurous even. It was definitely not

112

what they were supposed to do. Marcus and Rosalia had been matched from birth, he was to be her groom, not Hasboro. And Hasboro's wife Amanda was made his, everyone knew it and you could even confirm it by the markings on their ROPUs, serving as a sort of wedding ring, uniting the pair all their life. Two couples, two mismatched pairs it seemed, that age old story of love assumed, misallocated, and unrequited. Only this time there was no foul evil King behind it with a plot to steal land and pay no dowries. Even years later, when they both were living PTB, Rosalia longed for Hasboro's presence in her world. It was not to be back then, and it just wouldn't be proper now that everyone knew of their adultery. When she finally gave in to her lust and suggested they run away together, if only for an evening to be alone without their ever-present third wheel, Marcus, Hasboro had quickly agreed. Hasboro had ensured they would be safe and that their little trysts would go unnoticed. But after the incident at the Interval ceremony, her heartbreak and love for him were obvious to all on DZ: 23N and word travelled fast.

*

Marcus was present of course, and even held Rosalia's hand during their Interval, as was expected of a husband and wife. "I'm telling you something's not right, that baby hasn't moved in many, many seconds!" Rosalia whispered to Marcus as she pointed over at Amanda. She was bent over, frantically rubbing and clutching her protruding belly, searching for signs of life within. Hasboro and his wife Amanda were nearby awaiting their own Interval that they knew was coming. Mandy was there, head hanging low and standing hand in hand with her husband Hasboro, she was certain she wouldn't make it past her Interval.

That damned ROPU of hers had initially began sputtering a few months ago. Hasboro was the first to notice that she had started habitually holding her breath. Lots of people habitually held their breath especially toward the end. A sputtering ROPU was nothing new, but they were always a sign that Tranquility Base would remain elusive. Always.

Rosalia and Hasboro's Interval was three years ago, just like everyone on the Platform. They can both still remember their Interval like it was yesterday though. The waiting was over, mostly. 441 million seconds had passed and all the ROPUs on DZ: 23N had dried up and the Intervals had started. For some it was quick and for others the agony was even worse than the anxiety leading up to it. After three minutes and thirty-one seconds Marcus breathed a big sigh of relief, open mouthed and nosed for the first time in fourteen years, his useless hose dangling down under his cape. He briefly wondered what he would do with that constant companion in that ROPU device he had been carrying around with him all these years and he found he had a hard time letting it go even though he had no need for it any more. Both Marcus and Rosalia had passed, and they could breathe without their drained ROPUs. Hasboro had been living on the Platform without his ROPU for years, the dandelion mixture helped make sure that tonight was all about Mandy and the baby. No worries for his own breathing, Hasboro had that down.

Mandy was right and she wouldn't make it to Tranquility Base. That telltale sputter had announced it, and now she could hold her breath no more, she had failed her Interval. No retirement away and chance for her to spend more time with Hasboro. Three minutes and thirty-one seconds had passed, and she couldn't hold it any longer. She covered her mouth as she began to choke and cough. Some drones, standing by to oversee the procedures, just swooped down underneath her and started to carry her away with her stillborn child locked away inside her womb. Mandy floated away on a maglev cloud of drones like a teenager's rockstar dreams of crowd surfing her way back to the stage. Only no one demanded an encore, Hasboro just squeezed her hands, closed her now bleeding eyes and let the drones take her away. Marcus, however, was more moved by the scene, he had always liked Amanda, she was more than a Mandy to him. He liked and relied on her no-nonsense attitude. She would make fun of the trio's little antics but always seemed to have a few raucous ideas of her own for them to carry out. Marcus glanced over to Rosalia with a compassionate look because she and Mandy had indeed been close friends. They made a handsome quad, even jokingly called themselves a 'full deck', and Mandy had always insisted she was the Queen of Hearts, Marcus was the consummate Joker, and her King just played along, not wanting to be a Spade, they traveled together even on tech support calls and would Club anyone that got in their way.

Marcus called out "Rosalia!" and reached for her hand to comfort Rosalia and get a little sympathy himself in return, something to take away the pain of the horror he was seeing. Rosalia heard him of course, but she couldn't return his gaze. Rosalia was quietly taking little sips of air, holding tight her belly, and looking over her shoulder with a longing that Marcus quickly recognized and was certain – she loved another. It was difficult to describe the various ways their betrayal broke Marcus' heart that night. He had never been suspicious, but never thought of Amanda in any other way than his best friend Hasboro's wife. Marcus' vital organ was still pumping after the Interval, but it was split into three pieces. First was his longing for their relationship to continue on Tranquility Base, they made quite the group here and had big plans for retirement and how they would wreak havoc together during their final years. And then his trust in others and soul was just crushed. Hasboro was his best friend, they had been raised in houses side-by-side, how could he take away his bride? And what about Mandy? She was a catch that Hasboro never did appreciate. Finally, Marcus had revealed his deepest secrets and dreams to a love unrequited in Mandy, that sort of openness and transparency was rare and he would never have a chance to share his thoughts with another. The epiphanies hit him all at once as they usually do. He didn't say anything for an agonizingly long number of seconds and then Marcus pulled his cape around him trying to wrap himself in a protective blanket as he was feeling very vulnerable right about then. Rosalia thought she recognized tears in his eyes, but he looked away. She placed a hand on Marcus' shoulder, and he reached up to take it in his own. Marcus gave it his signature gentle but firm squeeze and turned around to say between tears, "I hope he brings you the happiness you deserve, Rosalia! I recognize I could never give you what you need, and well, I guess, see apparently, Hasboro can! And now you will have the freedom to love each other openly. I will stand between Cupid and no man. Goodbye my love." And with that Marcus strolled confidently away through the doors to the community center. He makes two strides and then quickly spins around as he stretches his neck out and whispers one word to her. She spins on her heels and is already on the move. But she hears him and knows Marcus is right. She must make it to Hasboro now and they must quickly flee if they will be together. Rosalia knows that the drones will be after them both and unlike the CDCG they didn't negotiate. The Collective saw no logic in just making a new pair with Hasboro and Rosalia.

That just wouldn't do. How would they get along with each other? Very well it turns out, in every way. Oh! She had indeed heard Marcus' last word and very much agreed – it was time to "RUN!"

Marcus sees her pick up the pace and Hasboro make his way over to her as well. Marcus takes a big step forward, but he didn't make it to the doors before two drones pop up from under the Platform. He doesn't fear death but is given no choice. There is no Davey Jones who is going to appear from the deep and ask him the age-old question, do you fear death? Davey Jones doesn't just show up on the scene as the sailors are drowning out calling for rescue and Marcus is not given that ultimate choice, will he serve a hundred years as a slave to the mast? Sail away on the Flying Dutchman and take on the mission of carrying souls to the end of the world? Or die alone today here on the Platform. No Jones doesn't appear to give Marcus that choice but what might as well be his dreaded beast appears. That fearsome and legendary monster of the deep summoned from fathoms below. Great electronic tentacles whip out from under the Platform. They reach out their tails like lassos and wrap around Marcus' legs and summarily drag him down to his knees. Two more jointed metallic ropes come out and secure his arms and try to further secure his hands as Marcus makes one last ditch effort at survival using his hose and ROPU as defense. He whirls the hose around in a circle, whipping back and forth at the lassos tying up his legs. He uses the hose like a fan blade then and keeps it up to protect his face. The hose is ripped away and three more tentacles zip in and cover his eyes and ears. The dusty cloud at the base of the Platform, the ever-present and looming blanket against the dark smog and sky above DZ: 23N, comes up with its mighty mouth open wide and toothless and a large cloud of dust fans out and encircles Marcus, bringing him down flat. He disappears without a scream knowing death is to come. He breathes a final sigh of relief as the dust overtakes him, he knows that binary unity rules all and an unmatched pair just wouldn't do. Rosalia watches in known terror, but this was always a risk. It was pairs or nothing. No three of a kind, full houses won't do, flushes are outlawed, and definitely no straights. Everyone knew about the mission of binary unity. Sure, there was some talk of a separate Tranquility Base, one just for singles, like a sort of hedonistic paradise, right? Heard it down at the CDCG gathering from a guy, been doing this a long time now, you can trust him. Of course, that was false, you couldn't trust anyone at the CDCG. Seats to Tranquility Base were limited to pairs, like big love seats built just for two. One-offs couldn't be tolerated, and this is how they are dealt with. Just make the problem go away went the programming. As Marcus slips below the Platform and finally really does go away for good, Rosalia's heart skips a beat. She did love Marcus in a way. They had grown up together, relied on each other, and had made promises to each other. Promises she meant for Hasboro but gave away to quiet the pain in Marcus' gentle heart. She is good at deception, in more ways than one and not just from her husband and lover, for Marcus believes she truly loves him back even at the end. She is good at lying to him and has had lots of practice. She is not a bad person but feels bad about being a victim of circumstance all the same. Rosalia does indeed love Marcus, truly does – but more like a close cousin or brother. Her lover and soul mate, whose hand she will squeeze forever in public now, was and always will be Hasboro.

Rosalia instinctively grips Hasboro's hand while she reaches out slightly, opens and closes her fist, and then it falls to her side, nothing she can do for Marcus now. Hasboro pulls her tight and whispers "trust me" into his sweet Rosalia's ears. He wraps his arms and big flowing cape around her in one deft motion. She gives into him, slides over and in, and she leans her entire frame and body weight against him as they both instinctively adjust to make room for her ROPU. He takes a big, huge gulping breath of air into his lungs and taps on her shoulder nodding quickly for her to do the same thing. She complies and her eyes get big as she steels herself for the four drones swooping in for the kill overhead and behind Hasboro. This mismatched pair are a complete disgrace to binary uniformity. Math must win, they bleep and boop as the drones come in, laser-saws buzzing and flickering, little sparkles of light dancing in the dark air. Hasboro can see the size of her eyes, dilated to nothing but pupils, all whites gone. Her eyes, the size of dinner plates, warns him of their impending doom if he doesn't do something, and whatever it was, he had better do it pretty damn soon. He wasn't sure it would work. Hasboro had heard about it but never tried it himself. It was too dangerous, and besides, he had no reason to tempt fate and try it out before. Well with those drones buzzing about looking to kill him and his precious Rosalia, Hasboro certainly had plenty of reasons now. He ducks his head as he pushes down to kiss her forehead and then pushes them both off the ledge. They were going to find out just what was under the Platform. The dilithium crystal dust engulfs them in an instant. Step, poof, gone. Drones satisfied, no one lives under there, and zoom away. These units are still on standby after all. Their mission is to keep binary conformity during the seat assignments to Tranquility Base. For those whose spouses don't pass the Interval, no sense in keeping an odd pair alive, take care of them quickly or so it was coded into the algorithms. The drones float off to continue their gruesome gaze over the community center.

119

Rosalia is still in a good deal of shock at what just happened. Her fourteen years of certainty that they would make it on the trip had kept her going. That and her love for Hasboro. But the Interval and seat assignment had certainly not gone their way. Rosalia decided she was okay with the end result, she was with Hasboro after all. She was actually relieved now that her Interval was over, and she had passed. But she was definitely not content with the ways things played out and of course she felt horrible about the consequences for Marcus and Mandy.

Rosalia is in many ways happier now though, more so than she has ever been, excepting that picnic that Hasboro had prepared for her just a few months ago. Even without Puff the Life[x] snack they shared seemed heavenly and was no doubt enhanced by the secrecy and lusty nature of their rendezvous. He has kept his promises and kept her safe and their affairs of the heart a secret all these years. She harbors no ill will toward Marcus and the marriage selection, he had been a good and faithful companion. The fact that love had given her away to another was beyond anyone's control.

Her faith in Hasboro is stronger than ever, but she does in fact blame him, thinks it is because of his puff addiction, or his run in with the CDCG, that kept them from Tranquility Base. Rosalia has long since forgiven Hasboro, but she has certainly not forgotten. She had made a vow to never mention it to him, and he certainly didn't want to remind her about it. The scars on his hands told everyone all they needed to know. He tried it, probably the Prime Rib dip, your classic 'first timer', got a bad popper, BOOM! Scars, probably found naked with his socks on sprawled out in a dimly light bathroom somewhere. Like almost all popper victims, including Kitteridge, he had sworn off Puff after his first and only time. Hasboro entered the bathroom all those seconds ago and emerged after a long time a changed and forever scarred man.

Rosalia had the same sense of relief as so many spouses do when their loved ones finally give up the ghost. She could relate because she had the hunger in her as well. But she had learned to control it as it turns out meditation and exercise feeds more than just the mind and body. A few 'down dogs' and a 'warrior two' and your belly and nose feel fuller too. Or maybe you're just so tired and sweaty that you can do nothing but be Zen about the world around you. Whatever it was it had been working for Rosalia and she would convince Hasboro to take it on with her now. He owed her that much. She teased him about his chubby 'little Life[x] baby', his pouch of extra consumed rations that kept him warm around the middle. He knew exercise and meditation was good for him, but he just needed her to help him set aside the time.

The journey through the dust and Platform, if you could call it that, had lasted only a few thousand seconds. Rosalia held it back, but Hasboro vomited a bit in his mouth from all the rotation, he had terrible vertigo even at this young age. The feeling of floating, sliding, turning, up, down, right, up, back left, turn. It was hard to know which way they were going. But just like house cats they landed on their feet – or rather a gentle maglev down, or was it up?

Even though they both needed it after what they just went through, the mix of emotions and tension running through them, there was no active stretching for Rosalia and Hasboro right now. They are on the run now and they must wait a little longer until they can be truly reunited and live off somewhere with no cares in the DZ. But what they need now is medical assistance. Despite all the commotion at the Interval and TB seat assignment ceremony the fact that Rosalia was still pregnant, and that her due date was today, escaped no one. They would need to find the Waster Kings and soon. Hasboro swings wide his cape but continues his firm embrace of Rosalia. He shifts her ROPU again and gently moves it as he slides his hands around her waist and pulls her even closer. Hasboro leans down and kisses her passionately. She returns his kiss and embrace. He gently pulls away and lowers his head down into the nape of her neck, he loved that spot between her shoulders and neck, so soft and sweet smelling, like that shampoo she always insisted on buying. "I'm so sorry about Marcus."

"Me too, he was such a sweet guy." Rosalia wonders out loud if Marcus could still be alive. They had to find out and save him! But Hasboro simply shakes his head because he knows that the Platform portals like the one they just took are few and far between. There was one in front of the community center, and they had just confirmed that. But the other gaps in the Platform did seem to just swallow you up, of that Hasboro was certain. He isn't sure exactly where they are, but Rosalia insistently taps him until he spins around and looks up; just through the fog he can make out one the Platform's navigational beacons. A big sign announcing they had made it "Welcome to DZ: 23S." Luck must be turning in their favor he thought. The Waster Kings were rumored to be holed up in 23S, but Hasboro thought 23N only intersected with 23A?

Some seconds pass and they have a heated discussion about what to do with her ROPU. Hasboro has had enough and tries to take the thing out of her nose in one big dramatic pull. She lets it dangle and even hit the dusty ground as he unshoulders the unit itself. He briefly debates trying to destroy it, burn it in a fire, something, like a glorious Viking funeral send off. Rosalia however isn't ready to give hers up just yet. She has grown rather fond of living and can't breathe without the hose, not just now, maybe later, she said as she picks the ROPU back up and puts it on. They both breathe a sigh of relief when the Waster King 'welcome wagon' rolls up. A bunch of scraggly looking teens holding light-guns at the ready pull up in a classic Army Jeep. Hasboro quickly relays the relevant, they are now PTB and need help, she is giving birth as we speak! They are quickly whisked away into the hospital triage dome where surgeons were waiting, they had been doing a lot of emergency c-sections today, couples desperate and willing to pay any number of credits. Hasboro is glad he had been pulling some extra shifts, he tipped the orderly and nurses, and made sure to grease the palms of the surgeon too. He is pushed out of the room, told there is nothing he can do now but wait, maybe go get some cigars to celebrate – he was about to be a Daddy.

*

Rosalia was glad that Hasboro was escorted out of the room. She had a new plan forming, and while he was an important part, this next step wasn't for him to know. At least not for a long time to come. If the plans worked out he would have more than enough love in his world to forgive this simple, one time, indiscretion. It would be her one little secret. She had heard it could be done; you could ask for the baby to be taken care of right there. They would whisk the baby away and euthanize it, although not sure the baby would choose the same path if given the choice. Now that she knew Tranquility Base was not for her she wasn't sure she could raise a baby on this planet. Rosalia had counted on Hasboro being around to help, the divorce from Amanda and

Marcus now no longer needed would just make everything easier. But she decided then and there that she needed a new plan now and one that secured her and her baby. She knew that the Collective raised all the younglings here and would see to it that they took care of her child. Rosalia would watch over the child from afar and reveal herself at the right moment. It wouldn't be odd; the Collective drones raised all the children. Hasboro wouldn't know, at least not right away. She wanted him to have the pleasure of helping to mentor and raise all the remaining children, together like one big family. Not just relegated to raising Marcus' baby with her. Only that much love could pull Hasboro out of the depression and sadness she could tell was settling in. He had never wanted to be a father, even though he knew it was part of his duty as a citizen on this planet, but he had resisted the idea. The moment he saw Mandy, clutching his baby, his love, seeing it be taken away forever, well his gentle heart burst right open. It was impossible to describe how he could love something so entirely that he had never met. Hasboro knew he was a good man, better than most, he had his run in with Puff, but had come out on the other side. He wanted to impart his wisdom, share the stories of his experience, teach another the cycle of life, love, and loss. Rosalia had found a way to give it to him, not just once but many times over. She hoped that would be enough. It had to be.

The cesarean section surgery is over and Rosalia gently awoke in the hospital bed. Her newborn baby, a boy, was lying bundled up beside her, swaddled in his blankets, rolled up with his ROPU, almost as large as he was. Rosalia blinks open her eyes, holds the little baby burrito close to her chest, and kisses his forehead. "Hello, my beautiful baby boy!" She raises him up to the sky briefly and then brings him back in close for a big hug.

She breathes in that distinctive smell of a newborn baby – trying to hold it all in because she knows she will never get this back. This time together, her baby in her arms, alone just the two of them, it will never be like this again. After many hundreds of seconds, thousands even, she pushes the call button and summons the nurse. As the nurse slides over to her bed Rosalia slips the extra credits into her palm. "Keep this baby safe and put it with the others. No one must know." The nurse nods, not her first rodeo, and takes the baby and credit bribe away. The baby, is placed with the others, to be raised by the Collective. "Here, for the surgeon," Rosalia says as tears slip from her eyes.

"Did you want to pick a name for him?" the nurse asks, pausing at the door.

"Sevrin," she says, and closes her eyes shut tight as her baby is taken away from her. It was her plan, and she knew it was going to be hard, but nothing could prepare her for this. She didn't know how much more pain her heart could take; first Marcus, Mandy, her baby, and Tranquility Base. Now she had to give up the one thing she had been living for, living with, for the last two years.

Hasboro is called back by the surgeon who explained to him everything did not go according to plan. She was okay he said, but the baby didn't make it. Arrived appearing healthy enough but couldn't ever seem to breathe, even with his ROPU. "Did you say his?" Hasboro chokes out?

The surgeon casts a look downward, suddenly interested in his shoes. "But yes sir, a boy. So sorry sir, I mean to say it was a boy," the surgeon whispers and puts a caring hand on Hasboro's shoulder. He pushes past the surgeon who is just thankful this terrible part of his job is over, lying to patients is not what he signed up for. Hasboro makes his way through the double doors and scans the hallway looking for her room. Rosalia is sleeping when he finds her. She is exhausted from the ordeals of the night. The lights in the room are dim, except for a bedside lamp, shining down and illuminating a letter on the side table, next to the spent Life[x] tubes. They were trying to keep her hydrated. He takes off his coat, slides his cape aside, and settles in to read the note.

"Dear Hasboro – Please know that I am well, and I have decided this is what I want. Our plans of living together and raising children at TB didn't come together, but I know another way we can still be with each other and still get the love of children. I don't want you to be restricted to loving just one, you have enough love in that big heart of yours for an entire orphanage of kids. And that is what we have here, a group of orphans, their parents gone back to Tranquility Base. And, well, they need you, Hasboro. They need your gentle wisdom and guidance, teach them how to survive here on this planet. I will be by your side the entire time, with you in this journey. People will talk, and we may get some resistance, but we will find a way to do this together.

I love you with all my heart,

– Rosalia."

Hasboro doesn't know what to think as he covers his eyes, welling up but locked behind forever dark opal over-eyelids from his popper run in. His eyes are heavy with tears that will never fall. Hasboro had already done some deep soul searching in just the last few seconds and had taken in everything that happened at the Interval. His Mandy, his unborn child, and his friend Marcus, all gone. Rosalia was here, however, and she had ideas about how to bring more joy into their lives. Something they could both use right about now Hasboro knows. He makes a vow out loud, to himself, for Rosalia, for anyone to hear. He would dedicate his life to raising the kids of DZ: 23N. He would be there preparing them for a life of tech support and making sure they are ready for Tranquility Base. He would indeed be a father but just with a bigger family. He closes his eyes and settles into the chair at her bedside. Hasboro sort of wishes they could stay at the hospital forever. While they are here no one questions why they are together. Everyone just assumes they are married and he kind of likes that. Likes the way people look at them when they think they're together. He drifts off to sleep wondering if they will ever find a way to be together, really together like in public for everyone to know.

Chapter 8

94,608,001 to 126,144,000: 10 Years until Tranquility Base

Kitteridge has lived a lifetime out here searching for his daughter. Four Earth years have ticked away draining her ROPU all the while he looks. Countless houses searched, Life[x] consumed, mock Intervals passed, and refilled ROPUs after refill, ransacked buildings and overturned sheds in his quest; too many "Goodnight, Rachel" and too many "Good morning, Rachel." He wonders sometimes if he shouldn't just settle down. Take one of these old resort hotels, with their manmade pools and amenities, and live out his days there. He had managed to find more than enough hidden Puff caches along the way. By now she would be dead, or thoroughly indoctrinated in the belief of the almighty Tranquility Base. Kitteridge still considered himself a believer, but he had begun to have doubts. If Tranquility Base was really all that, how come they never heard from anyone after they left? Surely parents would want to check up and chat with their children still here on this planet. If nothing else, to watch them hopefully become StatStars and compete in Derby Days. Give them guidance and coach them through the challenges of life on the Platform, even if from afar. I mean, wouldn't you want to guide your child through that difficult choice? Do they really want to be sterilized and dedicate their life to Derby Days? What if she never becomes a StatStar, will she regret it?

He could just give it up, stop the searching, finally see what that cinnamon bun thing was all about. Puff until he bleeds out, smelling like donuts and fried bacon, with a side of richly brewed espresso. No one was around to miss him anyways. Even if he did find her in time, she was destined for the trip to Tranquility Base, not him. The moment he showed up without Marianna his bachelorhood would not be tolerated – he would be summarily executed by a squadron of drones for sure. 63 seemed content to wait around and fill up his ROPU. Kitteridge had managed to avoid the temptation to quit, he pressed on even though he knew he could Interval it out here and the owl was all too happy so long as Kitteridge kept on living. Keep searching, keep going. He hadn't made his way all through DZ: 23N yet but was sure to be close to 23S. He had been heading that direction with constant course corrections due to the shifting dusty base of the Platform.

His first course 'corrections' were random wild ass guesses at best. His compass still worked so he could point South all right. The gently undulating waves of the Platform, the shifting sands of dilithium crystal, and constantly swirling smog made everything look the same. Only by keeping careful track of the lights on (not searched) and off (searched) he could at least prevent himself from going in a circle. Big random swoops across the DZ, going where the maglev boots take you, was no way to search for your one and only family member. Kitteridge had no other options, so yeah, clear a house and start walking left. Check the compass, ride the Platform wave 200-meters right and West. Tack. Jib. Hoist the main sail we are really making progress. Every scrub of duck to the wind me hearties; all fast and steady as she goes! Or so that is what he thought each night after he made his navigational decisions, confident that he would find her tomorrow, was sure of it.

63 had been beeping and vibrating on his shoulder since the beginning. It wasn't all the time, sometimes on the left shoulder, sometimes on the right. At first he thought it had something to do with his ROPU, like his little buddy back there was just telling him, "another one's coming big boy, but don't sweat it bro, I gotchu homie." Then they started happening in between gas station top offs with no apparent order or pattern. Then one pleasantly thirty-four degree and pitch black night, drone 63 beeps like crazy and jams Kitteridge in his left thigh with the tip of its metallic tail. Not so much as to puncture or wound but the motion and strength of the robotic appendage moves Kitteridge right a few steps as it bumps up against his pants. He instinctively follows suit and keeps going in his new direction, a few steps to the right. Beep, beep, stop vibrating, tail actually strokes his thigh right on the spot in a tight little circle, like a quick gentle rub on a booboo from a loving mother's touch. 63 is quiet again, like the whole thing never happened. It was so quick and subtle that Kitteridge didn't really notice, just his drone moving around under the cape and misfired or something he figured.

*

Fast forward a few hundred thousand seconds, more Life[x] consumed, more hovels and villages searched, and still no Rachel. This night as he walks about DZ: 23N drone 63 beeps and taps, this time on Kitteridge's left thigh. Oblivious to the intent behind these jabs, Kitteridge doesn't so much shift left as he stumbles a step out, then back to his ever-portly course West tonight. The drone under his cape beeps so loud that the owl on his shoulder screeches awake ready for battle – this time the droid is going for the kill the owl just knew it! Owl takes a quick glance, hears another beep from 63, this time oddly gentle sounding like a little blip from a toddler's nursery toy. Content that their third search party member is not out for bloody murder the family protector decides to search around, might as well now that he is awake and has already taken flight. As the owl flaps its wings and flies away Kitteridge gets another quick succession of jabs – right thigh, left, right. He can't help himself and like a little marionet doll he complies; a little toy nutcracker marching to the left ready for battle. "LEFT?… Is that it? You want me to go left!" Kitteridge walks a few more steps forward in his new direction and then stops. Drone 63 beeps and squeals with electronic delight – it was like R2D2 and BB8 had a baby, a robotic Elmo having just had his fourth espresso announcing its agreement. Kitteridge can't help himself; he laughs out loud for the first time in over four long years. It sounds strange, muffled by the smog of dust cloud around everything, but it felt good to smile again. Drone 63 tries its luck again and taps him, this time a gentle tap on the shoulder. Kitteridge calms himself and takes a deep breath. He felt it all right but waits for another just to be sure. Tap, turn, step. BEEP! Kitteridge was right, the little drone was signaling to him which way to go. Chuckling to himself he does a little dance number right there on the Platform. Drone 63 keeps time with its tail, clicking against his ROPU. He shuffles a few steps right, tap tap tap on his right side. 63 plays back and tap on his left, pivot left and jump a few feet just for fun. He wasn't sure why, or where, this little drone was trying to get Kitteridge to go, but he had a gut feeling he should check it out. They weren't getting anywhere with his sense of directions, so far anyways.

Just tickled with his new discovery and excited for the potential this new trick might reveal Kitteridge finishes his shift here, finds the lucky thirteenth house to camp in, and quickly settles in for his rest. Four hours of sleep and then back to searching for Rachel. He hopes he won't dream this time; he was still haunted by images of Marianna dead on their wedding bed, splayed open like the remains of a freshly carved Thanksgiving turkey. Sometimes he dreamt of cinnamon buns, and that wasn't so bad, even some nights made you want to curl back into your cape and dream some more. "Goodnight, frosting. I mean, Goodnight, Rachel."

They make up quite the trio by this time and they work together as a cohesive unit. Splitting apart and forming back together like big sine and cosine waves splitting apart and coming predictably back together. If they split up, they can search an area faster, and can clear almost an entire village in an evening, maybe two if it was a Capital community. Drone 63 continues to signal to Kitteridge their intended course and he obediently follows along. They have been seeing new towns lately, so at least they weren't lost and doubling back, might as well keep going. As long as they kept making progress in a Southerly direction, he was content to take orders from the Collective drone, he had been all his life. Towns, cities, and villages are mapped, swept, recorded by the drone, and then they move on. They never find survivors any more these days, occasionally come across some skeletons laying out across the street, left dead where they lay after the attack all those years ago. Left alone by the sweeper in their recycling push as a gruesome warning sign to others. What the message the Collective intended to send wasn't clear – work hard all your life, marry, carry a child, and then if you're good the drones will kill you first when they show up a day before Tranquility Base unannounced and start terminating everyone. But don't worry ma'am it will be efficient so long as your Puff addled husband betrays you. Or at least that was the takeaway

Kitteridge was left with when they killed his Marianna and took away Rachel from him. The random skeletons here and there are still unsettling even now. But the mass graves were the hardest. Bodies piled high in a reminder of the horrific roundup at the community centers. He would never do that to Marianna, but many husbands had. Extra Puff was too much to resist.

Kitteridge teaches the drone/owl combo to fly together in a low sweeping motion. Like a giant snowblower they clear dust and rubble in his search for clues, or even the unlikely survivor. The three of them swoop in and quietly maglev their way about before coming back together. They always started each shift with a scrum, a quick huddle to align on the plan for the shift. After drone 63 had paired with the owl, he taught it some new tricks of its own. Using the optical projectors and audio equipment inside the bird it would project rich three-dimensional holograms, maps of buildings or even the entire DZ. They would zoom in and out, pivot and pan, rotate and pinpoint their next target. All the while 63 tapping, bumping, and jabbing Kitteridge in a direction or another. They kept making their way South and from the latest hologram projection they had made tremendous progress. Well, lots of activity, but no meaningful impact. His Rachel, the girl with the thin scar on her left cheek, was still out there. He knew she had many seconds left before her ROPU ran out. And from the looks of it his present situation was sustainable long term, or so long as 63 kept refilling his own ventilator.

*

One day, night if you know what I mean, it was a Tuesday. "Definitely feels like a Tuesday, doesn't it?" Both the owl and drone 63 beep back a low reply, not really clear who he was talking to, they both respond. But Kitteridge talked to them a lot, helped keep him sane, or talking to inanimate objects was the sure sign he had gone crazy. He still had to figure out names for them both; family owl and drone or "hey you" just weren't getting it done. They are on their last home of the shift, and so far, unfortunately as expected, but not hoped, nothing. No sign of the girl with the thin facial scar. He gets the telltale taps on his right from 63 as they enter the two-story home just off the Platform. A gentle touch, barely a feather's weight here or there on his clothing, but they are a well-tuned machine. By just letting go and letting the drone take over, Kitteridge knows when to duck, dodge, jump, or just sit. He quickly learned to 'listen' to the drone after he nearly cut his own head off on that underpass those months back.

Kitteridge makes his way up the staircase on the right and enters the bedroom at the end of the hall. From the wallpaper and decorations, he can tell immediately it was intended to be a nursery for one of the lost children of DZ: 23N. A rocking chair on the side and a large crib in the middle of the room confirmed it. 63 was beside itself beeping and blurting at his side. He takes a step forward and then swings open his cape as the drone floats toward the crib. It shines a light and stops its propeller blades as it hovers just over the bed. Kitteridge reaches inside to pull out a bundle of bones. It was definitely a newborn baby from the size of it. As he looks inside the folds of the blankets he fumbles and the bones spill onto the floor. It makes a noisy clang as they scatter. Kitteridge leans down to pick them back up, doesn't want to disrespect the dead or anything. He picks up the bones, gently placing them back in the blanket on the crib. As he reaches over to take up the last rib bone he notices the little blinking sensor. It must have been part of, or inside, the baby. Kitteridge had heard the Collective implanted a tracker in everyone, that's how they kept your tech support stats. But he had never seen one, even had confirmation they were real, no one did. Until the night the drones took Rachel away. The vision of the tail implanting the device in the stomach of his still wailing newborn flash back across his mind's eye. Whatever this little device was, the red blinking light meant it was still on. Kitteridge had no love for its makers and certainly didn't like the idea of being tracked; to be honest he still wasn't entirely sure why 63 was helping keep him alive. What was clear is that the drone had led him here, to this house and this bedroom, heck it even walked him up to the crib and practically held his hand while showing him the remains of the baby and the tracker that was embedded inside. Drone 63 had wanted Kitteridge to find that tracker, they were here on purpose. That is what 63 had been pointing him at all along. "This? this device, a tracker I think, is that what you were trying to show me?" He didn't speak fluent drone yet but that was surely a "YES!" beep he just heard. "Are there more?" Beep, beep. "Show me," he demands and 63 quickly maglevs and airlocks back in place with a quick tap on his right. Time to move, Kitteridge floating along behind the owl+drone combo flying far ahead, scanning for the next shift ahead.

Millions more seconds pass, more Life[x] tubes consumed, their sticky texture catching in your raspy throat, and even more nightmares. Even when Kitteridge dreams of Puff all he gets is that stupid 'first timer'! He goes through the entire preparation ritual, even relives the meet-up with the dealer, and just as he hits the tube and is finally ready to smell the tasty flesh of a dead cow, it explodes in his face. He wakes up clawing at his eyes. It was just another dream he knows, but as he slowly lowers his hands Kitteridge knows the dark opals that center his face are no dream.

They are as real as his need to press on. "Good morning, Rachel."

Some mornings he wakes up having just done his pre-Puff ritual, the thirty-four degrees wakes him up quickly. Even lying next to his roaring fire, his other constant companion, Kitteridge sometimes wakes up naked. Thankfully, he still has his socks on. Usually. As the dust begins to settle down on the Platform behind him he decides it will be a short shift today. Maybe it is the weather, but he just isn't feeling up to more frustration and disappointment. He would simply find his thirteenth house and setup camp a little early this evening. He walks up the abandoned streets scanning for the nearest retreat and at this point anything will do. Probably going to scarf down some extra Life[x] today he thinks to himself as he opens the door, he isn't even certain which house he had chosen, just sort of lowered his head and went forward till he stopped at a door and opened it. But for some reason he hesitates at the doorstep and turns around, glancing over the left of his cape behind him down the street, stretching on for some ways and then rounding out into a big swooping cul-de-sac. Definitely that's his new hideout he settles it with himself and quickly makes his way toward the three-story mansion at the end of the block. One of the nicer homes he has seen in these last four and a half years out here. Millions of seconds and what seems like millions of houses gone by. Some nice ones for sure but nothing as palatial as this. Must have been a StatStar's home, only Derby Days winnings could afford you something like that. The iron fence gate out front had long since fallen into disrepair and is left hanging off the hinges. The house inside the complex appears to be intact and the lights are still on inside. From the size of it, bigger now from the inside, this must have been someone from the Credit Dealers and Collection Guild. Not even a rock star tech support agent, combined with the credit balance

136

of the best handlers, out there could afford a pad like this. Kitteridge makes his way to the front door and notices it open and clearly welcoming all with a large neon sign that appears to have been custom made for the occasion.

"Smell one, smell all. Come join us for the biggest Puff ball on the Platform!"

Apparently this house had other plans in mind all those years back, another way to ride out the Interval. Some people just knew they weren't going to be selected for Tranquility Base even if they did survive their Interval and so they chose to spend their Interval in a Puff filled haze. The house was absolutely destroyed. Clearly a battle had gone down here when the culling began. The corpses of people lay strewn about the house, furniture was haphazard in the rooms, and the lamps were all broken and still on the ground when Kitteridge entered the second floor; nothing but the bodies of old Puffers who tried to make their last stand here. Strewn about, some in defensive positions with hands over their skulls, while others appear to have been hacked down mid punch. Kitteridge knew enough about human anatomy, and the advanced aging of humans on this planet, to tell the bones belonged to older citizens of DZ: 23N; all likely living here still PTB. Why sit around and watch a bunch of babies be born, and your friends leave you behind, who wanted to relive that pain again? Just come to the big house at the end of the block, yeah right in the middle of the little roundabout. We are having a Puff party like no other, this bad boy is actually sponsored by the CDCG they said. The Waster Kings' own expert makers from all the tribes had shown up for the cinnamon bun smell contest. The ballroom in the basement had been converted into a showcase of different Puff smells, tastes, and textures. It started with the simple pop-up card table style booths with the

137

flower bouquet tubes. Pop a lavender tube in your hose and drift away my boy. As you made your way deeper into the cavernous room the displays got more and more outlandish. Garish signs in bold and flashing colors hawking everything you could imagine. Of course, some new textures that no one had ever heard of would be there, with limited availability. Everyone could smell roses just by hitting up their corner store backroom dealer. But to get the superSourSmash96, with the vanilla bean crust, you had to come to a party like this. More booths with an entire section dedicated to trying to perfect that first hit. Everyone relied on the trusty 'first timer' so it was like trying to invent a better mousetrap. Slow smoked prime rib dip couldn't be better they said. Until last year when someone from DZ: 23A showed up with a peppercorn crust. Now everything was crusted in black and red peppers. Kitteridge can't help but stop and check out the 'Junior Maker's Guild' show booth. Some just weren't cut out for tech support, or their parents were makers, and so they had a chance at parties like this to show their intern experience and hawk some cheap Puff. Guaranteed no poppers though, even from the new kids, trust me I been doing this a long time now.

At the end of the ballroom he comes to the last displays and there is one from each clan with their prized maker trying to win 250 credits for their cinnamon buns. Something that could finally crack the cold and get you out of bed when its thirty-four outside, like every morning on this planet. The Lion's guild was the clear fan favorite, and you could tell because their booth was twice as large as the other tribes. Spider clan had decided to go big or go home apparently – their booth sign announced, "with ORANGE frosting!" Why bust the record with just a plain old cinnamon bun when you could upgrade to orange icing? Years ago, at the height of the Puff party here, just before the drones came a killing, this flavor combo caused quiet the ruckus. They almost had to end the party a few days early when the Spiders showed up and people saw the orange colored Life[x] icing. The Bear clan, traditionalists as they were, went nuts. "Blasphemy!" they screamed as they stormed the booth. But almost five years later and all Kitteridge can see is that one booth looks just slightly more trashed than the others. But the difference between the colossal mess the poor hotel housekeeper has to deal with when rock band The Who checks out didn't look all that much different than when fellow rockers Guns and Roses stayed there, the ballroom was simply destroyed and this booth just like all the others. But oddly enough, unlike the rest of the house, there were no people here. No bodies and no remains of the dead. Just abandoned booths and a floor littered with the trash of discarded Puff tubes and Life[x] packages.

The floor was sticky and clung to the bottom of his boots as he made his way past the last booth displays and into the far corner of the ballroom. He reaches down and grabs a few Life[x] packages, he has begun to like the little crunchy red ones and notices a small glowing light from under the storage cabinet here in the back of the room. He gets closer and the glow appears to brighten, and his pulse quickens. He had seen that radiance before, when Kitteridge missed his tech support On-Call job all those million seconds ago. It meant a drone was past its maintenance window and was waiting for the sweeper drones, the ultimate recyclers to come and pick it up. But that wouldn't make any sense, how would the sweepers have missed it? He slides his cape back ready for action for something doesn't feel right. It felt like a trap. He looks around but finds it hard to tell if anything is awry with the room in its present state. The lights were on but nobody but him was home. The family owl had taken perch on the first floor after he had set up camp, it needed to recharge. Drone 63 had left him on the second floor and was scanning through the skeletons carefully looking at the skulls and examining the left cheek bones for any marks that would indicate they had found Rachel. A thought flashes into Kitteridge's mind, had 63 led him down here on purpose? Was this a hunter droid ready to spring out of the closet? He begins to slowly open the door, the glowing light quickly expanding and escaping out, thirsty for air having been locked up for so many years down here. Kitteridge takes one last breath and steels himself, ready for whatever comes next. Well 63 comes next, silently appearing about three feet away at waist height. The drone is either here to make sure Kitteridge doesn't escape, or it wants to see what's glowing in the storage closet too.

Kitteridge opens the door the final few inches and the light floods out. A gentle and warming light cast over the ballroom and the mangled booths sort of glow off in the distance. As the door hits its full stride a skeleton drops down from the left holding half a drone in his hands. The right hand hits the ground and the hatchet slides. Nice one! This guy had managed to cut the drone in two, well mainly cut the front sensor panel off. Rather the hatchet blow had damaged it completely. The remaining part of the drone just sat open on the floor, glowing away hoping that tech support could put it back together again. Poor Humpty Dumpty, without your sensor panel that must be why the Collective hadn't sent a sweeper to get you. You are dead, turned off, and off their radar. And so here it sat.

Kitteridge examined it closely and it appeared to be in mostly working order. The hatchet had only cracked the optical sensors but the little antennae for audio and all the other connectors seemed intact. Kitteridge manages to pull it out of the

140

closet and set it down on the Spiders' display booth. It might not be a cinnamon bun with orange flavored icing but a mostly working drone that wasn't trying to kill you was a rare sight these days.

Drone 63 agrees and zooms over to take a further look. It hovers down practically on top of the downed drone, and slowly scans it inspecting apparently for damage. It flips the drone over and inspects the propeller blades by actually spinning each one individually. Satisfied with review 63 must have decided he needed closer inspection as he brings up his scorpion like tail with the tip protruding and hovers inches away from the damaged optical panel. It is obvious to Kitteridge that 63 is about to join with this other droid and he can't wait to see what is going to happen. At that instant, his communicator beeps and vibrates. He still keeps the thing with him all the time. The dilithium crystals ensure it never needs to be recharged and he likes to look back at the pictures of Marianna. They hurt his heart and always make his broken eyes heavy and hurt; he can't tear up or cry since the accident with the popper. He reaches under his cape and looks at the communicator to see a message asking if he would like to pair with another drone. Wait, what? He thinks to himself as he quickly accepts the prompts, just like he did when Kitteridge originally paired with drone 63 all those second back. A few more prompts and the pairing appears to be complete. 63 removes its tail and floats off, making its way back to the ROPU on Kitteridge's back where it airlocks in place again, apparently content with their new companion. The new drone kicks into life, opens both its cargo holds with the telltale hiss of the airlocks, and begins collecting Life[x] from the floor. It grabs a few tubes, beeps a little back to 63, opens it pincher arms and drops the rations, and then closes up shop. The doors seal closed and it floats away out of the ballroom and joins the family owl still perched on the first floor. No more Life[x], we got enough, it seems was the message from 63, go join the bird upstairs and wait for us. Sure enough when he finished his tour of the ballroom, grabbed all the crunchy little red bags he could stow in his messenger pouch and went upstairs, there it was. Waiting next to the owl, oblivious and still recharging. Kitteridge decides to let it rest, he is sure to get a kick out of their introduction when the bird wakes up and realizes it now has double the robots to be suspicious of.

As Kitteridge gets close to the pair, 63 beeps a note or two and the new drone opens its cargo hold. Drone 63 messes around under Kitteridge's cape and then reaches into the messenger bag slung under his shoulder and takes the little crunchy red ring ones and puts them in the opened cargo hold of the new drone. So, he's supposed to put stuff in there I guess? Not sure what to make of his new floating backpack, but Kitteridge had to admit he liked having a party of four. Binary unity and all. If he could somehow find and pair more drones who knew what he could do. They could spread out and cover more ground as they searched for Rachel. He still wasn't sure how to get the drones to begin pairing mode and that signature glow. But he knew they could be paired and that 63 could control them.

Glad that he decided to finish his shift and set up camp early here, Kitteridge settled in for the repair work ahead of him. Like almost everyone on this planet he knew how to do tech support and a broken sensor panel was a nightmare to fix. He would have to scour for parts, but repair was his only choice, not going to find a 'New Drone Parts' shop anywhere that's for sure. After just a few tens of thousands of seconds he had finished. The new drone had all working sensors. The refrigerator in the attic didn't work, but no one needed that now anyways; in fact, it wasn't clear why you needed refrigeration at all with the constant low temperatures. But I guess they sell fridges in Alaska too. He ran through the usual series of troubleshooting and diagnostics and confirmed everything was set and good to go. Nicest house on the block had been a good choice. No Rachel but a new drone buddy was a real surprise. He stayed the evening and slept his usual four hours. But when he awoke he felt no burning desire to push on again that day. It had been five years and still no sign of his daughter. He had held a little vigil each year on this night, it was her birthday. The date wasn't a happy one, the memories of the slaughter still poured in even after five years. He whispers, "Happy Birthday, Rachel," and blows out the makeshift candle he placed on top of his new drone. Kitteridge had recently taken to calling them 'drone' and 'bird', not so much names really, but a way to distinguish who he was talking to when he talked to himself. Now with a third drone it just wouldn't do. He needed some proper pronouns in his world. He knows that anything with a name must give deference to his ancestral past, something animal like it had to be. Kitteridge thinks on this for a few days and not really liking anything that he comes up with. 63 has taken over his little storage unit now and uses it to store spare dilithium crystals. That way the drone doesn't have to fly away to mine crystals when another Interval kicks in for Kitteridge. Tonight, he sees his drone 63, the family owl, and the little floating suitcase ahead of him, clearing the dust as they go. It looks like a little donkey, a burro sherpa carrying the heavy load. Just like that it was decided then and that night, at camp after a particularly long shift, he etches 'J@ckA$$' on its rear cargo hold. Kitteridge still can't think of a good name for the owl or 63.

Chapter 9

126,144,001 to 157,680,000: 9 Years until Tranquility Base

She needed to focus and get to troubleshooting that drone before it had waited too long and started to glow – its eerie lantern a beacon for the sweeper drones to come and pick it up, and for the CDCG to come dock her some credits, or take a few rations, or both. Her current credit handler wasn't very forgiving, and she had been through a few already in her short time on staff here. Blavos knew how good she was and wanted her to keep up her stellar stats. He was the only one she felt she could work with and the only one that bet on her. All the other dealers just bet against her. Who wants to make those guys rich? Even though they set the odds and controlled the stakes, handlers were able to bet on tech support fix times, and she had made Blavos a rich man. His stock was rising at the guild. No one teased him about his last failed agent that was found sleeping on the job – you guessed it, naked except his socks, enjoying a 'first timer'. Blavos hit the roof because no way could he stand for his agents Puffing on the job. Everyone knew if you did right by them, your handler would take care of your every need, even that one. Especially smells. Just not on the job, man!

Blavos was tough but fair and got his wayward agent reassigned over to the Transport Center in DZ: 23A (where it intersects with 23N). If you didn't get to your drone in time, you knew it right away, and so did everyone at the guild. Your stats were updated and published in real time and a handler's job, massaging the metrics and controlling the oh so precious messaging, was a tough one. Most people didn't last until retirement. They usually just go 'under cover' and are never heard from again. Odds were good, and if you were bold and knew the right guy you could get double odds, even insurance if you were bold and dangerous.

All bets said Blavos was ruined after his agent spilled his au jus. Handlers took care of their agents, recruited and even poached the best ones from rival handlers, ditched and reassigned the baddies, usually to the TC. A handler with a good team was celebrated like a great sports coach from the past, directing and rallying his crew to victory. Blavos had a system, and as long as you followed his system, he ensured that all of the DZ followed you. System was simple, most solid ones are, just head for the lights. The pleasant, shining little drones, waiting in maintenance mode, making for an easy target for the sweepers. The sweeper drones would come and pick up the drone, the ultimate recyclers, and your job was to get there and fix it first. Do it fast, before the Collective noticed the unanswered repair and docked your pay for being too late, no excuses were tolerated. The Collective was efficient and there was no sense in having a drone stuck in pairing mode. So, get out there as fast as you can and definitely before the sweepers arrive, because then your only choice, well then, my dear you should flee the scene, Blavos had said. Sometimes if they can't find you there when they pick up the late drone you can avoid the fine for tardiness, the CDCG was a little sloppy that way. Blavos had made a few friends along the way and knew some gals down at the TC that could fix up a blemish on anyone's stats. For the right new texture experience of course. Most likely, if you're slow, then you get less credits per month. Blavos did too and he didn't like that. He worked the system but that meant he was a slave to it as well. If you didn't get extra credits then he couldn't pay out all his bribes. And no one at the CDCG likes to hunt and collect from their own handlers. No bonus for being fast though, that was expected from all agents. Plus, the Collective didn't need to give its slave workforce anything else. They had already promised the ultimate reward, Tranquility Base. If you do a good job at tech support on this planet that is, now run along and fix that drone before the sweepers get there. They seem to be getting faster at showing up on the scene these days.

*

She heard Blavos whispering in her ear, "Go, go!" The air was always chilly outside and seemingly stuck forever at thirty-four degrees. Just cold enough to almost ice over in places leaving the Platform treacherous to navigate at all times. She raced forth to the drone, her lights-sword at the ready just in case the sweepers showed up, or worse Blavos from the CDCG, the particularly unscrupulous handler she was assigned. Blavos, assigned to her after her legendary hat trick performance, thought a 'close relationship' with a firm handler would be good for her. Keep her on her toes he had said, trust me, been doing this a long time, but all the other handles had said that too. Blavos was not impressed with her hat trick, didn't care who she was no girl could do that, he was sure. He liked the money she made him, and she seemed like a good enough kid, but he didn't trust her. Something about the way she looked, her face, it was off ever so slightly, and it bugged him. But the money kept rolling in, she kept knocking her jobs out of the park, and Blavos knew a good agent and how

146

to hang on to her. He quickly reassigned or transferred his other cases. Being able to focus on one good agent was enough. It was the Rockstar client a handler always dreamed of. A whale that could set you up for life, and with all that dough, guarantee his trip to Tranquility Base. He vowed not to miss it this next time around. Blavos hadn't worked out in his mind the seating problem, how was he to get a solo ticket? His wife had failed her Interval almost six years ago and he had just barely escaped with his life. The Platform's tentacles even had him by the leg and had started to drag him under with her. But his Marcessa made her ultimate sacrifice and jumped on top of the tentacle, managing to rip it free, attention now focused on pulling her down instead. It was over in seconds, and she was gone in a single scream, swallowed in a cloud of dust. Blavos had already started running and made his way to the Credit Dealers and Collection Guild who took him in. Most of the ones living PTB worked at the guild and helped build a life for those sticking around. Plenty of odds to fix, drones to repair, and agents to extort.

Blavos grieved for his wife and unborn child that had perished all those years ago but was just glad he hadn't succumbed to the pressure and put her in the community center. They loved each other and he could never understand how someone would do that to their family, just for a few lousy credits. But Marcessa was no more, and he found he took to the bachelor life well enough. He liked to work and didn't have any distractions at home. In fact, he slept down at the guild house most nights. Blavos was a natural handler and his inner need to tell someone else what to do was strong. Stronger than his need for smell. I mean sure Blavos wanted to hit the 'first timer' and he loved to swap stories of cinnamon buns just like the rest. In fact, his stories of different textures and new smells always kept the crowd's attention at any gathering. Blavos prided himself on learning about the latest and greatest coming out from the Waster Kings and was a natural speaker. Miraculously, he had never succumbed to the Puff himself. He had seen firsthand what it did to a person, plus Blavos just didn't really like the sight of blood. Pouring from his nose and trying to wipe it away with a scarf? No thanks. Now cut your average fix time by three seconds and he can score some for you instead, do it for a few weeks in a row, build up a streak and a little name for yourself and Blavos could see to it that you had a fresh 'first timer' after every shift. He never minded doing this for his customers, considered it part of the many services he provided, a sort of one stop shop. Anything he could do that helped his agent focus and be their best authentic selves at work and Blavos would throw himself at it. He would try and get you the cinnamon buns, even heard orange icing was promising. Something was off, they said, smelled right, but tasted more like a dreamsicle frozen treat from an ice cream truck. It was supposed to be good but just not quite like fresh baked cinnamon bun hot out of the oven on a Sunday morning good.

With her flowing red hair and her cape flapping behind her she looked like a mighty Viking queen descending to devour the drone. The thin scar on her left cheek made her even more fierce as it glowed back against the pressing night sky. She got to work on the little unit, changed the tires, greased the rotators, sharpened the blades, and the drone was back in business. Before she turned it back on she left her signature trademark on the side of the drone. A quick flash of her light-sword and she etched a permanent tattoo across the side of the now fixed drone. She would mark it for the rest of the tech support guild to see, and so her handler, Blavos, could see how well she was keeping up her stats that were already the envy of DZ: 24S. The signature mark, that 'little miss hat trick herself' had been here, was Blavos' idea. He had heard about another agent who did this, genius idea, had all of DZ: 23N watching. And most importantly no one just watched the stats, they bet on them. Her little tattoos were fetching quite the premium and had even garnered a few copycats out there. No one had repaired as many drones as she did. The drones never seemed to come back to the same place, but she hoped if she tagged enough of them, they would one day return and she would earn the respect of the guild. All she knew right now was that Blavos demanded more selfies; fix a drone, mark it up, then selfie! She resisted the idea at first, but she gave in after he promised to stop offering her more freebies. That's right she didn't want more Life[x] or Puff. Blavos kept trying to reward her with Puff, but she didn't touch the stuff. Smelling sounded fantastic but not worth it. She had run into too many strung out tech supporters to know that once you hopped on that train you could never get off. She intended to get off this train, off this planet entirely. She had heard of Tranquility Base and was certain that her stellar stats would earn her a seat. She fully intended to bring her Puff addled husband along. Her stellar stats and rankings got her an invitation to be a Derby Days StatStar, with Blavos as her handler of course. It was a great honor and rare opportunity to be able to compete, even in just the qualifiers. No one can remember a StatStar who didn't make it to Tranquility Base: those who passed their Interval that is. When she first started getting recognition, the fan letters and free Puff tubes that started arriving, she just gave it all to her husband Justin. He wasn't working, he had broken his hand a few seconds back and was waiting for his robotic appendage to be repaired. So, he agreed to be her PR person, help Blavos make a name for her. If he did that, then all the extra credits, rations, and Puff Blavos sent

149

her way just went right to her husband. Justin did a good job with the media relations, and Blavos kept him smelling all right enough. Justin was an easy case, a long time meat lover he was content with the 'first timers', just keep 'em coming, and make sure the au jus is fresh and piping hot!

She had the fastest fix rate on the DZ, she earned more goals when she fixed a drone on time, and less errors against her when she didn't. Each tech support agent had their own fix rate stats. The higher you were in the rankings, the better your stats. With her near perfect fix rate, with just three errors, made her an absolute rock star. She is only six Earth years of age but already holds the record. That is why she was assigned the best handler, one with nothing to lose and everything to prove, Blavos.

No one ever got a hat trick before, most believing it was invented as some cruel prank to haze the new StatStar pledges. They went through all the hazing to join the guild, all the training and specialization, all the humiliation and stupid tricks. Like, which one of you is the idiot here that goes outside without a cape, really? Thankfully, that was a joke. Lying face first in dilithium dust and seeing who yielded first, that was serious. She was glad to have that experience behind her. She had earned her right and proper place and she was making a name for herself, fighting for it tooth and nail all along the way.

She heard about the hat trick at the age of four and went about practicing for it. She knew she could do it. So, one day, no one is sure the days or seasons here, but it didn't happen before and hasn't happened since that night. She took three calls, fixed them all in under three minutes a piece, over three days, back to back. Nine drones, under nine minutes. She did it at five years-old and was able to skip straight ahead to officer school when she arrived at Service Academy (the tech support guild's version of boot camp where they trained you to compete at Derby Days).

She aced those exams too and was now a StatStar. Of course, because of the legend of her hat trick, she was given absolutely no quarter when it came time to cover shifts and do the grunt work. She was the lowest of the low around the station and everyone had their hand in reinforcing it. The constant hazing made sure that she always knew her place. Many questioned her quick rise or outright denied the hat trick. She had earned the respect of only a few because that took time for these folks. But she trusted Blavos, he was tough but fair. She wasn't sure he trusted her though and he seemed to be always staring at the thin scar on her cheek. Whatever, she admitted it was unusual, but she figured it was just another thing that made her stand out, made her awesome.

*

A strong number of the guild, especially the fighting force, was here Past Tranquility Base (PTB). They had survived their Interval, but they were whisked away at the reveal ceremony and sent back to their tribes and clans. 1.43 million babies arrived at DZ: 23N but everyone knew the rocket to Tranquility Base only had a limited number of seats. Everyone knew that you had to earn your spot on the trip. Death from dilithium poisoning was certain, however. If you didn't get a seat you had some good years to put your affairs in order. Not much to do really here though, there is no such thing as personal property to distribute, credits were meaningless at Tranquility Base, no siblings or children to inform or grieve with.

The selection process was simple really, wait out your fourteen years and when your crystals dry up, remove your hose and wait three minutes and thirty-one seconds to see if you die a horrible death. Pretty straightforward. Everyone would have been gathered at the landing zone awaiting their moment. People would be lined up in waves shuffling forward to their own certain selection. Everyone is the hero of their own story. As the seconds ticked away the crowd turned from anxious to jovial, turning around and greeting, congratulating, and cheering for each other. They had made it! Seconds more now and the glorious trip would begin. A chorus of alarms, beeps, buzzes, and bells all go off at the same time, the Interval had arrived.

The hardcore would rip the hose out of their noses right at the very second the Interval started. Some thought it a sign of bravery to face the ultimate test without your trusty hose, the one that had been giving you precious life all these hundreds of millions of seconds. Others just couldn't wait to finally get the infernal tube out of their nose for good. Most said they would take their hose out when the Interval started, but a lot of folks held on, actually cupping their hands around their nose and clutching the hose in their balled up fists till the very end.

True to form, the entire process was very efficient, the moment the Interval was over people began to shuffle and spread out. They were slowly drawing air – just a sip. Little small test breaths to make sure they didn't melt from the insides. Just a gulp… swallow… exhale, it worked! A Little bigger breath now, yes it appears I am breathing. Maybe it was true, I was destined for Tranquility Base! More cheering, tears of joy, hugs, and high fives all around.

The eyes said it all. It is how you could tell if someone had passed their Interval. The first few breaths were the same for everyone. The same cautious joy quickly giving way to outright adulation was universal amongst those gathered at the DZ.

Everyone's eyes got big really quickly. After about five breaths – they were either melting from the inside as the dilithium crystal spores ate away at their lungs, or they were fine and just watched the slow pale of black shadow the eyes of their neighbors and loved ones, gulping away at their own destiny. The dilithium poisoning turned your eyes hard as stone and black, darker than even the perpetual night sky above. Great big white eyes tearing up for their neighbors' pain, or giant black ones frantically scanning all around, as things got even darker. You were either dying or watching as the world you grew up with died away, your over-eyelids slowly closing, fading in like a cheap slideshow dissolve animation.

Most people who failed their Interval didn't fight because they couldn't. They were physically overloaded, incapacitated, system in complete and total shock, shutdown imminent. That, or the heartbreak was too much for them to move, realizing that not everyone really is the hero of their own story, and that you, sir, are no hero. They shook their heads about in wide arches, trying to look for an escape as they slowly melted down, imploding in on themselves from the insides. Those with some fight remaining frantically waved their hands at their nose and mouth; some who kicked, punched, or stomped on their ROPUs, sure they could squeeze just a little more life from the units. A few would run around screaming like those proverbial headless chickens from yore. The collection of drones didn't seem to worry, they knew no one would make it far. A few paces at most.

The real movement was from those who passed their Interval. They quickly stepped over and around their remaining lumps of loved ones and neighbors knowing there was nothing to be done for them now. The trip to Tranquility Base had begun and those dead and dying around them were not on the heroes'

153

train. They would shuffle forward in big waves, making their way into the community center for the next stage, seat assignment. People who spouses didn't survive their Interval don't make it far; the metallic tentacles appear and pull them under. No unmatched pairs.

Those without a seat will flee and any who remain behind will either raise new children or fight for the protection of the group and their ways. A few become dealers, handlers, StatStars, or souls on the run constantly fearing a hunter drone will finally track them down. Some gave in and became full time Puff heads, wasting away as their borrowed seconds ticked down, smell after glorious smell. Maybe by the time the rocket for DZ: 23N arrives the Waster Kings will have invented the cinnamon bun experience. The ones who stay behind, live life Past Tranquility Base, or PTB as they called it. It usually lasted anywhere from two to four years. The oldest inhabitants of this planet were in their late teens, oldest ever to have lived PTB was twenty-one when the Puff overtook him. No one knew how long you could live post the trip, but they all go the same way in the end when it is their time. After the selection and trip to Tranquility Base, those left behind, living PTB, began another Interval; one that lasted years and not seconds. However there was no escaping the inevitable shutdown of your lungs and body. There was no surviving your second Interval they said, the dilithium crystals would poison you eventually.

With limited seats, by design and of course only available in pairs, there was always a guaranteed fight on the load out to Tranquility Base. Some say the Collective arranged it that way on purpose. I mean with all their skills and abundant resources couldn't they just build a rocket with more seats? Or send more rockets? Why couldn't they save everyone? It was rumored there

154

might, might, probably, but still not sure, had to be something. It was so massive this galaxy of ours, more than one Tranquility Base had to be possible. Build a bigger, or more, Tranquility Bases to send the saved to. Why not?

*

Making quick work of the downed drone she swirls around her cape in a flash and whoosh she is ready to return home to get back to bed. She knew it was time to go when her shoes changed from boots with spikes to the thin-soled 'slippers'. Her hair and features didn't always change day-to-day, but her clothing and shoes changed seemingly minute to minute or situation to situation. The clothing had been a gift from the Collective at birth. Always morphing and changing in size and shape it fit her perfectly. And no matter the situation her clothes ensured she looked fashionable as ever. She had her dust shield jacket and scarf now under her cape. She knew it was time to use her new slippers which were really just sneakers designed for sliding across the Platform. Sort of like the same principle as maglev, only closer to the ground. Super-fast, and super fun. And it left really cool groves and slices in the dust on the Platform. You could carve nice big puffy runs on your way out, and then crisscross them on your way back. These designs didn't last long though, they would be swallowed by the dust in a matter of hours. She loved making them, and Blavos had been sure to work with Justin and incorporate them into her ethos. More copycats out their trying to carve the same big loops she did. No one ever had quite the tight turns she made on her best nights.

Fast and fun, a timed objective with no rewards other than respect and glory, penalties if you error, individualism, and stats.

In a way tech support had become the 'sport' of this planet. Everyone did it and everyone watched each other and tried to best their neighbors. There were special skills that took time and patience to develop. Great meets and events were held with massive Puff symposiums for the Derby Days. Like all good sports of course there was plenty of betting. If you could imagine a scenario a CDCG dealer would let you put some credits on the outcome. Teams of great performers worked together, matching uniforms and all; heroes were celebrated, and legends spread. Especially the hat trick legend, that one had legs enough to make it to all the DZs. Tech support was all in good fun, but everyone was very serious about it, serious about their stats, and rankings. The skills demonstrations at the Derby Days were the best. That is when the slide races were, and everyone loved the slide races. Big fun, big stakes. Minimum entry fees for the agents themselves with stakes so high they had to be backed by a handler for sure. Millions were on the line with everyone looking to score enough credits for the true cinnamon bun experience.

The Derby Days were always held at DZ: 23A and all the clans and tribes showed up. Lavish Puff parties intermixed with tech support contests that lasted for many nights. Fortunes were won and lost at these events, and for the top agent the stakes couldn't be higher. Win the derby and you got a guaranteed spot on the Tranquility Base for you and your spouse. If you're in the final match, and you don't win, at least you knew from the beginning it was going to be a race to the death.

The Derby Days were held at the end of every Tranquility Base season, every fourteen years. For Blavos it was a way to earn more than just a quick coin. Last time around the Derby Days had been a doozy. A record setting turn out, and even though it was still thirty-four degrees some would swear there was a heat wave, and that night was its peak. Blavos had been to a few Derby Days qualifiers by then and had made a name for himself. Most importantly he had made a lot of money for his customers. His agents are the best at what they do and that was no accident. Join Team Blavos and you had to practice. Skill drills were a regular part of every shift, and the Derby Days were your big show, The Dance. Last time Blavos had made promises he couldn't deliver. His new agent at the time, a recent rockstar, was the kind of kid who always showed up with a mohawk for some reason. Cool, we can work with that, make a name for yourself, kid. Then when that guy, with his stupid mohawk, showed up high as a kite on rose-hips spiced Puff, he fouled up at the screwdriver races and lost to some chump from another handler's team. Started bleeding out and throwing up all over the event board – they had to cancel the match and return everyone's stakes. Not all that unusual, well the blood wasn't, nor was returning a bet after a cancelled match, happened every Derby Days. When it did the handler who backed the responsible agent was on the hook for the house's commission. Blavos' guy got pulled and that left Blavos on the hook for more money than he had ever seen.

*

Drone thoroughly repaired, she had to make it home quickly before dark. Just kidding it was always dark here. Her hair confirmed it was time to slide, no longer long and flowing, it was back to the short pixie cut from yesterday. This time it was blue, which went well with her matching fingernails now glistening against the glow of the crystals. She slid away as quickly as she had come. No sense rushing home, if you could call it a home that is. All she had to do was gobble down a little Life[x] and try again at the maglev evacuator. If it was fixed now, that was the third time this month. Justin was there, likely sleeping naked on the floor with just his socks on, safely tucked away in his bathroom 'sanctuary', very likely dreaming of beer. He had recently been reading up about hops and the guys at work had him chasing an IPA. The crisp smell and bitter bite of an orange rind on top to enhance the carbonated bubbles and really brings out the flavor. Way better than that African Amber ale he had been nursing for seconds. Sanctuary, what a crock, she hated when he called it that, or referred to the maglev evacuator as his 'throne'. He was a good guy and she loved him like a brother. A good PR agent it turns out and great at tech support. Not as good as she was but he could hold his own well enough. Blavos even offered to run a game or two on his behalf and float his name out there. Last year they had blamed the Puff incident at the derby on Justin, and so he had been laying low, even for Justin. He had been around on the force long enough that he got to choose his schedule shifts. She still got her choice, her hat trick had earned her that right, anything from the bottom of the pile was hers to choose, that's how much her skills meant. She knew she was tainted by continuing to have Blavos as her handler, he was persona non grata after last year's event. She would be dealing with the dredges of scheduling hell, probably forever, until some newbie came along that she could finally turn the tables and haze someone else. She was tired of being everyone's punching bag. Someone should get her a fresh cup of brewed Life[x] for a change.

Chapter 10

157,680,001 to 189,216,000: 8 Years until Tranquility Base

Kitteridge and his small army made their way through the gates of DZ: 23S. They had originally set a course due south but over the years had twisted and turned all across his planet and searched many DZs. They have finally arrived with mixed feelings. He was happy to have made progress and finally arrive in a location that he had been searching for, where he knew he would find the Waster Kings. On the other hand they have been searching for literally years now, millions and millions of seconds have drained through the hourglass of time, and still no sign of Rachel, or any girl with a thin scar on her left cheek. Not a clue of her, but Kitteridge pressed on. After all, when it really came down to it, unless he wanted to become a Puff head, he really had nothing better to do. Of course then again, maybe he would start a traveling show, complete with a run at the DZ: 23X casinos. By this point Kitteridge had mastered pairing drones and had a complete battalion. They cleared major sections at a time, grouping in the morning and reviewing the map, that ever expanding sign of their progression through and from DZ: 23N to here. It sadly reflected and reminded him of their lack of finding anything but dead bodies, a few trackers, lots of Life[x] rations, and more credits than Kitteridge knew what to do with. Over the years he had amassed quite a fortune and used more than a few of J@ckA$$ and his friends to carry it all. Sixty-four drones now followed Kitteridge and the family owl around, they had become a series of small teams all working toward one common goal, find Rachel. With a crew this large they were able to break down and assemble a new basecamp every night. All the creature comforts of this planet were at his disposal, it made the constant going and searching a little more bearable for Kitteridge. He never worried about his Interval, his ROPU always topped off, J@ckA$$ always on standby with a fresh load of dilithium crystals right from his storage bay, handing off to drone 63 to complete the lifesaving reload.

Assignments were given out at nightly scrum, and he still kept his eight hours on and then four hours off shifts. They paired off in twos and fours and made their way to all the homes in the area to continue the search for his long-lost daughter Rachel. The combined squad, like a finely tuned Navy SEAL team, would clear an area, mine some crystals, and grab a few Life[x] packets and any extra credits people had left behind; any little safes or hidden stashes were easy to crack open with the drone's laser-saws. In six years' time Kitteridge had amassed a large group of drones, all working together under his control, and had looted quite the fortune in credits. He wasn't sure it was enough to bribe their way onto the next Tranquility Base but close enough to give them a fighting chance.

Kitteridge made his way to the edge of the DZ and instructed drone 63 to set up here for the night; a quick series of beeps and boops and the other drones get to work setting up basecamp. He oversees the construction, looking for any way to optimize the load out and pack up, always looking to be more efficient to make better time, always lots more searching to do, no time to waste was his thought. Satisfied with the progress Kitteridge slips away on his maglev boots and through the nearby portal to the Transportation Center. In order to do a real thorough search, leave no stone unturned, he would have to find and take the portals to all the DZs and continue his reconnaissance there. At this point Rachel could be anywhere. He knew she was still alive, or rather that 63 kept tapping and vibrating on his shoulder, bringing them to new tracking devices. Which always meant dead bodies and always heartbreakingly young skeletons with garish little blinking black electronic pucks stuck in their belly cavern. Kitteridge and crew had come across quite a few trackers over the years, but none seemed to belong to a skeleton with a scar on the skull. Kitteridge plans to maintain basecamp here at the edge of DZ: 23S for as long as it takes. There comes a certain point where a man needs to settle down and for Kitteridge this was as good a place and time as any. He would set up a little homestead here and wait out his remaining years. He would never give up searching for it was a vow he planned to keep all his life. But now, with his team behind him and capable of doing the hard work for him, he would have his hands full just consuming status updates and directing the next search party. He already felt old, but if waiting it out here in his little hexagonal dome shelter means months, he is ready. Kitteridge is ready to hunker down for years, the rest of his life and many more to come, he has enough Life[x] stored away.

As he enters the TC he is not sure which portal to take first. The massive, cavernous hall echoes with the sound of his footsteps and the constant chatter of others; he was not alone, here with the dregs, the unwanted and discarded of the planet, hiding away here till they bleed out from too much Puff. It would take quite the effort to clear it all, with its intersecting tubes and twisted tunnels, swirling portal doors opening and closing, keeping time like some large metronome, eating away at seconds as it banged from side to side. From the Transportation Center Kitteridge would be able to access all the DZs and continue his search and he could truly scour the planet for Rachel. He knew he had to make his way to 23X eventually. But he was worried that with all that Puff around he wasn't sure he could resist the temptation. He knew the dealers would swarm him, take one look at his eyes, and offer him all sorts of free tubes of Puff samples. He could get high on 'first timers' for the rest of his life. One couldn't really settle down in 23X, you just partied until you couldn't stay awake, ran out of credits to pay your dealer, or by then you probably had a casino assigned handler who kept you chained to the table with free Puff and drinks, or you ran into trouble with the Collective and got arrested. Stay longer than three days they said, and you would never leave. Two days tops or you could feel yourself slipping to the dark side. He intended to keep his visit short even if that meant he had to come back multiple times. Kitteridge didn't like to revisit the same places, too many bad memories, and they all look the same.

DZ: 23A is a good place to start he thinks, and Kitteridge makes his way over to the portal. Next exit is coming up in, well would you look at that, just three minutes and thirty-one seconds and the maglev doors to the tube slides open. Just for fun he holds his breathe, makes it a full one minute and thirty-eight seconds, not bad, he had been practicing. His goal was a full Interval. He steps into the portal and prepares for the pressure change and inevitable ear pop. Kitteridge doesn't even look for a seat, not because the tube is crowded, quite the opposite. There is a singleton, a lonely Puff head in the back, dripping a fresh serving of blood from his nose, still dreaming and mumbling about cinnamon buns, it seems at least someone is a die-hard orange flavored icing man. Kitteridge had decided to stand because the ride shouldn't take long, after all DZ: 23N and DZ: 23A intersected somehow, he knew that much. The trip took many seconds too long, which was just weird. He makes his way out onto the Platform when the maglev doors unlock the tube, safely arriving at 23A, or so the sign says, everything looks the same. Kitteridge maglevs his way down the ramp and out of the Transportation Center. He steps into another hexagonal dome nearby. He is hoping to drum up some gossip on any survivors from the incident at DZ: 23N, years back now? He had learned to call it the 'incident', after finding out the hard way that it aroused less suspicion since the Collective had ruled the raid the work of a political terrorist group, radicals who wanted a life better than tech support. I mean, really? What better life of passion, education, skill, finesse, style, and panache could there be?

Kitteridge could tell that 23A had a series of wild and crazy nights and more than a couple from the looks of things. The ground was lousy with discarded Puff tubes. Apparently the sweeper drones were giving this area a wide berth for the time being. There was little, and some not so little, pools of blood scattered about, making muddy puddles mixed with all the dilithium dust on the Platform even inside the hexagonal domes. Some bloody pools were big enough to bring into question whether the victim could survive that much blood loss and still live? Sadly, there were a few bodies strewn about that proved they could not, their crimson and black soaked scarfs the only autopsy they would ever get. Kitteridge doesn't want to, but knows that he must, but can't help but shiver in disgust, as he turns over each body, all long ago stiff from rigor mortis, and the constant thirty-four degrees kept them preserved just on the edge of rotting. He needs to examine the heads and make sure there are no scars. Kitteridge carefully unwraps each body from their cape cocoons and looks for signs of Rachel. But of course, he finds none, relieved to again prove his daughter is no Puff head. Who knows how long these discarded and long forgotten bodies had laid there in their own filth? The dust could have preserved them indefinitely. But the lack of any crystals on the victims, and that they still had skin and hair, teeth and nails, all appear still young. Everything indicates this was a recent party and an event not to be missed for sure. No doubt it was a minor symposium. The Waster Kings hosted these to suss out all the best makers across the DZs. They needed to find the best combinations of taste, texture, and smell to win the Derby Days tournament. And everyone was vying for that 250 credit reward for the perfect, fresh from the oven, frosting melts in your mouth, cinnamon bun experience.

He makes his way through 23A, searching the homes best he can, and marking others to send a recon drone or two. He gets stuck in a portal loop for a bit, not sure which exit to take. He makes a wrong turn and then quickly course corrects. For some reason, all the evidence of the party he missed here saddens him. It makes Kitteridge want to search the area quickly and be done so he can move on to another DZ. He had decided, there was nothing to find here and was ready to write the whole thing off, get back in the portal and head back to the TC for the evening when from behind the concrete barrier he hears a loud raspy whisper, "DO it already, dude, that is just a myth."

"No WAY, man, you got a popper for sure, look at the hardened black crystal inside. They are not supposed to have lumps and be puffy like that."

"Why do you think they call it Puff dumbass?"

"That's not what they mean, and you know it." Kitteridge locates the voices, coming from deeper in the tube, no doubt some Puffers left over from the party, likely getting high in the maintenance shafts. Kitteridge didn't want to go find out because they were all probably doing 'first timers' and would be naked except their socks. He briefly considers going up there anyways, when is the last time he had some fun? Six years of all work and no play makes Jack a dull boy. Kitteridge decides he will just scare the socks off them. They already aren't wearing pants.

"Okay, here's what you do," The first one says. "Trust me, I learned this from the dealer, he has been doing this a long time he said, and I trust him. Something about his face." It is all Kitteridge can do to stifle back the giggles as he hears that, "There is this special thing, a ritual sorta like, you know?"

"Oh yeah, everybody has heard about the ritual."

"Ensures no poppers, guaranteed if you did it right." Agrees the third. Kitteridge continues to listen and decides yes sir he would join in and see if he could have a little fun with these kids. They seemed naive enough if they were cool with getting high on 'first timers' out in the maglev tube for everyone to see. Kitteridge decides to approach the crew to see what sort of stories they knew. To make things more interesting he decided that he would just have to invent a few outrageous things for these boys to pull off and see if he could get them to do it, a little ritual of his own. And he agreed with himself right then, there would most definitely be dancing. But best to see if he can get them to put their clothes on first.

It doesn't take Kitteridge long to win them over. "Yeah, hold the hose like this and spin it around sixteen times. No, bigger circles. See, watch me, like this. Okay, you try. Good. Yeah your arms are definitely going to be tired, but better than one of those infernal tubes blowing up in your face, am I right?"

Just like that Kitteridge yells out the encouragement. The three kids all huddled together with fresh white scarfs at the ready to soak up any blood. They had heard the first time was the worst when it came to the bloody side effects of Puff and that it was like a nonstop geyser from your nostrils. But better to do the ritual right, be sure, or the nosebleed is the last thing you will have to worry about. Kitteridge had spooked the boys initially for they started to scatter, running away buck naked into the night, their stockinged feet kicked up little clouds of dilithium dust. Remembering what he had heard about the dealers and how they sometimes sent people to 'help' you through your first high Kitteridge tells them to stop. "Are you the guide?" the raspy voiced one asks him, his knock-knees clearly shaking.

"What's a gui… Guide you said? Well, yeah sure! That's me, your guide. Dealer sent me to watch over you kids." That seemed to put them at ease a little bit but they all still just stood around exchanging glances, trying not to look at each other directly in the eye. Thinking quickly he slides the pouch from under his cape and tells the kids he brought extra Life[x] with new textures in there to try. Free of charge but only if they wanted, Kitteridge explained. These kids had never seen so many rations in one place.

"Pazzos sent you?" He nods and begins to try and convince the kids to put on some clothes, at least pants. The little guy declines, wants to let it hang he says, and Kitteridge imagines he is one of those kids who goes shirtless all the time, practically the reason they invented those signs on convenience stores that say, 'No shoes, no shirt, no service.' It wasn't clear whether it was from the fear or the cold but the other two decide they don't want to just shiver and shake and so quickly dress back up. Well two out of three ain't bad, Kitteridge feels, decides he will provide service despite the nakedness, and lets the little one dangle it all out there, except for his socks which remain firmly on his feet.

"Yeah, put the tube in the hose mod sideways. Yes sideways. No, here let me show you." Kitteridge grabs the tube and pushes it sideways into the hose mod and really crams it in there which renders it useless. Okay, now briefly hold your nose, squeeze the trigger on your mod, and squish the tube with your other hand he tells them. They do it all in unison and he watches in satisfaction as the Puff vapor dissolves harmlessly into the air. It is a good thing he did because two of the three tubes turn out to be poppers, big nasty blow your face right off ones. One of the tubes explodes in the hose blowing out the recent modifications from the dealer. They won't be needing that anyways he thinks, not after I am done messing with them tonight that is. They are going to go back home to their wives, embarrassed and ashamed, but still unscarred and in one piece; the whole trio would swear off the hard stuff from here on out after tonight. He decides to make this their one and only high and he was going to make it a good one. He takes them through the rituals, runs out of zany ideas, and has them sit cross-legged in a circle. He wants them all to hold hands, but they are still too immature to imagine touching anyone other than their wives. Kitteridge guides them through a little meditation journey as he set the stage for their dinner to come. He builds it up and allows the anticipation to continue growing. Kitteridge dutifully melts some Life[x] for the au jus cup, even further drawing out the event. He goes a little far out there and has them do some breathing and deep nostril stretching exercises. "CAN YOU SMELL IT? The slow roasted prime rib, fat soaked with bloody juices, meat melting in your mouth?" he asks. "The piping hot au jus, steaming in its fancy little cup right where you can reach it?"

"ITS RIGHT THERE!" one of them screams in delight, reaching for a rock nearby. Sure, I'll give you a rock Kitteridge giggles to himself, but first he smells it, breathes in real deep, then passes the cup of beef drippings around for all to witness, like some holy relic recently found after centuries buried away in a distant desert. The 'first timer' experience is amazing for this little trio, they had never dreamed a sourdough roll could be so good; the crispy crunch of the crust, the squishy gentle white dough in your mouth, and they loved the way it caused your cheeks to buckle in, a little hug on your tongue from each bite.

"Don't forget the crumbs. Yeah, look down, you're filthy with them, all on the front of you." He laughs and they gobble up the little crusts of bread, licking the last remains of absolutely nothing from their greedy fingertips. Kitteridge couldn't help himself. He stuck around with the kids for a little while guiding them safely through their placebo trip because all the Puff vapor disappeared now without effect or side effect. It really did smell good, if you could smell, an olfactory mixture of the best Sunday brunch; right after church in your good clothes ready to eat with recent haircut and family pictures out of the way. Kitteridge and the boys don't smell anything of course, but that doesn't prevent the boys from living out their own first Puff experience. Kitteridge does feel bad about tricking them but know it's for their own good.

Kitteridge described his 'first timer' to the boys. He goes into all sorts of details, and he stretched the truth way more than just a little bit, left out some key info about the poppers and broken hose-mods. They are his captive audience, and they eat it up. Kitteridge takes the time to give them a little Life[x], he has plenty, and it helps them along on their trip by making it more real, something tangible to bite into. Kitteridge, the consummate storyteller, goes on a little bit more and then even makes a few recipes up, some do sound pretty good, so much so that he takes in a bit of Life[x] himself. He takes the time to dramatically stop the story, hear from the boys some, one keeps talking about cinnamon buns. He even sells them on the idea of orange-iced cinnamon buns, something they swore off after hearing about pineapple on pizza. They felt both were an unnatural combination and an unholy abomination.

The kids are weary at first, they had heard about some unscrupulous dealers that sent people out to 'help' you through your first time. But these so-called 'guides' usually just beat you up and steal your credits, likely your hard-earned Puff tubes too. Kitteridge had won them over with his stories and imaginary foods and smells, even managed to talk away around his over-eyelids, apparently these kids weren't experienced enough in the ways of the world to understand how he got those peepers of his. The kids are shy at first, but they quickly open up and argue over each other for Kitteridge's attention. They of course talk about food and smells, tastes and textures, mouthfeels, and bite size. Some kid goes off on a lecture about flowers, clearly enamored with the Stargazer lily. The one in the back, the small one, can't help but talk about cinnamon buns, he wants to know just what kind of orange were they frosted with?

"Blood orange? Navel? Did it have pieces of pulp mixed in it, like marmalade?"

"Oh I love marmalade," chimes in the second boy.

"You've never even had toast, much less jam, or even come close to marmalade!" cries the raspy one. They all laugh. Hmm, marmalade with pulp in it, that would be great, Kitteridge thinks to himself, and then he quickly makes up the name of some new variety of produce, and the guy buys it wholesale, sets back down and begins to literally chew the pulp in his teeth from the imaginary spread.

They continue to talk for a while, many seconds pass, and the light outside never changes from pitch black, so who can say how long they have spent with each other? He likes his new companions, was tired of all those years only running into dead bodies, or Puff heads, or worse the insane ones who still don't know which way is up much less if they have seen a scarred girl around. It was nice to have people with you that you could talk to. It was hard to be alone. It does something to a man when he is alone for a long time. It changes him from within in a way that can never be undone, like some big red switch that breaks when you pull it down, the spotlight now forever shining on what is missing in your life. Someone to share it with. He had found someone, and was one step closer to being with Rachel. Life wasn't so bad living PTB, he was still alive, had passed he doesn't know how many Intervals. And sure, he had the sweetest camp setup around, and drone 63 and the owl kept him safe. But the human soul needs companionship, even the Collective understood that, which is why they assign you a companion, a spouse at birth – so you never have to be alone. Kitteridge had to learn the hard way but by now he was good at it. Like most who live an isolated life he talked to himself all the time. And the years of solitude had ensured that Kitteridge not only talked to himself but that he argued back. But he also talked with the drones. He couldn't exactly beep the same tones and pitch, and he is sure there are signals too high or low for him to hear, ultrasonic voices that only the drones make sense of. But he had become very good at whistling and could direct the drones to build or dismantle the most complicated of structures. He would pucker up and whistle a few notes strung together and the drones would beep back an acknowledgment and get to work.

Kitteridge is enjoying his time just hanging with his new bros, and the silly conversations, and lets it continue on. He doesn't care that he is in the back of some dingy tunnel, stuck in DZ: 23A. He almost forgot what he had come here for, almost. There are more areas to clear in this tube here at 23A before he makes his way back to basecamp and more people to meet and talk to. He can hear others talking and laughing further down the tube, and a few vomiting and what sounds like spewing fresh blood, the choke and cough followed by the spatter of blood soaked spit hitting the dust. He hasn't had anyone to talk to for years, and this is nice, he will make his way to the others eventually, he says, even if he must come back. Admittedly not talking to anyone else for six long years does something to your social skills but Kitteridge was managing to get along just fine. It helped that his listeners were high as a kite or at least he had convinced them they were. Just to make sure they didn't question their euphoric state he made a point to mention a few times that the high can last only seconds really so it might go away as quickly as it comes. Well yeah, everyone knew that they agreed. They never once seemed to doubt or question the fact that they never smelled any roast beef tonight, slow-roasted or otherwise, and they still didn't know what a peppercorn was. He sort of felt bad about it, all the tricks he played on his new friends, the stupid rituals and all that. Although the little dance he made them do, how they all held hands while they tried to twirl together, that had been worth it, he didn't feel the least bit guilty about that. Kitteridge decided to make it right and ensure these boys live the straight and narrow. To finish off the evening he extols the evils of Puff and how the boys should swear the stuff off, never touch

171

it again. He's really getting going, something about don't hate the sinner hate the sin, when he can't help but stop as he sees they have lost interest. He pauses and the boys go right back to their nervous banter; he eavesdrops on the conversation between two of them. He glances at the third, off on his own, who was still mumbling on about orange icing. Kitteridge leans in and listens to the other two talk.

"...The Ghost? Oh yeah, man, she was there all right. For sure. And she was looking fine! So fine. Man, I had never noticed before, but you get up close to her and you can see the sexiest little scar. A deep but thin line right there on her left cheek, just a nudge under her eye."

"Really? Bad ass!" says the little one.

"You know it man."

"Badass is right," says the first, wanting to be back in the limelight, "I saw her, you two dweebs only dreamed and read about her," claims the first one. "I don't know if it was the way the light was catching her hair, or what, but man that scar shined out in the dark, like a little light-sword right on her face."

"So bad ass!" chimes in the little kid. All four are leaning in and paying attention now and none more so than Kitteridge. He jumps to his feet, hands in the air, and then practically shouts.

"YOU SAW A GIRL WITH A SCAR?" He lunges down and with one motion brings the first kid up into the air, clutching him by the collar. "TELL ME," he screams and then recognizes the terror in the kid's eyes. He is just a boy, and this big scary man is yelling and threatening him all while he is tripping his face off. Kitteridge gently settles him down and smooths over his collar and cape. But that isn't enough, the guy is nearly in tears, and the other two are getting into a defensive stance as they slowly rise to their feet. Yup, this guy was a guide all right, sent by that crappy dealer to beat them up, he had already tricked them out of their Puff, made them waste it they lamented. But they decide it isn't Kitteridge to blame, no he was on their side, he had walked them through it and made sure they did their 'first timer' right. It was the dealer's fault, I don't care if he has been doing this a long time, I knew we couldn't trust him they all agree. Sold us a bad batch, even had a popper in it they cried out. Amidst all the commotion Kitteridge did something that surprises even himself. He pulls the group in together wrapping them in his big cape and initiates a big group hug. Everyone leans in, glad for the personal connection and they hold each other in silence. Thankfully, the final boy has succumbed to the pressure, or the cold, and is fully dressed now. The naked thing was a rumor, Kitteridge had finally assured them all. They settle back down as Kitteridge apologizes and encourages them to go on and tell him everything they know about this Ghost character.

"So, I leave the TC right? Going to meet that dealer Pazzos and then… what? Don't interrupt me, man, I was just getting to that. You good? Okay then shut up and let me tell my story, you go back to dreaming about cinnamon buns and your god forsaken orange icing. That dealer Pazzos is recommended by everyone, great for 'first timers'. Pazzos is a busy man, and his clients like their confidentiality and the anonymity that only a man like Pazzos can provide. Don't get there early, he says, and definitely don't look at them, they aren't some freak sideshows in a carnival zoo cage. Just don't gawk is all, yes at the goddamn customers! And whatever you do don't talk to them even if spoken to, he glared. So, of course I plan to get there early, hit the showers after my shift. Man, let me tell you, what a shift, I get topside all ready to fix up my drone, I been on a streak lately…"

"Dude, get to the point. Did you see any StatStars with him?

He is supposed to be the go-to guy for celebs and trainers."

"I thought I told you to shut up? Will ya let me go on with my story now? Thanks. So, I take the three portal hops like I was told so I make sure no one followed me. Pazzos needs to ensure secrecy he says. For a guy that is that well known across the DZs, especially in a place like 23X, all the cloak and dagger nonsense seemed silly. But whatever, I play along just to get the goods ya know? Yeah man, I get to the spot, showed up a little early just like I said. And I see Pazzos, looks just like them ads you see, yeah the dealer idiot, who else would I be meeting? And there are two others talking to him, a pair who I can't quite place although they definitely look familiar. Sure I had seen 'em in the newsreels or something. Anyways, I stroll up to 'em and get close enough to see. At first, I don't believe my eyes, it can't be. But then I make sure not to blink because I don't want to miss her if it is her. And it most definitely is her. From up close there is no doubt. And I can see the scar to prove it. The Ghost is real, and she is here, close enough I could almost touch her. Almost, she has never been tagged in a professional slide race you know that? So good, so fast and nimble, one second she is there standing right beside you, and the next she has flipped and twisted away, sliding across the Platform in a little cloud of dust. I can't believe she is really right there, and I am briefly frozen. They have all stopped their conversation and are just staring at me now. So, I get a little closer and recognize the guy they are talking with, her handler, that guy Blavos. You always see that dude in the background hanging around next to The Ghost wherever she appears on camera. Except on the track, and then she was nothing but a Ghost, a trail of dilithium crystal powder briefly showing you where she had slid off to. Blavos was the one on the hook to fend off and answer all the dumb questions from those pesky reporters.

"Does The Ghost have a boyfriend?" they would ask, full well knowing she was married to Justin, heck the guy was in the room most of the time they asked. Her marriage did nothing to stop all the attention, and the rumors."

"Yeah, yeah, she's great and all, man, we know all about The Ghost. Did you get to see her? Talk to her? Touch her even?" the little one wants to know, back from his cinnamon bun trance.

"TOUCH her? You're a creepy, pervy little man. Don't touch me with those hands, they are tainted. So anyways I take a quick step back, just then remembering I am not supposed to be seen, the plan was to look only. Even though his back is turned, Pazzos hears me first and spins around. He whips his cape open and draws a rather large and menacing light-sword. His clientele cowers behind him, not clear if for protection or for secrecy, they hide their faces in Pazzos' cape. Emboldened by being so close to a real StatStar I just bumble on forward a few more steps until I reach the little group. The clearly pissed dealer says hello, apparently a signal to Blavos and The Ghost to disappear, their business for the evening has come to an unfortunate and untimely close, brought on by this rude intruder. And just like that they are gone. I manage to close my mouth, whip the fanboy drool from my lips with my scarf, and I start really pressing the dealer, right, asking all kinds of questions, like does he know her? Can he get me an autograph? Has she really done a hat trick? Pazzos says he doesn't know, man, barely knows Blavos, the casinos just hooked the two up as he had a line on the next races. My guy Friday there doesn't want to talk about it any more, clearly not a Ghost fanboy or anything. The dealer lowers his light-sword and swears a little at me. 'Let's get this over with.' So, I give him all our hard-earned credits, the ones we saved and rationed for, worked extra shifts for. I give him all that and he gives me those lousy popper Puff tubes we wasted."

Kitteridge is stunned and glad he was sitting down. Here he was, six years of searching and now he finally had a lead, a real solid clue to follow up on. Surely there was more, especially if this gal with the scar really was a StatStar, she would be all over the place. He had never been much of a gambler and didn't really follow Derby Days. And in the last years he has more pressing things to find than keeping up with a StatStar. She would be easy to find for sure and Kitteridge could see her tomorrow he realizes. Kitteridge can't help himself and begins to pace the room in excitement. He had done it, kept his vow and seen it through. He was so close he could taste it, if he could taste that is. A second thought occurs to him. Kitteridge knows that if his Rachel is famous then that would mean she was hard to approach. People would be constantly harassing her, trying to get in her good graces, and her wallet. She would be leery of new people. Especially some crazed looking old man with bug-eyes going about telling everyone he is her father. He might find her tomorrow, but it could take years to earn her trust, even to get a simple meeting would be hard.

Kitteridge knew he didn't want to leave tonight because he was still having a good time with his companions here in the dirty tunnel of the Transportation Center. There were more people to talk about, more stories to tell, and who knows maybe he could get some more info? If his Rachel really was that good, was a StatStar, then everyone would know about her. This fires him up for some reason – it isn't fair that the whole DZ gets to know Rachel's favorite color but Kitteridge. Just not fair at all. But tomorrow night he would make his way over to DZ: 23X. If he wanted to find a famous person, especially a StatStar, that is where she would be. Rachel likely lived there, when she wasn't traveling around swooping up maglev slide racing trophies, cashing in her prize purses, or traveling around the DZs on promotional and press junkets. Yes she would be easy to find there among all the lights of 23X. He was sure he would even find some Puff head willing to sell Kitteridge a homemade map straight to her little hovel, although with the money she was most definitely raking in, it would be more than a simple hole in the ground with an old grungy army-green plastic tarp for a roof. Perhaps he wouldn't even need a map, he thought, as Kitteridge made his way back to basecamp. He had a few things to pack up and some good news to relay back to the team. All their hard work had paid off and had not been in vain. Perhaps I will give drone 63 and the owl a fresh drop of oil and maybe even paint the drone. The drone was getting hard to tell apart from all the others in the mix, but it seems to have settled on keeping its scorpion tail out all the time now, which helped. It is docking with the owl and taking to its wings at almost every shift so no sense in extracting and retracting that control probe I guess the programming went. The group would be as excited or as motivated as a robotic army of sixty-four drones can be. Six years of searching and now they had a new mission. They had located Rachel and now they just needed to find her. He still had to come up with a way to talk to her.

*

The night had finally arrived, and they were going to run away together, if only for a little while. Rosalia had waited in anticipation and had been making lots of small little arrangements to pull it all together. She wanted tonight to be perfect even though she knew Hasboro was already madly in love with her. He told her so all the time. Wrote her letters attached to drones for her to find on her shift. Sometimes she would show up on scene and he would be there having already fixed the drone. They could use those brief rendezvous to steal a kiss or exchange a secret. Linger any longer and people might talk even more than they already are. Now, after all this waiting and planning, she was going to get to spend some special alone time together. It seems like lately all they do is hang out in groups or talk over and over again about Derby Days and what their strategy should be. Rosalia was so shivering with excitement that she could barely button her scarf. They had agreed to the plan and both of them had been rationing Life[x] to prepare for a feast together. They weren't going to actually Puff together but the ritual of sitting down to a dinner experience was fun to act out anyways and you could still imagine it when paired with some fun new textures. Textures was Hasboro's job and he wanted something special and would have to meet her at the Transportation Center after he met the dealer. She wanted something crunchy and flat. Had to be flat, those little red rings were driving her nuts, kept getting stuck in her perfect teeth. She had been giggling with the girls and had been hearing and lately dreaming about potato chips. Without the sea-salt Puff it wasn't the same experience but crunchy was still fun. Hasboro had more in mind, he wanted something bubbly and sweet: a nice crisp Moscato d'Asti paired with a ripe juicy peach. If he could score it all that was. A proper picnic like he promised her was a daytime activity she knew and somehow her clothes knew as well. She was all ready to go and twirled around in her sun dress, with the cozy cashmere tights and thigh-high boots with the furry balls on them, because it was still thirty-four degrees outside. The outfit complimented her outlook perfectly and even matched the water and dust-proof blanket she was bringing. She knew that it would all look fine and put together, but she breathed a sigh of satisfaction as if she had a choice in the matter of what she wore anyways.

Hasboro was just as excited, and his fashion choices of the day matched his enthusiasm. But was still weather appropriate of course. He met her just outside the Transportation Center; even though he and Rosalia lived close together they had agreed to meet here so as not to arouse any further suspicions. Plus he had to meet the dealer first and insisted on going without her, it was too dangerous he said. Tonight, the center was hosting an electorate rally in its attached convention hall, and those rallies always ran long, giving them the extra time they both desired. He slides into his maglev boots wearing a blue and tan seersucker suit with the hat to match. His job was to bring the extra Life[x], and he didn't forget, and he slides them into his messenger bag as he leaves the house.

Hasboro arrived at the TC a little bit early by design and he was out of breath. In order to get there ahead of the dealer, scout the place out and all, Hasboro had to run up the station steps two at a time, the early train having already passed through here. He was sweating under his seersucker suit. He thought these were supposed to survive a picnic in the grueling heat and drenching humidity of South Carolina back on Earth and he thought it would breathe more under his cape. The Transportation Center was the central hub of the Platform connecting all the DZs together through a series of tubes and portals. The entire underground network, or under Platform would be a more accurate way to describe it, had been used as a mining center for dilithium. It thrived and a little community built up around the TC. Stores and shops, restaurants, Puff dealers side-by-side with bookies and handlers, all were here, and you could be sure to pick up the latest textures. The Transportation Center tunnels were a meeting ground for new wares from afar. Some say the Collective had to build another Platform above this one just to contain all the growth. After too much unchecked expansion the base had become unstable. This is the seventh generation of the Platform and the third with universal connectivity to all DZs. The Collective had been busy working on an eighth generation in preparation for the next Derby Days. Some sections of the TC were shut down for the construction, maintenance, and upgrades. This caused a bit of a convoluted route but thankfully there were no delays. Hasboro had to transfer and switch portals at DZ: 23A. It was weird that it took him so long from the station as they were supposed to intersect with 23N. But once there, it was a quick transfer through the tubes, and onto another portal before Hasboro arrived at the designated meet up. Profant was supposed to be waiting inside. He was the dealer who his buddy from work hooked him up with, had been doing this a long time, you could trust him. Well, Hasboro didn't trust easily, a byproduct of a life of secret meetings and little lies had made him suspicious of everyone. All the portals and tunnels, all the restaurants and service shops, all are supposed to be back up and running in time for the Puff symposium, held on day three of the final Derby Days celebrations.

Hasboro makes his way through the grimy restaurant that Profant had chosen as their meeting place. It wouldn't be long, quick exchange really, the best way to do it, didn't want to get stuck with the dealer trying to tell you his life story. Look, man, I am sorry to hear that about your mom, must have been tough growing up on DZ: 23X and all, but just give me the Puff and I will be out of your hair. At least that is how it usually went, they say. Hasboro didn't quite know what to expect or exactly what he would say when Profant did show up. He had heard the guy knew his stuff, had been doing this a long time now, and you could trust him. Sure well we'll just have to see about that, Hasboro thinks to himself. He had it all planned out. What he was getting and how to order the special mixes he had picked for the evening's occasion. The instructions he had been given were throwing him off just about now. He was confident enough in his manhood, one look at Amanda and it was clear he was getting it done. He did hate it when he ordered a cocktail, and it showed up in some stupid Hurricane glass with an umbrella or some nonsense. But he did as he was instructed and motioned over to the robotic waitress. As it wheeled over, tray balanced on one of its eight arms, the others holding dirty trays and a full coffee refill service with cream and sugar, Hasboro cleared his throat and from under his breath he whispered, "I'll take a fuzzy navel, extra fuzzy around the navel please. And throw in an orange spiced rim for my friend." The air hangs heavy in the back of the restaurant and not just from the smog that had escaped and made its way through the dust shield. Voices stopped and all heads turned down suddenly super interested in their meals in front of them.

Just then, as if on cue, Profant strolls in from some hidden backroom; how long had he been waiting there? Profant is dressed head to toe in crushed dark red velvet with a dark red stained feather in his cap, felt fedora and all. Dark shades of crimson, hues of rose, and tints of pink highlight around the cuffs and trim. The man looked like a pimp from the '70s, straight out of Harlem. Hasboro notices he doesn't walk straight, sort of a looping curve hitch to his left, and he swings his cape wide and catches himself with a jut out of his cane to the right. He steps-hops-shuffles-post-swing-hops-walks over to Hasboro's table and hits the robotic waitress on its metallic bum and takes a seat right next to Hasboro. Weird, there is an entire booth across from him, but this guy saddles up in the shotgun seat beside him. Profant lays his cane down on the booth across from them and slides his cape over, silently and effortlessly, as if he had done this hundreds of times, probably all in this same booth. Profant pulls the Life[x] textures out from his vest and quickly slips them into the messenger bag Hasboro was instructed to bring. He even managed to throw in the aluminum metallic tube to hold the potato chips. "Be careful once you pop you can't stop." Profant whispers in his ear. "You have no idea what I had to go through just to get that stupid can," Profant declares. "I should take all your credits just for this dumb tube." He then goes into a long story all about how he had to keep the can away from the sweepers, the ultimate recyclers appeared to always be on the job. "Sure you don't want to smell all that? I can throw in a 'first timer' and you will be able to enjoy the full meal? Give you a discount because I like you. Michael told me you were coming and about the special picnic you have planned. You dirty minx you two! But I can't turn down a lover and a true romantic like myself. So just three more credits and you will blow her mind! What do you say, friend?" Hasboro was overwhelmed and actually considered the offer, he had the credits after all, and they were burning a hole in his pocket right about now. Hasboro resists as he manages to whisper a no thank you back to Profant and then pushes himself out of the booth. His business was done here, and he didn't especially care to stick around and try his first fuzzy navel, orange spiked rim be damned. Hasboro knew he had to make haste if he was going to make the portal exit in time back to meet Rosalia. He hurries off down through the wide and vast corridors of the TC.

Rosalia is there waiting just as they had planned. She had

grown a little bit worried but not too much. She knew Hasboro was careful, plus this dealer, some guy named Profant, had been doing this a long time, and we could trust him. The grin on Hasboro's face, and the triple foot toe-tap-click that Hasboro does when he sees her confirms it, he got the goods. Mission lovers' picnic was a go! They both instinctively look around when they meet. They are sure that everyone is still at the community center 'enjoying' the debates. Just a bunch of blowhards arguing and yelling over each other, hard to tell what the point was they were supposed to be making, or even the question they were supposed to be answering. What a waste of time, Hasboro always thought. But Amanda was into it, and he supported her. The fact that he betrayed her almost every time she was gone now was a convenience, that while often utilized, always left them both feeling guilty. Rosalia and Mandy were friends after all. He steals in for the kiss she was waiting for and had been preparing, actually saving it for Hasboro, it was his to take, she had kept it away just for him and had even just hugged her actual husband before she left for the evening's tryst. Just a hug for her husband, the kiss was for Hasboro. She didn't want to give Hasboro's kiss away to Marcus even though he probably had earned a kiss or two. She slips her hand in Hasboro's and they make their way down the hall to the portal heading to DZ: 23X. They won't have time to take in the shows there but the people watching was fantastic.

When they arrive at DZ: 23X they are quickly encased in lights and sounds all around them, a generous helping of visual and auditory stimulus prepared for even the hungriest of appetites. Casinos, a great way to lose some hard-earned credits, Puff dealers, bookies, and all the handlers for the tech support stars, those StatStars, all had their offices there. Rosalia wanted to spend some extra time walking around, looking around and taking in all the buildings and their unique architecture. These weren't simple hexagonal domes but massive complicated structures. Tall skyscrapers housing guests dwarfed big convention halls right next door, with restaurants, shops, and more scattered all about. 23X was a place of debauchery and sin and your every wanton desire could be met there. There were pools, saunas, hot tubs, spas, and even a lazy river. Those were all inside. No one wanted to wear a bathing suit outside when it is a constant thirty-four degrees out, and besides, the dilithium dust was murder on your skin. Most of the occupants were Puff heads themselves having long ago given up the ghost and succumbed to their overwhelming need to smell. Puff parties and conventions were held here and of course the Puff symposiums for the Derby Days finals. All the Waster Kings' makers were here collaborating and constantly mixing and experimenting. If the cinnamon bun is ever to be cracked it will come from 23X. There is even a place getting ready and seemingly preparing just for the symposium. They already have signs up promising a true cinnamon bun experience. They even had a name for the place – 'Cinnabon'. It wasn't ready for visitors, not even a soft opening, when Hasboro and Rosalia arrived for their picnic.

They make their way to the one of the hexagonal cabanas in the park. Everything had been going according to their lovers' plan, the night seemed to belong to them, in on the little secret and willing to bend the rules just once, for them alone. Hasboro rolls out the blanket and begins to set out his plunder. They would start with a bite of peach each and let the juices run down their arms. Who cares? There was no one to see them. Hasboro had arranged for a cabana overlooking the pools at the Lion clan's Casino, it was the nicest in 23X. The service staff arrives, arranges the lounge chairs, gets towels, sets up the heater, and arrange for the massage therapists to come promptly after dinner for their couples deep tissue massage – tech support could be murder on your back, shoulders, and hands. Hasboro had been going to a chiropractor for years now, without an adjustment and over time he can't move his neck to the right, must look like Batman when he turns from the hip instead of the neck. But a regular quick snap-crackle-pop and Hasboro was good for another one hundred drones. After the peach they would pop open the Moscato d'Asti and share some bubbles. They won't be able to taste its sweetness without the Puff but how it enhances the feel of the peach as the taste buds expand to consume the bubbles of the wine is magical. Both lie back in ecstasy and slowly sip their special drinks. Hasboro always liked a special drink, especially one with a little snack: like the perfect Bloody Mary he dreamed about, complete with candied bacon, celery, cocktail onions, cucumbers, pickles, celery, and a sea-salt encrusted rim. He knew it would be best tonight, because they would put the A1 sauce in there instead of Worcestershire. The A1 really brings out the Kobe beef slider delicately balanced with a toothpick on the edge of the glass. Snapping back into focus and the present, Hasboro knows he doesn't want to miss a moment of this precious time with his Rosalia. He encourages her to save some of her bubbly for later when he opens the chips. She can't help herself and tonight she gulps it all down hungry for more. He shares his still mostly full glass with her and reaches for the chip can brushing away the accumulated dilithium dust that even got into his bag under his cape. She sees the bag and her eyes open wide. "You didn't?" She giggles and tickles him a little under his chin, right where he likes it, and deftly steals away the chip can. She opens it up, POP! And laughs in delight. He can't help but smile and is glad he sprung for the stupid container. He briefly thinks about telling her how much trouble it was to get, the story from the dealer seemed sort of charming, but Hasboro doesn't want to risk it and spoil the moment. The guy had said it was worth it, and Hasboro felt like he could trust him, he had been doing this a long time, you could tell from the crimson stains on his scarf that he was no newbie when it came to Puff and textures, the guy probably chain-hits 'first timers' like it was his job. Well, in a way it sort of is his job to know the product and his customer base but the 'first timer' sort of sells itself. But no Puff in their experience today. They hold out their temptations for something better – each other. Letting their togetherness be enough, he wraps Rosalia up in his cape. He was wearing the faux fur-lined one for extra warmth. She wished he would wear that one all the time, but this will do for tonight, she thinks, and they both drift off to sleep in each other's arms just for a few precious seconds.

The potato chips don't last long, and he agrees that they are better flat. Somehow they are crunchier that way they agree. They don't get the salt hit but that's okay. This night has been special to them both. It was one of the few times they could just be together. Conversation came easily between them as it always does and was just as comfortable as the pleasing silence. You had to try hard to find people in this world that you could just be still and silent with. For Hasboro that was Rosalia, and he was her silent sounding post back. If you manage to meet someone, and you can be with them, in the same room, without saying a word just to break the tension, if you can do that for an hour or more, than by hell or high water do whatever you can to keep them by your side. That was what Hasboro's dad had told him, and it stuck with Hasboro. Mandy was great, but she was always talking.

Mandy didn't care so much if you responded, interaction was not required. Hasboro just had to be in earshot, and she would wax on for hours, talking his ear off. He would sit patiently, waiting and listening, for he truly did listen when she spoke. It often felt like Mandy was straining, looking for topics to bring up, as if she couldn't handle the silence with him. Mandy was like that with Rosalia too and it was exhausting to keep up with her. No matter what you did, how you engaged in the topic, or brought your own material to the discussion, the tension between them was always there. It was different with Rosalia, Hasboro felt comfortable in his own skin and enjoyed the silence with her in it.

They take in some more people watching and admire the comings and goings of all the people in DZ: 23X tonight. The parade rivals something from Carnivale back in Brazil on Earth. Huge flowing costumes and a rainbow of colors fluttered by. Some have won big and feel like they have stolen from the Casinos like they had just pulled one over on the man! Their faces and wallets would be fat and flushed red with greedy satisfaction. They would be back tomorrow sure of their continued success. And then, by day three, they would look as haggard and downtrodden as the rest of the residents here, blood-stained scarves revealing their new pastime. Hasboro and Rosalia were just visitors. They know that even if they had more time they wouldn't want to spend it here. Get out while you can, and they did. The pull of Puff and gambling, the rich and easy life, wasn't very strong for either of them. They had each other and their love was a force stronger than any other on this planet. They were buoyed up and carried on by it. That and the hope of Tranquility Base. It didn't matter that they were mismatched with their spouses, just make the seat to TB and then you can actually get a divorce back there. Amanda would resist but Marcus would be okay, fold his hand gracefully, and probably help her through it. Who knows, Marcus might even end up with Mandy in the end. They would make a great couple, Rosalia always thought.

Their wristwatch alarms go off in unison. Their night was coming to an end and the signal that it was time to head back home blared annoyingly on, cutting the silence, and building romantic tension; the bubbles had gotten to their heads. Their time together is finished, and they must depart each other's side. They will take separate routes again not wanting to risk it. Hasboro makes it back in time to meet Mandy home fresh from the rally and wanting to talk to someone about it. She had made a great speech and had really got all up in the speaker's face. Something about a new community center and how it would better for Derby Days. She didn't like the new track, could prove it was slower through her training times, the new surface held back her maglev tricks that made her famous. She fought against it and the committee agreed to bring the matter back for further discussion at the next meeting. That bought her a few more months where she could focus on training and not have to worry about this nonsense. It was a victory she would take and needed to celebrate! Marcus is asleep when Rosalia slips in the door. He usually didn't wait up for her for she could be a bit of a night owl. He certainly helped Mandy win her little battle tonight, but he had no need to stay up and relish the win with someone. He enjoyed his quiet time and was able to celebrate in solidarity. Anytime he got to help Amanda was a win in his book.

Chapter 11

189,216,001 to 220,752,000: 7 Years until Tranquility Base

Fourteen years between Derby Days was a long time but there were lots of things to prepare for. A multi-day celebration that took place across all the DZs, the event culminating in the Interval and seat assignments for Tranquility Base. Fortunes were won and lost daily betting on the Derby Days qualifying events. You could take a long view and make an early bet on a contender before they even had names or learned to walk you could put your credits down and bid for them to win it all fourteen years later. But few had the stomach for such a long shot. Most of the action took place at the training and practice events, the minor rallies and qualifiers that led up to the final matches before TB. Gambling was a weird addiction; you could bet on anything. Parlay, straight win, team win, place, and show, a trifecta was a possible bet if you had the right gal, usually just reserved for handlers. Yes, Virginia, sometimes you bet on just a slide race and that is all you need to make your fortune. Bet enough and you could make your way to Tranquility Base some say. Whatever you thought, you could bet on it; if it happened, might happen, or even if it didn't happen, credits were changing hands. You could make credits predicting the color of the cape on the victor. Or you could lose credits if you thought that newcomer from DZ: 23G had a chance at the screwdriver races. People even bet on the number of events, which is dumb because seven, it was always seven. The real smart ones though usually just bet on the weather though, 1:1 odds, and most didn't even blink about the one percent fee the CDCG charged. Another game of life where you lose by winning. Why would you pay to have the Collective tell you it was going to be thirty-four degrees outside? It was always thirty-four degrees, always. But people paid. The mini events, those fourteen years of minor battles won and lost, all leading up to the final war, those events were only a tad smaller key than the big Derby Days. They were still usually a full day or two of matches and revelry though, and truckloads full of credits and Puff moved around with them. All the handlers would be there barking off their latest champions and arguing with the robotic refs over stats and bad or missed calls. The Credit Dealer and Collection Guild would most definitely be present, setting odds, making lines, and yes, taking bets. All the Derby Days qualifiers held their own Puff symposiums showcasing the latest and greatest experiences one could ever dream to smell. Even the Waster Kings' best makers had to secure an invitation to the gala event at the final Derby Days, on day three, right before the Interval. If you're going to fail your Interval, maybe that ROPU has been sputtering awhile now, might as well try a cinnamon bun first. Everyone is saying they are close and going to have the real McCoy at the next Derby Days, still perfecting that infernal icing though, but they'll get it.

Blavos shows up late and meets The Ghost at her trailer. The mobile units follow them from each DZ qualifier to the next and serve as their constant home away from home. He is normally a very punctual guy and gets pissed when she is even a second off her time and she wonders where he might have been? Come to think of it Blavos had been missing a lot these days. Just last week, at DZ: 23J, after she almost scored another hat trick, he was nowhere to be found at the press briefing. Thankfully, Justin had been there, and his quick thinking saved the occasion. He invented her now famous Ghost-selfie trend that night. Anything to distract the reporters away from that guy Bishop who won the last rally and get their attention back on his wife. It worked and teenage girls all over this planet have been making the same lame, awkward pose The Ghost did as she scanned the crowd looking for her handler, caught by the camera transfixed between two moments. Blavos was always there, what gives? She needed him too now. That guy came out of nowhere and she had never seen anyone jump that far. Maybe she really did need to rethink her strategy… maybe there was more to the slide races than just pure speed? He absolutely scored a bunch of points with all those rings he brought down. Got close enough to see his name next to hers on the scoreboards. Judging by the attention of the press, all the casino handlers, and the CDCG big-wigs sniffing around meant somebody had just won a bunch of money off this new guy and his fancy big leaps. Or somebody had just lost big. Real big. Either way The Ghost needed her handler right about now to, well, go handle this. She needed to focus on her next race. Blavos finally shows up and dismisses her concerns off hand, he looks a little disheveled and she can't help but notice the new scarf around his neck. God help her if he turns to the Puff, she thinks. He waves off her questions and concerns and they quickly get down to talking about strategies to handle this new Bishop fellow. He was cramping her style. She was scared, no one had come close to her in the slide race qualifiers, and then this guy shows up out of nowhere. Plus, who backs themselves in a race these days? The Ghost thinks to herself. "Probably has some shadow handler from another DZ pulling strings behind the scenes," Blavos blurts out loud before he can stop himself.

"You think so?"

"Makes sense, but who could it be? Large Marge got out of the game seconds ago, who had the kind of juice to back a guy and fix odds against her?" Blavos knew he made a critical mistake as soon as he said it and wished he could take the words back. She bought the idea outright and was now a dog on the hunt looking for some shadowy handler. It wouldn't be long till her curiosity lead right back to him, and then what? Blavos didn't want to think about that, he had enough problems to deal with, he didn't need her to be distracted looking for someone else. She needed to focus on the race, and he brought her back to attention with a snap of his fingers – that was their cue. Blavos was patient and listened but when he snapped the conversation was over and he got his way. A quick loud finger snap always had that effect on people, trust me, been doing this a long time.

The DZ: 23B Derby Days qualifier had an especially large Puff symposium this year and of course all the Waster Kings best makers had RSVP'd. There was to be your standard set of new textures but how many times can you recreate those crunchy red rings? A slightly bigger and more pink colored O still tasted the same. Soup had long been a big thing here and not just on 23B. The warm, melted down Life[x] was soothing after a long cold shift working tech support, fixing drones was cold lonely work, and soup helped warm the bones. But this year a new recipe was unveiled, Clam Chowder, and it turns out those little red ones are the perfect substitute for oyster crackers on top. Mollusks had long been a popular snack; the perfect little slimy appetizer slid right down your throat when simulated with the already gooey Life[x]. But combine them and melt them down in a rich cream based broth, add some carrots and potatoes, a little parsley sprig, and BAM! Peppercorns had a resurgence solely due to the popularity of chowder. Crispy black peppercorns were plentiful. Some say it was just little charred dilithium crystals, but they were a must as a chowder topping. The real treat, the ultimate prize part of the meal, was the bread bowl. In no other magical concoction, no mix of taste and smell, was sourdough better used than as a vessel for clam chowder. Somebody got wind of the new dish and two different makers showed up each touting their own soup made with clams. There was the cream based soup which is a rich and hearty dish that stuck to your bones and weighed down your spoon. But a lot of people found they really liked the 'Manhattan' style, with its tomato base and clear broth. Better for bigger clams like razor clams they said. The only thing having a better showing at the symposium than clam chowder was sea-salt. Maybe because peppercorn grinders were hard to come by, I mean who could have been prepared for a run up on grinders? A new condiment was in town, one that when sprinkled liberally on top, will bring out the true smell and flavor of a meal. Sea-salt arrived with a bang and was clearly here to stay. It was good in food, good in drinks, easy to carry, and never expired, or went stale. It was the perfect complement to make even raw Life[x] bearable. People even saw a niche and started making individual pocket-sized sea-salt shakers with extra-large openings for the big crunchy flakes. Everywhere you looked at the symposium you saw vendors hawking their wares. Surely everyone sold sea-salt just like everything will be all 'salted-caramel' this and 'salted-caramel' that in a couple of years. By the end of the last day all the vendor booths were sold out of sea-salt, and the chowder bowls were all empty. Except one fellow, a maker who found that the perfect complement to clam chowder, and the smell of sea-salt accompaniment, was the smell of sunscreen. He sold little tubes of white goo, clearly just scented Life[x] in its original form, and had people rubbing it all over their hands, arms, and faces. This vendor called himself Coppertone and from then on was a marquee attraction at all the Derby Days qualifier Puff symposiums. Coppertone made quite a name for himself, he could get you way more than just sunscreen and soup. Need some info on a gal? Think your man's been cheating? Want a line on the next slide races? Coppertone was your man. He knew all the best handlers and somehow managed to keep on the CDCG's good side. All the StatStars were there at the 23B qualifiers but the real stars of the show this year were clam chowder and sea-salt.

Chapter 12

220,752,001 to 252,288,000: 6 Years until Tranquility Base

These days there is a protectorate force that patrols the dust shield and eliminates drones. It is staffed mostly by volunteers, washed up old sterile StatStars still living PTB or bulky Puff heads out to make a score. Some of the elite guards were on staff and were paid in credits or Puff by the Waster Kings. These elite guards paired up with the current running StatStars. The guards would join the entourage and become the fulltime bodyguard for their StatStar. Most guardians are old, living way PTB, fat slow moving organisms consuming too much extra Life[x] rations. Then there is a singular specimen that does stand out – your 'bad in the garden, great at the mall' type, a man named Darrenhoe. He was the leader of the detail assigned to protect Blavos and The Ghost. Nobody was excited about it, well except Blavos, he sorta liked how it made him look like a gangster when he got to start arriving with a protective detail, Blavos felt like some high ranking corporate executive, or a foreign ambassador sent from DZ: 23X to negotiate terms for the upcoming qualifier. The Ghost is not happy at all about this at first, she hated the detail, but after what happened at DZ: 23F, when the fans rushed the stage at the press briefer and three StatStars plus two handlers were trampled to death in the madness, now she understood the need. But that didn't mean she had to like it. There were few people in this world she liked to practice her new disappearing tricks on more than her protective detail – who better to ghost? Of course they hated it, and all would threaten to quit if Blavos didn't yell at them first. The Ghost got a kick out of making them look like fools, but no one loved it more than the press.

The Ghost had come to an agreement, an arrangement of sorts; Darrenhoe would allow her a closed door and some privacy, give her more than the standard "within eight steps at all times, ma'am. I know I can leap the width of six grown men, but any farther and I just can't guarantee I will get to you in time," physical space bubble he usually demands. In return, she agrees not to dust him in public any more, leaving him standing there looking like a fool literally holding her handbags. It was a quick negotiation with both sides getting right to their demands – "Do that again and I'll kill you, no one makes me look like a fool. I don't care if you're a freaking StatStar," was met with a "Let me piss in peace for once!" and the deal was set. True to his word Darrenhoe left her alone and even permitted her to run her own Life[x] trace-purity test before she ate after practice. She used to just gobble them down, racing really took it out of you and she was starved after her trial runs. But now she was convinced, Blavos had been on her for some time, she had to be sure no one tampered with her rations. That happened last Derby Days and the entire team of StatStars from 23Y were disqualified. It didn't matter that their records were expunged years later when the jig was up and the poisoning discovered. She could do the drops, set the timer, measure the bubbles, yeah he would let her do all that, but he had to watch. Good thing he did because on more than one occasion the bubbles didn't pop fast enough from the punctured Life[x] tube. Could be nothing more than just settling air... but then again it could be anything. Better safe than sorry. And she had missed it both times. Darrenhoe was there to protect her and it wouldn't be the last time. He had made it his life's work to protect the people around him, which was a vow he took deadly seriously after what happened to his wife all those seconds back.

*

Kitteridge keeps playing with his Interval by pushing it back further and further. It's not so much that he wants to die, why would he when he had just discovered Rachel some millions of seconds ago? But he needed another goal, something to conquer again, bigger than himself. Having spent the better part of six years on the move, challenging and chasing a goal, when you get it, finally reach the reward, it can be crippling. The creature habits have become engrained so deep. And for Kitteridge he has to know if he can pass an Interval on his own, without an always full ROPU, as crazy as that sounded. He had already missed his trip to Tranquility Base and so it shouldn't matter if he could breathe without his respirator – but it matters a great deal to him. He was able to hold his breath for over three minutes by now but wanted to stretch himself even further. When he does decide to stretch it is usually spur of the moment. The owl helps him fight back the drone and helps trying to hold it off while the seconds tick away. That is when we all discover that 63 isn't done showing us new tricks. His tail's end splits open and three small barbs protrude, making a trident with razor sharp points. Oh, and the sparking arches and crackling lights make it clear to everyone that this new weapon is electrified. It jabs the owl in the back of the head, right in the same control port drone 63 has been using all along. The bird lets out a little screech and then proceeds to fold up into its own wings quickly and quietly. It lands softly on

197

the ground and side to side it waddles away on its little legs like an ashamed and guilty penguin. Kitteridge can't help but laugh out loud as a little chuckle escapes the folds of his scarf – it takes a special kind of idiot to fight off someone trying to save your life he thought to himself, and even more comical was that his family owl, his lifelong protector, would help him do it. But they could never fend the drone off in time and no one wanted to see if he had more tricks or tools. There are probably at least another eight deadly appendages in there somewhere. In all the times he has tried to pass the Interval, in all the times he and the owl fought back the refill order, no, no this prescription has expired, you need to call your doctor. In all their struggling they were only ever able to hold 63 off for more than a few seconds after the Interval had passed, and that was just once. Once paired, keeping a fully stocked ventilator was a task that drone 63 took very seriously.

*

"NOT THE FACE!" Blavos cried out as the big guy's fist approached his face, but thankfully he is able to do a quick dodge to make his point. "I need this kisser for the crowds, man or how am I going to ever pay you guys back the credits you say I owe?" he reasoned with the large and menacing thug towering over him. The handler's life is a tough one, no doubt, especially the fast and loose full tilt way that Blavos played the game. He always bet big, bet it all-in, and often borrowed and extended himself to try and cover more. You could bet with other people's money so long as you won. But if you lose somebody else's credits, on a race you promised you had set the lines and odds just right, well that called for a visit from your not-so-friendly Credit Dealers and

Collectors Guild associates. This guy called himself Drew and was definitely a Collector.

"You're not getting away this time, shorty." Drew threatened and promised at the same time. Blavos had been living bet to bet and the strategy was of his own devising born of necessity. He would bet it all on The Ghost and make the less-than-generous pay out and use it to pay back just enough of his debt to limp on, with no broken limbs, till the next qualifier. At that event he would bet it all again only this time a shadow bet, through Profant, and his outrageous 33% cut for the confidentiality he provided. Darrenhoe had offered to place the bets as he had been the first to figure out who Bishop's silent backers really were. When the Bishop won, and he almost always did, Blavos would pay out a few more bribes and the cycle would start all over.

But his lifestyle did catch up with him and true to his word Drew gave Blavos a beating he wouldn't soon forget. All part of this crazy game we call life on this planet, he thought, as Blavos took his beating like a man. No crying, Drew kept away from his face and he agreed to spit the blood back to the left side. Drew didn't mind the stains on his cape and said it was good for business. The blood stains on Blavos' scarf and vest told another story and this one is full of wild debauchery and 'first timers'. Drewski, Blavos is sure that's what the other thugs at the CDCG called this dude. Drew knew he had to take something back to the guys at the CDCG or no one would believe he had paid the wayward handler a visit tonight. Blavos knew the standard ante menu and quickly chose from the usual menu of; lose a thumb or a finger, give me an eye or an ear, your tongue as a last resort. No toes though, Drew hated feet. There was another option, strictly off menu and only reserved for the disenchanted handler like Blavos. "Take a molar, nothing from the front of my grill,"

Blavos begged. Collectors weren't Dealers and seldom negotiated but the victim always got to choose his offering back to the CDCG dispatchers. Better to give it up than have it ripped or gouged out they said. There were a lot of Puff heads running around with less than a full hand or just three toes and everyone knew they were deadbeats with big balances on their head and most had bounties out for them. Some said the long term effects of Puff cause vertigo and dizziness, you would see lots of people stumbling about in the late hours of the night at 23X. But the real problem was their balance. Do you know how hard it is to stand up straight for any length of time with just three toes?

Blavos didn't really go all-in and he was never fully leveraged. Otherwise, he couldn't go all-in next time and make it back if he lost his original bet. In fact he kind of relished this part of the cycle. He always started a broke day with just fifteen cents in credits. He would bet that with some guaranteed fast mid-race action on the screwdriver events. He would take his dollar, turn it into four, and then sixty-four. And so on till he made his purse, always the same ten thousand credits that he would use to bet all-in. Blavos had done this rodeo a few times before and preferred to just grab the thing by the horns – he could usually turn a fifteen cent ante into ten thousand in just a few hours and even sometimes less depending on the odds. Blavos was such a predominant figure in the Derby Days circuit that lots of smart folks started following this little trend. Need a quick 10K credits for an upcoming Puff gala? Just wait till he goes broke and then bet with Blavos.

Chapter 13

252,288,001 to 283,824,000: 5 Years until Tranquility Base

They made basecamp just outside of DZ: 23R which was some back country outskirts requiring two transfers and a three mile hike just to make it to the event center. The Ghost had been doing well in the other qualifiers and had long since secured her spot at the finals in all events. All events except the infernal screwdriver races. She had the other ones down cold and can maglev slide the short track like no one has ever seen. No fancy flips, loops, or tricks for her. Just heads-down, arms flying, legs pumping, cape fluttering through the smog as she slides across the surface of the Platform, blowing up billowing clouds of dust. She left the tricks to the show-boaters. Try as she might she just couldn't seem to master the screwdriver races. Perhaps it was the 'slight but noticeable' electric shock corrections that dinged you if you got off course, or worse stripped a screw. Slight my ass, she thought and all the other participants agreed. Some yokel a couple of seconds back tried to beat the system and wore protective gauntlets around her wrists. It seemed fine at first until she got down to the sixth and final layer. She slipped up and hit the guard rail inside the screw-head. The cuffs grabbed down on her wrists, pinning her hands to the table with enough pressure to splay out all her fingers, giving her hands a turn upwards as the fingers stretched out wide. The resulting electric shock ran all through her fancy gloves and caught fire. By the time they were able to free her and peel the now smoking gauntlets they had melted little rings around her wrists, permanently disfiguring the girl. She would forever be called 'Jazz Hands' for what was left of her fingers and the limited mobility she retained all shook back and forth like they were still pulsing with electricity. "Wave high to Jazz Hands," a Mom would say to her son knowing full well that she always appears to wave back.

Blavos tells The Ghost to rely less on her laser-saw and focus on finding the right bit and matching them. A lot of people thought that was the sucker's way to play the game but all the best usually took this route. It was more boring to watch but effective and most importantly safer. Cutting right through heads of the screws and bolts tended to shoot all sorts of sparks that could damage your eyesight permanently. Some of the best screwdriver men and women actually preferred to work blinded either because of an actual disability or just with a blindfold and eyes shut. The focus helped with the tedious task. One slip up and if you hit the guard rails you would get a nice little 'reminder.' ZAP and boy did she hate that!

Tonight's qualifier is a standard six-ring affair, no demos with the next three ring obstacle tonight, just the official match. Time was the goal. Contestants had to unscrew and remove all six rings to reveal the final button and press it to lock in your time. So simple really that even a child could do it. Most time trials are done with a drone, and almost everyone but the real sickos practices without the electric cuffs, but the qualifier events are paired against a real opponent, another StatStar. And some of these cats specialized in screwdriver races. It was worth enough points in your all-around score that a big win often pushed you over the top and into the winner's circle. Fail your race, or get a slower than expected time, and you were guaranteed not to finish in the top twenty-five. And right now this dumb event, one stupid time race, really a show-boater's paradise, was the thing holding her back. She had a respectable enough score but couldn't best the top five and this new guy Bishop was annoyingly good at the screwdriver. That bugged her most of all. By this time in the season the agent fees and the entry purse were pretty steep stakes. A newcomer like this in his first year on the circuit couldn't have amassed that much credit. Somebody was backing Bishop and she needed to find out who. She had heard the recent rumors and didn't like seeing Blavos talking with his apparently new chummy associate. Some old dealer turned handler creep named Profant. Profant was a known gambler himself and was a strong shadow backer. He always left the Derby Days qualifiers loaded down with newly won credits but would never say who he backed. Of course Blavos loved the mystery and it was just another thing to brag to the press about at the next briefer.

But The Ghost wanted to brag about qualifying for all her events and Justin was sure the public would love that. He planned to put up a new social media story all about it. Blavos loved the idea because any attention on The Ghost meant action on the betting lines. Blavos began following Profant's team too, not so silently backing them and making some quick credits himself. The Ghost didn't like the idea of Blavos betting on another StatStar. He was her handler at the end of the night and she needed his focus and dedication. No one disliked the idea of Blavos backing other racer more than Justin — just bad for her image, man, he would whine. "And STOP hanging out with that Profant fellow, he gives me the heeby jeebies," Justin insisted. This caused a little lover's spat between the two men in her life, but she crept up to Justin from behind and kissed his ear, whispered for him to let it go, and then promised Blavos she would double down on her screwdriver training.

Bishop took the seat beside her and was clearly delighted to be paired up against such a well-known opponent. He knew the visibility would be good for his reputation whether he won or lost. But he planned to win at all things and this was no different. Bishop rolls his sleeves, exposing his wrist to the cuffs, and lowers himself into place in the chair as he is strapped down. He bites down on the leather bit in his mouth to prevent him from biting off his own tongue in the case of a 'gentle but noticeable correction'. He slides his cape to the side exposing his constantly running ROPU. The Ghost takes her seat next to him and vows to ignore the distraction. Head down and stay in your lane she swears as she is strapped in. Bit clenched down between her teeth she glances around at the other contestants, paired off and strapped in, all biting down and waiting for the clock to start.

BUZZ and they are off. Everyone sets in and begins to make quick work of the top ring. It was a large square piece with just four little screws, one in each corner. Before anyone can finish the first layer a cry goes up from across the room. Apparently, someone slipped already with first ring jitters, no Mulligans here. He is rewarded with a 'correction', and by the sounds of it the threshold is turned up well past the initial BUZZ, and even beyond the subsequent JOLT. Another contestant is whimpering, and it sounds like unconsciously and clearly uncontrollably giggling between choking sobs, pinned down by the electric cuffs now pumping voltage through him. His face begins to go red and the skin and muscle tissues start to stretch and peel back from the tops of his hands exposing the pumping blue veins. They start smoking and the fire spreads up his arms. Thick clouds of black smoke waft up from the scene as this man is burned alive. He clearly hit the guard rails more than a few times already and probably had gotten his screwdriver stuck on the rails continuously triggering the alarm for more and ever increasingly strong 'corrections'. The man is corrected down to a smoldering heap. Seems clear to the crowd that getting stuck on the guard rails raised the correction level to CHAR and then followed by a quick BURN TO A CRISP setting. Whoever bet on that guy just lost something fierce and no trifecta is going to cover that mess.

Not to be distracted, I mean who would be, nothing to see here, move along, the other combatants lower their gaze back to the table in front of them and the remaining five rings of the puzzle. Seconds continue to click off the clock overhead as they marked the time so far in this screwdriver qualifier. Top layer off first now across the tables and everyone makes their way down to the large triangular ring. Easy to hold and work with but the eight-inch long screws make it challenging and painstakingly slow to undo. Most contestants can't pass this stage without a volt or two to remind them to stay on course. Bishop is halfway through his triangle when The Ghost looks up. She is just a little bit behind and can quickly catch up if she just focuses... ZAP! She gets a little singed around the cuff as just the fuzzy layer burns off in a quick pop of white smoke and it brings her back into her own lane where she knows she should be. The Ghost finishes off the triangular layer by placing all eight screws in the little recycling collector by the side of the table. And now for the tricky part; the triangular ring was oversized on purpose and she needed to twist it just so and slide the rest of the puzzle through. Hit the sides and you get corrected. Drop a screw and you get some amps and a few thousand watts of arching pain pinning you to the table. Bishop was the first to push his puzzle through. Damn it, she thought. Onto the third layer now, the hexagon.

Terribly small with a whopping sixteen screws, the binary math ensuring the screw count doubled each layer. But these were tricky and required a special purpose star-shaped bit. Most of the time she didn't even take the seconds to find the bit and swap it out. It was allowed of course but took precious time away from the other rings to do. Even though she practiced this all the time. Heck she never left the house without her screwdrivers and bit-set slung neatly around her. Most people just kept all their tech support tools in a shoulder satchel but she preferred to keep things strapped to her body and loved her utility vest – you would be surprised how much you can hide under a big flowing cape. Tonight The Ghost uses one of her signature moves as she unsheathes her light-sword and begins to simply cut a large divot into the top of the screw-heads. She makes quick work of the sixteen screws and leaves a little cut still burning red hot in perfect little spaced glowing dots around the small black circle. She makes quick work of them all, just three turns now with her big-bladed screwdriver and they are free and into the recycling bin. All those screws will be important for the sixth and final layer. But she had to make it to the next ring and she could see from the arms held high that Bishop and another contestant are already in the thick of it on the next layer. She swears a little under her scarf and tries to do it as low as she can as she remembers last qualifier when she told the audience and the rest of the world her prolific vocabulary of curse words through her forgotten chest mic which was always hot during these events. This time her murmur of frustration was inaudible enough but those paying close attention to their video monitors could see the concern in her face. It was almost like the little thin scar on her left check glowed hot, shining a little in the night sky. Whatever it was she was back in her lane and quickly dispatched of the remaining screws, being sure to place them all in the recycling bin strapped to the left side of her competition table.

Four minutes on the clock already and all the contestants except one are onto the fourth ring. This is another larger circular one taking up the full size of the puzzle hiding the rings underneath it just like the first. Thirty-two screws this time and another special purpose bit is required. The Ghost knows she can't cut her way through this layer because the ring and screws are made of pressed dilithium crystals. If she tries to cut through them the resulting shock will blow her back six feet off the table – rather her body and legs would fly back and her arms would be ripped from their sockets and left dangling till they slide down in bloody stumps, hands and wrists still pinned to the table. She switches out the bit and begins the slow tedious work of removing this ring one four-inch long screw at a time. The ring had to be turned like a dial to find the proper hole alignment to expose and remove each one. Twist, turn, turn, more turning, and then finally pop. The spring-loaded screws jump out of their hole slot and fly into the air; none of the other rings are booby-trapped like this, just this special ring. Catching the long thin metallic pieces as they launch into the dark night sky, and then quickly hiding them away from the contestants, was part of the fun for the crowd and why everyone cheered as all the StatStars move onto the challenge of the fifth ring. The crowd gathered around the competition tables had been waiting for this layer and they really got into it.

An additional six long minutes pass by and the contestants are all struggling with the fifth ring. Bishop is almost done and at this point every single one of his screws has made it safely into the recycling bin. The Ghost, or rather her crowd, was making it a rather tough go for her though. Each time a screw flew out some new ruffian would grab it and disappear into the crowd and in a dust cloud. There was a reason this event was Blavos' favorite. He relished his job as a handler here because he got to get physical with these ever-present miscreants. Onlookers running off with the screws you needed was a problem for every StatStar and one that someone else was expected to handle. Ten minutes and thirty seconds into the qualifier and the contestant directly diagonal Bishop is getting stronger and stronger corrections. He keeps hitting the guard rails and it doesn't help that he let loose his bladder, his urine-soaked pants setting off the shock sensors embedded in the seats. Thirty-eight agonizing seconds of yelling, screaming, and burning pain, with the audience cheering for more with blood lust in a full pitched frenzy at this point. Lots of credits and Puff were on the line. The screwdriver races were one of the few events that the betting booth allowed bets during the event, you could put in new bets to try and cover any losses from earlier ring rounds, or double down on a combatant that isn't crispy fried yet.

Bishop finishes his penultimate ring first, go figure. Say what you want about him and his shadow backer, he was continuing to get the job done, and had already qualified for all Derby Day's events. The Ghost had to finish in the top three this time to clear all her requirements and check off all the qualifiers. And all throughout this layer no one messes with Bishop's wayward screws and they all go safely into the container, for all screws will be needed to undo the final ring and reveal the button. To win all you had to do was just press it to lock in your time. Profant had long been the suspected shadow backer for Bishop and Profant had decided it was high time to make some credits in the open from this unspoken alliance. And he didn't mind stepping into the role publicly because everyone assumed that

Profant was the Bishop's handler already. So the old dealer turned handler began to put his name on the winners board by fixing lines and making money. Blavos was good at this job as a handler taking care of the crowd; he was part goalie and part wide receiver as he kept the screws safe for The Ghost. Blavos had been practicing his martial arts and he was really good at tripping people with his 'pimp cane' as he called it. Call it that when I am around and I will show you just who is the pimp here she reminds him whenever he brings it out and feigns another limp. Justin keeps reminding him that he stumbles better on his left side, yeah that's the Crip side. But one side-eyed glance and a snarl from Profant with his piercing eyes burring deep into your soul made the crowd question whether getting a screw from this particular StatStar was worth the beating. Some other StatStar might lose it and put up less of a fight, they decided. The sign Profant wore around his neck that simply stated, 'Touch the Bishop's screws and none of God's mercy will save you' proved that the pen is truly mightier than at least a pimp cane. Everyone stayed away from the Bishop's table and decided to swarm The Ghost instead. They would steal her screws because they were more valuable because of her higher StatStar rating. Her ratings and subsequent betting odds had blown up leading to this qualifier and everyone knew she had to place in the top three. The mid-match betting hit a new peak as she dug into the ultimate and final ring. While Bishop is frantically spinning the ring looking for the final hidden latch to remove the ring, Blavos proves his worth as a handler saving all screws and placing them snugly in The Ghost's own recycling bin to be used for the ring to come.

As she finished the blasted fifth ring and places the final two screws into her bin, quick tally, and verification from the ref, and she finally makes it onto the last layer. Twelve minutes in total and she was happy for a second because at least she was hitting this tricky sixth layer well ahead of her personal best. The ultimate test of dexterity you had to keep the claws away while also unscrewing sixty-four different locks each with four different bits required to loosen the special purpose heads. She lays out the bits in a row after a quick glance at their order, it changed every time they hosted a new event. Fun for practice and kept the match interesting. But this is where she always tripped up. Last time she lost one of her bits in the dust and was disqualified. The media and fans ate it up though and delighted in watching her take out her frustrations on the event space with her light-sword. She destroyed three tables before Blavos and Justin could hold her down. Profant and Bishop couldn't help but laugh at the three, Bishop had finished first again. Seems he was as good with his hands and fingers as he was twisting and turning in maglev boots. He had been improving and inventing new tricks, he particularly liked the double back flip and how it allowed him to grab all but the final ring. He kept begging The Ghost to follow him and give him a boost from underneath. He needed just enough force to grab that high ring and get the all-ring bonus. It was enough to catapult them both into victory and she would get points for the assist. But she wanted the win and her technique on the track was flawless and nobody was faster. But sheer speed was not enough. She had to get better about remembering to collect the rings, watching Bishop rise through the ranks over these last millions of seconds has proven that. She had proved she could get them all except the last and high ring towering above the track teasing you to try and grab for that bonus; most racers simply didn't even try. You didn't have to collect rings to win, but it sure helped.

The claws come up from the four corners of the table and pin down the final ring securely locking it in place. You can't move the ring to reveal the screw-heads and align the holes without first removing and pinning back the claws. This step is where you need all those long screws and yes they had different bit requirements. Just to bring up the challenge level the wrist cuffs tighten a little more restricting both movement and blood flow as the locking buckles slide back and in six-inches pinning your arms and hands back. Muscle or bend back the claws and screw them down and only then could you make it to your final layer, twisting and turning the ring like a dial. Fourteen minutes had gone by and The Ghost was still in fourth place. The Ghost briefly slides into fifth as a nearby player overtakes her. But he gets a little too excited and his cheering and high-fiving. The guy bumps his whole screwdriver and bit set onto the puzzle and it hits all the guard rails at once. He doesn't so much burn alive as the electricity all pumps into his head and neck. It pops back like a Pez dispenser, and his insides spew out a hot and steaming mess, burning embers of life spill out onto the table. The Ghost is in fourth place and the Bishop is almost onto the next step having successfully pinned back the claws.

Sixteen minutes on the clock and Bishop has the ring clear and just in the nick of time too. The claws on the left side snap free from their screws having been jogged loose by the constant twisting and turning to remove the last ring. He slips the ring free and opens the little glass door exposing the red button about four-inches in diameter buried a few inches below the base of the puzzle. Bishop brings his hand high in dramatic fashion right at the nineteen minutes thirty-eight second mark. The crowd erupts in cheering and applause. Bishop sees the nearby Profant, standing next to a secretly satisfied Blavos who knows his underhanded bets on Bishop beating The Ghost will pay off. And in his usual style Blavos had bet it all, leveraged everything he had on the line, on a full can't-stop-me-now-mamma tilt worthy of a heady drunken spree at DZ: 23X. Bishop pauses and lets the joy wash over him. He had an undefeated record on the screwdriver races and this was going to boost his stats right to the top, just under The Ghost. Right where he wants to be going into the tail end of the qualifiers. He doesn't want to debut at Derby Days as the top ranked StatStar. He wanted some decent odds and betting in his favor.

The Ghost had prepared for this and her practice paid off. She made quick work of the thirty-two screws and to her luck got the ring lined up on just two spins, all the way left and then all the way back right to center. She practically throws the last ring on the dusty ground and tries to slam the button as her wrist cuffs unlock the moment the last layer is free. She decided to skip the part where she gracefully opens the glass door covering the button and she just slams her balled up fist through the glass and smashes the button down first and most importantly right before Bishop. He is dumbfounded by the loss; she came from nowhere it seems as she leapt from fourth to first. It helped that competitor number three stripped two screws and the resulting blow back from the bumpers ripped him right in half as predicted. Some folks gasped and a few others had cheered – they had bet on the longshot. An injury sideline bet was sort of insurance on your original bet. If someone gets injured and has to be disqualified your first bet is returned in full. Bet on someone losing an appendage and if you could predict which one you would win big and were guaranteed to triple your original bet, and then if the poor sap lost both body parts, bigger payouts for binary unity and all. Number four jumped into the third spot but didn't see the claw on his right side come lose. Its barbed and jagged teeth slammed into his arm at the wrist and completely severed his hand. Hard to win a screwdriver race with one hand but a few other gambling addicts won big and began taking turns waving around the bloody severed appendage.

Profant had spread his bets so much across all the StatStars he had pretty much every outcome and bet covered. He never won a big purse of credits at these qualifiers. Profant preferred to slowly build up a bigger and bigger cache to bet so he could go all-in on Derby Days. The leap-frog first place finish from The Ghost threw off many lines and beat a lot of odds. Lots of credits were on the table and big sweeps were made by a few, most lost. Betting on the Bishop had become a sure thing lately, but that luck ran out tonight. None, however, suffered as big a hit to their pocketbooks and bottom line as Blavos. All-in, double down, borrow from shady bookies at the CDCG, forever slanging fast and loose, go big or go home, with great risk comes great reward had always been Blavos' style. It was exciting with the sort of adrenaline rush and public attention he craved. It had become a thing not just to track, watch, and bet on his StatStar, The Ghost, but also on how much each event impacted Blavos and his precious treasure chest. Some people just bet on Blavos. Blavos had backed his silent associate, backed him big, and lost even more tonight.

Justin and The Ghost were happy as they practically jumped into the room for the post event press briefer. Everyone wanted a quote, "How's it feel to have finally qualified for Derby Days?", and "Tell us what you did during practice to prepare for tonight Ghost," they asked. "Did you think you would win?" She had secured her top three spot, better than that. Her stats jumped up to reflect that. At least two people had won at this qualifier, she won the event and had her spot. And another had bet, sure she would win the whole thing. Darrenhoe it seems was always betting on her.

Chapter 14

283,824,001 to 315,360,000: 4 Years until Tranquility Base

Rosalia had been a blushing baby carrier as she glowed in the way that some women do when they are with child. And for her it was never the early trimester sort of glistening as the sweat drips down and mats her messy and tussled hair sticky from the morning sickness kind of glow. Thankfully Rosalia had nothing like that because she was just happy and didn't mind getting plump. She literally lit up a room back when she was pregnant and practically raised the temperature by at least a few degrees with her radiant glow. She rather liked it and couldn't stop smiling and rubbing her belly. In another home, Amanda was constantly messing with her midsection just like Rosalia. Rosalia would gently caress her own belly in big little circles as she smiled and sometimes even hummed to herself a little. Mandy was always wincing in pain as she clutched at the growing person inside her as it stabbed away at her insides; the last trimester, when it really started moving around in there, was the worst. Amanda would cry out little gasps and whinnies like a downed and wounded horse. Rosalia enjoyed being pregnant and spending time with the other wives, some liked to dream about Puff, others just wanting to talk about their babies, and all they would do to make it to Tranquility Base. They were doing their part and had made do with some lousy husbands, and were doing their expected role here on this planet. Be a good tech support agent, always work hard to improve your stats, marry your pre-assigned spouse, avoid the Puff, and keep your balance with the CDCG on the plus side of the ledger. Be a good girl and your seats on the trip would be all but guaranteed. Mandy was no peach however, she had been throwing up pretty much non-stop since her pregnancy was confirmed, almost as if the very idea of a baby growing inside her made her literally sick to her stomach. She and Rosalia always kept a close confidence but their shared experience allowed them to grow even closer, more like sisters than friends or cousins. The only downcast light during the germination period for Rosalia was the guilt at betraying her friends, her affair with Hasboro was forbidden. Sure lots of people felt like they were mismatched with their spouses. And they bided their time, waited until Tranquility Base till they could get a divorce and be with the one they truly loved. Provided that she passed her Interval that is, usually nature had its own way of dealing with mismatches.

She had been putting this off for hundreds of thousands of seconds and was not sure how to tell him. No, that wasn't right, she had written down her thoughts in a letter to Hasboro, she wanted to ensure she said everything she needed. He seemed to take well to the letter last time, understood that she had things bottled up inside her, things that needed to be let out, they just couldn't be expressed with the voice or tongue. The issue wasn't telling him. The worry was how he was going to take it. Hasboro had been devastated when Mandy and their unborn child were taken away from him that night Mandy failed her Interval. He had carried on though, right in the way she had planned, and it worked out wonderfully for them. Rosalia and Hasboro could still not be together but he was surrounded by people who loved and depended on them. He thrived here, even though he was living PTB, and his one true love was kept always at an arm's distance. Hasboro was a good father and she had been right he had a heart big enough for all of them. She just hoped he had some space saved in there for their baby boy. Not so much a baby now, he has been alive and well for the past ten years, living with the Waster Kings since the raid when he was rescued along with the others. The little boy, well into adulthood now, was raised by the Collective and would either be a StatStar, or great tech support agent. Hasboro liked all the children equally. I mean sure he had some favorites; some kids are just more fun to hang out with. But then again you don't take those same kids when it is just chill and watch a movie time. Rosalia just hoped that her boy would stand out to Hasboro, he already did to her.

The thing that weighed heaviest on her heart, and her mind, was how to eventually tell her boy that he had a mother and father still here. And that they had been watching over him the whole time, right here. Would he understand why she had to keep him estranged? She was confident that Hasboro would be okay, and would come to embrace and love the idea of her own flesh and blood still alive and giving 'em hell! Would her boy Sevrin? She knew her boy had become a StatStar, one of legend because of how fast he came up the ranks. Would he be too famous to even talk to her? I bet there are people who say they are related to a StatStar all the time, some for the credits and some just for the short-lived notoriety. I mean how many people get to shake hands with a screwdriver race legend? Rosalia would have to find a way to get a message to him. She was good at this sort of thing and already had a way in mind – she would write a note. But first things first, she knew she needed to tell Hasboro. Not sure why now was the time but it just felt right. Or, more accurately, for

Rosalia no time was right to admit her deception, all these years of lies and deceit. Hasboro would forgive her but could her son? Focus, she tells herself, get Hasboro on board and he will find a way to connect with the boy. She had to keep reminding herself they were looking for a man and not a newborn child. Ten years was a long time and he had certainly grown at an accelerated rate. All children long for their mother and father's love and attention: if only to hear and know where they came from. It somehow helps ground people in the right moral compass to have an understanding of their heritage. She knew this, and not that she and her adulterous lover were such great people, but it was time to meet and become a family.

"Dear Hasboro – I hope you have an ounce of forgiveness left in your heart for me. I have lied to you, and not just once, and these are no harmless white lies. I hope you can find it in your heart to forgive me these indiscretions. For the last ten years I have been orchestrating a conspiracy to keep the truth away from you. My child, the one you thought had failed his Interval all those years ago, he lives. Here, with us on DZ: 23S. He knows of us and we have a deep and loving connection. He doesn't know I am his mother or that you are to be his father.

My son, our baby boy, is a grown man now. He sees us around him, teaching him and supporting him. Just like you do with all your children, those lost souls of the DZ, who you have taken under your wing. But now the time has come for you to pay special attention to just one child, my own flesh and blood. Your boy is a fine young man now, and before he goes to Tranquility Base, I want you to spend some father-son time with him. You need to connect with him soon because with his success he is sure to get a seat. Tell him your stories, teach him our ways, let him understand what's important and how to keep it safe. You have done this for all of us but now do it anew with him.

He is a good tech support agent but that was not his calling. He is one of the Blavos' StatStars of course. He is rich and famous, has people all around him, pushing and supporting him. He has a great handler from the CDCG and is said to be a contender to win the Derby Days slide races. But he needs your special touch, your unique skills and approach to sportsmanship, and he needs you to take him to the next level.

I will always love you with all my heart. I give it to you freely. Take it, and me with you.

Yours forever,

Rosalia."

She wrote the note down, then quickly tore it up. It just wouldn't do, she worried. But she knew there was no other way and that no amount of talking with him would allow her to say what needed to be said. Rosalia rewrites the note and leaves it on the desktop then turns the little lamp on, moving it to focus the light on the letter. Seeing it now all written down it wasn't that long really. It will have to do, she knows, and leaves the room. She turns back and rushes forward as she grabs the letter and slips it into her satchel under her cape. She will give him the letter when the time is right, maybe at their next picnic? Most people knew about the affair, and surprisingly to both of them, few cared. Rosalia didn't care for the people who did care.

Tonight at their celebration of life picnic she wanted some more to celebrate. He takes the letter and takes it all in. There is room in his heart for someone special to keep closer than the rest. Hasboro relished the idea and when they returned to the DZ there was a new pep in his step. He awoke well rested now and no longer haunted by the dreams of Mandy being pulled under the Platform. Rosalia sleeping next to him now calmed all that.

218

Hasboro approached practice with more vigor and was the first to get all decked out in his new swag every time the teams changed up colors or styles. Rosalia had been worried that he would pay special attention to just the boys but that was not the case. Hasboro had decided not to try and figure out who it was: which StatStar of theirs was actually her son. Instead of picking out a special agent for his additional love and attention Hasboro was capable of opening his heart to treat them all like his special children. It was more than Rosalia could have hoped for in his response to the letter.

*

Living close to Rachel has been hard for Kitteridge. He takes comfort in seeing her as he and his drone army follow her to all her qualifying events. He cheers her on but doesn't bet on her or against her or anyone else for that matter. He has already looted enough credits to last him three lifetimes. To Rachel he is just another face lost in the crowd. She has long since stopped trying to recognize her true fans, those who follow her around from event to event. They all just sort of blend in now, she likes them, and knows that having loud cheering fans helps her keep her competitive edge.

It has been a no-go trying to get in touch with his Rachel or even get a word in edge wise. He tried many different routes, both direct and some not so subtle. He even hosted an elaborate presser right after the Derby Days qualifier at 23T. He knew if he invited all the media that Blavos would insist on her being there, Justin would tolerate nothing less. She had already been a household name because of her hat trick and facial scar, but qualifying all those seconds ago, and her dramatic last-minute finish over Bishop, had given her broader fame and recognition, if that was even possible. Kitteridge finally decides to write and send her a letter, that will probably be the least intrusive. Rachel can read and think about it, really digest in her own time with no pressure to respond back to some hopeful stranger sucking on his ROPU hose while he awaits his long-lost daughter to fall into his loving arms. That won't happen, but a simple letter can't hurt. Naturally his first thought is to mail the letter. He tried just posting it and leaving it in the box at the Transportation Center. But the machine took one look at the address, cross checked it with the registered StatStars' addresses and denied it, shredding the letter right there on the spot. Not to be deterred he wrote another letter and decided to hand deliver it. He tried to get into her home or rather would have been satisfied enough with just leaving the note inside the perimeter. But try as he might couldn't ever seem to get in. Ever persistent Kitteridge figured he could hire a trained professional, an in-person courier to handle the logistics of delivery. The CDCG had these guys on staff that usually delivered credits and Puff back and forth. But you could rent them for a small and reasonable fee and a lot of goods moved around the Platform that way. All the messenger guys and gals that Kitteridge met only had to glance at the address on the letter and they would laugh him away.

At one point Kitteridge even gets up close to Rachel's finishing tent at the last slide races but she couldn't hear him over the whiz of her maglev boots. Plus, what was she supposed to do after hearing some crazed fan yelling out "I'm your father!" did he expect she would just stop the race and come over and hug him and they would be together forever? A lot of creeps kept telling her they could be her daddy, or some offered to be what they called a 'Sugar Daddy'. Decidedly she didn't want that kind of daddy in her life as she had what she needed in Justin and that was enough. Although lately the glances from Darrenhoe had become longer and more intense. The Ghost found that she welcomed the attention, even though she had fanboys drooling over her all the time, this was different. Darrenhoe knew her deeper somehow, understood her unmet needs, her fears and a way to calm them that only he seemed to know how to do with her. Justin was oblivious, too invested in his social media work, always increasing her stats which were directly correlated to her followers, it just ate up any and all of his time and attention.

In recent events The Ghost had noticed her competition suits were getting tighter and tighter, especially around her chest and buns. Blavos had agreed after much convincing from Justin and her handler just rolled his eyes and demanded she put it on. Sadly Justin was right, the new more revealing suit had improved the odds in her favor, just the sort of strategy they had planned. This is how she wants to go into the final Derby Days – on top of the leader board, maybe not number one, not good for the betting lines, but up there.

Not to give up Kitteridge decides that his next best option is to give the note to Blavos. He had tried screaming at her at some more events but against the impressive drowning effect of the crowd noise it was pointless. Blavos denies Kitteridge a meet up flat out and says he has no interest in talking unless the guy wanted to be a shadow backer. For enough credits Blavos would let you put an angel investor's size stake on a secret, never to be named but sure to pay out big newcomer, up in the ranks with great stats unless you were a backer. Blavos was all whispery secret about this point but Kitteridge knew it was Profant who had the line; Kitteridge's little drones had ears everywhere. Kitteridge gives the guy one quick look-see at his credit balance and says he's sure he can afford a few bets in return for one simple letter delivery. Blavos seems to be coming around to the idea once he digested how many credits that really was, but Kitteridge gets ahead of himself and blurts out the part about being The Ghost's long-lost father, thought to have gone to Tranquility Base but had been following and searching for her all these years. Blavos just freaks out at this revelation, tells Kitteridge to stay away from him and The Ghost or there would be trouble. It is at this point that the protective detail, assigned by the CDCG to each StatStar team, appears out of nowhere and steps in at the first signs of trouble. Blavos gives one quick exchange of some secret looks and gestures over to Darrenhoe who inserts himself between Kitteridge and Blavos the handler. "Listen, bub, I don't care about your story or who your daughter is, I need you to get and stay the hell away from her and the rest of us," Darrenhoe insists politely and gently but with a firm resolve that Kitteridge knows he means business. "Okay give me the letter if it means you leave this alone from here on out," Darrenhoe tells him and snatches it, safely storing it away, albeit somewhat wrinkled but still readable. It was farther than Kitteridge had ever gotten and he left the TC portal that night feeling like it had been a success.

"Her name is Rachel, will you be sure and tell her at least that?" he begs as Darrenhoe and Blavos walk away, meet up apparently over.

Time would tell, but one thing was certain, if Rachel did decide to reach back out to Kitteridge, he would be easy enough to find. There aren't many, okay just the one man, Kitteridge, who walk around the Platform with a small battalion of drones at the ready to do his bidding. Finding him would not be hard but knowing what to say would take some effort. Blavos hadn't told her about the run in with Kitteridge in the past because he didn't want to disturb her and steer away her concentration from Derby Days preparations. She had heard the media, it was hard to ignore, the story was everywhere because Kitteridge had gone on such a wide tour broadcasting about his search and hoping for someone, anyone really, to help him contact The Ghost. He got some initial attention and it always replayed whenever she won another qualifier, which was often. The world knew Kitteridge not only as the guy with the drones but as The Ghost's father. All the DZs were united in cheering for him. Fans had even taken to chanting "Hi Dad!" during races whenever she made another lap and zoomed past on her maglev boots, sweeping past and lapping many of her slower competitors during the slide races.

Darrenhoe keeps the letter for he is a man of his word. Having opened and read the letter he feels it does warrant The Ghost's attention. Mentally he agrees with himself that he will deliver the letter to her when the timing is right. He needs to give her space to be by herself and absorb something like this and for longer than just her few standard seconds of privacy in the bathroom. This was heavy news if it was true. He knew the last qualifier was coming up and makes the call that it is too close and would just make her slower. She needed another top three showing in the screwdriver races to keep her stats up. Darrenhoe had reason to keep this quiet because The Ghost had started becoming suspicious and asking him questions about the rumors that kept cropping up. Had he heard anything or had anyone approached him claiming to be her father? She probed him on more than one occasion. He was always able to side-step the question and redirect with an, "it doesn't matter what I think so long as the guy doesn't try and hurt you, that is always my only concern," and if that didn't work the classic, "well what do you think, do you want a relationship with a newly discovered father now at your age?" and that always stopped her questioning.

She had begun to wonder more and more about that specific nagging thought; she had lots of questions but at the end of the night it didn't matter that he was her biological dad, of course she had one of those, everyone did. So, he showed up a little later in life, better late than never, they say. That part didn't faze her but one thing that did keep pestering her, like an exotic beetle from deep in the bowels of the jungles hidden in the distant mountains of Peru. The kind of bug that you had to sleep completely inside a mesh netting that tented your entire bed like a canopy shield to keep the beetles away. Without full netting the little pest would crawl into your ear and begin to burrow its way through, scratching and eating its way into your brain where it settled and gorged itself. The sound of pincher claw picking little pieces of grey matter as a snack, and the subsequent chewing sound inside your head that only you could hear was so intense it would drive you insane. If you couldn't get the bug out suicide was the most commonly prescribed remedy, if the hot and painful ear-candling didn't push the beetle out. That little hungry insect chewing away at her brain was the question of whether she wanted a relationship with Kitteridge. He and his story, about his search and supposed relationship to her was well-known. He was generally considered a good dude, always trying to help people out, his squad of drones would do some impressive things on his say so. And the real kicker is the guy went around paying you credits from his own stash anytime he did something nice for you, like you were doing him the favor, said he had more credits than six men could spend, even if they were high-stakes handlers going all-in on a Derby Days event. She didn't have a father and Blavos wasn't the sort of balanced and well-rounded father-figure for her. He was no wise sage she could learn from or hero to look up to. If she could even just be friends with Kitteridge she might like that. Nothing romantic, she had Justin, and Kitteridge was way too old, plus what if he really was her father? Gross! If she wanted a little side action, Darrenhoe was apparently all too happy to oblige her, and to be honest she wasn't entirely sure that Justin would be against it. The Ghost fooling around with her protective detail captain, man the media would eat that up Justin would no doubt think, good for her lines. But there weren't many people she could just be her authentic self with, too many people wanted just to get next to her for her fame, or to beg her for some of her hard-earned credits. And this Kitteridge fellow, true biological father or not, had garnered enough fame and credits of his own it was clear he wasn't after hers.

What if all this guy wanted was to be a part of her life and cheer her on, somebody unselfishly in her corner? Maybe she had a place for that. At least recently, she thought more and more that she just might be ready for that. She said nothing of this to anyone, least of all Darrenhoe. The two of them had become close no doubt about it. Maybe it was a matter of repetition and proximity, or just convenience but Darrenhoe was a mystery, a lock worth turning. She felt like she had known him all her life but what did Rachel really know about her bodyguard? He was married before, obviously, but had said his wife died young. It was clearly still a painful memory for him for he always changed the subject whenever his late wife Tiana came up. But should she probe deeper? Who knows just maybe she would be able to confide in Kitteridge, lord knows she was confused with how she felt about Justin and Darrenhoe, and he seemed like he, or at least one of his many drones, with all their sensors, would be able to lend a sympathetic ear. He was no doubt married in the past and maybe he had some experience to share that would help her.

She let the idea of a relationship with Kitteridge marinate in her mind for a few thousand seconds and decided that now simply wasn't the time because she had Derby Days to think about. Perhaps she could use his help, but for now she would just be watching him from a distance, she knew he would be at the upcoming qualifiers, knew he had been at almost all her events.

Chapter 15

315,360,001 to 346,896,000: 3 Years until Tranquility Base

They are all set to go on their annual picnic where they always celebrate Rosalia passing her first Interval. It was a combined event and yearly tradition they used to commemorate their life together and to morn their lost loved ones. Rosalia still kept a special place in her heart for Marcus. She was happy for the dedicated time they spent remembering and swapping stories of past antics. Marcus had been quite the crack-up and Hasboro had them both rolling with his jokes remembered and still fresh from beyond the grave. But for Hasboro the event was more about wanting to spend time thinking about his unborn child and the life they would have led together. He never talks about it, just spends his time pouring love into all the of the lost orphans of DZ: 23N. She knows it hurts him every day, and this time together does seem to soothe him. At least some parts of him deep down seem to settle if only for just for a little while.

Hasboro has made the arrangements and they have their own little private cabana reserved at DZ: 23X. They went for the great people watching, taking in the atmosphere and seeing the lights and sounds, and of course all the different fashions from around the planet are always on parade for all to see. This time Rosalia had wanted to get the Life[x] textures herself because she wanted to prove it to herself more than anyone else, Hasboro knew she could do it if she set her mind to it. Just in case though Hasboro had called ahead and made sure she was going to be meeting with a reputable dealer and not some chump who is going to try and sell her on a 'first timer' or swindle her with promises of cinnamon buns. She gets the goods all right and quickly passes them off to Hasboro for safe transport to the picnic. This tradition had a few important elements to get right, the location here at 23X, the night, the two of them together, alone without a care in the world. Except for smell, they both missed that, even though they never had it. They were a strictly texture only experience kind of couple and that suited them both just fine. The meal was to be the same every year as well. Moscato d'Asti, almost too ripe but just perfectly juicy with gentle fuzz on the skin peaches, and of course some potato chips. Hasboro always insisted on getting the special can, that long tube that you could just almost fit your hand in, but probably good you couldn't do that because the can was so large it would swallow half your arm, right up to the elbow if you tried to get the crumbs at the bottom. The thing always reminded him of the ways he had read about how one used to be able to catch a raccoon back on Earth. If you cut a small round hole in a log and then put something shiny in it the raccoon cannot resist; he puts his hand in the log and grabs the glimmering object, like a quarter credit piece shining in the sun. He squeezes it in his little fist and tries to pull it out of the log, but his fisted hand is now too big to pull out of the hole – the racoon could squish together his fingers and easily slide into the hole but try and bring anything out clutched in your fists and the animal was stuck. All the raccoon must do is drop the quarter and then he can remove his hand and be free. The stubborn little mammal won't let go and he would rather chew his own hand off to escape than drop the quarter. That was a dark thought and

Hasboro can't help but chuckle looking at the can and imagining getting his hand stuck fishing for crumbs. He was glad he won't have to chew his own hand off tonight because these fun Life[x] textures would be enough. Sharing them with Rosalia was always enough for him.

They arrive at the cabana and this time they decide to be bold and travel together through the portals of the Transportation Center, Rosalia was tired of sneaking around. Hasboro always brings the can out from under his cape like a magician with a rabbit or some other unexpected magical prize. He lays down the treasure like he bested it from some fearsome she-devil in the depths of a cave, a prize he found and secured just for his Rosalia. She always pretended to be surprised. That's the part he liked most. She made sure they always tried to get every last bit of crunchy out of there, the crispy, and they say salty, goodness, even all the way down at the base of the can. They had learned to tip the can up and tap the bottom but keep your mouth wide open or it would spill all down your shirt. "Better not stick your hand all the way down there," he warns her.

"I know, I know," she whines back in a little flirty voice and bats her eyes at him. Hasboro always bumped her elbow to make sure some spilled down her vest, she knows it is because he likes to nibble the little crunchy bits off one by one, crunching out loud with his teeth. She likes it and holds him close.

Tonight is no different, same great people watching, same special place quietly secluded and reserved just for them. Hasboro had always taken care of that and he did so again this time. The wine is fine, tiny orbs of effervescence burst in their mouth and slide down, popping a little bit more in their throat, before they land in the belly, giving them a warm glow that makes Rosalia's cheeks all red and splotchy, giving a big rosy blushing smile across her lips. The peaches are sweet and juicy like the best produce picked fresh from the farm and sold on some backwoods country road on a hot July day. It drips down their chin and the Life[x] even dyed a little pink and orange to make it look like peach nectar. And this year Rosalia got the texture down just right – you could feel the little fuzzy hairs on the peach rind tickle the inside of your mouth and tongue as you bit into the fruit. Adam and Eve didn't throw away paradise for an apple, the serpent no doubt gave them a peach. And Eden was not in Africa or Pangea but in Southeast Georgia where the peaches were sweetest. Tonight Rosalia would be the angel of deception and she slips the note into Hasboro's hand. He reaches for it and begins to unfold it. "WAIT!" she says. "We haven't finished our second bottle," she whines in that little schoolgirl whimper that he also kinda likes. It twists his insides up just so. She had made up some convoluted story about how this year was a special celebration, and that they had a lot to be thankful for, so drink up my man! Hasboro puts up no fuss because he likes the wine and the heady feeling it gives them both. Plus she doesn't mind his wandering hands while they 'nap'. They curl up in the warmth of his large cape, she's a little burrito wrapped in hers, and together they succumb to the wine and sleep for a while in their cocoon.

Many seconds pass by, but they are not worried, there is no one at home to miss them any more. They mourn that for a while, Marcus and Amanda were good spouses, and most of all friends. They shouldn't have gone out like that. And they mourned over the loss of Hasboro's unborn child. Drifting in and out of sleep, they cuddle up and exchange kisses, whisper sweet nothings into each other's ear for comfort, drifting in and out of cuddly slumber. Hasboro awakens and raises up and he is sitting cross-legged now. He gently shakes her awake and Rosalia smoothly rolls over and says, "Now is the time. Read it, but know that no matter what I love you." He takes in the gravity of that statement and unfolds the letter, carefully reading it, taking it all in slowly word-by-word. It takes him some seconds to read the note, and then again. His hands are shaking by the time he reads it for the third time.

"No one knows?"

"Nope," she shakes her head.

"And he's here?" Hasboro wonders out loud. Rosalia bursts into tears, she had been worried about this, how he would take the news. Would he hate her? Would he hate her child?

"Come here my darling," he whispers and takes Rosalia up into his arms. "I don't understand, or even care. I don't need to. I have more important things to care about now." She continues to let out a few little sobs, she can't hold back the emotion, all those years of secrets, plans and coordination, and now it was out. She felt reborn, like she had passed some other Interval, only this time she had been doing it every day for the last ten years. Rosalia breathes a huge sigh of relief that is so big it pops her hose out of her mouth and it just dangles down by her ROPU. He lovingly kisses her nose and places the hose back. He brings her close like she wants right now and whispers, "I forgive you, my love." She embraces him, not quite knowing what comes next. Rosalia needed him for that and he showed her he was ready to take on the challenge with one single simple phrase, "I'm a father. I have a son!"

Chapter 16

346,896,001 to 378,432,000: 2 Years until Tranquility Base

DeathMatch is what they lovingly referred to the event as. Much as she loathed the event, she was good at it, fiercely so. The Ghost would usually deal a fatal death blow with one of her leaping and twisting 'finishing moves' as the blood-thirsty fans called them. She usually just cut off their heads, it was fast and efficient enough for the crowd, and it left a glorious messy reminder not to mess with The Ghost. These light-sword duels were no sparring match. The laser arc was real and it would cauterize you right in half with a quick flick of her wrist. She had already qualified a few times over and the body count this Derby Days was adding up. She had the leader board and no amount of killing would best her scores. That also meant everyone on here at DZ: 23W had only one thing in mind, get the lucky card, bet big and long on yourself and try to beat her. Most fighters just tried to make it out alive and last as many rounds as they could. Some gal from 23W managed to last fifteen grueling rounds against The Ghost but she struck her down in the end. Justin had designed the move and intentionally made it a crowd pleaser – The Ghost powers down her light-sword and places the hilt right up against her victim's forehead. With one deft flick of her finger the laser springs to life and pierces right through the skull in an up close and personal assassination style and sure enough the crowds eat it up.

Blavos loved any violence and was even part of the committee lobbying the CDCG to allow pushing and shoving if not outright beatings on the slide races seeing no reason to leave the carnage to just this event. Spice it up a little bit, they say. DeathMatch was just that, a fight till the final end with one combatant left standing. The fighters at this qualifier, here on DZ: 23W, were bound to be a set of matches that did live up to all the hype. 23W was a hub for martial arts training. It is the only place on this planet to get the supplies for it; one had to make and master their own light-sword creation. Dedicated blacksmiths and electricians teamed up to make some sponsored light-swords a few seconds back. They were unbalanced in the wielder's hands and made for big sloppy sweeping arches that when they connected usually resulted in terrible limb severing blows. Blavos ate it all up, silently watching and cheering from the inside; he was so entranced it was one of the few and only times he kept his mouth shut. Darrenhoe was equally interested, but he used the matches as a way to study and pickup new fighting moves. He would stand ringside and shadow-box the moves happening from inside the caged and electrified octagon. Always on the lookout to pick up any new fighting style, drunken monkey was Darrenhoe's favorite, it really threw the Puff heads off their game, and balance. He made the silent swift moves on the side, quite the show himself when it came down to it.

The Ghost steps into the ring and takes off her cape and exposes her new blue leopard-spotted and skintight pleather leggings shining in the lights above the ring. She feels silly, more like the night-walkers of 23W looking to score some quick Puff in exchange for a roll around, than a true warrior of heart, mind, and body. Blavos counts on this and knows that when she dresses sexy it increases her odds and has the added benefit of really pissing The Ghost off. It fires her up and, well, just makes her want to kill someone if she's honest. She complains in her usual fashion about Justin and his behind-the-scenes nonsense with the live-streaming social video chat running non-stop. You would think people would have better things to do than watch her get dressed.

The bruiser is introduced over the loudspeakers as The Almighty Drewski and clearly has the backing of the Credit Dealers Collection Guild members cheering on wildly from the audience. Her opponent comes in from the back left side of the event center and the audience gets deadly serious as a gentle hush falls over the colosseum. The guy towers over The Ghost and this monster is her physical better in every way. He is a muscle bound giant and displays smooth grace as he brings forth his light-sword, already arcing, while he flings off his cape and throws it gloriously and dramatically into the crowd. They eat it up and everyone watches on the big Jumbotron while people tear the cape to shreds. His handler must keep quite the wardrobe budget going on the side she thinks. No matter though, his size will just make it easier, she knows she can jam her laser right into his throat with just a slight overhead uppercut motion.

Not wanting to waste any time because she knew Blavos and Justin had bet on her to win in the first round, she makes three quick swipes with her light-sword but he manages to dodge and block them all. "I'm gonna tear that little sexy scar wide open!" the pugilist promises as he parries back. The Ghost quickly dodges out of the way, rolling to the left and taking out his legs at the shin. He drops down to the ground clearly in agony as his maglev boots fail to whisk him away to safety. Just as she approaches him he reaches under his vest and deploys two daggers at her waist. She didn't see them coming and had no way to anticipate the attack – projectiles were illegal and could not be used in the qualifiers and not even allowed in the final DeathMatch at Derby Days. Not since the last two Derby Days ago when a crossbow arrow killed one of the Waster Kings from DZ: 23R. The guy is big and close enough that no one sees the daggers pierce into her sides. They are small enough that they embed right in and their barbed tip ensures it cannot be easily pulled out. "All right, you want to play dirty, let's dance you fool," she threatens him out loud. Miraculously he finds the strength inside him and rises to his full height, buoyed by the sneaky and underhanded advantage. If she breathes too deep the daggers push farther into her belly. And every boxer knows if you can't breathe you can't fight. "Enough of this, I am taking this sucker out," she yells at the crowd. But they push back, they want more rounds. Some just can't get enough and want to see another person beat down and murdered right before them. Others just want the match to go a few more rounds so they cover their bets.

Lunge, swipe, block, thrust, parry, dodge as the DeathMatch at DZ: 23W continues. Six rounds in and there is no sign of stopping. The big ruffian keeps going for her face mumbling over and over about how he is gonna get that scar, and he keeps whispering the scar part at the end which added an extra layer of creepy. When the crowd started chanting "cut her face!" she decided it was enough. Time to finish this bozo and collect her winnings. She was hungry and wanted her post event Life[x] snack. She had sprung some of her own credits loose and bought a can of potato chips. She enjoyed exploring new textures just as much as the rest of them. No Puff for her, thanks, although she couldn't help but see the longing in Blavos' eyes, and she heard the deeper meaning every time he moaned how much he wished he could smell the damn thing. She is not sure which fight will be over first, Blavos' battle against the Puff and his need for smell, or this little DeathMatch in front of her.

She goes in for the kill with a spinning attack followed by a quick one-two counter parry. She dukes left and strikes at the right side of his head. As she had learned in the first nine rounds he was fast but for this blow not fast enough. He moves his head out of the way but the big block exposes his ROPU and she doesn't hesitate. She buries her sword into the device on his back and it immediately starts spitting little clouds of spent dilithium spores and begins to sputter something fierce. The audience gasps, you were allowed to take out someone's ROPU during a fight, but it was frowned upon and considered dirty. But popping a buddy's ventilator meant a big mid-match bonus on your high odds bet. The force of her swing, empowered and emboldened by the crowd and the itching of her new uniform caused her to bury the light-sword so deep in the ROPU that she could not remove it. The guy rolls over onto the ground and knocks her sword lose. She quickly hovers over on her maglev boots and picks up the weapon. She jams down pinning him to the deck by piercing his shoulder. He howls out not so much in pain but in recognition of his defeat and the impending death. She leans in close and whispers into his twisted face, "Boo," and she kisses him on the forehead. Blavos and Justin will be miffed because they had bet on death. But since she already qualified she could skip the contestant culling until the final Derby Days. The only thing that pays out bigger than a lost appendage during a fight was if both contestants are able to leave the ring of their own accord. Two enter, one leaves, but if they both left then you get paid big. The tide of emotions shifted in an instant from blood lust to compassion and hope for the victim.

But this man was born to be a fighter and destined to win Derby Days to make the folks back home at 23R proud. He was supposed to win, not go down as a failure, bested by a woman no less. He would be laughed at, beat on, or banished for life out to DZ: 23U. Drew manages to grab The Ghost by the lapels, pulls her close, and tells her to just kill him. "I don't care how you do it," he says, "but just make it a show, and please let me stand up first. I want to die on my feet."

She does more than let him stand up as she offers a hand and helps pull him to his feet and even places a reassuring hand on his wounded shoulder to steady him. She tries to shake his hand as a signal that the match was over and he could live to fight another day. He just shakes his head and juts his chin out as he points his nose upward in pride. "I am done killing for a while," she appeals to him, "think of your wife back home," she implores. His self-worth is too much for that so he lunges at her and screams an obscenity, something about her being a harlot and wanton hussy. Now harlot is a moniker you don't hear much these days, Blavos thinks, and he is ringside all the time and hears all sorts of profanity thrown about amongst the crowd, coaches, and especially the contestants as they try and egg their opponent on. Darrenhoe has stopped mimicking the fight but he does give her one signal – he draws his finger slowly across his throat. That Drewski chump is not Almighty enough to survive The Ghost that night, Darrenhoe's eyes tell her.

It isn't Darrenhoe or even Blavos chanting "kill him, do it now, take this loser out!" that puts her over the edge. Not even the degrading outfit or the bloodlust of the crowd. His mumbling out in what sounded like some foreign and possessed tongue, screaming out his sermon against the evils of women and what they can do to a man. That did it, that is enough of that, she finally concludes. He lunges for her to try and provoke an attack and this time it works, all too well. She just simply kicks him in the groin and steps behind him as he falls to his knees. She grabs The Almighty Drewski by the hair on the top of his head before the horrible aching feeling moves up his legs and settles into his stomach, the wave of cramping pain like a massive bout of diarrhea rushes into him. A terrible quaking feeling brought on by a well-placed maglev boot right to the scrotum. He resists and shakes his head back and forth, pride too big to be woman-handled this way, "and especially by a little slut like you," he yells loud enough for the crowd to hear. The tide had shifted quickly back, let's see The Ghost do away with this slimy one, he was a cheater they could tell by the blood coming out of her stomach, no mercy for him. The Ghost obliges and takes two quick steps around behind him. He is still fighting her trying to push her on even farther past her breaking point. It works and she digs her fingers into the bloody hole she had gouged into Drewski's shoulder with her light-sword. The pain is immense and he hollers out as he raises his head involuntarily up to the night sky. She glances over at Darrenhoe now and he makes the motion again. She understands and at this point is so incensed and fired up she decides one more death count on her record would be fine because this creep deserved it.

The Ghost takes a small blade from her maglev boots and ever so slowly cuts the guy's throat wide open. The crowd absolutely loses it as his life blood spills out over the Platform, and that takes a good couple of long seconds to fully drain out of the bloody and oozing gash where Drewski's throat and neck used to be. It took thirteen rounds but this DeathMatch was over and only one fighter exits the ring. "Let's get out of here," she tells Justin and convinces him to skip the press briefing just for tonight. Besides a little radio silence after just cutting that guy's throat and letting him bleed out like that would create a definite air of mystery and dread from the other StatStars.

"Let's let that play out," Blavos agrees with her. She didn't know that she had just taken a good bit of heat off Blavos and he was very glad to keep the last of his molars. Maybe he will give in after all and celebrate with a caramel apple. He looked forward to being able to chew down the crunchy bite knowing he gets to keep the last of his back teeth now. They make it back to the house and she settles into her Life[x] treat. But not before she gets the kit and tests its purity, Darrenhoe reminds her. He is always looking out for her wellbeing. She manages to wait it out and go through the procedure because she knows the added attention leading up to Derby Days has increased the attacks and threats to her life. By this point in the season any StatStar worth his or her salt had to have a protective detail twenty-four-seven. She had that in Darrenhoe and his team. In every way he was there for her.

Kitteridge was at the matches over there at 23W because where else was he going to be? At first he was all for the DeathMatch, cheering Rachel on but not wanting to see her get cut down, but also just to see her moves. He had been watching her for a while now but was never tired of seeing her grace and all the new tricks and moves she would employ without knowing the reactions of her contestants. Consistent as the night, Kitteridge hadn't made any bets on the match, but he had loaned out a few of his massive credits to others. He never accepted a payout in return though, said he had enough credits stashed away safely in the airlocked storage bays of his helper drones to last a man for twelve lifetimes. But when the DeathMatch was finally over he had a mix of pride and disgust. She was a tough fighter all right, but did she have to slit his throat like that? I mean it was just humiliating not to mention gross. But she didn't allow herself to be pushed around and he was proud of her; he could hear all the degrading and disparaging things Drewski had said to her. Kitteridge was so fired up by it that he might have taken the guy out in the parking lot after the qualifiers, but she took care of that herself. He might be her father but she didn't need him to fight her battles for her. She could handle that just fine all by herself thank you very much, long-lost father.

What she couldn't handle and knew had to be taken care of immediately, like tonight, was the barbed daggers slowly digging deeper inside her. She finished her Life[x], savored the crunchy potato chip wedges, and then said she was ready to get this over with. The little knives twisted a little further with every breath, each was wincingly hard to take in and pretty sure I heard her ribs splinter when he stabbed her, Justin said. This was way beyond the combat medic training that Darrenhoe had but Blavos had arranged for Profant and one of his bribed doctors to come and take care of the blades. They did as advertised and she was well on her way to recovery in a few thousand seconds. Her ribs would heal over time without any medical intervention, but the little swords would leave permanent scars on her belly, like two little crescent shaped moons. Just another to add to her growing collection it seemed. Blavos took one look at the already healing wounds, the faster growth rate here on this planet also impacted the body's immune system in a positive way, and he had other ideas. The whole planet had seen her fight and assassinate this guy in a brutal finishing move. Some held that against her, said it was 'unsportswomanlike'. But if Justin let leak that she had been cheated, stabbed illegally by the projectiles, the tide would turn and her stats would jump. Justin agreed to the plan when

Blavos took him and Darrenhoe aside. Post a grainy photo of the doctor leaving and make sure at the next qualifier her outfit shows off the little scars. "Yeah I don't care if she likes it, the crowd will love seeing the sight of the crime across her chiseled stomach." It would be a mid-drift top for The Ghost at DZ: 23E. Darrenhoe sorta liked it that way, he for one appreciated her increasingly revealing outfits. He knew it made her mad, which helped, and his secret lust didn't mind the extra eye candy.

Hasboro and Rosalia had been at the qualifiers that night. Initially she wanted to sit separately, not because people would talk, but because she needed to concentrate on her bets. She had been going big on Bishop for some reason Hasboro didn't understand. Of course Hasboro knew Bishop and rooted for him, but the betting and resulting credits held no sway over his mind. Hasboro helped all the StatStars prepare for these qualifiers; he didn't have any personal experience for he never participated in them. But his general calming approach to any problem meant he could help you surf even the biggest waves. Rosalia got a big return tonight, all her bets had paid off, especially the one backing The Ghost. She didn't expect her to slit the guy's throat, but knew The Ghost would walk away the victor. Hasboro watched in awe for he had no idea that she had so much inner rage locked up. She was impressive and he decided he liked her a little bit better than that newcomer Bishop that Rosalia was always raving about.

Bishop had won his fight that night as well, double payouts to Blavos and Profant due to the long twenty-five rounds. For the first five Bishop's opponent just ran around the ring avoiding any contact. The girl wouldn't even look him straight in the eye. She would just give long staring side long glances as she moved around in a big circle within the octagon. The ref finally stepped in and warned that she would be disqualified if she didn't start engaging. That seemed to fire her up, a disqualification meant elimination from life itself, it was a fight to the death. The girl kept dodging and making little parry jabs right at his stomach. Thankfully, Bishop was able to jump, twist, or roll away for about ten rounds. In round twelve things changed and the girl got some momentum. She had slashed his vest into tatters in just the last forty-five seconds. In the end his prowess and experience in the DeathMatch won over. He took the girl out in a quick and painless fashion by cutting her head clean off. Somebody won big for that because everyone knows heads got an extra bonus from the house if removed after the twentieth round.

*

Midway to the next and final qualifier and Kitteridge has lost his patience with Darrenhoe. He didn't want to blame Rachel although it was entirely possible that she had read the letter and decided to do nothing about it. Couldn't believe or didn't want to believe? He decided to put it all on Darrenhoe because Kitteridge needed someone to take his frustrations out on and pushing for more seemed easier. And so that is just what Kitteridge decides to do, push Darrenhoe to understand just where this situation is at. If he ever was going to give her the letter than just give me a timeframe. I deserve that at least, he thought. Kitteridge wanted to be sure he was around when she read it, not there with her in person, but in close enough proximity if she decides to engage he can bring a few drones over and visit with her. They have a lot of catching up to do and he can't wait to say "Good morning, Rachel" when they do finally meet. Or maybe "Goodnight, Rachel" would be a more appropriate catch all for the occasion, what with the constant darkness here on the Platform.

Chapter 17

378,432,001 to 409,968,000: 1 Year until Tranquility Base

Blavos is done for, they all say. He was extended beyond his limits and his name is mud these days. No one is willing to extend him any credits and the other handlers won't back his lines. CDCG has been crawling all over him lately and he has resorted to using his own teeth as his payback currency. If they kept this up that scumbag Drewski would have been able to make a sweet necklace as a trophy for all to see as a warning sign of the beatings he handed out. But the CDCG hadn't been sending any follow up credit dealers to visit him late in the night. Blavos has been making more of a show of backing Bishop, now no longer in the shadows. His name was right up there next to Profant's on the betting booths. He could only bet limited amounts at the qualifiers, always relying on his trusty ten thousand dollar nest egg. Blavos had wagered his way out of troubling spots in the past, he would handle it, he was one of the best handlers there was on this distant and desolate rock in the outer edges of the galaxy. Darrenhoe didn't like the split attention and neither did The Ghost. Kitteridge and Rosalia had been following along and were surprised to learn Bishop had now joined her StatStar team. The crowds had long ago started wishing and chanting for them to team up – the couples slide race was worth big points at Derby Days. She never skated with anyone, she swore, but Justin kept pushing her on the point. It would be good for her stats he says. "Yeah yeah I know," she says back. "I am not racing with another guy especially not that newcomer Bishop," she declares. "He would just get in my way with all his twists and turns, always greedy and trying to grab those point rings." I guess with her speed and his skills and agility they could make quite the pair. They would make a worthy combo that the betting lines said could, just might, be able to win the whole thing. But only if they worked together and even Darrenhoe thought it was an idea worth trying. She finally agreed to do it in a practice run, try it out, she agreed, and if they didn't finish with a top three score Bishop and The Ghost would remain sworn enemies on the track. Bishop was thrilled with the idea and approached The Ghost first that morning, right out of the locker room when she was still putting on her maglevs.

"Stay the HELL out of my way," is all she says as she strolls onto the track as if nothing is happening, just another practice run.

"That won't be a problem," he assures her. The plan is for The Ghost to hit all the time gates, make as tight a turn as possible and then build up the needed speed to make it through the three-sixty-degree twisted loop de loop toward the end of the track. If she managed to do all that she could simply maglev slide all the way down the finishing hill. She needed to be careful not to cross the finish line without him though. It was a couples race they both knew and they had to cross together and holding hands to boot.

She hits all the first-turn gates no problem but has to extend her right leg out to the starboard side to clear the first timed gate out of the straightaways. She did as promised and made ultra-tight turns being sure not to touch the jagged toothed spindle gates. Bishop followed along close by, watching and avoiding her every turn as she carved out big S-turns into the dust covering the track. Justin kept time on the sidelines while Darrenhoe and Blavos kept back the gathering crowd. Lately everyone seems to love to watch practice and they had bigger attendance this evening than they had for the fan-favorite screwdriver races back all those seconds ago over on DZ: 23F. Bishop grabs for all the extra point rings and collects quite the bounty as he slides along the track. He is careful to go through each of the timed gates so he doesn't lose seconds post-race. A lot of people went for the rings but missed their timed gates. Even though their partner had cleared the gates already and kept their time bank going as a pair each of them had to clear the gates otherwise you suffered a ten second penalty after the race. If a contestant has amassed enough missed gates and it could knock the pair down the ladder a few rungs. Something that was definitely not good for your stats. The CDCG kept track even during practice now that Derby Days was quickly approaching.

After the first three laps around the track the drones are let lose to chase down the laggards and remove them from the track. The slower racers just got in the way when they were ultimately and predictably lapped by The Ghost and Bishop amongst others. Eight drones hover across the track and zoom toward the slowest two from DZ: 23I; an old-timer living and competing PTB and her up and coming teammate. They fought valiantly with their light-swords, a mid-air collision of swinging, beeping, and slaying tail waving about trying to rip apart an ROPU or three. The couple managed to down a few drones into maintenance mode with their light-swords, always a crowd favorite in these events. Usually people just cheered for the drones and waited for them to play their deadly position in this race tonight. Fanboys relished the idea for deaths on the track paid out double. The

CDCG had even designed and distributed mobile betting booths at practices all over the DZs. Eight drones are too much for anyone, even a pair can only handle about five or six at any one time, more than that and you were just overwhelmed and overpowered. The remaining drones are putting up a valiant fight, but the couple manages to hold them off by taking wing and passing the pair skating in front of them. Now no longer last, the drones back off and shuttle toward their next victim, who realize in horror that they have drifted next onto the Collective drone's deadly accurate radar. Last place is no place to be and it doesn't last long for these doomed last place finishers. They don't finish the race too busy finishing dying as the drones split them in half clean down the middle. That seemed to be their preferred way to dispatch a racer, more of a show for the audience gathered as always to see the carnage. Every event at Derby Days is a sort of population control but that is okay because everyone knows there aren't enough seats on the trip to Tranquility Base. Better to go out fighting and standing tall and defiant on your own two feet, in the heart of a DeathMatch battle was the hero's way to go. Fatal mistakes on the slide racetrack wasn't a bad death either but no Viking pyre and funeral for you.

*

Darrenhoe gives in to his better instincts and decides he will give her the letter. She had seemed distracted already, whether from the constantly swirling rumors surrounding Kitteridge, or the fact that she had to couple slide with Bishop, and they had been good. Real good. So that was a thing now, they had competed in and won every qualifier since, and their continual practice was paying off. They still couldn't get that final high ring. Bishop insisted that he could jump higher and therefore it made sense for The Ghost to be the base and boost him up. But she resisted the idea, plus she didn't want to get stepped on by anyone's maglev boots, much less her new partner. Justin, Blavos, Darrenhoe, and his crew of protectors was enough companionship for her. And now she had to be all buddy-buddy with Bishop too. It was exhausting. Thankfully Darrenhoe said he had arranged a special quiet evening of alone time. Justin agreed it was a good idea, she had been testy and not sleeping well. Last thing they needed was for her to be drowsy and lose her edge; one slip and she would be impaled on the time gates. And if she were stuck on the track Bishop couldn't cross the finish line without her. It didn't matter how many rings he had collected before she got grabbed. They only counted if you finished the race and there were no points if you didn't finish. Usually, the drones got you first, and recycled those slow-pokes off the track.

The plan was to finish practice, test and eat her daily Life[x] ration, and then they would leave together to the Transportation Center and onto their undisclosed and secret location he had arranged for her. A lot of people ate their Life[x] and squeezed the tasteless, colorless, but rumored to stink to high heaven, tubes directly into their mouth. They usually did this once a month, a single serving of Life[x] had enough nutrients and vitamins to keep you satiated for thirty days. The stuff was so powerful and had been prepared to such an exacting recipe that many folks could stretch their rations out for forty-five even sixty days. But she was like many of the other StatStars in that she liked to spread her rations out evenly and take a little bit each day. She liked to eat the small bites directly off the sharp end of the knife as she cut the slices off, imagined an exotic pineapple, mango, or other tasty fruit, and she savored each bite. There was a physical benefit beyond the mental one, daily Life[x] consumption was shown to be good for muscle growth and recovery not to mention hydration. It was a dry and dusty planet and without Life[x] the population of humans couldn't survive here. Complete nutrition and tons of caffeine, guarana, ginseng, vitamins B12, B6, and some manually extracted horse urine from a rare and dangerous mare who only lived in the treacherous jungles off the Amazon. No doubt it would be pulled from the beast by a nude virgin who would be sacrificed to the gods as part of the ceremony. Yup Life[x] contained all the important nutrition a high-stakes athlete needed to compete in Derby Days. Darrenhoe was convinced and told her as much that the daily intake made her hit harder and swing faster, all important to winning a DeathMatch.

Life[x] down she was ready. She kisses Justin a friendly goodbye before heading out, no one will be suspicious of her going about town, even through the TC, if she was with her protective detail. In fact she would draw quite a bit of unwanted attention if she went anywhere without them. So Darrenhoe accompanies her as they leave DZ: 23X through the Transportation Center and its many portals. They don't have to change tunnels where they were headed because the rehab facility at DZ: 23A intersected with a lot of places. It might intersect in the portal sense but the journey was a long one. The Ghost noticed that Darrenhoe was much more talkative than usual and he was cracking jokes and asking her all sorts of deep and introspective questions. She didn't know if she needed a relationship with a father-figure, why did he ask? And what's under your shirt she asked back as she noticed he kept rubbing and fingering on his left side, like Darrenhoe was hiding something.

They check into 'The Facility' as it's called with no incident.

Darrenhoe had called ahead and arranged everything so it would be ready for her stay, ensured they could enter through the quiet VIP door at the back so as not to be recognized and photographed by the media. StatStars in rehab for Puff addictions was nothing new, but the handlers didn't like to pay out on the bets that their star racers would give in to the hunger. Some stayed at the rehab center for just a few days, and others lived out a few months, checking in and back out as they went in and out of recovery from Puff and its bloody side effects. The moment The Ghost steps through the door she is instantly recognized by the scar on her cheek and her stats drop a little bit. Justin noticed the dive on his monitor at home and watches in shock the articles and posts coming out. Darrenhoe was supposed to take her out for a special evening to get her mind off Derby Days. But bringing her to a Puff rehab center could only mean one thing. She had decided it wasn't going to eat away at her competitive edge to try it a little. Blavos caught wind too but wasn't worried. He knew she wanted to smell things, but her burning desire to win would carry the day.

"Come on, my last race times were great, and my stats are up. And I don't do Puff, never have, never will. Why did you bring me to this place and just what do you think I am going to get out of staying here for three days?" she asked him once they had checked in and been led to her new home away from home. She was used to sleeping in new and strange places because the life of a StatStar meant a life on the road. Home was wherever you hung your hat for The Ghost, but not here, she thinks. Darrenhoe quietly arranges the one single chair in the room and places it directly in front of the small single bed. She sits down quickly because he is all serious now. She could tell he was nervous before, he kept asking her all sorts of stupid questions, she felt like it was some post-race presser. But he was quiet and all business as he began his story.

"There is something I need to tell you and it isn't going to be easy for you to hear. What you make of it and how you want to respond is entirely up to you. I will support you no matter what you want to do, I hope you know that."

"You're scaring me," she says and he whispers back a gentle hushing sound to quiet her.

"I want to tell you about my wife, Tiana, or about what happened to her."

"You don't have to, that doesn't matter to me," The Ghost tells him. But this is a part of Darrenhoe, it shaped him and how he thinks and interacts with the world, and he needs to share that with her. He knows she will never give in to the temptation for smell, but she doesn't know just how dangerous or tempting it can really be.

"I've never told anyone this story so forgive me if I leave out some key points. It is true I was married once. Of course I was, everyone on this planet gets married. Some arranged marriages are of convenience: a cool roomie you grow up with and would grow old together on Tranquility Base. Others were tolerable at best and many couples lived out separate lives. But Tiana and I were different. We were one of the lucky couples: the kismet two whose marriage assignments matched harmoniously. The perfect pair and we complemented each other like Rocky and Adrianne. "Everyone has gaps. I have gaps, Tiana had gaps, and together we filled gaps." She listens intently, sitting perched on the edge of the bed. Darrenhoe is visibly uncomfortable as he shifts around in the bland room's solo chair. She puts out her hands palms down and places them in a reassuring gesture on his knee but he pulls away slightly and gently brushes her hand off. "Not for this part."

Tiana and Darrenhoe had been longing for smells like everyone else on this planet, they were of course not immune to temptation. They had shared stories of different recipes, what they thought a 'first timer' would be like, and of course they talked about cinnamon buns. Looking back on it now it was hard to pinpoint a specific situation or event that led them down the wrong path, more just a series of build ups over a long extended period of many, many seconds. Darrenhoe had actually been the first to suggest they experiment with different Life[x] textures and he had heard from some of his coworkers about this thing they called a 'potato chip'. Tiana was excited about the idea of trying something new but she was leery of working with any dealers. Darrenhoe knew a guy who had a recipe for making chips at home. So they rationed their servings for about a month and when their next supply drop came they were ready to try. Darrenhoe explains all this in the dingy little room and she is transfixed – she had heard him preach on about the dangers of Puff for so long she couldn't believe he would have even gone down this road. Realization passes over her face as she begins to understand where his long-held hatred for smell comes from.

"To make the perfect at-home chip, with just the right crunch, you really had all you needed right at home. Take the little red O-ring Life[x] rations and heat them up slowly... then just as they begin to soften and melt spread them out in thin little rounds on a baking sheet." Not sure all of this is important, but she lets him continue. The words are flowing and he clearly has no plans to stop his story any time soon. "It is an agonizing three hours of baking where you just sit around and think about more smells. Still wonder what salt and vinegar tastes like, that unique blend of taste on the tongue that combined uniquely with the pungent sour in your mouth and the sting in your nose." She couldn't help but get hungry and her mouth watered a little as he explained more. "We made the chips, a big ol' batch of them, like two dozen or so. And it was true what they said, once we started we couldn't stop, it was impossible to eat just one."

"I should have known right then and there the mistake we had made," he tells her. "Tiana went completely silent after her first bite. She just slowly chewed and chewed with her pretty head tilted back and her eyes closed tight. I couldn't help myself because I was so excited I just kept talking and talking between big crumbly mouthfuls of chips. She was completely lost in herself, alone with her silent thoughts, and immersed in the experience." She could see the pain in his eyes as he told her that Tiana never looked at anything the same way again. "I blamed myself for introducing her to it," he laments "and I could tell by the way she wouldn't quite look me in the eyes that she blamed me too. I had awoken a demon inside her that she would never be able to control." Darrenhoe goes on to tell her about the long and painful seconds that passed between him and his wife. It wasn't long before Tiana started wanting more and more textures but none of them quite satisfied her cravings. There was always something missing, she would complain and they both knew what that was. Smell was a large part of taste, and no matter how crunchy you baked the chips they still tasted like dried out old moldy cardboard. "The fact that she didn't start Puffing right away was a surprise in retrospect. But it didn't take long at all." She made finding new textures and smells her full time job as she ignored her tech support shifts and did her best to avoid the CDCG. Tiana had no problems making friends with a whole bunch of dealers; a young vibrant Puffhead was good for business. Nobody wants to follow some strung out has-been of a StatStar as they stumble on to get their next fix. It started slowly but quickly became all consuming. When she wasn't high Tiana was planning how and where she was going to score next. Even after replaying things over and over in his mind Darrenhoe isn't sure how many seconds she lived from score to score, at least a few years. Her scarves were stained almost black from the constant nose bleeds. Like most spouses of Puffers he was patient, he had the same desire and knew how tempting it could be. He even cleaned up after her, washed her scarves, and at the end had started following her on her outing, just to be sure she was safe. Well, safe as she could be. Darrenhoe knew it was only a matter of time before the side effects overwhelmed her. The need for it already overwhelmed everything else for Tiana, even her beloved Darrenhoe.

Darrenhoe found Tiana in the usual circumstances, midway through her high, splayed out on the bathroom floor. Naked except for her socks, the studded kind for extra traction. She was laying face down, again not that unusual, but Darrenhoe immediately expected something was wrong. There was too much blood even for a 'first timer'. Darrenhoe tries to awaken his sleeping bride from the ride of her life but she doesn't respond to his voice or his touch on her shoulder. His worst fears are met when he rolls her over to see only half her face still attached and the other part still hanging from her long flowing hair. It was clearly a popper and a very bad one at that. He knew this day was coming and had prepared for it, even had a folder with clear instructions on who to call and what to do when she finally did succumb. Almost all emotion was gone from the equation now. Darrenhoe had said goodbye to his wife many long seconds ago. The lifeless body before him was just another cautionary tale and not his dear Tiana. "I swore off the Puff and textures forever that night I found her on the bathroom floor," Darrenhoe takes a long pause and then confidently declares, "and I make a point of pushing people away from it whenever I can!"

"Is that what you wanted to tell me? About Tiana? I'm so sorry. That sounds like it was awful. I can understand why you hate that stuff," she tells him and takes his hands in hers and tells him. "But you don't have to worry about me, I wouldn't touch the Puff."

Darrenhoe gives back a gentle squeeze before dropping one hand and he fishes the letter from Kitteridge out of his waistcoat. The letter is crumpled and faded with the envelope a little torn at the top edge. "No, I don't know why I told you all that. I guess I wanted you to know some of my secrets, because I know yours." Well of course you do she thinks, it's his job as her bodyguard to know all about her. "This, it... well it isn't about Tiana, or Puff. This is about you, Rachel." He turns the letter over in her hand once he gives it to her so she can see her real name for the first time.

"Who's Rachel?" she asks Darrenhoe.

"Just read it and you'll find out," he says back.

She cautiously opens the letter and spreads it out, smoothing the wrinkles as she lays it on the bed and begins to read, slowly and deliberately taking it all in. She is a fast and efficient reader and she doesn't have to even scan it a second time. Rachel exhales a big breath of air and blows it out intentionally through her ROPU hose. She had thought and been worried about the letter once she saw it. Darrenhoe had been acting weird on the trip over here to 23A, talking and joking a lot. He was clearly nervous about something and The Ghost worried this letter was going to be a confession of his love and longing to be with her always. In all ways she wished this shy guy would just grab her and kiss her already. She couldn't take the flirty glances any

254

more. Oddly enough, it was Justin who brought it up to her. He had been watching Darrenhoe and seen how the two acted around each other. Justin wasn't mad and in fact had pushed the two to have that special night together. He even knew she might be gone for a few days with Darrenhoe. Justin had in mind just what they might be doing and decided that frankly he didn't care. As long as she maintained her stats, and also didn't mind who he spent his time with, he didn't care if she had an affair with her protective detail captain. In fact it would be good for business. Justin shared his little plan with Blavos and as expected he agreed. Nothing would bump up the odds in her favor like a little tryst.

Thankfully, it wasn't a love note, at least not in the physical romantic sense. What she holds in her hand, and is still digesting, is the letter from someone claiming to be her biological father. She didn't need to read to the end to know who the letter was from, and in fact she had been waiting for something like this. The Ghost had been watching at the qualifiers and sure enough he was always there hanging around. She liked that and had started even exchanging glances with him. After her last race she even nodded to him, just a subtle tip of her chin, but the scar glowed out and it was obvious to Kitteridge that the signal was meant for him. He gives her a sideways smirk out of the corner of his mouth and raises an eyebrow in return to her. Rachel had been debating contacting Kitteridge herself. She shared the idea with Darrenhoe and he looked down, ashamed that he had hidden the letter from her for so long. I mean who was he to keep her from a relationship with Kitteridge? Even if he isn't her real father he was a stand up kinda guy no doubt about that. He would be good for her Darrenhoe had decided. She just took his reaction as a sign it was a bad idea. If the communication were intercepted the media would have a heyday, Justin made her aware, and she dropped the idea of getting in touch with her new super-fan.

Rachel gently folds the note and stuffs it back into the old and tattered envelope. The note wasn't long, apparently Kitteridge was not a man of many words, or at least not in the written form. The entirety of the letter was just a few lines long.

"Your name is Rachel; your mother Marianna gave it to you.

I am your biological father, but I want to be more and be a dad to you if you will allow it.

I want nothing in return but to know you and spend more time with you.

You won't hear from me again. I will leave you alone if that is your wish.

Love,

Your father Kitteridge.

PS. I'm the guy with all the drones living on the outskirts of the DZ. If nothing else I would love to show them to you, I think they could help you in practice and best your own times."

"Well, Rachel, I should say, you can stay here as long as you need. No one will bother you and you can think this over."

I don't need much time; she thinks to herself. Rachel, she says in her head, still getting used to the idea. It had taken her a while to get used to being called The Ghost. It had been that way for so long she doesn't even remember if she had a name before that. Rachel wants to meet Kitteridge before Derby Days. It isn't a whole lot of time to get to know him and develop the new relationship but she liked the idea of him in her corner cheering her on to victory. She knew she was the best there was but Bishop kept nipping at her heels. Perhaps just one more cheering fan, someone other than Justin, Blavos, and Darrenhoe, not to mention that sleaze-ball Profant. It just might be the boost they both need she decides, might get them to that infernal last ring, way high up there at the end of the track, just when your physical reserves would be all but tapped. She says she is ready to go back now. She wants to talk to Kitteridge tonight. "Take some time, hun, think through this. It is a lot to take in. If nothing else, use some seconds to come up with what you want to say when you do meet him," Darrenhoe tells her. Rachel doesn't need any additional time on this one, she has been thinking it over for a long time now it seems. Yes she did want a relationship with her dad. Time to go find him, she wanted to meet his drones.

Chapter 18

409,968,001 to 441,504,000: Trip to Tranquility Base

"Your mother and I are very proud of you, Bishop. Now go get 'em!" Hasboro tells the racer before the slide track finals. It will be the short track race first, then the mandatory rest break, and the final extended track event, followed by the couples slide. Bishop had been doing better and better and he was already besting his time and moving up the ranks at each qualifier. He had the second fastest times at many DZs and only Rachel was faster. The short track was her signature race and she was so fast and focused that she left most of the other racers in the dilithium crystal dust. Rosalia had convinced Hasboro it was time to make themselves known to the StatStar and she would do it with another one of her letters. He had to admit they had been pretty effective in the past so he didn't resist her. She delivered it to Blavos at the press briefer after the last qualifying match. Blavos told her he doesn't do letters but the real truth was he couldn't read. He had a knack for numbers that helped him set the best betting lines but never could make heads or tails of letters and sentences. He got the basic concepts but couldn't sound out or properly pronounce the written word.

"Justin takes care of all her fan mail," Blavos tells Rosalia. Hasboro takes over and figures the magnitude of a man-to-man talk will ensure the delivery of the letter to Bishop. And he is right, Darrenhoe has learned his lesson not to keep secrets from the StatStars he protected, he can't take the guilt and it almost ate him up from the insides keeping Kitteridge's note from Rachel all that time.

The captain of the guard gives Bishop the letter after arranging a few nights at the rehab center for the poor guy first. By now Darrenhoe was considered a regular at the facility and was able to check him in right away, no waiting list. The rehab places across all the DZs, especially 23A, were all full of washed up StatStars trying to get clean and gain their edge back before the final Derby Days. They had been training all their life, made the tough choice to be sterilized so they can focus on training and not growing a baby, and had thrown away their seat to TB for some Puff, time to get sober and go earn that trip ticket. Bishop was a little more shook up by the idea of a living and present biological mother and her lover. He knew them both, had his entire life. Hasboro was the one always coming up with new track tricks for him. They had been working together just a few seconds ago on his leaps. At this point given even just a small boost from The Ghost and he would be sure to get the last ring. Bishop spent two nights at the facility, returned for about a week, and then decided it was better for his nerves to check in for the remaining time before Derby Days. He didn't need more practice and Rachel refused to do the couples slides until the final event. Bishop had spent the last thirty nights at the center and left ready to face his parents. Blavos didn't care, more people to bet on his boy was all he took away from it. So long as the old couple didn't dip into his share of the credits he didn't care if they were Bishop's parents. Just make sure it doesn't hurt his performance, Darrenhoe was instructed. That was all mental. What was he going to be able to do? A little solitude, some alone time to rehearse all of his events in his mind, mentally doing and redoing his tricks would be good for him.

Kitteridge was at the final qualifier, he wouldn't miss it, just one more leading up to the DZ event at the big Derby Days colosseum built just for the occasion where it connected at the top to the towering casino with unlimited betting all during the days-long affair. His team of drones was needed for the construction and operation so he had to be there. By this time Kitteridge and his battalion had been steadily growing as he downed more wayward drones into maintenance mode and then paired them. Rachel met him before when he had sixty-four drones he could introduce her to, but had now amassed a collection of two hundred and fifty-six little robot helpers. Kitteridge had told Justin that he had been hearing about a special device. If they could get their hands on it for Rachel and Bishop, it would give them the edge they needed to win their couples race. The added points from that optional event is sure to post them to the top of the winners board. It all depended on the action from the field how many credits they would each earn. They all wondered if it would be enough to buy their way to Tranquility Base. Blavos had been bribing people for years, shady folks who could promise they had a way in, a guy on the inside, they said. Blavos had missed his first trip to TB and was willing to pay anything to be picked up this time around. His all-in strategy was at play and Blavos even went fully leveraged and bet his never-touch-this reserve and bet all ten thousand just on the fact that Bishop would get a boost from The Ghost. The racer didn't even have to grab or really touch the ring, the fans had been wanting and even chanting "Boost him! Boost him!" at the last couple of rallies. If Bishop's maglev boots even so much as smooshed her nose in just a hair for a little lift then the resulting payouts would be enormous. Some few went the hard road and took the sucker's bet on Rachel jumping that high all on her own to take that final ring, no way was she going to let some guy step on her face, even if it was her StatStar teammate. After all, did you see what she did to that guy at the DeathMatch over on DZ: 23W, he said a disparaging thing about women in general and she opened up his throat with her little serrated blade and just stood there while the blood spilled out of the big red gash that split his neck sideways, hitting the ground like pieces of candy that had exploded from a smashed piñata. Step on her head just to get some points they probably didn't need, no sir, just not gonna happen. Might as well just give your money to me or burn it up with a lighter if you're going to bet on Bishop hitting the ring. Trust me, been doing this a long time now.

Chapter 19

Derby Days Screwdriver Race

The screwdriver races were always the first event and nothing fires up the crowd at the start of Derby Days like a few burned crispy contestants. A surprise to the fans and the racers they would have to do the three-ring puzzle followed immediately by the standard six-ring. Sure, your hands weren't pinned down at the wrists for the smaller layered unit but the device's rings spin so fast you need all the reach and dexterity you could get. Instead of being on top of one another the rings on this little puzzle were concentric, narrowing into the center like a bullseye, and placed vertically sideways at an ever changing angle. It was tricky going, just when you had found the right position and locked in place the outer ring and moved onto the center, it spun back lose four turns the other way. Like interconnecting cogs on a great and complicated moving machine you had to line them up just right. A lot of people loved this new event, but a few complained it should be called a 'bolt race' because there were no screws. Contestants had to work both the top and bottom side of the bolts at the same time all while keeping the rings held in place. Naturally, the little corrections and occasional 'WAKE UP' zaps from the sensors in your seat made it all the more challenging. Much to the crowd's dismay no one was burned alive from the inside out at the bolt races. Save those bets for the six-ringed race.

Bishop manages to finish second by just beating out Rachel.

She still secures her top three finish that she needs to qualify for the final slide race and is happy with her showing considering she has never done the three-ring event. The Ghost even manages to choke out a congratulations and a handshake. "Be sure and get it on camera," Justin blurts out. The constant reputation manager he even makes them do the whole 'good job teamie' thing again so he can livestream it. Say what you want, that guy Justin is good at his job and knows when and how to juice the stats and their odds of a big payout. Images of the two glad-handing each other is broadcast on the video monitors overhead. All the attention in the ballroom hosting this race is on them, including from the other racers. One gal on the far end of the contestant tables, just sitting down to her six-ring, can't help but stare, clearly a big crush on Bishop. He gives her a big smile and she just loses it as she trips over her own boots and goes headfirst onto the race table. As she goes down the claws are still up on the corners because they only go down when the event starts. She loses an eye, and someone gets paid, she wails out as the claw jams into her socket. She didn't so much lose the eye, as it lost its entire shape, crushed by the solid dilithium crystal formed claw. That does it for her, she can't compete if she can't see, and so is disqualified. The crowd boos her away for they would have rather she tried and get stuck on the guard rails, the resulting correction would be impressive and immediate. Wonder what it would look like to peer into her skull through her missing left eye while she was burning up from the insides? The drones snatched her up and nobody got to find out.

The screwdriver races are in full swing now and Bishop and The Ghost are the only two on the third ring. Three other contestants have gone up in flames and a fourth was ripped in half after stripping a screw on ring two. The second ring, the oversized triangular one that had to be maneuvered over and the puzzle passed through before you could remove it, that ring was just huge at this Derby Days. Big, slippery, and heavy. It was hard to move and even harder not to hit the sides – people all over the tables were getting corrected. ZAP! Even Bishop, who never got zinged, got a jolt or two removing his. He makes quick work of the third ring and now he was onto the fourth ring and was busy removing the thirty-two screws. Blavos, Profant, and Darrenhoe and his entire crew were busy running after and catching the popping screws as they flew into the dark night sky. Each one was recovered, a fanboy beat down and carried out, and the screws placed carefully and exactly back into the recycling bins on the side of the tables.

Somebody from the mass of onlookers cries out "BURN HIM ALREADY" and it works, the noise distracts another player and he gets stuck on the guard rail. His trusty all-metal to protect against the elements screwdriver is the absolute perfect conductor as the voltage melts the dude right there. It sticks him to the event surface. The smell of the burning body is overwhelming and makes the contestants' eyes water. A few tears even hit the table and the seat sensors delivered a quick BUZZ in response, shocking the unlucky contestants who had welled up.

Bishop gets stuck on the fifth ring and slides from second place, right behind Rachel who is now on her sixth and final ring, to fourth. He knows he must hurry up because he needs to finish in the top three. Bishop finally makes it past this layer and onto the final ring. The pressure from the wrist cuffs becomes too much for him and Bishop loses feeling in his fingers. The numb digits are worthless and before he drops the screwdriver and becomes pinned to the electricity he calls out to the judges. They rush over and just as he is about to give up and accept the disqualification he hears Rosalia's voice calling out from the edge of the watcher barricade. Relax and let your mind solve the problem, she whispers in his mind. Close your eyes and let the muscle memory take over she soothes him with her eyes. Bishop starts to feel the tingling sensation in the tips of his fingers as the blood flow corrects and begins to bring feeling back to his hands. He grips the screwdriver even tighter still not maintaining full control or precision over his digits. As he brings off the final ring and reaches for the button cover Rachel slams down her button with her numb fist, just in time as the electricity on the table shuts off right as her screwdriver falls and lands resting right against a guard rail. Bishop is right behind her and secures his second place finish. The event is over as quickly as it had begun and everyone is excited about the first day and wants the events to continue. As the sweeper drones come in to clean up and recycle all the discarded bet slips the crowd make their way to the grand Puff symposium. Had they done it? Was the cinnamon bun finally ready for mass consumption? And if so, how many credits was it going to cost? All these questions and more were top of mind for everyone at DZ: 23X as the first events of this season's Derby Days comes to a close.

All the StatStars make their way back to their basecamp tents surrounding the casino because the events are over for the day. The Puff parties, however, are just getting started and the revelry permeates the DZ. The parking lots are littered with little geometric domes scattered about. Blavos was practically running and it was clear at this pace he didn't know what to do with his cane. He slips the cane under his left arm as they approach the entry to their tent, actually more of a compound now that Kitteridge's drones were in charge of the setup and takedown. He had something to show them, something Justin had swiped from one of the exhibition booths. Justin had just got the devices back from Kitteridge who ensured him that they most definitely probably work. Well at least one of them. Maybe. This new device would help them stay hidden in the final parts of the race. Everyone knew that clothes would shift form, style, and especially color all throughout the event. At a certain speed, by turn two and on the straightaways and long finish hill a racer got up enough speed to make the surrounding cloud of dilithium spores in the air glow. The color always matched the tint and hue of the racer's uniform, which meant that you were always a different color. Somehow, probably cause it made for better viewing, it was more exciting to see your racer turn the corner and almost cover your bet, and the speed glow certainly did the job. But what Justin had swiped, these little gizmos that attach to your belt, in the back under the cape, well they were to be kept hidden Blavos insisted, not so much from the judges, but from the other StatStars. These babies would give them an edge and he didn't need any followers digging into his bottom line. The fact that Justin had to promise a picnic for the vendor's daughter didn't really matter to Rachel; the girl was hot. Besides Justin and Rachel had a pretty much open relationship. Now that her companionship with Darrenhoe had been revealed they were free to see other people. Rachel just wanted to be with Darrenhoe, but Justin found lots of fans willing to keep him warm under his cape. He had stopped wearing the fuzzy one The Ghost liked so much, it was his one way of showing his wife respect.

Chapter 20

Derby Days Death Match

A few more events are queued up for the next couple of days, and Rachel easily gets top marks. She makes quick work of the diagnostic testing and by this point in her life could spot a leaking storage bay or rusty bolt better than anybody. Hide and seek with the sweepers on day three was always fun. She made Bishop look silly which she and the crowd always enjoyed. Profant was a bit miffed when Bishop's odds took a dive but decided he would just go deeper and bet wilder. Most of the betting booths were pretty quiet as everyone had been saving up their time and credits for day four's DeathMatch battles. This year was a big one with more entrants than ever before. There was sure to be blood and the audience anticipation was palpable as they all gathered in the big top tent put up by Kitteridge's drones. The undercard matches are brutally long slug fests between very unevenly matched opponents. It was during these early rounds that men and women fought against each other. There was a bit of a bruhaha during the tag team match, somebody got the bright idea of throwing combatants out of the ring and meeting them with a swift folding chair to the face. The final death blows would be delivered after dragging the writhing victim into the stands. Killing someone yourself at the final Derby Days would rob the crowd the pleasure of tearing them limb from limb right there in the stands. The sweepers were quick to clean up the mess, and with the overrun of fighters this year, were kept busy all night. The tag team match was the last undercard fight before the main event. Bishop got the short end of the stick in his draw and was to face the big bruiser from 23D – Death Dealer they called him. Rachel faired only slightly better, she was to fight the judo wrestler, the gal from 23Q that was more likely to want to break your arm than see you bleed out. When her opponents finally did submit and try to tap out, usually crippled by her signature arm-bar or a figure-four leg lock, she even resorted to a full Nelson hold if they went a bunch of rounds, she would return with a quick tap to their heart, burying her light-sword up to the hilt.

Rachel spun around and swept the legs out from under her opponent sending her crashing to the floor of the mat. It was already stained red from the previous matches and made for a sticky slippery surface that made it hard to put any weight or heft behind your punches without sliding back. Just for tonight, and like all other finals, the last two bouts, the heavyweight matches, for the belt and the title, were both fought at the same time. Bishop and Rachel had couples skate enough that they unconsciously mirrored each other's movements right down to the fighting style and technique. Jab, cross, hook, uppercut as Bishop connects on the big guy's chin. Rachel at the same time throws her corresponding one-two-three-pow and sends her opponent to the floor of the ring again. It makes a sickly squishing sound as the blood spatters out, both from under her head soaking her hair and as it spews from the large cut above her right eye that Rachel had given her. Bishop is gobbled up in a big bearhug but head butts his way free. The big guy howls out and grabs his face, Bishop had broken the dude's nose with the force of his skull. Blood pours out and new fresh puddles gather on the mat. The guy spits out a tooth or three and charges Bishop.

Rachel rolls away from the girl's quick parry and springs right back to her feet charging in unison with the big guy in the ring one over. The two pairs of bodies crash together connecting in a big arc and splatter of sparks from their light-swords. The battle is intense and Bishop manages to knock the light-sword free from his opponent's hands. Bishops lunges in for the kill and looks sort of like a bowler hitting his tenth frame strike as he juts his foot out behind him. He hits the guy again and again in the bloody hole on the middle of his face. Where his nose used to be. Bones crack and splinter as Bishop keeps wailing away.

Kitteridge is standing ringside looking all stoic next to the concentrated and strained face of Blavos. True to form as always the reckless handler had bet it all full tilt, now he had more on the line than even Profant. He had side-lined and limited his exposure with a little insurance, courtesy for all his years of 'business' with the CDCG, so when the gal in ring seven cut the head off the lifeless body of her already dead opponent Blavos got paid out triple: once for the post-mortem dismemberment, one for the lost appendage because hey, heads counted, and finally the bonus kicked in for the sheer brutality of it all. Not to be outdone, Blavos goes back to the betting booth all flush and lays it all-in on the next matches – a double header with The Ghost and Bishop both fighting high ranked pugilists in their own right. He needs both his StatStars to win, or at least one of them to lose an arm or be permanently disfigured, otherwise he wouldn't cover the spread. And convincing either of them to snatch that last ring with so much as a broken finger was going to be an uphill battle that not even Atlas could handle: continuously up the hill two steps and then sliding back three. Profant had said it was a foolish bet and refused to follow suit, even though that old dealer had credits spread all over some outlandish calls. Darrenhoe remained busy on the sidelines, shadow boxing and copying every move from Rachel. Kitteridge gets closer and leans into the ring during a break in the action because both fighters have been sent to their corners after the bell signaled the end of the round. Bishop has his guy pinned against the ropes and continues to swing away in the opposite ring, alternating between slamming his clenched fists into his broken nose and then back to the ribs. The crowd went wild with every bone crunching blow as Bishop decided to stop this man from fighting back altogether; he knew you can't fight if you can't breathe.

The crowd surges forward in all the excitement, rushing the ring and even pressing up against the ropes, invading the territory previously reserved for the combatants. The rush of motion behind him pushes him forward and he topples into and then over the top of the big brawler from DZ: 23D. As Bishop rolls forward a few additional feet he spins around, cartwheeling his feet to spring back up, and all in the same deftly agile motion brings up his light-sword and takes a defensive horse stance, feet spread out beyond shoulder width to stabilize him. By this point in the night both Bishop and The Ghost are into the second half of their eighteenth round and everyone, including the crowd, extreme fanboys and high rollers notwithstanding, was simply exhausted. The cabanas and spa tables would all be reserved for a brunch complete with an IV drip for extra hydration. All the Puffers would be recovering from their hangovers, pushing around their wheeled apparatus with hoses hanging out, sucking on pure oxygen to try and soothe their inflamed and still bloody nostrils, raw from the side effects of trying to hit that cinnamon bun too hard. It turned out to be a disappointment in the looks department when it was all lumpy and viscous like oatmeal. It was as if the whole thing remained an unbaked mess that was waiting for its turn at three hundred and fifty degrees for eighteen minutes. But scoop it up and swallow it down all in one big bite and it was pure heaven. You could feel the sides of your tongue curl up to take in the icing as you bit down on the squishy and raw dough, just a small bit in the middle. The rest of the mouthful is the sides of the bun, crispy and crunchy from the caramelized cinnamon crumbs. A few brave, or depraved, people freed the extra credits from their wallets for the orange icing. Just by itself it had become popular after the last symposium as people would just squeeze it directly into their greedy gullets; the citrus flavored goo had become somewhat of the texture only man's 'first timer'. Start with that and after a few more texture experiences you'll be ready for the potato chips. Don't spring for the stupid can, you could get your hand stuck in there. Trust me, been doing this a long time.

The sweet appearing old Puff head in the front row appeals to The Ghost. The old bird keeps tapping her left wrist and then rolling her right hand over and over slowly in a little circle. Rachel understood that motion meant the lady had money on this going another few rounds or so. That was fine with her, and Justin liked it when she picked folks out of the crowd, of course it boosted her stats a few points and encouraged the early and continual mid-match betting on the races tomorrow. The Ghost quickly brings her hand out and shoulders up in an 'I dunno' gesture; how many rounds more you need me to push this girl around before I can finish her and be done with this guilt inducing event she wanted to know from the old hag, who by the looks of her had clearly been living here way past Tranquility Base, maybe even on her second or probably third round, how long she had been on the Puff no one could tell. The woman raises her shriveled fingers, three of them to be exact, Rachel has great eyesight and can make it out even with the blinding lights from the DeathMatch octagon piercing through everything below them. The crowd heated up the big top at least thirty degrees, their sweaty breath and perspiring bodies thick with the lust for violence and easily won credits. What with the heat from the contestants' bodies pouring off and the lamplight glow, one hundred and twenty thousand lumens, and it gets downright balmy in the ring. It was pretty toasty in there for sure. Rachel had a plan, quick and dirty, but that went out the window twenty-three rounds ago. This was turning into the barnstormer that Blavos had needed and Justin all but demanded. Put on a good show and you could win us all seats to TB he assured them. Twenty plus rounds and still going, bets were now only paid out in rounds of five, one couldn't even get 1:1 side-bets with the most crooked bookies for them to duke it out one more round, bet on five or get out of line. Like the famous heavyweight boxer Mike Tyson always said, everyone has a plan till they get punched in the mouth; this little girl was quite the competitor and fast as lighting. Rachel suffered blow after blow to her ribs and it had become her own Achilles' heel. Hit her hard and fast, over and over, right in those two little scars, yeah the moon shaped ones you seen all over the video replays tonight. If she can't breathe, she can't fight. Rachel had been watching and learning all along. By the twenty-sixth round The Ghost could anticipate and mimic the gal's moves. Rachel's defense became attack and the girl didn't know what to do and was quickly overwhelmed.

Ring nineteen, where Bishop is fighting that dude from 23D, is pure red from the bloody nose, a veritable open fountain now after Bishop's nine round slug fest on it. The big guy can barely stand up and is wobbling from broken rib-raddled side to wheezing side. He was sucking in big gasps of air and was only getting little sips of relief as his lungs were pressed in by every rib on his frame. Yup, Blavos had been right all along, if you can't breathe you can't fight. This guy must have been paid to last because he just stood there, slowly moving side to side, like a dumb pendulum keeping beat. On Bishop's next blow, a crushing, jumping, round-house kick aimed at his opponent's ROPU, the man surprises everyone. Not because he draws his light-sword, for the guy has been helplessly holding that thing limp at his side since the very first round. On this occasion it seems as though he has been training with something special just for Derby Days. He slides his left hand down and rotates the hilt of his blade, a quick turn and it extends another eighteen-inches, becoming perfectly balanced across the width of the man's arms. He spits out a big old loogie of blood and snot from the hole in his face where his nose used to hang out as he begins to spin the now double-bladed light-sword in a circle in front of him. His weapon has been transformed from a light-sword into a bow staff. With his weapon now a full twelve feet in length the brawler steps forward and rotates his shoulders pushing the deadly blades toward Bishop in huge arching sweeps that surround him on each side caging Bishop in. Well, I know what I am asking for my Tranquility Base parting gift, Bishop thinks, I need to learn how to build and use a sword like that! Bishop is no slouch when it comes to thinking on his feet, and he had prepared a special trick of his own, reserved for just this DeathMatch. Darrenhoe made him swear not to deploy the special attack because the weapon was to be kept a secret while he trained the rest of the protective detail. Bishop slides his battle cape to the side and a thick black chain lowers down from where it was coiled like a whip on his hip. The trident-pointed tip hits the ground with a thud and the big guy looks down. Thankfully, he doesn't see the eight pound spiked mace ball on the other end of the chain whip around from its tight circular spin until it knocks him upside the head and right over on his left side. Putting some space between them so he can really wield his custom-built ninja assassin's kusari-gama Bishop slides back in a sweeping crane's backward motion, wide sweeping backward lunge after another, mace ball swinging all the while in a tight circle. The pronged eighteen-inch razor sharp spike at the far tip of the chain was aimed right for the guy's ROPU when he spins around and uses his double-blade to block the attack. He springs up onto his feet with one quick kick of his legs and arch of his back and hops from laying to standing in one deft leap. A little too much momentum so he almost falls straight forward as he stands up. Kitteridge had been standing by with his attention focused on the match with Bishop because his Rachel was busy pounding away at her combatant's ribs. "Atta girl, Rachel!" the proud father yells out and for some miraculous reason his voice carries through the other sound waves and she looks over at him. Kitteridge slams his fist into the palm of his other outstretched hands a few times and Rachel understands. Time to go back to work, and she does. He doesn't mind the violence so much as long as she is the one dealing out the punishment, Kitteridge hates to see The Ghost get hit. Bishop continues to invoke his Shaolin crane-style that he employs with the perfect form and movements to use when wielding the kusari-gama. He dips and dodges, moving his arms out and around in distracting motions, he lunges forward and lets fly the mace ball, hitting the other guy right in the middle of his gut, doubling him over. The sound of air expelling from his belly is almost as loud as the whooshing sound of the long chain as it spins through the fog.

Wow, my man over there really knows how to spin that thing, Justin live-chats with the audience on the side as the big guy twirls away, defensive block after two offensive jabs and a quick third parry by whipping the hilt back up, bringing the laser inches away from Bishop's face. He slows down and appears to have finished his flag girl routine, in the main ring and not on the sidelines any more. The kusari-gama is the perfect weapon against the laser-edged bow staff and its big swoops. It was the only way he could get inside the protective shield from the spinning circles of the double-blades. Bishop brings the mace back and spins it in another tight circle but this time for momentum he hangs the spiked end down and lets it swing from the chain like the pendulum of a big grandfather clock in an old and haunted mansion on the barren hilltop on the outskirts of the village in the mountains. He spins the mace ball over his head and lets the other end fly out to the side reaching its full length. It hits the peak and a flash of metal glints, sparking off the lights of the monitors hovering over the action in the ring below. Bishop brings his right hand down hard and pushes all the way to the Platform. He assumes the classic super-hero just landed to save the day stance – supported by a clenched palm slammed into the ground and down on one knee with other arm out just for balance and of course crowd appeal. As he does this the pointed business end of the stick makes a perfect circle and comes down right in the middle of the spinning blades of death, the center lane being the one weak point. Darrenhoe is right and tons of people exclaim shouts and cheers at Bishop's new weapon. The judges call is quickly convened, ignoring the contest for a few seconds, until they ruled that it would be allowed because it was still held in at least one hand it could not be categorized as a projectile. That was a good thing, a very good thing indeed, for Bishop and all

275

those in attendance betting on him to just kill this guy. Finish him off in under thirty rounds and we can all go home fat and happy.

But Bishop isn't worried about how many rounds he has to go still before the match is over. He is just trying to stay alive and away from the fence of sharp toothed death that threatened him at every step. The pointed end of his chained weapon wraps around the center of the guy's double-bladed light-sword. Bishop pulls up and then down and the sword snaps in two. Not only did it become two swords, which would be useful, and the guy could even use it to his advantage, but the blow broke open the hilt and spilled out all the laser producing dilithium crystals tucked away inside. The light-swords were useless little nubs now and 23D dude quickly throws them down, well he chucks one at Bishop's head and it makes contact. Bishop wasn't expecting the guy to strike back. Heck just a few rounds ago he could barely stand and now he was all Johnny on the spot!

Back in ring eighteen and Rachel is on top now literally sitting on the girl in the middle of the ring for all to see. She isn't punching the girl, not really, but she is squeezing in with her knees and thighs, crushing the girl's broken ribs into her lungs. The Ghost was no stranger to leg day and this girl got to know all about it. The tactic worked, while Rachel took turns slapping her across the cheek, once with the right hand, now with the left, even a backhand just to mix it up, she squeezed the breath and life out of her opponent like a python would a large rodent. The resulting pressure from the muscles in her legs against the girl's sides caused her opponent's already shattered rib bones to pierce her lungs in not less than nine places. As her lips turned blue from the lack of oxygen from the power of Ghost's awesomely strong legs a shade of purple overcame her opponent's face from the blood spreading up and out. Bishop was back in the corner wolfing down some extra Life[x] to see if it gave him the boost he so desperately needed going into the thirtieth and final round. If one of them didn't kill the other before the three minute bell rang then they would both be disqualified. Delay of game would be the official call and all bets cancelled. DeathMatch was as advertised, a fight to the death either way, for one or both of you. People made money either way and an overtime disqualification was always fun to talk about. Something to reminisce on your long trip to Tranquility Base. Rachel's match is over and the media has already stormed through the ropes and onto the ring. "Will she be ready for the couples skate?" and "We haven't seen you at practice, just hanging out with Darrenhoe. What does Justin think of that?" they wanted to know. Rachel simply ducks her head and begins to quickly make her way over to Bishop's corner. She hadn't been able to watch his progress and only glances every now and again between rounds. He appeared to be winning if the blood coming from the other guy was a reliable sign, and as she sits down ringside she knows it is. From the crowd, it is hard to tell whose blood it was. Both of their uniforms and capes were stained crimson from the last thirty rounds of duking it out and cutting each other open.

Blavos is standing dead still and is trying to take it all in. He has so many bets going across the DZ he doesn't know if he is up or down. It doesn't matter, he lived and bet like he always had nothing to lose so long as he kept his couple thousand nest egg safe from the CDCG. At this final Derby Days he figured he really did have nothing to lose and had even bet that little nugget too. Blavos wasn't so stupid after all, he would proudly show Profant later, Bishop had made his thirty rounds. This one was too good for even the usually chaste Rachel to get in on the action. "He makes it all the way and you get a kiss from me in public: one for each round he's still standing." She smiled at Darrenhoe. He gladly accepted the bet because he had been training stamina and cardio with Bishop for years now. The guy could race an entire track length breathing through a little narrow metallic tube – good for his lungs, Darrenhoe explained. The fact that it was sponsored by a new flavor of Puff didn't matter, Justin tried to assure them. Darrenhoe bores of his ringside practice. All this punching and kicking in the air had him tired out. He takes a seat next to Rachel and she begins paying off her debt. The Ghost blows right past her no PDA rule because the whole DZ knew the two were an item. And she didn't know which she found more disrespectful, the fact that the media ate it up and sold pictures and videos of them in the act sometimes, or the fact that Justin encouraged it and even smacked faces with a few of his fresh 'social media influencers and engagement management interns'. When they did pull their faces up from the blue light little digital assistants they kept on hand, blogging and chatting away, posting and posing for their next selfie, Justin's interns were actually quite pretty.

Back up in the ring both guys are still sitting on their benches in the corner. The bell for the thirtieth and final round dings and both guys rush to meet in the center. The near certainty of impending death hypes them both up and they have more energy than when they first showed up at Derby Days. They are both completely amped as the adrenaline courses through their bodies. Some more mid-air gymnastics from Bishop and a few savvy blocks from 23D and they are no closer to seeing the Grim Reaper. The kusari-gama hits a few more blows and knocks the guy's hose right out his mouth. He had been biting down on it ever since his nose disappeared all those rounds ago. The mouthpiece is soaked red and dripping down his chin as he attacks. Bishop whirls his cape and the chain around and crouches down as he sweeps the large fellow right off his feet; the spiked mace ball crushes the combatant's ankle in the meantime. The guy lands sitting upright and as it happens that is right where Bishop wants him. He wraps the center of the chain around the brawler's neck, choking off his air supply. And he knocks the hose free for good measure, it droops and flings around in the battle sky. For his final blow Bishop sinks the pronged end into the man's chest, buries it deep and then yanks it up, hanging the guy in the air like a side of frozen beef stored from the ceiling in a stinking freezer in some dimly lit back room. The crowd, already on their feet and standing on their seats, lose their collective minds. Men hug men and women cry as they realize their man is the victor here tonight. Many had bet it all and had been stretching and skipping rations and saving credits just to bet on Bishop winning his DeathMatch.

Rachel had stopped kissing Darrenhoe, her debt all paid off, and the cameras had panned away now more interested in the final blows of the match over at ring nineteen. "Make a good show of it and we all get tickets," Blavos had said and Bishop does as he is told. As the life drains away from the man's face and his soul packs its bags, ready to depart, Bishop takes the weighted mace ball and begins digging away at the bloody nose socket. He delivers punishing blow after blow right in the middle of his combatant's face.

"Mister, mister! He's not going anywhere. I think you can stop hitting him now," the little girl said through the noise of the cameras and feedback from the boom mics overhead. Bishop agrees, nods and mouths a thank you her way, and then walks back to his corner. His body and mind tell him he is the victor and the smiles and claps on the back of his ROPU from Profant confirm it. But his heart and soul tell a different story. He didn't like this aspect of the Derby Days because he didn't agree or understand why people had to die. Couldn't they just watch and bet on the sport of it all? The display of skills and years of dedication and training? Marvel in a well won race… no, kill her or I don't want any action it seemed was the law of the land around here.

After the DeathMatch presser is over they all make their way back to the compound. There will be more events and the Puff symposium would be in full swing. But the next three days were set as mandatory downtime for all the StatStars. Nobody but the betting public complained about the rest time and the quick recovery times for the human body on this planet meant two days was just enough for the body. Leave the last day for the mind they all said, see yourself going through the paces of the race, feel the track underneath you. Some of the real superstitious kind would even don their race uniforms and sleep in them for the final three days leading up to the game. That was stupid, Rachel thought. She made public fun of everyone who showed up in their lucky maglev boots which clearly stunk to high heaven and hadn't been washed since they first qualified back at 23K. You gotta wash your Derby Days gear, kiddos. Especially your maglev boots.

Rosalia was happy, she had bet their savings on Bishop to win, and the insurance she purchased against dismemberment had luckily paid off. His choke-out at the end saved her big credits. Hasboro was pleased as well, he loved seeing the enjoyment on his adopted son's face. They had made it official just a few seconds ago, days before the start of Derby Days. Hasboro, Rosalia, and Bishop all signed the papers. He was officially and legally a dad. They make their way back to their tent for some rest. They will hold up together, enjoying a picnic of Moscato d'Asti, peaches, and potato chips, complete with the can. No one will bother them about being Bishop's parents. Even if they were star-crossed lovers from a past Tranquility Base season, the media just wasn't all that interested. They were at first because Justin and his 'influencers' made sure of that. But as the interns quit or were fired for not putting out enough and Justin brought in more, he stopped fanning the flames and the media's smoke for Bishops, Rosalia, and Hasboro just died out. The real action was a picture of Rachel, and these days she could be doing just about anything, and the photo taker got a credit reward. Get her with Blavos and it was a quick five spot. Smooching up to Darrenhoe was an easy fifty credits. The big payouts went to photos of her with her old man. She had publicly admitted they were seeing and talking to each other, had formed a loving relationship and she wished all her fans had someone like him in their life. Rachel had her suspicions at first but Darrenhoe had talked to a guy named Coppertone. Coppertone said he didn't smell anything fishy after he dug around. He had contacted his guy who knew a girl that would take the job. The young gal met him outside during a whistle-snort-sniff chat with his drones and swiped some hair from his vest. Coppertone's gal Friday checked it out and confirmed Kitteridge was indeed her father.

Chapter 21

Derby Days Big Puffer

Day seven of Derby Days was called the 'Big Puffer' and you didn't have to guess too hard to figure out why. Even without a ROPU hose-mod you could get high just hanging around outside the 'first timers' tent. The whiff of roasted beef was hard to resist. New flavors and texture were all about and freebies were plentiful. If you didn't have a bag stuffed full of free Puff tubes and crunchy or squishy Life[x] rations, then what are you even doing here in this convention center? Ranch was back, had never left really if you asked Blavos, that guy poured the stuff on every Life[x] tube he consumed. Sea-salt and peppercorns were there of course and some vendors in the back are giving out automatic shakers and grinders complete with a little light so you could be sure to get just the right amount. The big draw, the real hit of the whole symposium, voted on by the Waster Kings themselves was a new drink called 'coffee'. Hot or over ice, with cream or black as the night's fog it was the perfect morning wake-up and afternoon pick-me-up. The vendors couldn't keep up with the throngs of people that wanted it or the crowd's willingness to wait. Long queues stretched for thousands of feet and looped all the way in and around the outside of the entire event campus. Some real enterprising gals took to their legs and began biking around big thermoses filled with the hot liquid and was making serious side credits dolling it out to people waiting in line with hours still ahead of them.

Justin's interns were good for a few things with most of those reserved just for Justin. They were also in charge of getting the team all the cool swag at Derby Days and so far they had built up quite the collection. There were people hawking shirts and hats, keychains and magnets, shot glass and t-shirts made with custom "I saw some guy get choked out by a ninja!" fresh off the presses. They had them all and that perky little intern Rebecca had become Rachel's favorite. She had an eye for fashion and always brought her the best stuff. The Ghost didn't complain when she offered her a piping hot and steaming cup of coffee. "'Joe' they call it," she says, and slips the warm cup into Rachel's outstretched hands. It felt great and warms more than just her fingers as her body soaks up the heat, she was still stiff and frigid from the constant thirty-four degree temperature. Even without the Puff accompaniment she enjoys the newfangled concoction and Rebecca agrees to get her the recipe. This would become her go-to drink after practice. She couldn't help but wonder if they had coffee on Tranquility Base. After her big win in the DeathMatch Darrenhoe said her seat assignment was all but guaranteed. She wasn't so sure now as she had been worried about passing her Interval. The social press had long ago started blogging about her ROPU. On her third trip around the track at the DZ: 23L qualifiers it had started to sputter. Kitteridge was the most alarmed, he had been worried, watching and carefully tracking her seconds left till her crystals dried up and Rachel would have to prove, yet again he still believed, that she could breathe on this planet without a ROPU. He had been chatting with her about it in secret. Kitteridge had told her about the massacre, showed her how he learned to pair the drones, and how he would swear that he saw her breathe without the hose when she was born out of the bloody c-section. Just hold your breath and try it out he encouraged her. Plus, the breath work and lung workout will be good for your stamina. That made sense she had agreed, but try as she might, couldn't help but take a big gulp of air right around three minutes and thirty-one seconds. She had the timing down right and when her time came she knew she could hold her breath all the way up until the end. Then we would all see if she could. And the dirtbags who took the long bet on whether she would survive her Interval would finally get to see if their bet slips were winners or recyclable losers.

Hasboro stops by each night just to check in and say hello. He and Kitteridge have become good friends, they are kindred spirits, both seeking just to teach another and make the world a better place. Kitteridge had been over earlier but had to go back to check on his drones. After some seconds away he was satisfied with the scaffolding that would hold up the track base, a collection of about thirty-two drones, and made his way back to enjoy the camaraderie of his teammates. The drones that hold up the scaffolding could shift and rotate with the Platform as they surfed the ground tides that threatened to push the racers off the track and into the depths below.

Rosalia is a bit shy with strangers it turns out. She likes Rachel but worries a little bit every time she is around her. Something about that scar turns her off, makes her worried someone will rip it open. Rosalia has seen The Ghost fight so she is not sure why she believes her to be so vulnerable, the woman is no weakling and when she slit that man's throat you could tell she was no pushover either. She was always friendly with Rosalia, she had come to enjoy the woman's company and relished her stories. She told of picnics and long-kept letters. Lovers on the run was the tale that hit closest to home for Rachel.

Rosalia had become sort of a grandma figure in The Ghost's life. She was a nice complement to her father-figure in Kitteridge. She had Blavos and Justin, but they were more like brothers or annoying cousins. Darrenhoe had sworn himself to her in every way and she could truly appreciate that now, and in public if she allowed it. All those kisses had been nice, especially the long one at the end.

"What time are we out of here, doll face?" Blavos asked one of the interns. Not Rebecca, maybe Lindsey, could be Sabrina, or even the newest one who wore those oh so short skirts and knee-high boots, she would know.

"Hold your hose man, I'm almost there," called out Justin from his room at the back of the compound. He and Rachel had split rooms a while back and truth be told they both preferred it this way. Even if they were hanging about in someone else's bed these days, when they were back at their home compound it was nice to have the space all to yourself so you could make those big angel-in-the-snow motions under the covers and you never got accused of hogging. No one cared about your snoring and the fact that you awoke by inhaling the smell of dried drool on your pillow and got to stay in your own private secret den when you had separate bedrooms. Justin comes out and into the foray dressed to the nines. He couldn't control his style but it could be influenced by the number of layers he put on. For tonight's special party he had even borrowed Hasboro's fuzzy cape. That intern Monique would just have to get warm some other way tonight, and with her looks that wouldn't be hard for her to pull off. Justin looked great, he always did, Rachel knew. With the five layers he put on he was in a full dinner jacket and waistcoat, but no tails. They just got in the way of his dance moves and the frantic arms waving legs akimbo movements that you could roughly call dancing were another side effect of Puff inhalation. There was no music on this planet so your moves could be anything you could string together; you didn't even have to stay on beat. Darrenhoe wants the opportunity to spend some alone time with Rachel, to talk strategy for the slide races and all that he says.

"Sure, man, whatever. We both know full well what you're going be practicing," Blavos teases as they make their way out the door and off to the Transportation Center. Rachel had asked and Kitteridge was all too happy to supply four drones to watch over the little party. The gaggle of interns struts out after the handler and husband.

Profant greets Blavos at the door and motions him in. "Sorry, man, can't have the cane in here," the bouncer tells him as he is searched head to toe.

"Whatever," he says, "I will leave it at the coat check," Blavos tells the guy and walks into the DZ's largest Puff Party. Coffee is everywhere and the caffeine boost is visible in the white and enlarged pupils of the attendees. The place is packed full and the swirling fog from smoke machines fills the air as the laser-lights bounce around the room. A classic disco ball lowers from the ceiling as the spotlights hit and expose the dance floor. The entire place seems to break into motion, swaying and stepping to and fro. Justin and his throng of interns take up a full quarter of the dance floor and begin to whoop it up. The two in front bring out and share a 'first timer' right there on the stage and everyone around them seems to be inhaling and spitting up blood as they take in hits of Puff.

They had all been given a number and a ticket when they went through the front doors, don't lose it they were told. The symposium director had been calling out numbers over the loudspeakers and giving large black velvet envelopes to those who could provide a matching ticket. Fraud meant death, but nobody tried to fake a winning number tonight. No one could see what was inside the envelope, very important. No not even your spouse can look at it. Right this way and you can wait inside the VIP lounge, we have all you need for a pleasant stay. Yes, yes we really must insist on keeping you overnight. Your handler has been notified and we will get you to the track in time for the warmups tomorrow. Off you go the director sang.

"YOU HAVE TO FREEZE IT!" calls out the symposium director. He had just been given a note and the thing was still clutched in his outstretched left hand as he held it high overhead. He waves it back and forth and makes the announcement he has been asked to deliver. Anyone holding a black velvet envelope had been invited to try the world's first authentic cinnamon bun. The stupid maker was nervous and forgot the most important step in the recipe. The Life[x] tube had to be frozen overnight otherwise it melted into mush. Good tasting mush to be sure but choking it down without the crunch of cinnamon just wasn't a real cinnamon bun now was it? They wouldn't serve you that crap at Cinnabon, people agreed. After freezing it, apparently the makers had cracked the code and come up with a winner. They were rare of course, and too expensive to afford on your own, even if you were a high-stakes handler. Cinnamon buns were only to be gifted once every fourteen years. They couldn't be bought or earned; Lady Luck had the only say in the matter. But get a smooth envelope from a booth and you were in like Flynn. The media begs to get in and film the reaction, but only one reporter, some pimply faced kid from 23C, is allowed. He got first and exclusive access, do a good job and we might even let you smell it yourself. That was the best part after all was said and done, lots of things tasted like cinnamon and icing, and you could gorge yourself on icing from any old cake. The smell of the fresh baked delectable was enough to get you out of a warm and comfy bed. It was enough for even the StatStars to risk missing their races. If they were one of the few on this planet to eat and smell a cinnamon bun then losing it all would be worth it the thinking went. None of the winners complained as they were rounded up and shoved into the next room like cattle.

Hasboro and Rosalia saw Justin at the symposium and waved in his direction. Hasboro was subtle enough at first, but when he saw Victoria, the intern from 23U, he practically started to jump up and down as he called out her name and waved his hands overhead. She heard him and skipped right over, slipping her fingers between his and swinging hands with Rosalia on the other side. They liked hanging out with the interns, made Rosalia feel young and pretty, and Hasboro liked any excuse to cut a rug. His moves were classics he said, never goes out of style. And the girls agreed, giggling and fighting over who got the next slot on his dance card. Sorry, all full, he told the girls and grabbed Victoria for a twirl. The people watching was fantastic tonight as expected. And the party's bellies had grown full. They were stuffed from all the new Life[x] texture they tried. The taste was that of wet moldy cardboard and it stunk to high heaven, but they couldn't tell. The different recipes gave the rations a unique mouthfeel. It was fun to try them all but now Hasboro couldn't take another bite. Rosalia was still carrying around her second bottle of Moscato d'Asti, offering sips to all the other girls on the dance floor. The interns were a thirsty bunch and they were on bottle three right before bottle four arrived. It came complete with sparklers going off and sticking out the top. Eventually the older couple say their goodbyes and depart to rest up in their cabana, the final track event will start in just a few seconds. Their Bishop would do his final public couples slide and they had ringside seats to see him take down that final ring.

*

Blavos pulls back the curtain from the back room as the heavy smell of 'first timers' takes the air. There is enough Puff floating around that he can get just enough of the scent to draw him further into the room. He is motioned over to a large cushion on the floor by his own personal 'Puffstress'. Profant had assured him this place had the best hired help and would walk him through every step. Sure, dude, they will even do the ritual and get naked with you if you're into that sort of thing. No touching of course, but a little eye candy never hurt anyone, am I right? Profant wanted to know. Blavos isn't interested in anything she has to offer and doesn't even take the time to read over the extensive menu. He is of course interested in the 'first timer' because everyone always is. But he didn't have time to do both and didn't want to miss the scene at the VIP lounge. He motions his hostess over and shows her the vast number of credits slung at his waist in his large messenger bag. "This is enough credits to get me one of those black envelopes, I think, and if you're a smart negotiator there is some left over just for you. You can leave this place and never have to wipe another bloody nose again for the rest of your life," he convinces her. She slips out the side door and quickly comes back with her own handler. The guy makes it clear right away that he wants a cut or no deal. Blavos pulls one of Profant's tricks and pays for his Puffstress to give the handler his 'first timer'. The guy agrees as everyone knows a little au jus is good for the soul. The girl comes back with a black velvet envelope, but this one had a big blood smear on the back. Had she just killed somebody to get him a ticket? Probably but Blavos didn't care. He wasn't above a little bloodshed to get what he wanted. And what he wanted right now was to smell and taste a cinnamon bun!

Bishop declined Justin's invitation to the Puff party. He was still bothered by that guy from 23D's double-bladed sword. Why hadn't he thought of that? It bugged him. Sure the kusari-gama had been worth the training and he liked the crane style it implored, it worked well with his height and long arms and fingers. He wanted some time alone in the dojo, he was going to work on his nunchuck technique. The racetrack was no place for a long-range chain weapon. Here what you needed to get ahead in this race was a quick stiff hit up the head with a nunchuck, that was sure to knock a racer off course. Darrenhoe stopped by and they sparred for a bit, but then both turned in. They had been preparing for the events of tomorrow for years now, and they weren't going to let a little shut eye be the end of it all. They had come too far to walk away with so little. Bishop was after the win, not just for his own pride, but he hoped that the prize purse would be enough to get the three seats he needed for Tranquility Base; he vowed not to go without his mom and dad.

Kitteridge doesn't get the luxury of sleep. He spends the better part of the cold night moving back and forth between the Puff symposium booths and the racetrack hill. Both had to be able to withstand massive amounts of friction, movement, and weight. A few drones under each post wasn't going to cut it. Thankfully, there were drones aplenty at the Derby Days and he had been going around pairing all he could. In total he had one thousand and twenty-four drones spread out across the DZ. He didn't mind at all, Kitteridge thought it was his way to be useful, and pay some of it back. He couldn't give enough credits away, it seems. Blavos kept betting for him after he gave Rachel access to his accounts. More money is the last thing he wants and Kitteridge would do anything for more time with his daughter. That sputtering ROPU of hers had him worried. Everyone knew what that meant.

Blavos goes to the VIP lounge and makes quick work of the place; he is such a well-known handler that everyone wants to get a picture with him. They all tell him about their best Puffs and how excited they are about the cinnamon buns, I can't believe I won, the lady from DZ 23:M keeps exclaiming. They will all be given the same Life[x] ration and Puff tube, each in private, all at the same time. The Waster Kings wanted a true review from each of them and couldn't risk them influencing each other. The group of sixteen was quickly and efficiently separated and lead into their own private rooms. Blavos enters the room and begins to immediately undress because he knows the all-important ritual is the next step. Crucial to the process, man, they all had said. He strips down naked, except for his socks, she reminds him. His constant Puff companion had followed Blavos into the back room and helped him out of his clothes. She started to take her own clothes off but Blavos stopped her. Just let me lay my head across your lap and I'll be fine, he said and she agreed. She takes his hand in hers and lays Blavos' head down as she begins stroking his hair and gently scratching his head. The action causes the hair on the back of his neck and arms to stand on end and a shiver runs down and through his body. He likes it and lets her continue on for some seconds. It isn't romantic in any way but it calms him and prepares him for the trial ahead. He has been waiting and wanting a cinnamon bun his whole life it seems, but the fear of a popper had kept him away. Somewhat. It was obvious Blavos puffed from time to time. But he had seen the popper victims walking around the Transportation Center with their zombie-like stare and enlarged dark over-eyelids, and that was a sufficient warning not to try too much Puff.

"Are you ready for the ride of your life, sweetheart?" she asks him. Blavos is genuinely excited now. All the anticipation and years of good behavior were about to come to an end for both of them. She plans to lean in right at that critical second just as she jams the Puff tube into his hose-mod built just for inhaling Puff and simulating smells. If she gets close enough and fast enough she will be able to at least smell the cinnamon bun, she could tell Blavos had been cheap and his modification wasn't airtight, it would leak just enough. If it really is as good as they say it could be that would be enough. Even though she worked here, or maybe because she worked at a Puff house, she had never touched the stuff. Sure the little tubes tempted her, with their rainbow of bold pretty colors and vivid pictures, even fun to just sit and read the description of the experience it would lead to. "Not yet baby," he whispers back and closes his eyes. He hasn't felt this at peace since he started being a handler, maybe ever. But he was finally ready, but not before a quick and passionate kiss with his new mistress, stuck inside this little room with him while he takes it all in. She agrees quickly and leans in for the kiss wholeheartedly. A kiss was a great idea, no other way to get closer to the escaping Puff vapor. Like everyone she had been hearing about and waiting to smell something, anything, her entire life. And if her first and best time was to be here and now, with this guy and his still shiny white scarf that had 'Team Ghost, Team Bishop' embroidered on it then let's do this thing she thinks. If it were to be with a cinnamon bun she would kiss a thousand toads. And even though he was a bit older, Blavos was good looking, and thankfully he had left his pimp cane back at the compound that night, convinced by the intern Lindsey that it didn't make him look like a bad boy, but like a cripple. She leans in so far and hard for the kiss she pushes him back and lies on top of his naked body, except for the special nubbed socks he had donned for the occasion this evening. As their lips connect she jams the Puff tube in hard and the vapor explodes out into both of their faces, each of them getting a full sized hit. Their newbie senses are overwhelmed with the smell of thick cream cheese icing.

They are done smelling the Life[x] and begin to unwrap it ready for a bite. She had been so overwhelmed, just overcome by smells, tastes, and overall emotion that she forgets to take the now spent Puff tube out of the modified ROPU hose still in Blavos' nose. He doesn't know any better and inhales again in a deep breath to be sure and take all those wafting smells in. He takes in a massive lung-filling breath and he sucks in deep through his nose. She hears it and it registers in her muscle memory before her mind even recognizes what had happened. As a Puffstress one of her main jobs was to make sure the clientele didn't die. You had to turn them over on their side so they didn't drown in their own blood or worse yet double-inhale and take two hits back to back. This girl, still in her early years, had heard what could happen after a double but it had never happened to anyone in this house. The head mistress had drilled it into them and they always took the spent Puff tube out after the first hit. If you didn't the still smoldering crystals in the tube were almost certain to explode in a glorious face-destroying burst.

The spores in the tube backfire and shoot straight up the hose and into Blavos' nose. They burrow deeper and deeper in there as the heat melts his nasal cavity. She had been ready for blood, they all bleed. But not even his big new scarf was enough to sop it all up. A spore lodges in Blavos' lung and he clutches at his heart. It is all too much for his system and the girl rolls off him. Smoke begins to rise first from Blavos' nose and then his ears and eyes. The blood dries up from the heat billowing up inside him and comes out in thick black chunks. And just like that, all those years of wanting and resisting, are gone in a moment's temptation. He had bet big wanting to get enough credits to go to Tranquility Base this time. When he heard about the VIP invites he knew there was a better spend for his fortune that he had amassed backing Bishop in the DeathMatch. And death and bloodshed aside, Blavos had succeeded and smelled a cinnamon bun before he died. If only we could all be so lucky Profant wondered out loud from the private room next door. He heard all the commotion and could smell the burning flesh from his neighbor and suspected what had happened. It wasn't until Blavos didn't show up for practice the next night, and Justin hadn't seen him since they got to the Puff party, did everyone make the connection to the news story about the burned body of one of the VIPs. Apparently even the chosen few are vulnerable to a double hit popper explosion.

*

Kitteridge finishes the setup at the convention center and makes his way back to the compound just in time for Rachel's pre-practice Life[x] rations. He had promised the night before that he would be there for her, he liked to do her purity test, enjoyed watching the bubbles pop and had a knack for guessing if it were going to be a good one even before he tore it open to inspect the color, always a good litmus test. Darrenhoe and Justin are there, one of them well rested and the other just barely hanging on, still busy trying to whip the dried blood away from his upper lip. Bishop joins them after a bit and shows them a few new nunchuck moves he had been working on. He hadn't slept much, just a catnap between practices here and there, but the adrenaline would carry him on. Today was a big day, but tomorrow was set to be even bigger. Tomorrow his ROPU would dry up, all four hundred and forty-one million seconds gone, and he would have to pass his Interval. Rosalia, plus lots of other PTBers, had done it, and he was pretty sure he would as well. But if he was honest with himself, and he was very open and honest in his interview at lunch, he even fought back a tear or two and choked up when asked what he thought about his partner's sputtering ROPU. "Woah, watch it with those things," Rachel yells at Bishop as he brings a nunchuck around his waist and almost takes her hose out of her nose. "If you touch me with those on the track I will shove them so far up your…"

"Yeah I got it, take it easy," Bishop says and goes back to lay down before warm-ups.

Hasboro and Justin have been messing with his new toys or the 'cloaking device' as he kept calling them. Don't let anybody see them and don't touch them till the last lap right before the hill. And only then if someone is close. I don't want to spill the beans on this if we don't need it to win. Justin figured if he didn't get a seat to TB he would just hang around and make a fortune in credits selling his new devices to other StatStars. Rachel says she still isn't sure about it and Kitteridge agrees she doesn't need to cheat to win. It isn't cheating, Justin retorts back, having done his research he was ready for this avenue of resistance. Bishop was fine with it, but he was sorta show-boat like that, I mean who carries around nunchucks anyways?

Warm-ups go off without a hitch, like they each had done this the hundreds of times they really had in all those years of practice and qualifying events. They were StatStars and had this part down cold. Cooling off period over, all the racers line up on the track. For this Derby Days they actually have surprised the contestants and the audience with three tracks all side-by-side and then converging into a single track on the straightaway before the loop. There were just too many sliders to have them all on the course at once, unless they turned this hallowed race into a roller-derby beat down. Blavos is nowhere to be seen and Justin is the one to deliver the news. For some reason Darrenhoe seems to take the news of Blavos' death the hardest. Darrenhoe had become a bit of an abstinence evangelist and took pride in providing protective detail to the only StatStar on the circuit who didn't Puff at least occasionally. Blavos would listen to him preach on for hours and it really did help keep the handler away from the stuff. For a time. Puff, and even the harmless 'taste testing' was forbidden fruit for Darrenhoe, and as far as he was concerned anyone within earshot. Darrenhoe should have gone with Blavos, he was supposed to protect his team, that was his job. Rachel assures him that Blavos would want to be alone, or at least with a nubile young Puffstress, for the event. There was nothing Darrenhoe would be able to do to save him and he knew that. It was hard for all of them to get their heads back into the race ahead. Warm-ups worked out a few kinks in the timing system too, for some reason they didn't get the memo that there were going to be three races all running simultaneously. Keep track of the fastest times for each track and winner takes all.

Chapter 22

Derby Days Slide Race

There is a four hour window while the betting booths are open. They close ten minutes till post and the CDCG agrees to a one hour delay, more bets still coming in on the slide racers. It was always a mad frenzy because unlike the other Derby Days events there were no mid-race bets accepted. Pick your person and make your line before the gun goes off or step aside, chump. The booths all close up and the lights around the track go off in unison; just the overheads and glowing lines along the track begin to shine the way around each twist and turn of the magnetic track. With their special racing boots the contestants will reach up to a hundred and eighty-three miles an hour, protective helmets and polarized eyewear were a must on track. Each racer, starting from the lowest track and then up to the top, takes their place and lines up their maglev boots. The special boots, are custom made and fitted to each StatStar's prized, and no doubt insured, foot. There are guard rails about three feet high that light the track and they are just high enough to bounce off of in order to get those higher rings. These guard rails weren't electrified like in the screwdriver races, but they did pack a nasty little six-to-eight foot blow back if you so much as breathed on them or looked at them wrong. Bouncing off of the bumpers to grab a ring was standard part of the repertoire almost as much as bouncing your opponent's face into it as you push over them. Or another fan favorite was to bounce them off the rails and over the top into the dust below.

All the contestants start to hover and get ready for the fastest maglev race of their life. The resulting hover of all the racers causes the resting dust to kick up and briefly shields the racers from the cheering crowd below and around them. The stadium seating towers are even higher than the top of the loop near the end of the track and there is not an empty seat in the house tonight. Never was at these finals, not to be missed for anything, well except maybe cinnamon buns. But just like the betting booths, yes even the automated ones way far in the back with the crummy odds, the Puff symposium was all sold out.

The hometown favorites, the fresh-faced couple from DZ: 23X, had just finished their second lap around and were into the short curves at the first turn of the dreaded third lap. After three laps on their own track the racers start to enter and converge onto the rest of the singleton track. Paxton leans way far over to the starboard side of the track and slides her right hand along the ground for support. She zooms right past her nearest competitors, they were dumbfounded as she passed, locked hand-in-hand trying to take up as much room on the track to prevent any passing. Paxton and her teammate Laughlin had beaten their personal best set at the last qualifiers, and someone has won big. No mid-match bets at the booths didn't mean no mid-match calls or payouts from the sidelines. The lines and odds might be set already but bet away, big momma. This was Derby Days at 23X, you could bet on anything you wanted, so long as you had Puff, or credits, those will do too. The guy goes off in the third row and the field splits apart in an instant, everyone surging forth, pushing and shoving, trying to make room against the pulling tide of people and for the lunatic. The guy makes it to the track refs and when they reach out to validate his tickets crazy-eyes becomes suspicious thinking they want to take his ticket and claim the booty themselves. There is only one way out of this, one way to secure the ticket so no one but the CDCG betting booths could validate it, only one way to be sure. Bulge-eyed dude chokes down the ticket, eating every last dry bite. He takes in the gravity of what he has just swallowed, lowers his head, and holds his hands protectively over his belly to make sure the ticket stays safe until he can fish it free. Man makes the long and lonely walk of shame to the bathroom; he'll have to wait a little bit longer till he's rich.

The ground tide, a huge, massive swell that caused the Platform to dip and rise a good fifteen feet, had settled in and was making its way across DZ: 23X. All the buildings were unscathed as the wave rolled through, their construction requirements and the municipal codes ensure they could withstand the perpetually moving Platform of this planet. The movement wasn't a problem and even the fans and racers knew to move with the tide and swayed back and forth like tugboats on a turbulent sea. But the fans nearest and actually underneath the tracks, those elite and select few who had scored the really expensive seats directly underneath the transparent Platform, best view to see the track, could really get a sense of the speed, they said. "Trust me, been doing this a long time, and under the hill is where you want to watch The Ghost shoot by. Buy them now and I will throw in some seats and a 'first timer' for you to enjoy the show with." Good seating indeed, if you like to see the track hanging above you come crashing down on top of you. The tide change had been so dramatic that the hill pushes up at the bottom of the slope until it flattens the little fanboys below, with their cheap looking VIP badges. It all happens in an instant, track goes down and then back up, then back down, and settles right into place. The drop of the bottom from the track causes all sorts of noise and interference, giving the tried-and-true magnetic levitation boots hell. All the contestants feel it before they can see what happened. It was like stepping down two or three flights of stairs all at once, unawares that there was another rung to assist your descent. Half the peloton of racers tumbled into a jumbled mess of arms and legs, broken helmets, and twisted, shattered protective glasses.

Rachel wasn't paying attention to all the commotion and blasts past Laughlin. He and Bishop are busy fighting it out over a lousy extra credit ring only easily accessible now because the ground had dipped and bottomed out. An easy mark Laughlin knows as he leans down to swoop it up just in time to grasp the ring credit, he and Paxton were still in second and just one ring behind Bishop and The Ghost. Now he lunges forward just in time for his face to break as Bishop connects with his nunchuck across the now shattered cheekbone. The blow was strategically and expertly placed just under the lower edge of Laughlin's helmet, right in the blind spot from his glasses frames; poor racer never saw it coming. Bishop had been practicing that, he and Darrenhoe had taken turns practicing knocking off Justin's stupid hat since the DZ: 23C rallies. The nunchuck blow Bishop hands out to him, complete with a signature Bruce Lee "Woah!" and nose thumbing, causes the guy to have to spit out a few teeth. Laughlin has to shake the pool of blood and spit from his ROPU hose. Paxton joins in the fray, wielding her twin sai blades, the ninja weapon with the trident shape and two guarding points on the hilt. She unsheathes them from under her cape, perfectly balanced out in front of her as she begins to swing those two-feet long swords, jabbing and prodding Bishop and Rachel back. DING! The butt of one of the blades hits the rings on Bishop's hip and sends the last hard-fought credit flying away. No one is worried about the official race time at this point, everyone from the refs right down to the other racers had stopped to see what would happen to Rachel. If she could continue on, could cross the couples slide finish line hand-in-hand locked in time with Bishop, they might just have a chance still. Paxton and Laughlin are now two rings ahead of them and the high one at the end of the race was worth three. Fresh from clearing their next time gate Paxton wheels about to face off with The Ghost. Bishop follows Laughlin as he goes back to fighting for rings in the roundabout. Always the fierce competitor, she tells her partner to "Suck it up, cupcake!" as she maglev bounces off the guard rail behind Bishop who was safely tying off that ring he had stolen from Laughlin. But he was fiddling around with nothing, he had forgotten they just stole it and he was two rings down now. He had to catch up but needed to get Rachel moving first. They had to get moving because if they didn't cross together it didn't count. Bishop hadn't seen it when the ring rolled away and neither did Rachel but Laughlin's maniacal laugh had given him and its location away. Bishop was all too happy to take it away from him again. He had been spinning his nunchucks waiting for something besides rings to hit with it. Paxton twists 180 degrees mid-air and calls out to Laughlin, "Formation Delta. Number seventy-two starboard, not port!" And Bishop lunges off toward the roundabout and its pit filled with rings. Had he remembered the moves from practice and moved right the first time he would have been able to roll out of the way but Paxton's sword hilt hit him right in the nose, splintering it open. It might be bleeding like a mother but at least it wasn't broken. Justin reminded him to be extra careful because they both know what a broken nose can do to a man's blood supply. And if you don't have any blood left, you can't race.

The Ghost isn't worried about rings, times, or even credit. Well, there is one timer she is worried about and it isn't the one on the jumbotron. She has bigger problems to think about, particularly 441 million seconds of them. Her ROPU keeps sputtering and finally gives up on the third lap, just one more to go. She didn't think her Interval was till tomorrow just like everyone else. Kitteridge must have seen the panic in her eyes or saw the stoic look as she prepared to face her demons and flung the ROPU hose from her mouth. The audience gasped as they saw her actions and time seemed to stop all around them. Justin, Darrenhoe, and Kitteridge are standing by. They wait on the sideline medical tent for the agonizing Interval. Her noisy ROPU had been announcing to everyone that her crystal juices were drying up faster than anticipated. Bishop comes up to her at the start of the straightaways where she is now kneeling on the Platform, having stepped off the track completely just then as he and Justin join her. Darrenhoe is busy keeping the crowd, and those perky and annoying little Interns, at bay. Justin and Kitteridge nod and her husband starts to livestream the event. Hasboro and Rosalia had come up. She takes Rachel's hand in hers and begins stroking her hair. It had been glowing and flowing red tonight and Rachel looked just like a Viking and she liked how fierce it made her look as her locks flowed around the track. Hasboro put up a fuss about the camera and how close the crowds had pushed in. "Let her breathe," he hollered out.

And Rosalia responded, "Oh lord, if she can."

Rachel was very worried about time now. She had just three minutes and thirty-one seconds before she would have to face her ultimate test. No amount of practicing could prepare her and she couldn't qualify her way out of this event. At most she had learned to hold her breath for over three minutes: just take a big lung-filling breath first. Once that was gone would her final exhale be her last? It was something she wondered late at night. And since her blasted ROPU had started sputtering Rachel had been having lots of late nights recently.

Three minutes left and the CDCG make a surprise announcement; "We are temporarily opening the betting booths for some rare, but justified, mid-race betting! Step right up to your nearest betting booth and meet your credit dealers!" Everyone who was anyone took the new odds. Double or nothing on any previous bets, no matter the amount, if she survives her Interval. Yeah man, all she must do is make it to four minutes and we are rich men! Everyone has been watching the social media streams and knows she has been holding her breath and practicing building up her stamina for this. The Ghost prepared for everything and she didn't believe this Interval of hers was the one test for which she couldn't study. She wasn't going down without a fight, Rachel swore.

Two minutes on Kitteridge's watch timer and Justin's social media broadcast has a little clock in the top right to confirm they are in sync. Rachel is calm, she can do this, she thinks. Bishop looks cool as a cucumber, chilling under his vented cape. He needed the extra airlift under there if he had a chance of making that high ring he told Justin. Bishop didn't care what it looked like or what it did for his image and stats. Bishop was pissed enough about Rachel's new outfit for Derby Days. After the scars on her stomach had healed into those little moons Justin insisted that she officially adopt crop-tops as her new about-town uniform. "Pair them with a shacket if you must, but you better well match that thing with some of those cute little heeled booties, the ones with the wings on the heels yeah good idea, Auletha," he tells one of the interns over his shoulder. "Cute booties, or I am making Darrenhoe revoke your late slide-outing privileges, my blushing bride?" Justin was teasing Rachel, but she knew he was serious about the boots, Justin never joked about fashion. He was right that it would look great, but then again she had no control over whether or not she wore a jacket of any kind. Clothes took the shape, color, and style of the occasion. And nobody could control it. Come to think of it, Rachel had commented to Bishop about clothes the last time they tested their Life[x] purity together. "Have you ever noticed how that intern Rebecca, yeah the one that looks like Rosalia sometimes and is always harmlessly flirting with her older beau Hasboro? She is always wearing that red shacket." Justin, always quick to defend his harem, told them both that she was just trying to cover up any Puff stains from the blood of the bender last night. I know you can control some of the look by how many layers you put on, but how does she keep the same things and in the same color night after night, Rachel wonders out loud.

Fifteen seconds disappeared in a flash and Hasboro takes Rachel's other hand and puts something inside it. "Just in case," he whispered. She nods, eyes still closed tight, waiting for the remaining two forty-five to go. It had been Rosalia's idea and she convinced him that even though he always did the ritual in private people knew about him and his dandelions. "Remember that girl, the little one, Tammy, who had stowed away in our compound?"

"Right the one from 23E."

"She sees you harvesting dandelions one day, and those yellow streaks across your face don't exactly scream Puff head," she tells Hasboro one night after another successful picnic. Hasboro had been tending his large field of dandelions in private for years. He rotated the crops and always had a harvest to attend to. Lately he even had Kitteridge's drones taking care of the vast underground caves where the fields flourished. Hasboro had a surprise this last time at their picnic and they enjoyed a peanut butter and banana sandwich. They shared it and savored each bite. The thick substance, Life[x] was the perfect simulation for anything gooey: caramel, marshmallow fluff, and especially creamy peanut butter. You could pay extra to smash and grind up some crunchy red rings and make the peanuts. Moscato d'Asti works pretty well at clearing the cake from the roof of your mouth Hasboro found out that night. But the southern delicacy was a hit and they swore to make it a regular part of their picnics.

Waiting for another two minutes to pass on the clock is driving the audience absolutely looney tunes with excitement. "You can do it, Rachel!" Kitteridge cries out because Justin had encouraged him to rally the crowd's support for her. The audience is happy to oblige and picks up the chant. They don't have the betting booths or the CDCG dealers to worry about or distract them. Eyes are all fixed on Rachel, crouching just under the hill bottom, with Bishop at her side. The media announcers call out by name and role everyone in their entourage at ringside.

One minute and thirty-eight seconds slide by like a short track racer, 247 mph was the current Derby Days record. Three girls in front of the track's turn argued with the interns about whether The Ghost was gonna make it or not. If she doesn't, the drones will kill off her teammate, Jessica informs those within earshot. "You're stupid, Jess, the Platform would swallow them both up like some Kraken from the depths of the ocean coming up from deeper than hell."

"Either way, if the Interval doesn't go Rachel's way Bishop's done for," said a competing high-stakes handler to intern Lyndsey. That handler, some big wig from DZ: 23L, she has been enamored with his cowboy hat ever since she met him and follows him around. The guy pisses Justin off something fierce, but he has a big follower count and always does a share-for-share when it mattered.

Sixty-eight seconds are all that remains for Rachel as she takes this planet's final exam. Paxton and Laughlin have left the gathering of other racers on the far side of the straightaways, this is where the Jumbotron keeps replaying Rachel's hose being torn asunder in 4K slow motion. Laughlin kept batting down Paxton's hand as she tried to get Rosalia's attention.

Thirty-five seconds is all that is left on Kitteridge's timer strapped strategically to his wrist, his left one; Rachel's dad was left-handed just like her. Which was just one more advantage for the pair. Bishop could jump a full eighteen important inches if he posted off his right boot and hit the guard rail. If he did that just in time and Rachel bumped up against the opposite rail. "We would hit each other right in mid-air. Great plan, Bishop. Did Justin put you up to this?" she pressed him.

"No and then you boost me even higher, right up to that sneaky little ring."

"Just don't step on my face and make me look like some patsy. I'm not your pawn you know!"

"Relax, we've practiced this," he reminds her.

"Yeah but you did hit her in the face with your cape that time." Kitteridge had been standing by watching. He knows Rachel had been nervous about the couples slide. She had the short track and had made it her own, the long race was no picnic either, but Bishop always picked up enough rings that even if she didn't clear all the gates he could go back and touch them as he caught up to her with the rings safely attached to his hip. They would wave to the cheering and adoring crowd and then hold hands outstretched high overhead in victory as they broke the ticker tape and crossed the finish line. The only thing needing a photo finish would be Bishop's gleaming eyes and the thin scar on Rachel's face declaring for everyone to see that they had won Derby Days and it was true, the whole StatStar team would be going to Tranquility Base, or at least that was the plan. If she could last the final Interval.

No one blinked twice at the fact that Kitteridge was close by for the Interval, Rachel was his daughter, they reasoned. What father wouldn't want to be with his daughter, hold her close, and reassure her that the dark and scary things in the night wouldn't get her. The dilithium crystals spores might lodge into her lungs and burn her up from the insides out. But there was no boogey man or anything like that. But when drone 63 hovered over and onto the track people definitely took notice. Drones were most certainly not allowed on the track and couldn't even be seen at Derby Days at all. The Collective sent their sweeper drones to clean up all the discarded samples from the Puff symposium, and the Transportation Center, rather these days it went by the more accurate 'Bloody Nose Station', needed cleaning regularly with a thoroughly strong astringent and a lot of bleach. Nobody could smell it anyways and it was a better cleaner than vinegar. Trust me, been doing this a long time.

As her alarm kept wailing on Rachel could hold it in no longer. With exactly eight short seconds left Rachel opens her now bloodshot eyes. She refuses to cry, but Bishop is taking care of that, enough waterworks for the whole team to stay high and dry. "That sputtering didn't mean anything honey, you'll see." Rosalia tries out her act of little harmless white lying, she had talked with Kitteridge about the supposed miracle he saw those fourteen years ago when she had been born. She had breathed without her ROPU and was about to show the whole world if she could do it again. Before, the Collective drones had been standing by with a fresh ROPU and gave her the hose pretty quick. But he knew what he saw and leaned into kiss Rachel on the forehead. See you after the finish line he said.

Rachel pays attention to 63 now. The drone has crawled up and is nestled right on her chest. With only five seconds left it starts a long low and slow beep, followed by another in a slightly deeper tone. Hasboro had been meditating as part of his daily ritual for years now and he knew guided box breathing when he heard it. Drone 63 walks Rachel and the entire world watching through Justin's livestream as they imagine a single ball of air in their belly. They count to four in unison as they inhale a large ball of air and hold it in their lungs and chest as it makes its way vertically up and into her chest. They hold the ball tight up there on the right side of the lungs for another four count. Four more as the powerful ball of air moves to the left across the front of the chest, all the while expelling out through your mouth. Filling in through your nose for another four count and the ball slides down the left side. Hold for just four more and then the ball slides back right to the starting position as you take another breath and start the rotation again. The whole ritual makes a large imaginary square. It is a breathing, focusing, and relaxing technique used by the US Navy Seals back on Earth. Only Rachel doesn't exhale, she has been holding her breath tight in her lung this whole time but still follows the imaginary ball. They had done this a few times in practice. Hasboro motions everyone to sit down and at least three hundred people all go down in unison and sit crisscross applesauce just like good little kindergarteners. They are in rapt attention, quiet except the barely audible murmur from the crowd. "She can't breathe without that hose" and "Nobody can hold their breath for that long" filled the night air. Rachel catches on as Rosalia starts to squeeze her hand, keeping time with the sounds coming from 63's little stereo speakers. One thing Kitteridge had learned from his time on the tech support force was how to upgrade an audio component or two. Without music there wasn't much use for a subwoofer to amplify but Kitteridge liked the sound it gave to liftoffs and landings. Plus it was easier to tell 63 apart from the over one thousand drones he had under his control now. Not sure what he was going to do with them all or if they could learn many more new tricks? The drones had taken to maneuvers on their own now, inventing new formations and adapting on the fly. Kitteridge just made sure they always had something to do. If left idle they liked to take turns circling the family owl and taking its control board over. They were after the wings and apparently liked how high they could get. Kitteridge's drones would make an amazing Kamikaze battalion if they ever needed one.

63 scares the Interns, especially Lyndsey and Amy, when its long extended metallic tail begins to lower out of the drone's body cavity. Kitteridge guesses what is about to happen and worries more for his drone than for Rachel. All 63 wanted to do was give her a fresh load of dilithium crystals and to top up her ROPU so she could breathe again. 63 knew the protocol and had been keeping Kitteridge alive for years, ever since he left home all those long and cold dark nights ago. Thankfully, the family owl knows its mission too and flaps its mighty wings, beating back the drone with big swooshes of air. Kitteridge and the owl manage to hold off 63 for good this time. Kitteridge just stands up and let's go of the rotator control board he had ripped out and leaves it still dangling by the power cable. The drone can operate just fine with six blades and I will fix it later he thinks to himself.

Kitteridge simply says, "Hey, dummy, she doesn't want one right now. Thanks but maybe later. I'll just keep this safe in here for you, little buddy." And he taps the satchel's side as he drops the dilithium crystal he took from 63's pincher arm where it was holding it crablike high over its head. Oh, not now, maybe later you say? 63 seemed to understand and backed away to join the rest of the drones, hovering and recording all the action for the bookies that had approached Kitteridge with the deal. "Forget about your credits, and I for sure don't want your Puff," he told the CDCG guys. "Just make sure my Rachel, what? Yeah she's the one they call The Ghost. Be sure the cameras get her good side. No man are you crazy, people dig the scars."

"Let's have some close ups of those cute belly scars," the little fellow in the back pipes up. Kitteridge agrees and sees 63 take formation as the leader of the pack of drones filming the action.

It has been an agonizing, on the edge of your seats, popcorn still hanging from your lips, beer spilling on the ground as you watch, four and a half long minutes since her ROPU stopped sputtering and finally dropped a big load on the bed. Rachel had taken another breath, mostly because she was afraid that Kitteridge's drone, the one he calls '63', was about to propeller blade her face off, but also because she had heard the alarm and seen Rosalia bury her head in Hasboro's cape. She didn't need to see what was happening to know what was about to transpire. The Ghost choking on her own steaming hot blood would be enough to tell Rosalia all she needed to know. Rosalia held out hope that the betting lines and odds were right. Of course, she put some credits down on it, a lot of them in fact. Even though Hasboro tells her that their place is here on this planet and not Tranquility Base. "We need to continue to live here past

Tranquility Base so we can raise and train another generation of StatStars." Hasboro can't take his eyes away from Paxton. Hasboro thinks he knows what she is trying to do and he keeps motioning her on because he thinks it is a really good idea right about now. Who knows, maybe the ROPU will kick back to life? They never do. Paxton shakes her hand away from Laughlin who goes back to counting the rings stored on his hip belt, still three rings up on Rachel. Not that it would matter anyways, Paxton thinks. If you can't breathe you can't fight. And this final Derby Days race was going to be an all-out slug fest; Bishop had practically guaranteed that when he brought out the nunchucks.

Bishop sees Paxton edging forward and is suspicious as the very last thing Rachel needs is for this bird to start talking some smack. He can tell from the expression on her face, the furrowed brow, downcast eyes, and the single tear welling up in her left eye, Paxton is looking for a way to soothe Rachel, not taunt her. Maybe not so much Rachel, as soothe her own unrested soul. Paxton's Interval will be tomorrow, just like everyone else. And if she could pass that then she would make it on to the rocket home. No not DZ: 23N but her new and improved home on Tranquility Base. It would be a long ride but she would have Laughlin. The two were one of the only StatStar couples that were actually married. They had grown up and trained together all while living together. Sadly, Paxton and Laughlin were both sterile just like most StatStars and without a child to raise they focused all their time on training for tonight. Bishop would be swallowed whole and disappear in a cloud of dust if Rachel doesn't pull through tonight, Paxton knows. At least they don't have to worry about their seat assignments. Everyone suffers an Interval; some make it and many more don't. Those who do aren't always whisked away to TB possibly but seats were limited. Now in the past most of the StatStars had earned a spot, especially those athletes that managed to literally keep their noses clean. Even then, and Paxton and Laughlin had been angels on the smell front, even preferred their Life[x] rations straight and gooey right out of the tube. Paxton shakes free from Laughlin and he goes back to join the whispering, wondering, gossiping, and inevitable side wagering going on from the rest of the racers. A few had slowly continued their slides, taking little baby steps up the track in the right direction with some of the other more timid competitors relenting a step back when Justin called them out. Paxton grabs Rachel's ROPU hose still dangling from the now spent and busted backpack container. Paxton takes it in her hand, blows through it to clear it out, and then wipes it clean. She tries to put it back in for Rachel's but the fierce competitor shakes her head back and forth, preventing Paxton from trying to insert the tube into her nose. "I can do this." Rachel closes her eyes. She needs to believe now. Kitteridge had told her about her first Interval and how she passed. She wasn't sure about that, no one had ever heard a screaming baby around here.

The Ghost takes in one more gulp of air and holds it a surprising and crowd pleasing thirty-eight seconds as they all count down. Her lungs are bursting, stretched out beyond capacity, but she can't find any oxygen in all that multi-breathe volume of air pressed down inside her body. She lets it all out in a long slow release and 63 beeps a sliding scale down along with her. The sound somehow soothes her and she closes her eyes. Nothing to do but wait now and we all will see. Her Interval is long over and it's time to see if she can breathe on her own.

She takes in a baby sip, just a swallow of the near freezing night air. It pierces her lungs and makes her cough as she involuntarily brings her hands up to her mouth to stifle the resulting cough. Big hacks come out but no chunks of lungs, blood, or little black dilithium crystal spores. At least they weren't coagulating yet, which is saying something. If you failed your Interval it was the crystals that got you, or rather their extreme heat. Ninety-eight point six degrees is normal for the human body. It can stretch a little, a fever of a hundred and four is alarming, but no need to rush to the hospital. If a fever goes unchecked and continues to raise the internal core temperature it can be life threateningly bad. At a certain point, and medical science either hasn't tested it or refuses to publish the results, but after some seconds of cooking from the inside the body gives in. Blood runs backwards in your veins and starts to drain from your eyes and nose just like it did when you hit your 'first timer'.

First one done and no worse for wear, so Rachel decides to take another little breath into her fragile lungs. 63 is all up in her business, inserting a thermometer into her mouth to monitor her, checks her pulse, listens to her heartbeat with its ultra-sensitive recording equipment, and the drone even monitors her pupils for dilation while it listens to her lungs. "BEEEEP," then a slow corresponding "BOOOP," and 63 instructs her to breathe deep through this next part, the little sips of oxygen aren't fooling anybody.

Hasboro spins around and starts high-fiving the crowd and hugging strangers. Kitteridge is on one knee and quickly rises to join the celebration. Rosalia had already snuck out from under Hasboro's cape where she had been hiding her eyes. She thought Rachel had lost the battle, but was worried that war was just beginning when she heard that first cough. Once she saw that Rachel was all right, stable, standing and breathing big take-ins in time with Kitteridge's metallic pal she was relived. Rosalia made her way off to the betting booth; that was traumatic and all but this woman had credits to pick up. Rachel had passed her Interval, showed the world just how special she really was, not just some 'roided up jock. Bishop is still counting rings because he knows there is nothing he could have done for his teammate. And truth be told he was a little on edge thinking about what would definitely, most surely, happen to him if she couldn't breathe without a hose in her nose. The poor athlete can't stop beating himself up for that lost ring at the bottom of the hill. He should have blocked the attack with the sais. I mean come on, does everybody have a ninja weapon nowadays? He thought the kusari-gama had been cool, and was stoked when Justin showed him the videos of the kids practicing in the streets with their homemade ones – Life[x] ration cans tied with butcher string or a lamp cord to a tennis ball. The bigger, meaner, kids would cut a little slit in the tennis ball skin, break the heads off strike anywhere matches, and then throw them. The little projectiles would burst into a glorious flame when they collided with another solid object. Nothing says fatal death cage like flames. Too bad we can't use any projectile weapons, Bishop thinks, as that would be an enhancement to my new go-to weapon. Tonight Bishop had been going to his trusty new nunchucks and Laughlin was tired of getting beat upside the head with them. He swore that his next opportunity he was gonna snatch those things right from Bishop. "Who's all Bruce Lee now?" Laughlin had rehearsed in his head and was now just waiting for the right opportunity.

After several minutes, the track heated back up. The gal in the front at the end of the straightaways saw Rosalia heading for the betting booth before she even looked up at the Jumbotron to see if Rachel had passed the Interval. One girl finishing up on track three just maglev spins on her snazzy boots and takes off, clocking in a cool 153 mph with her partner, helmet down and face up in the night's fog causing little water droplets to billow up and run across the lenses. The extra-loud buzzer goes off signaling that all the racers are going again, some still finishing their third lap and were about to hit the straightaways. There were other racers still duking it out on the other two tracks.

Physically and emotionally The Ghost was fine. She was right as rain and ready to slide. But mentally Rachel was another story. She had listened to Kitteridge's story about her birth and decided right then and there to believe it. She could breathe without her ROPU. Just to be sure she had been practicing holding her breath. She was pretty good at it, but apparently not even close to her and Hasboro's old friend Mandy, that little girl could hold her breathe for over seven minutes if she wanted. Needed it to suffer though the contractions of her baby, that thing almost killed her. After deciding she could do it, now she was going to breathe without a hose, Rachel was sort of Zen about the whole affair. Mostly that is, it was hard not to think about it, everyone was talking about it and the fact that the DZ's final test was scheduled for tomorrow. It was enough to give her pause to reconsider her position on the whole matter. Hasboro must have sensed something like this was coming so he motions to Rachel beside him, opening and closing his hand as his lips form the words "Open." Hasboro closes the distance between them and whispers "Just in case." Rachel opens her hand and takes the small leather satchel from its lanyard. She had seen Hasboro wear this before, but he never talked about it and she never saw him open it. She tries to see inside, pinches the sides of the pouch and tries to peek in, but it is too dark and she can't see what it contains. She sticks her pinky finger in the satchel and as soon as she brings it out knows what to do. The deep yellow color stain on her finger tell her this is the stuff that streaks Hasboro's face. Not sure if it's for courage or something else, and definitely not aware that this dandelion powder mixture was what kept him alive. Rosalia had her doubts about the recipe, she had been living PTB without a working ROPU for all this time and she was fine. She wasn't fine and Hasboro didn't like to remind her when he saw more and more fine hairs in her brush on the bathroom counter in the night. The side effects were creeping in slowly but surely. Hasboro is glad she is gone for the moment. That means she was collecting credits. No doubt it would be enough to spring for a can of chips. He just hoped she saved enough for them to get their seats. Hasboro sure wished he could keep his promise to Rosalia and take her there. It didn't matter if they had to use her high-stakes gambling credits to get there. They would finally be together, everywhere, and always. Rosalia said she didn't need all that, they could be together forever right here on DZ: 23S. Deep down he knows she doesn't mean that. She had missed her last chance and would do just about anything to try again.

"Wait, I see another ring over there, or at least I think I do. Ima gonna go check it out," Bishop says and quickly hovers over, leans down to examine a dark corner of the track, then unsatisfied with his reconnaissance, Bishop rejoins Rachel and tells her it's time to go. "If you are up for it," he warns her. He might have to do something underhanded but he could get at least enough credits to tie Paxton and Laughlin. That would force an overtime match, whatever that turns out to be. Bishop and Rachel knew about the surprise rule – if two or more teams finish with the same time and extra ring credits, the same combined score, there will be a surprise and secret event. One that guarantees high payouts and awesome death, something special for this Interval's Derby Days, the CDCG organizers had thought when they devised the little rulebook twist.

All the racers are back on it now, sliding and bumping each other through the straightaways. The lanes are so close on this section of the track that if you falter and bump one of the guard rails you will ping pong back and forth between the opposite rails until all your ribs are broken and you're dead. At 213 mph a racer was pretty sure he was going to make the loop de loop, and they all pumped their legs in unison as they tried to pick up speed. Some loser, last-minute entry from DZ: 23O, this guy pulls a hammy and goes down in a heap. The not-so-graceful approach of 23O ensures more than a few other racers go down as they get caught up in the mess on the tracks. The sweeper drones come out of nowhere and physically push and shove four guys right over the edge.

Paxton and Laughlin are in the lead now after having overtaken the pair from 23L. All three tracks are still going but one only has a single racer. Cancel that, Justin tells the livestream audience. The Platform just swallowed up the final remains of that pair. Track two has fared a little better but after the last ground tide has twisted on itself and now resembled somewhat of a Mobius strip, an impossible geometric anomaly puzzle, made famous on little black and white line drawings from a little tear-off desk calendar, usually sold at a mall kiosk staffed by some foreign woman. They were always situated somewhere within sniffing and whiffing distance of a Cinnabon. Laughlin has managed to get all the rings but one, the high one at the end of the track. Rachel is catching up speed now, 223 mph. Her polarized glasses have all but glazed over from the fog mist, but the scratches and cracks from the little spores congealed and floating in the air made it especially hard to see.

While they all know the loop is there, most racers have built their own version to practice on or they wouldn't have qualified, the loop de loop still leaves the faces of some racers looking surprised. Maybe because of the sheer size of it. At fifty-five feet tall it towered above the track. The second track's loop was pressing against the track above it, when the Mobius strip twists two full rotations the other way, wrapping it up counter-clockwise. Paxton, then Laughlin, and Bishop now proudly sporting an extra ring he had snapped up and away from Laughlin at the end of the straightaway. Bishop zips right through the loop, maintaining close levitation as he slides over, up, and then he's upside down, slides left, down, back on his boots sliding upright now and he peels through the other end of the loop. Bishop hits a new speed record of two hundred and eighty-seven miles an hour. He decides his glasses are worthless and throws them aside. "Bad move, honey, did you see that?" Hasboro asked Rosalia.

"Badass, keep 'em off, man!" Justin throws out and the interns all agree.

"Badass!" A reckless move like that and if one of those crystal spores gets jammed into your eye then you're gonna have to start shopping for patches. Going blind is the best you can hope for if you get a spore in your eye. That's what the glasses are for, Blavos had told them over and over again. Blavos had liked it when they wore the 'look at me' glasses off the track. She hated how he was right when Justin told them how much it had boosted their stats, especially Bishop's. She motioned him to come on, she had passed him in the loop when they were both upside down.

Laughlin pauses on the side of the track and pushes for Paxton to go on. She has a few more time gates to clear before they try and hit the high ring. Unlike the other extra credit rings you didn't have to take this one and bring it back to the refs at the end of the race. Not for the final high one, way up there above the top of the track. All a racer had to do to get the two point credits was just tap it and not even with your hands, anything will work. "So long as you don't throw anything at it you are golden. No projectiles remember," Rosalia had told Hasboro and Kitteridge one day after practice. Laughlin can't believe the count, he thought he was ahead. But sure enough the number on his belt matched the Jumbotron. The big screen also displayed the captured ring count for Bishop and the two rivals were tied.

Bishop screeches through and gets a cheering round of applause from the crowd as he turns starboard and leans way down, way past forty-five degrees from parallel, purely for show. His mid-race stats jump a little for the pizazz. On the track's surface his slide-gloves give off huge sparks as he maintains his balance on the razor's edge of magnetic levitation. The Ghost has the gall to even pat Paxton a little on her ROPU as the pair slides into the lead. They approach the final turn before the hill and the entire course bursts into glowing orbs making huge waves and throwing off dust as they zoom along the racecourse. The tracker lights have been triggered and the crowd alternates screaming "My ten to one is green tonight" and "The purple one, that's her!" The murmur that comes up from the fourth row, the bald fat guy who has clearly had too much Life[x] these Derby Days, is the first to notice the missing pair.

"What color is the Bishop," the man asks his wife.

"How many times do I have to tell you, Scott, it is just 'Bishop', not 'The Bishop'. She's 'The Ghost', he's just plain old Bishop! How many times do I have to hammer that through your thick skull Scott?" His old lady is letting nothing hold back because she is tired of all his questions. It is more than enough actually for her to have to listen to the constant drum of her brain aching for smells. She just couldn't listen to his insipid voice any longer and decided to try and figure out what was going on herself, she began to make loud motions to the crowd around her. The media saw the commotion and cameras zoomed in on the woman.

"Yes, Kate, just where are The Ghost and her Bishop? We haven't seen them since loop de loop," the mass eyeballs and ears glued to their consumption devices all agree. We can see their life sensors are still tracking a pulse and they haven't crossed the finish line because the big race clock on the Jumbotron is still ticking away.

See? I told you! Justin is beside himself; the little cloaking devices were working beautifully. He takes all the credit and immediately starts a new livestream where he shares all the stats and details about the device. To hell with secrecy he tells the audience, these things were going to make him a fortune in credits, Justin thinks. His interns-turned-call-operators are standing by and taking preorders. The fact that he can exchange the credits from any sales into Puff for him and the ladies in his throng doesn't escape him. In fact, Justin should be thanking the interns, they were the ones who lead him into the 'Hall of Miracles' at the symposium. But really it was Rebecca that had spotted them and suggested the plan to strategically swipe them. It hadn't cost the vendor a lot to shut up shop that day, Justin made sure Lyndsey paid the man out well. The extra-long kiss she left the inventor was just an extra juicy tip from Lyndsey. For some reason Lyndsey was the only person in the entourage that Justin would allow to carry and handle the credits for the team. She wasn't the brightest, quite dull in the brains department, but was a wunderkind when it came to numbers. So he let her handle the finances, among other things she and the interns did for him.

Paxton, as fierce a competitor as Rachel in her own right, is not to be outdone and reaches for her waist belt, behind her back and under her cape. She hasn't been using weapons on the race much yet, but everyone knows what is coming when she brings her wrist forward, spinning her hands and the sai blades she had retrieved in each hand. Paxton could never be seen at a presser without her deadly weapons. Paxton reaches out with one of the blades high and drags the other in a semicircle low. Both blades connect, but the bottom one slides off, I guess that pleather was good for something Rachel remembers as she plays the race back in her head later that night. Things definitely didn't go according to plan in this event but they sure did give the Derby Days slide race watchers quite a show to remember.

*

"I can do it, I don't need to see it, I can feel it in the air," Bishop screams through his hands as they cover both his eyes but only his left will be permanently disfigured after tonight. People close to the track would later tell the story this way; they could actually hear the sparkle from the dust crystals as Laughlin threw them in Bishop's face when they begin to take the hill. Without his protective eye shades the scatter shot did its cruel task. One of them with the barbed tipped end of the crystal's surface exposed burrows right into his left eye. The only thing Bishop sees can only be described as 'white hot'. Bishop and Laughlin had been sliding side-by-side, too far away for Laughlin to reach him, but well within range of the mercilessly accurate nunchucks that flew out from Bishop's side. They connected somewhere on Laughlin's leg. If you can't stand you can't fight, was the clear reasoning behind the strategy and it seemed to be working. Laughlin had slowed noticeably and the big digital displays floating above for all the crowd to take in showed that the racer had fallen three seconds behind the pace time, one that he set in the qualifier back on 23R. Laughlin should have gone down many blows ago but just kept getting hit from the side and he would lose his balance and kilter off toward the guard rails. He kept coming close enough to riffle his cape, but would stumble back up, shift, correct, and then back up. Bishop was making Laughlin look like some novelty blow-up punching bag that bounces back and forth from the hits. Laughlin was always a smug faced clown ready to get popped up against the side of his dumb plastic blown-up face again. Laughlin kept pumping his legs and Bishop kept pumping him with crushing blows to his opponent's ribs, cracking more than just a few in the process. Apparently this guy didn't miss leg day either, Bishop thinks as he takes his offense upstairs to the midsection. If you can't breathe you can't fight. A few times he couldn't catch himself and leans back upright in time and the bumpers gave him a shock blowback, Bishop was all too ready to meet his face with a wood block to the nose. It was true Bishop loved to break noses apparently and nobody loved it more than Profant. That creepy old dude always made money when somebody bled at Derby Days and there was always a lot of blood from a broken nose.

As they begin the slow crawl up the hill both racers bury their heads down and focus, big thighs and calves pumping as they try and maintain speed up the long slow incline. Coming down will be blistering fast and if you didn't practice the timing right you would speed right under that crucial ring. But the hill was an event all by itself. In fact up until a few Derby Days ago it was its own separate race; lots of side action would take place mid-race as the climbers shifted position, moving up six only to slide back two, the twenty minutes long hike up the side of the mountain leaving plenty of time to keep the CDCG betting booths open. Bishop decides another volley of beatings from his sticks-tied-together-with-a-thin-chain tool. Bishop's new chucks were quickly becoming a fanboy fave, surpassing even the now legendary kusari-gama. After watching more of the spin, twirl, swing, smack exposition from Bishop and the involuntary participation of Laughlin as his pugilistic assistant, the crowd started to refer to Bishop as 'Ninja'; "Ninja and Ghost, Ghost and Ninja!" Either from exhaustion, Derby Days had been going on for many nights in a row now, or from sheer arrogance, Bishop wants to make sure that his nunchucks are turning at the right revolution per second, getting enough speed and momentum. He lifts his deadly apparatus high above him. The weapons were once simple farming tools reserved for beating down rice and sugar cane in the fields of Asia. It is impressive to watch the artistic display of spinning and twirling from Bishop and the crowd loves it. However it is also a clear and unmistakable signal and shadowing of his intent. It is a move that no racer, especially not someone as in tune as Laughlin, would ignore. Laughlin sees it clear as day and duck-walks under the blow. While he is low Laughlin scoops up some dilithium spores into his gloved hands and as he comes up on to his full stride you can tell for the first time just how tall Laughlin really is; he towered a good eighteen-inches above Bishop and bested his teammate Paxton by just slightly more. The Ghost had been complaining to Justin that he was too tall and that it had to be against the rules. At that height, with that arm's length reach, the guy was gonna grab that last ring before Bishop, and Paxton didn't have to even be around to give him the boost that Bishop would need. Blavos had been pushing the pair to do a couples slide ever since Rachel found out about his silent backing of Bishop. Blavos thinks he finally got it through to her at their last practice that she was stronger as a base than Bishop and he needed her to give him that little bit of extra oomph. She had said she might do it but only if they needed the points. And starting up the hill, with a tie race, and everything on the line, if there was going to be a time to truly make this a couples skate, and not just two teammates whizzing bye and loosely holding hands as they beat the time, then it was at the Derby Days finale. Here. Tonight at DZ: 23X. She just wishes Blavos could be here with them to see it. The old handler always had a soft spot for the couples slide.

The force of the dust throw was doubled by the maglev blowback that arched off the track and the spore burned a neat smoldering hole right through Bishop's eye as it lodged into his retina, just above the optic nerve. Laughlin shook his head low and redoubled the pumping motion he had already put into his legs, he needed to dig deep to beat The Ghost up the hill. Paxton was all high and mighty about racing, talked about the purity and the speed. But Laughlin was more of a realist, he had seen Bishop's new crane fighting style at the last expo and knew that he needed something of his own up his sleeve in order to compete. It wasn't pretty, but he was happy with his improvisation on the course. Sure, later on Laughlin might feel bad about Bishop, hard not to notice what you did to the guy when he stumbles past you on the Platform somewhere, blind and gazing away into white nothingness. Paxton vowed she would never forgot his actions on the track tonight. Laughlin was all steel resolve, he had done it and would do it again if he got the chance, might even shove some dust into the guy's nose or throat. If you can't breathe, you can't fight, and no one can breathe with dilithium melting your innards.

Laughlin knew he needed a clear runway in front of him to

build up the necessary speed in order to snatch victory. Bishop never falters as he brings his hands up to wipe away the remaining crystals from his now useless eye. Finished wiping he then lowers his head and begins pumping double time himself. He doesn't need to squint any more, his eyes are protected now following the attack. It happened so fast and the dust particle had gone in so deep that Bishop's over-eyelids never had a chance to even flutter much less close over and protect his eyes. They didn't cooperate like Hasboro's or Kitteridge's did, those dark opals forever closed against the night but still allowing the viewer behind them to see. The inner eyelid had closed just slightly too late; the dilithium buried deep enough to cut Bishop's cornea and render him permanently blind in both eyes. But the inner eyelids closed tight to prevent further damage as the crystals burrowing deep in the back of the eye were stopped by the helpful mutation to protect sight on this harsh planet and to preserve the eyes against the dilithium poisoning and its horrible side effects. Rachel sees the underhanded incident on the Jumbotron and immediately whirls around back over to help him, crouching down beside him in the center of the track. The seconds are put on the big stopwatch and she doesn't know what to do. Justin had them prepare a plan, if one of them goes down then just forget about the rings and hit those time gates. You're fast enough and you can go back and drag your partner across the finish line if you have to. Rachel starts to slide her hands underneath Bishop to lift him up, she can do the time gates with him on her shoulders, she knows. But as she leans in and gets close he says it again. "I can do it, Rachel, I know this track better than I know myself!" So he is that cocky huh? She doesn't know why but she isn't surprised and helps him steady himself as they both maglev rise back up into racing position. He can't see but doesn't even need to see to do his part. Well let's see about that, she says to Bishop and then mouths it over to Kitteridge who has been watching from the start of the hill climb where he had moved the drones. Kitteridge had to make sure nobody else got crushed. That was bad for his new burgeoning 'friendly drone helpers' service he had informally started.

"POP IT OUT ALREADY!" some young hooligan called out from the audience near the track. All the DZs had just watched the probably should be but technically not a disqualified dust throw and now all everyone could do was watch them in living color on the big screens overhead and all around the stadium seating. "POP! POP!" came the uproar of the crowd. Bishop's eye was useless, clearly, just jam a finger in there and pop that sucker out, and every one of us that bet on dismemberment would cash in. Disfigurement or even permanent injury like blindness was a sucker's bet, but a lot of suckers went home richer that night. Everyone always got antsy during the hill climb. The anticipation of the resulting free fall on the other side of the hill was just too much and the crowd swayed side to nervous side at the contestants' orbs glowed in the darkness. Except for Bishop and Rachel's light which was pitch black now. Bishop's eyes, oddly enough both of them even though the injury had been just to the one, both of his eyes had cast over a ghostly white pale. He looked more like a Ghost than Rachel. With her skintight pleather uniform, cropped top and high cut shorts and paired with thigh-high maglev boots she looked more like a Go-Go dancer. But again, Justin had been right, not just about the sex sells part and everyone secretly likes scars. No he had been right in insisting she wear the skimpy thing. When Paxton had shot at her with the sais the first one glided off and even the other blade just barely snagged and tore a little rip in the top. Had her clothes been any looser, or flowing and casting a cool silhouette for the cameras like Hasboro had suggested, then that knife attack would have hit its mark. Sliding nude around the track was frowned upon but Rachel liked the competitive advantage of not giving her opponents anything to grab on. The fact that bookies took bets on the chances of grabbing something, or more than that, did little to bother Rachel so much as it did Kitteridge. Even if it did protect her and give her a slight advantage no father liked to see his nearly nude daughter up on the giant video screens for everyone to ogle over.

The Ghost helps her partner up off the track base and they hold hands as they hover up again just below the fog. As they slowly begin to build up speed they overtake some of the lesser competition, their eyes are set on only one thing, the glowing blue orbs lighting their way and allowing the onlookers to follow the blazing fast action. At Derby Days the sight of those glowing athlete tracker beacons as they made their painstaking and lactic acid inducing ascent up the one side and the corresponding reward of watching those same lights slide down the other side and over the finish was what it was all about.

"Come on, come on!" Rebecca was chanting out loud to herself. She had been the one to see the devices and convince Justin they could be put to good use. She wanted to see what they could really do and by this time, final lap and midway up the hill, the time was as good as any she knew.

"Wait! What? Where did they go?" the entire bleachers let out a gasp and hold their breath, peering anywhere and everywhere looking for Bishop and The Ghost. They were right there, center track, passing 23J invisibly on their right. One moment the two skaters from 23J are doing everything they can to stay in tight formations up the slope, and the next moment another team is using their tight strategy against them. Staying in a thin single-file line might be good for wind resistance and eliminate some drag, but it also made plenty of room on the side of the tracks for someone to bumper slide right past you. And that is just what Bishop and Rachel do here tonight.

More cries of foul and concern from the crowd and everyone decides that the best thing to do is watch the Jumbotron and all eyes rotate up. The missing contestants are still up there and judging by that fancy graphic in the corner they have a chance at winning it all, the ring count is the same amongst all top three racing teams still in this. A little graphic in the bottom right corner shows the outline of the track and a colored number indicating each racer's relative position around it. All eyes are transfixed on that infographic, on Bishop and The Ghost. Their reassigned race numbers now just hovering inside a black circle have gone from way back in the field to third place as they pass another team in the shadows. The little toy devices from the symposium are working and finally in full swing now. The crystals, when powered by this device on their belt, expand and begin to swirl and hover mid-air due to their ultra-light weight. Once they collect enough crystals it creates a handy little cloud of its own, completely hiding you from view but still allowing you full movement to do their evil deed unnoticed. When Rachel learned about them one night over dinner after practice she had a lot of questions. And worries, she had a lot of those lately. Was this the right way to win, she had wondered? What other surprises await us at the bottom of this hill? She felt bad about potentially using the things at first and had told Justin she wouldn't do it. If Bishop wanted to use his that was okay, it would probably help him wrestle away more rings in the roundabout pits. Rachel felt all she needed was raw speed and for all the other racers to stay out of their way. But he insisted on both keeping them on. If only one of them had a noticeable bulge from under their cape it would draw attention. If they both did everyone would just assume it was on purpose, some style thing that the garment had decided was a necessary last-minute change, just to look your best for Derby Days. It worked and no one asked about the little bumps under their cape fabric.

Lots of fast moving glowing clouds of crystal dust and then two pitch black figures of encased racers zooming ahead, zig zagging around like no one sees them, come from behind and overtake their next rivals in line toward Paxton and Laughlin. They had catapulted ahead as the audience was all abuzz trying to figure out what happened to the two anticipated winners. Bishop and The Ghost were nowhere to be found on the track, which is exactly the case because the resulting effects of using the device kept them undercover. So long as they stayed quiet they could come and go whenever and however they pleased within the protective effects of the cloaking devices under their belts and kept safely hidden under their capes.

Paxton is the first to figure it out. She knows the Jumbotron keeps tracking Blavos' pair as they make their way ever closer. Laughlin is still busy counting his rings and watching out for new ones. Paxton knows there is nothing left to do but stay in her own lane and focus on the time gates. So long as she kept those clear they were in a good position. Laughlin can grab the high ring with no problem given his extended arm's length, and Bishop knows this all too well. Justin and his interns had taken it upon themselves a few qualifiers back that the best way to motivate their champion was to tease him about how tall he was, or wasn't when compared to Laughlin. It didn't even take Tina long to start in on the hazing, the mean-spirited little one that recently joined the group, loaned by one of Profant's associates from DZ: 23H just for Derby Days. It is not like the ribbing could actually release some chemical agent that would encourage localized bone growth, but the placebo effect seems to have kicked in; after a few rounds of jesting from the ladies on the sidelines Bishop had added an extra eight-inches to his max vertical height. It still wasn't going to be enough distance so that he could hit the ring and he would need the boost from Rachel for sure. But could he even find the ring? His white-veiled under-eyes had obscured most of his vision because Bishop could only see shadows and faint movements. The spore had lodged itself deep inside his eye socket on the left side; the dust would eventually work its way out. The exposure would no doubt begin to poison him from the inside out. Tonight would be his last race, if not his last night on this planet altogether.

"Whatever you do just don't put this guy in charge of naming if I fail my Interval tomorrow. Modular Drone Services? You gotta be kidding me, Kitteridge, that has to be one of the worst names for a business! Even the acronyms on business cards sounds like some sort of long forgotten and cured muscular skeletal disorder." Justin was beside himself, a constant verbal outpouring of every possible different name for the drone construction and operation outfit that Kitteridge had put together over these last few years. Derby Days would have gone on just fine without them. The Collective and the Waster Kings always saw to a good show. But Kitteridge's little team of drones had been busy all along the floating tiered track. Construction up against the rising and falling final hill, none of that would be possible without the drones. A lot of people around the DZ had been suspicious when he first showed up and many still are. There was a growing concern amongst the citizens when he started pairing more, and then even more, drones. People quickly came around when Kitteridge started, and kept, using his drones for the good of others.

"There is some wacko with dark over-eyelid shields going around paying YOU his own credits to let him do something that helped you or made someone else's life better?" People sought him out now, including the Waster Kings who were all pestering Kitteridge on the side lines. The runners were now cresting the hill and we couldn't have more crushed audience members, bad for business. CDCG briefly considered opening a line and letting people bet on the overall body count at the end of Derby Days, not your standard number of racers left, but a new bet on crowd deaths was an interesting, and tonight a very lucrative, wager. But sanity prevails, with a body count they might as well just put up a bounty, some genius had tried this before, no doubt the same idiot in the back hall of the CDCG headquarters that brought the idea back up to the group. The plan seemed like a good one, a new viewing opportunity and a chance to encourage audience participation: always a big money maker. The continuous vertical pressure and pounding from the force of the racers' maglev boots had been swaying the track severely, but it held.

Years later and all the analysis, research, active and passive simulations, and re-enactments would all come to the definitive conclusion – The Ghost and Bishop were entitled to the high ring and that there was nothing differently that Rachel could have done. All the recounting of tonight's Derby Days final event will include a detailed blow-by-blow of her mid-race Interval, no one was paid out after her sputtering ROPU was discarded and she was still breathing. Or at least she was breathing well enough without her own ROPU hose pumping purified air into her lungs through her nose. Most people had bought insurance and the carryover rider so the overall betting field momentum didn't swing that much between the losers and winners bracket.

Paxton and Laughlin's glowing dust cloud showed the crowd right where they were, both by the matching color's icon on the video monitors high above, and they could see the shiny fabric tape that stretched across the track, a sort of intermediate finish line being broken. Paxton leaned forward just a nose, hers was clean and unbroken, Laughlin's looked like a messy omelet centered in his face from all of Bishop's attacks. As the top-of-the-hill tape breaks, another timer goes off to track just the split time for the downhill blast. After the grueling twenty minute climb up the hill the racers had a hair-raising one and a half mile slide down to the finish line. By the time the racer's had made it to the top of the long hill they had slowed to a crawl, one to two mph. But as soon as the tape breaks the lead racers bend forward and begin their slide down. The dark, unlit, and uncolored cloud of dilithium dust that came following right behind Paxton was about to catch up. The cloaking devices had continued to obscure Rachel and Bishop. They were working a little too well though, the third and fourth place teams had pumped and pumped and managed to get within striking distance, or more accurately within cloaking distance. The effect from the devices was intended to be calibrated and customized to the exact dimensions of the wearer. The crew hadn't stuck around the demonstration booth to hear this part. She swiped the units and ran as soon as the guy turned around to get his slide clicker. The uncalibrated mechanics were propelling out a nice little hiding hole that gobbled up the nearest six other racers. The crowd was beyond confused. It looked like the dark dust cloud was beginning to pick up speed as it started to pour down the hill and was gobbling up and snuffing out the other racers. Maybe that's what happened to

Bishop and The Ghost, people wondered? They were still on the boards but could not be seen on the actual track. Everyone decided that the dust cloud was just another surprise, an obstacle of sorts that the racetrack threw at all the racers equally. CDCG agreed on one thing, people could now bet on whether the cloud would catch up and swallow Laughlin and his teammate, both still in the lead.

Bishop was gliding on pure instincts now. He could see nothing but big lumpy white shapes quickly moving all around him; the same dilithium ravaging his skull was protecting him from the view of the other racers. Rachel was happy about that at least. Seeing how close the race was still would have put Bishop on edge and he doesn't jump as high when he is nervous. Once the cloaking devices worked and clouded a racer they couldn't even see a few feet down to their maglevs. Rachel was right next to him and they had already started to hold hands. It was Rachel's idea and she reached over to take his palm in her gloved hand. She knew he was strong and could handle the eye damage and still make the ring, he was that good. As he squeezed the blood out of her hand in return she could tell he was scared. She gives his hand a little 'nice to meet you' shake and squeezes gently three times, reassuring her teammate that she is there right beside him. Bishop feels the pressure, returns the gesture, and the crowd sees them both surge forward with renewed energy. They don't know the places but their burst brings them right up beside the third place racers with Paxton and crew just a few slides ahead.

Laughlin has nothing to do now but coast, try not to stumble and hit the guard rails, and post when he first sees the glint of the ring. Any sooner and he will jump right over it. If he waits too long he will slide right under it. "White Ninja!" The crowd cheers a homage to Bishops' new look. Bishop calls out, but she can barely hear him over the sound of air and crystals spores flying by as they reach near maximum speed. Bishop really isn't at all that much of a disadvantage. Not really when you consider how fast these racers are zooming down the hill; the racers themselves can only see the same patterns and shadowy moving shapes that will plague Bishop the rest of his life thanks to Laughlin and his dirty tricks. Bishop, just like all the other racers tonight, glides by more on faith and instinct than visual navigation and sight line reminders of when to lean and when to cut. The Ghost and her teammate were sliding on pure faith – they must give in to the speed. No human being was meant to go over three hundred mph unprotected and the little crash helmet and glasses do very little to protect against the elements and hazards of the racetrack.

"MARK ONE!" came the sideline call out from Justin. He was the official coach and race captain now that Blavos was gone. Profant insisted that because he had backed Bishop all along it should be him in the race director's chair for the whole team. At that Darrenhoe had enough of the arguing back and forth and said he could allow Profant to champion the team, more publicly now than ever before, but he wouldn't stand for anyone but Justin to call the shots on the track. Justin knew better than anyone just how high the stakes were tonight. Profant had leveraged all he had on the Bishop and The Ghost to win, he kept reminding anyone and everyone within earshot. He had made enough on the side action that he would be whole tonight no matter what happened. But Derby Days is about getting rich, not about getting even. Rich enough to buy your seats to Tranquility Base.

At the sound of her husband's voice Rachel jumps high and leans hard right to hit the timer gate a quarter of the way down the steep descent to the finish line, just like they had practiced.

She hits the gate and the scoreboard reflects it. So far Rachel had managed to hit all her gates and Bishop had collected all his rings. Especially the hard won ring at the bottom of the hill he manages to scoop. Or rather he nunchuck whacked at it and then swooped in to snatch that all important ring. The ring count is tied and the racers make glowing dazzling colored dust clouds as they continue their ear-splitting trajectory.

A lot of StatStars are Puff heads and that is a well-known fact on this little planet. Most Puffed all season long, drying up a few days for a qualifier just so they could barely squeeze by and keep their stats and rankings high. There was a contingent of racers who are on the track tonight and these competitors have no interest in rings, timer gates, or even the supposed goal of crossing the finish line. These fools, a group that calls themselves the 'Derby Days Party Posse', were just here for the hill. Not every StatStar was addicted to the search for new highs like smell and taste. But they all were addicted to speed, and nothing generated the momentum like the hill. This group gets lots of attention and betting action as these people zoom past, into, and around all the other racers. The Posse is content on pure chaos and ever faster speeds. They bring up the back of the pack, more a roaming and hovering party, than serious contenders. The Posse takes out the middle group of racers, a glorious clashing of bodies, helmets, and the force of mid-air magnetic levitation collisions as boots become weapons.

More than a few of the Posse had adapted and made a certain reptilian inspired move of their own and the crowd jumps to their feet when some guy screams out "TURTLE POWER!" Three guys and six gals all form a tight formation. They go down and take one knee, then both, and then they pirouette their legs in big crowd pleasing swoops of light and dust, and stop face up on their backs, legs and arms held up in the air as they rock back and forth like a happy baby, feet grabbing ankles as they wait to be pushed. Bets are paid out quickly, there have never been so many 'shell bombers' on a Derby Days course before. A big guy, clearly the leader of the Derby Days Posse, goes around to each little turtle, snug on their back of their shells. He grabs each by the legs, being careful not to come too close to the maglev boots or they will blow back with such force as to send them all flying off the track. He wants the maglev force but not yet. He gets all the little human-turtle look-a-likes into a tighter ball, and then he tells the participants to put their legs together, all in the middle at once. "ON MY MARK... Five... Four..." But he doesn't need to continue as his part is over and the audience takes the baton and continues the countdown. Right at one all the racers in their shells bring their feet into the middle in one motion. The resulting magnetic confusion, the universal and guiding force that literally and physically holds this galaxy together, those extreme opposites all try and jam together and "BOOM!" The thunderclap echoes across the auditorium and the at-the-ready pyrotechnics and huge fireworks burst into the night. Someone had tipped off the CDCG about Turtle Power and all the shell bombers that would do damage on the course tonight. The shells zoom down the track and take out a few racers about to hit the halfway mark. The remaining turtles all spin wildly out of control, some bouncing like pinballs off the bumpers, colliding with and destroying the chances of other racers crossing the finish line. The pack leaders are on edge and not just because with the proper form and technique, lean in just far enough forward, but not too much, and you were easily over 375 mph by the time you hit the mid-point of the hill's descent. More Posse race down the track and most are dedicated to trying to fly off the track.

Maglev is great, fast, efficient, and easy on the joints. But you could only hover a few inches, maybe a foot or two, off the Platform before things became too unstable and shaky to balance upright. Floating, a human skill that eons of evolution still haven't gifted the species with, wasn't good enough once experienced. The human mind always wants more, bigger, better, faster, higher. Flight was indeed possible with this speed, and those hardcore racers who dedicate themselves to the Posse are wearing special winged suits to extend their hang time. As the Posse's dust cloud crosses the mid-point down the hill these racers all stand up tall and extend their arms out in a shoulder width 'T' as they puff up the wings of their flight suit. Projectiles weren't allowed at DeathMatch, but as you screech past 413 mph, enough to counteract the forces of gravity here, flying racers could be a deadly accurate projectile as it practically melts into the back of a competitor unlucky enough to be in front of the flier. Longest hang time was a bet, as was highest flight. These bets were big, partly because they had to pay out the handlers who would lose their racers forever if they achieved liftoff because they would simply fly straight off the back of the racecourse and into the depth of the Platform for an up close and personal tour of what lies below. Achieving flight was great and all, but everyone knew it was a suicide mission.

The event's participants have all fought bravely up till this point, but just about three quarters of the way down the hill, they reached maximum velocity and flight was possible. Lots of the Posse floated away up into the night air and the crowd is beyond pleased at the display. The turtles have all finished their slides now and as predicted everyone has gone over the edge. But going out in a blaze of glory on Derby Days was the entire point for them. More fliers take off and wreak havoc with the flow of things, bumping back and forth and generally just blocking the traffic lanes, not like at four hundred and seventy-eight miles per hour lane lines mattered. There was just track and speed, stay on the track and get more speed. Rinse and repeat, cross the finish line, and then Tranquility Base.

"MARK TWO!" Justin screams into the mic. He knows that Bishop hates to be reminded where he is on the track but Rachel needs the reminder, they all know. Bishop and Rachel, still holding hands, make their way to…

"JUMP PORT!" Darrenhoe yells and the team follows the instructions without question, narrowly missing the Posse member careening right toward them trying to take them out for good. If turtling your way to glory wasn't for you and the idea of taking wing sounds a little too scary then the Posse relegated you to either timer gate duty, or role of 'deep slider'. Keeping balance while hovering and also screaming down a giant hill was quite the challenge indeed as you had to fight the force of forward momentum and gravity constantly pulling you down. Lean just a fraction of a razor's edge one way too far and you were reduced to a spinning body of arms and legs flaying out as you spun out of control; death was certain if you faltered. A fate that is easily bypassed and was proven to make you go even faster, just lie down and slide on your belly face first. Most of these deep sliders had specialized coating on the front of their suits to ensure they glide even faster. Boots, ankles, and calves were all good targets for a deep slider to take out – but the big payouts came from a knee shattering collision. The third place racer's lights go dim signaling a deep slider had connected. The remaining slip past, right off the edge of the course.

Rachel managed to avoid the deep slider who just missed her on the starboard side of her boots. She couldn't see clearly at this speed and didn't know just how off course their little evasive maneuver had sent them. She squeezes Bishop's hand and yells that she can't see the timer gate, although in retrospect his vision isn't going to be any better, even in perfect conditions. "There it is," he says as Bishop raises their enjoined hands and motions a few feet ahead just slightly off course. He can see it by the shining and dazzling display of the time gate guards from the Posse that are there poised and ready to make sure no one gets to hit the gate. If you don't clear a gate you have to sacrifice your position and go back which eats up even more of your precious time. The alternative and route most racers take is to just skip the gate and take the fifteen seconds penalty. But Rachel was maniacal about hitting all the gates and she was the only racer to hit every gate in all the Derby Days qualifiers. One of the interns had rolled her eyes and said that wasn't a big deal, but when there is a group of three or four Posse members guarding it was another story. Five guards stood watch over the wayward gate as Bishop leans in and takes them closer. All guards have their light-swords out at the ready, and some just even hold them up in random locations, swinging blindly at any passing shadow. Two guys take position on each side of the gate edges and block it with their light-swords held out still like a baseball batter trying to bunt. Bishop sees them and gives Rachel four squeezes from his hand; she was clearly thinking the same thing and resolved to let the gate go bye uncleared. She knew Paxton and Laughlin were ahead of them now and the ring count was tied. If they hit all their gates it will come down to whoever can touch that extra credit ring first. The bunt works as two racers in eighth place are beheaded in an instant, they had seen the guards and had decided to split the gate and each take a side. But the crouching Posse members hiding behind the front guards simply stood up, raised their arms, and off with their heads. A wave goes through the auditorium. Both of cheering and applause, and of actual audience members standing and raising their hands in a series of subsequent motions, the wave rips through the crowd at the big double-beheading payouts to come. Rachel and Bishop take the fifteen second penalty and miss the chaos at the last gate.

The rest of the field doesn't matter at this point, it is down to just these four racers and the crowd is loving every second of it. It is a good thing that team Blavos doesn't need their cloaking devices any more as they peter out and the racetrack takes over giving Bishop and Rachel a pleasing deep purple glow. Paxton and Laughlin cut a glorious sky blue, although here the sky is black, not like the effervescent wispiness of the atmosphere on Earth. All four racers are past the three-quarter mark of the descent downhill. "He can't see, he can't see! How can he race if he can't see... there's no way you can find that last ring blind!"

"At those speeds none of them can see, ma'am." Rebecca holds her hand to try and comfort her; Rosalia is beside herself. Hasboro and Rosalia had been right up close to the action and didn't need to see it on the big video displays to see the dust throw into their son's eyes. Hasboro was the one to explain the white under-eyelids to the group because he had become a sort of resident expert at eye variations around here.

"Just watch and wait, my love, he knows where it is," Hasboro assures her, and himself.

"Let's finish this thing and go get you a doctor to check on those baby blue eyes of yours," Rachel tells Bishop through her earpiece.

"Just get me close to Laughlin and then you out race Paxton," Bishop commands.

"Close to Laughlin? Why? Just get the ring!" Rachel

exclaims but Bishop assures her, and Justin listening on the teams comms channel, that he has a plan. Paxton is just a few pushes ahead of Rachel and with her newfound mission she easily catches up. The four racers are side-by-side as they approach the critical jump point. Paxton and Rachel on the outsides and Bishop and Laughlin battling out for the middle lane.

"MARK THREE!" comes the call from Justin and all his interns in one musical chorus. Laughlin is focused on the ring constantly scanning the sky above him looking for an imaginary marker to tell him to jump. He finds it and makes the leap, briefly squeezing Paxton's hand as he flies up. He jumps straight port and hits the guard rail bumper but he is ready – Laughlin puts both feet out to that side and bounces a good eight feet into the air the other way as the bumpers blow back against the maglev's opposite polarization. Bishop follows suit and Rachel buries her head into her chest and gives it all she has. Paxton follows suit but The Ghost has her by a nose. "NOW!" "Jump Bishop, JUMP!" And "…well I don't know either, man, why isn't he jumping?" comes up from the sidelines. Bishop hesitates just a final second before leaping in the same direction, but instead of hitting the bumpers with his boots, Bishop swings out his nunchucks in a glorious arching flow, like water jumping from pool to shining pool in some outlandishly large display meant to distract and soothe the tired shoppers. The weapon blow works, and Bishop jumps just as high as Laughlin. The force of his nunchucks against the bumper catapults Bishop right into Laughlin but that was all part of the plan. Bishop kicks down with his left foot and then his right in a quick one-two stomp. His left connects with Laughlin's head knocking him unconscious, and Bishop's other foot punches right down on Laughlin's ROPU, sending Bishop flying up and over the top of Laughlin. Bishop deploys his nunchucks at the ring, gives them a whirl around to build momentum, and then lets them extend out toward the ring. They shoot out across the sky and make contact with the extra point ring, pulling Rachel and Bishop ahead and into first place. Paxton is oblivious to what was happening up above her and Laughlin's precarious state; he is free falling now unable to balance his levitation while he is still passed out. He drops lifeless the thirty or so feet to the racetrack surface and lands with a thud. Death on the track paid out triple in the final lap of the race so few complained. Paxton leans ahead sure of her victory in the slide race part of the event. Rachel pulls up and ahead right as Bishop lands, extra ring secured to his hip with the others. They join hands and cross the finish line together.

She didn't need to give him the boost after all. Bishop knew she would do it in the end but he found a better way. Later on, during the post Derby Days press event, when all the reporters wanted to know why she didn't boost Bishop for the final ring, Rachel simply had to tell the truth, "I was ready and willing to do it, but he just didn't need it, he found another way. Blavos had wanted us to win this race together and we did!" The Ghost and Bishop later talk about the race, replaying every twist and turn on their way to victory. Bishop had the same question as Justin and the rest of the crew; would she really have allowed Bishop to boost her like that? Obviously, the boot-stomp to the head and bounce off her ROPU wouldn't be the same approach he would use but they both agreed Laughlin had just made an easy target dummy and even better ladder. They both knew the risks and that is why he told her he didn't want to take the chance. "Besides, kiddo, that scar is badass enough already, don't want to risk it," he would say with a wink any time it came up later.

Chapter 23

Derby Days Short Track Race

But Derby Days isn't over, not just yet. All betting payouts were suspended while the CDCG reviewed the tape of the event. This was standard procedure, especially in the final event. It was rare for a match to be overturned and had only happened a few times. The CDCG finally makes their ruling with a simple, "Betting for tonight's tie-breaker match, the short track slide, will be open for the next thirty minutes." The video monitors hanging in the air above the track confirm the ruling by just showing a replay of Rachel gliding by and ever so slightly nudging a timer gate. But the light doesn't go off because she didn't lean in and hit the gate hard enough. It meant that they incurred a two-point penalty, enough to nullify the extra ring and crossing first. Had they known during the match they would have sent Rachel back to properly touch and clear the gate. Bishop and Rachel never brought it up with Justin, they didn't have to.

Rosalia was furious and laying into Justin. "How can you have missed that? I mean counting gates is the simplest thing you had to do!" It wasn't worth making him feel any worse than he did Bishop tried to calm his mother down.

"If you want to be mad at anyone go give that cheater Laughlin a taste of your ire," Justin suggested. Hasboro agreed and led Rosalia toward the racer's medical tent.

"Better get you patched up too, Bishop, while we are there."

They both knew there was nothing to be done about his eyes; they would forever stand out and mark the pair. Dark opals for the father, and white pearls for the son. But the thought that someone would at least look at Bishop was a small comfort to Rosalia as they entered the medical tent.

Kitteridge and his drones had been preparing for the unlikely event of a tie and the race organizer had him set up something special. The bottom-most track, closest to the Platform, shrinks down as you see some drones peel away from the base. The race is to be decided on a very short, all out, run as if your life depended upon it, because the special surprise tonight at Derby Days was not that there was to be a tie-breaker but that it would be a race to the death. To confirm and inform all audience and the racers of the seriousness of the final match large steel walls covered with four-to-six jagged spikes rise up from the surface of the track. There are two walls of death. One is behind the starting line and the other lies in wait in just beyond the finishing line. Both block the way and the racers have to enter the track from the side gates. The fans took the new setup all in: a quarter-mile straightaway that is sure to leave you pierced and hanging from a spike. The strategy would be interesting. Run straight ahead as fast as you can and the momentum from your maglev slide would surely push you into the spiked wall. Or stick around too long and either your opponent takes a small step just to cross and win, or the spiked wall closing in behind you is your next worry. "The distance started at a quarter-mile long but as soon as the race starts the walls will ratchet closed just a few feet at a time. It will be slow at first but then will gradually speed up until it runs both racers through," says the announcer as he explains the new rules.

"I have made my decision and it was an easy one. It will

obviously be The Ghost vs. Paxton for the finale. Bishop is in no place to race, maybe ever again," Justin told the group and they all agreed it was the right decision. Rachel was indeed faster than Bishop in the straightaways and Paxton was almost just as fast. Hasboro, Rosalia, and Bishop wish her well as he rubs at his left eye where the crystal had lodged itself from Laughlin's underhanded throw.

They had come back from the medical tent because the visit to Laughlin was a quick one. He had lost too much blood from the constant barrage of blows from Bishop. Rosalia thought that justified the matter and refused to say anything more about the subject to anyone again. If that Derby Days final race ever came up in conversation Rosalia would loudly declare, "Laughlin got what he deserved when justice was served by my son Bishop!"

And anyone within ear shot would quickly drop the matter when Hasboro stepped in to save anyone from a verbal tongue lashing from his Rosalia with a "So, thirty-four degrees tomorrow again you think?"

Paxton comes out of her tent, an image of grim determination. She nods to Rachel and takes her place at the starting line. Rachel adjusts her maglev boots ensuring they are tight and will give her the support she needs to really lean into her strides. The Ghost is the fastest racer on the planet at the quarter-mile sprint, she has invented and mastered a one-two-three step sequence that builds up incredible momentum and speed. Rachel usually won most races by a clear and wide margin as she was usually pushed by the bumpers at over a hundred and twelve mph. But Rachel and Justin had been trying to wrap their heads around this new course. It was the short track all right, just fourteen big pumps with her muscular legs and it would be done. Tonight must require a different tactic though because with an all-out sprint she won't be able to stop herself from connecting with the spiked wall. She wasn't exactly sure what the right move was going to be and Bishop had an idea as he explained, "Just listen for my voice and I will tell you when to step forward and when to jump back." Justin had a simpler plan and he wanted Rachel to borrow Bishop's nunchucks and as soon as the race gun goes off just beat Paxton into submission. Even though she was still not entirely sure of this new strategy Rachel had agreed to keep the comms channel open. She normally closed it down and preferred the silence. There just wasn't time for any instructions on the short track and she liked the idea that it was just her with her thoughts on the track.

The gun goes off and neither racer moves an inch. For a long crowd-on-their-feet period of seconds both of them just stared ahead. They were both not entirely sure what to do about those spikes ahead and behind them. "See if she goes for it, Rache," Bishop tells her over her headset comms. The Ghost swings her cape wide to show her opponent that she has her teammates nunchucks, still smeared wet from Laughlin's blood. It was Darrenhoe's idea to train with them and Rachel was good. She makes a quick little demonstration of her skills and gives the nunchucks a final turn before sheathing them by holding one end in her armpit and the other held vertical in her outstretched fist and pulls the chain to its full extension as she juts her arm out in front of her. Darrenhoe was a good teacher and the crowd went wild. Enough with the theatrics and just start wailing on her, Justin instructed her. But the display was just to let Paxton know she had the skills to wield the weapon. But instead of attacking, Rachel raises the chucks up over her head and then promptly throws them off the track and over the Platform. Paxton seems to understand and agrees to play along. This race will be decided by

346

something other than unbridled violence because they both had just about enough of that. Paxton nods to Rachel and drops her sai blades over the edge.

"Ok great she's in, now time for your first move. Take one small slide forward and then stop and turn around to face her," Bishop said over the comms channel.

"What? Dude that's the dumbest thing I ever heard you say. Ghost, listen to me, this is your husband Justin. Go and go now, I don't know what you think you are waiting for but those spikes do not look forgiving. Run, Rachel, go now and she won't be able to respond in time. If you wait she is bound to take off and will have the jump, and legs, on you. RUN I SAID!" Rachel shakes her head at the order and instead tries to follow Bishop's plan and takes a small slide-step forward and then pushes her heel down to stop. Paxton is confused at first, but the sound of the spiked wall coming at her pushed her forward, and she takes her place at Rachel's side.

"This part is critical; you have to make her take the next two steps. If you do one you will be off count and will walk right into those spikes," Bishop tells her and waiting is the hardest part for her. The short track was supposed to be all about speed but now it was all about waiting and strategy. Paxton hesitates and does the math in her head; it's like picking the petals off a flower… she steps forward because she loves me, she steps backward because she doesn't. Backward seems like a good idea but the wall practically pressing up against her makes Paxton reconsider her plan. The Ghost is one hundred percent Zen now, waiting and watching for Paxton to move.

"OH MY GAWD GO!" The crowd took up the cheer all together and it quickly became a recurring chant. Paxton is distracted by the sounds and when she hears the wall behind her whir into motion she breaks the spell and steps forward, or rather side steps and shuttle slides. Maglev sliding is all about long strides that gobble up the course. Even just a slight push off the heels of your maglevs would hover you forward two-to-three feet. But it was possible to break the magnetic tension between the two boots and make a single solid step. The boots weren't designed to move sideways like a crab and the resulting shuttering of force makes balancing terribly difficult. It wasn't an all-out leg-pump fest, but the racers both got their leg-day workout equivalent tonight on this final surprise course.

"Again, Rachel, your turn, nice and small," Bishop tells her and she does. One quick step forward, thighs quaking and shivering to balance upright, and she motions toward Paxton. The steel wall in front of them complies as well and Paxton steps forward just as the spikes do and shorten the track.

Eight steps remaining before the front spiked wall closes in on the racers and Kitteridge takes over. He is following along with their new strategy and knows Bishop cannot see well enough to guide her without impaling her. Kitteridge takes to the comms channel and encourages Rachel to take the next step. Seven more to go as she looks back at Paxton to follow suit. Paxton hesitates at first, clearly sensing the new step-by-step game they are playing instead of racing. The spikes are moving independently, sometimes the front wall creeps ever so close and reduces the distance to the finish line, making an all-out sprint to a first place finish a deadly conclusion. Other times the back wall starts moving and closing in behind them. One thing that is clear is that the walls are moving in faster now. Paxton is moved forward one step and then when she hears the wall narrowing the gap behind them she moves one step backward and then another forward. Rachel is ready and starts to step but Kitteridge whispers for her to stop and just hover in place for a bit and she does. Paxton responds by joining The Ghost and matches the hover only a few feet away, but Paxton is careful to maintain the imaginary line that binds the two together.

Rachel takes a small step backwards per Kitteridge's play-by-play calls. He has taken over the mic from the rest of the team and make it clear he was the only one with a plan and was going to see his daughter through this. Justin protested at first showing a false sense of bravado. It was clearly a display for the interns' attention. But the bigger man in Darrenhoe made it clear with one steely gaze that only Kitteridge had the comms now and he was going to walk Rachel through their new strategy for this tie-breaker event. Rosalia is still trying to play nursemaid to her son but he keeps pushing her off. Hasboro notices Bishop continually rubbing at his left eye where the crystal had lodged itself and would swear later that he thought he saw Bishop wipe away droplets of blood with his scarf. One look at the crimson stains spreading on his competition scarf confirmed it.

Two more steps forward both initiated from Paxton and clearly patience was not her strong suit. Four steps from the finish line and the back wall closes in a few more feet. Paxton and Rachel are now hovering in place sharing the ever more narrow space on the short new track between the fatal walls. Bishop has begun to cough a little bit and when he is not distracted by the race and the fate of his partner alternates between long drawn-out clearings of the throat and rubbing, no clutching now, the space under his left eye. The dilithium spore is continuing to heat up the area on Bishop's face and it seems with every heartbeat that delivers fresh blood it is fuel to the raging fire going on inside his skull.

"Now quickly drop to the Platform and take your starting

stance. Yes that's it. She is going to follow I guarantee it, she will be worried you will simply sprint the last few steps and beat her outright. But you have to wait for her to stop hovering if this is going to work."

The back wall has closed the gap to the starting line where Rachel is crouched just a few precious feet in front of it. She looks briefly back over her shoulder and sees Paxton drop down to the Platform. She is straining with all her willpower not to spring forward, it is only four or five strides; she is so close she can almost smell and taste victory, if she could smell. "Okay, now take a big step backwards and get situated in your starting stance again."

"That wall is awfully close," Rebecca whispers to Kitteridge and he agrees.

Darrenhoe overhears and leans in with an, "I think that's the idea." Paxton seems more afraid of the back wall than the front, she seems to jump forward every time it kicks into motion. And that was exactly what Bishop was counting on. Rosalia squeezes Hasboro by the hand and points to Bishop who has his head in his hands and is messing with that eye. After a few moments he looks up and makes eye contact with Hasboro, and then Rosalia. They can both see the peppermint candy-like swirls in his eyes, the mix of blood on top of the white under-eyelids, only the mix in Bishop's eye was all twisted, like the maker forgot which way the red candy swirl was supposed to go halfway, and then started the other way.

"One more step backward, Rachel," Kitteridge commands but she hesitates and complains.

"Any closer and if that wall moves again I am shish kabob!"

"The race will be over by then, trust me. That girl is all wound up and ready to slide," Kitteridge replies. The Ghost takes a slow and deliberate back step slightly beyond the reach of the spikes. Paxton does exactly as predicted and moves a step forward, just three big pushes and she wins the race. Rachel is too many steps behind. If Paxton can overcome her fear and simply slide ahead without stopping she would win. But stopping is the point tonight, you can't just break through the finish line at the speed of sound or you will be torn to shreds by the front spikes. But you can't wait around forever either with the back walls offering equal comfort and forever's dark solace.

"Okay, on my mark I want everyone to scream together 'Now', okay?" Kitteridge has asked the team to rally together and help with one last instruction. "Take your stance," he tells Rachel, "and when I say so start to hover and act like you are going to sprint. You have to get into it, kiddo, really exaggerate it, she must be convinced and buy it for this to work. Sell it with everything you got." Paxton is clearly agitated and still can't get her mind over the fact that they are not racing, this is a different event. But Paxton wants speed and all eyes are on The Ghost including hers. They watch as Rachel takes big motions and slowly begins to crouch down and no one is watching closer than Paxton. The Ghost takes her position and waits to see what Paxton does. Paxton quickly follows suit and retakes her starting stance. Let her sweat it out says Kitteridge, wait for the walls to move again. As the sound of the spikes behind them kick in Paxton involuntarily flinches a step forward and falters a little in her stance. Kitteridge and Darrenhoe both recognize the stutter, get her now while she's off guard, and Darrenhoe acknowledges the timing with a quick nod over to Kitteridge.

"NOW!" The screams break through the silence, so loud that even Paxton hears it, which is exactly what Bishop and Kitteridge had been hoping for.

"Okay, Rache, time to do your thing, stay in your starting stance and hover up on your maglevs," she hears through the comms and does just that. The Ghost reaches maximum levitation and hovers just waiting to see how her opponent will respond as her legs shake to maintain balance that high. Paxton is sure that Rachel is about to make a break for it, everything from her starting stance position to her hovering height signaled the move. And Paxton knew that if The Ghost got just a single stride ahead of her there was no way she could catch her, there just wasn't enough track left. Paxton can't wait any longer and decides that this is going to be a footrace after all. Paxton had decided she had enough of this step forward step back nonsense. Paxton quickly reaches maximum hover and still in her stance doesn't hesitate, she takes off at full speed, sure she can beat Rachel to the punch.

"Don't chase her, kiddo, you've already won," Kitteridge tells her and she lowers down to the Platform, completely relaxed now as she watches Paxton surge forward. Almost as soon as she does Paxton realizes her mistake. She is only two strides from the finish line and tries to slow her forward progress. But she cannot and the forward spiked wall moves a few feet to meet her. Paxton wails out and flings her arms and legs forward to try and push back the wall. But she is immediately impaled as the crowd watches, not a sound amongst them. Paxton is pinned to the wall and quickly bleeding out onto the Platform. Some drones come forward from the sides and begin the gruesome process of cutting her free. Rachel takes the few steps toward the sideline gates and steps off the track to meet her teammates, all huddling and cheering her on. Rachel makes her way to the post-race medical tent to check on Bishop.

*

The crowd quickly disperses and jams the queues at the betting booths; everyone now trying to collect. All the Derby Days events, those days-long competitions and celebrations, years of preparation, practice, anticipation, and havoc came to a close tonight. Most people are hoarding their credits now hoping to bribe and buy their way to Tranquility Base. Some have already started their Puff party to end all binges because they never really thought that they would make the trip. They just want to try out the new cinnamon bun, they say it might be getting there, close now, you can trust me, been doing this a long time.

But no matter how they were preparing for their Interval everyone on this planet was preparing for something tomorrow. They have been sucking life away from their ROPU hoses, breath by little breath, over these last four hundred and forty-one million seconds. After fourteen years of struggle on this forsaken Platform and now the ultimate next test is coming for everyone, ready or not. All the camaraderie from the fans has all disappeared as everyone turns inside themselves and makes their way home to prepare. You're not supposed to be able to bring anything to Tranquility Base but then again passengers have been trying to stuff full size bags into the overhead compartments as long as storage space has been limited. And on these trips there was no room for luggage. In fact, there wasn't even enough room for everyone to even take the trip. The horrible and always efficient selection process would take place tomorrow. The waiting of a lifetime came down to three minutes and thirty-one seconds, an Interval. And they would all take place tomorrow.

Chapter 24

441,504,000: Intervals before Trip to Tranquility Base

"I am not gonna make it, Rachel," Darrenhoe tells her as he pulls her close and wraps her in his cape. He has been dreading this and now the night was finally here. Darrenhoe was utterly convinced as to how this was going to work out for him. Rachel is persistent and keeps trying to use her own experience, her very public Interval out on the track. "I have done everything in my power to keep you safe. But my time is up…"

"Don't say that!" Rachel cries out and begins to sob. She had become so close to her bodyguard that she couldn't imagine a life on Tranquility Base without him. She only wished Kitteridge were here, he always seemed to know just what to suggest. Rachel hasn't seen him since the post-race presser, no doubt still busy with finishing up the Derby Days cleanup but also finishing the last-minute preparations for Tranquility Base. Rachel had been on Kitteridge to come up with, or at least share with her, his plans for the trip. Kitteridge dismisses any opening on the topic and just said he had something going and that it was enough for both of them.

Everyone is awake throughout the night, worrying, pacing, praying, really any way to try and make peace with an outcome you cannot predict or control. Even the die-hard Puffers are up, shuffling about scrounging through all the discarded Puff tubes that litter the Derby Days grounds, looking for a little hit left. The Transportation Center is full of people making their way back to their own DZs to prepare for their Interval. In just a few short hours the entire Derby Days event series will be nothing more than a memory for these people. Kitteridge's drone army makes quick work of the cleanup. It is more of a tear down and sweep out really, as a big section of event space, racetracks, abandoned betting booths, discarded Puff tubes, and even the occasional dead body were all simply pushed off the nearest edge of the Platform. What had taken years of preparation and planning was gone in a single evening in an efficient series of little dust clouds as the massive event disappears under the Platform.

There is the usual gathering at the convention center as husbands and wives all huddled in masses to experience the Interval together. Perhaps because everyone had to go through it, but very few people kept their Intervals to themselves, after all they just didn't see the point. After those terribly long three and a half minutes you were either alive and still hoping to go to Tranquility Base, or there was nothing left of you to worry. If you are dead, who cares what the neighbors think?

"Besides, you don't need me any more. Now that Derby Days is done you will be able to live out the rest of your life in peace. CDCG handlers won't be trying to convince you to take a dive in the next race so their guy can bump up a few notches in the ranks, fanboys won't swarm you at the TC, and just think, babe…" Darrenhoe kept talking, just a spew of diarrhea from the mouth. Words and incomplete sentences flowing out non-stop; he did that when he was nervous. The only thing Rachel had left with him was potentially a few precious minutes and all Darrenhoe could do was wonder out loud which of the interns was going to pass.

All across the DZ alarms started going off all at once: wrist watches, custom-built timers, wall clocks and clock towers all signaled that the Interval was starting. All everyone had to do now was wait. Those fourteen-year-old ROPUs had all stopped working in unison because their dilithium crystals all dried up and were no longer purifying the air. Some characteristically brave souls stood with their hoses hanging out of their noses for likely the first time ever, still like steadfast little soldiers awaiting orders, only they were waiting to see if it was okay to breathe again. As the seconds ticked away, more than a few of those change their minds and shamefully put their hose back in their nose. They join the countless others doing the same and even some join those who are now clutching their hose between two clenched fists around their face, sucking in huge breaths of air, as if that made any difference in the end. Sirens are still blaring out like big metronomes keeping track of the ominous soundtrack to life on this planet.

Rachel has already passed her Interval, but now she must take her turn and watch and wait helplessly for the fate of the others. She is standing close by her teammate Bishop and she is holding hands with Darrenhoe. She managed to convince him to stop talking with a slow kiss and he stands silently watching the former StatStar struggle to hold on. Bishop's eyes are completely clouded over with streaks of blood cast against his pale opalescent under-eyelids. Poor guy can't even see shadows and shapes any more, just a world of crimson and white. His prognosis is unclear at best, the dilithium has lodged itself in his skull just under the left eye, where it sits and constantly burns and plagues Bishop. It is a constant painful annoyance, like an itch under a full cast that, try as he might, cannot reach even with a long straightened out coat hanger wire to scratch. No one can say how long until the side effects of the dilithium lodged under his skin will poison him from the inside out; not long now, they say, trust me, been doing this a long time now.

Rosalia and Hasboro have decided to sit this Interval out, they have seen enough succumb in the past already. She has new purpose now, to care for her son, Bishop will need her now more than ever. Rosalia doesn't care how long he has left because she knows she will do everything to make it as good as can be. Hasboro is more optimistic, he has been successfully battling back the side effects of dilithium poisoning for years. Rosalia didn't like the idea of the dandelion ritual Hasboro did, but there was no denying its benefits. Hasboro had tried many times to get her into it, but she just wouldn't do it. Finally, after watching a demonstration at one of the Derby Days qualifier's Puff symposiums, Hasboro had distilled the recipe down and was able to make swallowable capsules for her. She took them regularly and insisted she felt better than ever. Hasboro was busy tinkering away in his head with new forms to deliver the dandelion potion, perhaps in an eyedrop form would work best for Bishop, he thought as Rosalia quietly worked away at getting the compound ready for Bishop's return. "If he passes," Hasboro gravely reminds her. But the thought that Bishop wouldn't pass his Interval never once crossed her mind, she simply wouldn't allow it.

Less than one minute remains and everyone begins to start holding their breath, still holding on to the notion that if they are going to stop breathing soon, better get it all in now and hold on to it. But no amount of deep breathing exercise is going to hold out here, not tonight. Couples are seen hugging each other closer and closer as the seconds continue to burn into the night. Even the most curious amongst them are deeply introspective now.

Everyone is a hero in their own story but even the most confident begins to question their ability to pass this test with just thirty seconds left to go. Having thoroughly convinced themselves that for them it was nothing, everyone else's ROPUs that started sputtering months or weeks ago were a problem, but their own wheezing device was just fine. But it never was.

"Stop. Please. Just stop talking, you're going to need all your air here real soon." Darrenhoe had started his nervous chatter again and Rachel just couldn't hear more of it. Justin and his gaggle of interns are all huddled together in a big group. They had been hanging out and partying ever since Derby Days started actually, and they saw their Intervals as no time to quit. Profant had tried to convince them all to come with him and Puff the time away; go out with a bang if that's how your gonna go, he kept saying. Surprisingly, and disappointedly for at least a few of the more hardcore partiers amongst the interns, Justin had opted out. Said he wanted to be present for these last moments and "…just, like, take it all in, man." Rachel was glad he had decided to stick around for she still loved and cared about him. They had discussed it many times over; if they both pass and make it to Tranquility Base then they would get an official divorce. It was a simple formality for them because they had been living separate lives with other lovers for more than just a few seconds now. Just because she didn't want to be with him and him alone that didn't mean she didn't still want him around. Justin was an important part of her life here and she would love that to be the case in her next chapters as well. "Just don't buy my seat, man," Justin tells Kitteridge, deadly serious. Years of Kitteridge dismissing Tranquility Base and teasing Justin that he had enough money to buy out all the seats just so Justin can't go. Kitteridge was playing around of course as he never intended to go to Tranquility Base himself much less prevent others from going. Kitteridge had other plans for himself, and for Rachel. He didn't mention anything to Rachel, for all she thought he really was planning to buy a seat for himself. Everyone knew he had the credits for it but couldn't be sure; you could never really iron out a clear purchase price, seems everyone needed a cut just to talk about it.

Under ten seconds to go and many in the throng begin to chant and call out loud each passing second. As the numbers roll off Justin and his interns enclose their circle a little tighter, everyone joining hands and leaning in. Rebecca, Rosalia and Hasboro's favorite intern, is sitting just slightly out of the circle and scanning the crowds. She is looking for Darrenhoe to see how he fares. She heard his ROPU start to sputter a day or so ago. It was just after the screwdriver races, and it could have been just noise from the competition tables still going. But whatever it was, he had heard it too. Rebecca saw the worry in his eyes when she approached him that night. He shrugged it off and said it was nothing. She didn't want to make him more nervous than he already was; besides there was nothing either of them could do about it. As she walked away from his tent that night, she could swear she saw him take his ROPU off from under his cape and begin to examine every inch. At last Rebecca sees Darrenhoe in the crowd but his back is to her and all she can see is Rachel with her head bowed down and resting on his chest while the final seconds tick bye. As the last second fades away and the last final chime of every alarm sounds the entire planet takes in one big collective last breath through their ROPU hoses.

Slowly but surely, everyone expels the final bit of stored oxygen in their lungs and cannot wait any longer. Involuntarily they all take their turn at taking one small, tiny little sip of air. Most people still clutch and cling to the hose in their nose while they consume tiny breathes though they know their ROPU is done for. Some can hold out longer than others, but eventually they all need air and once they try and take that first breath without a ventilator the eyes say it all from there. Justin opens his in the nick of time to see almost all the interns wide-eyed in terror. He jams his eyes tightly shut pushing back the sounds of screaming coming through choked coughs from his ladies. Justin's fate is quicker than most and Rachel was happy for that. Anyone close enough would be able to quickly see that the interns are not going to make it. They are all gasping for air, trying to dearly hold on and make every stinging swallow of oxygen last. But each one is more horrible than the last. The interns all hold hands together and make their tight circle even smaller, encircling Justin in the middle. They all bow their heads together and blood begins to seep out of their eyes and noses. Rebecca has her head hung low but is still moving side to side scanning for other possible survivors. She isn't sure for how long, but Rebecca has passed her Interval and is able to breathe on her own. As the rest of the party loses their brief but intense fight against the dilithium crystals Rebecca slowly rises to her feet. The same powerful gemstones that have been powering their ROPUs and keeping them alive all this time had turned against them. The crystal spores embed themselves in the airways and passageways of the body. The little nuggets burn hot, and the crystals heat up and melt you from the insides out. Rebecca scans the area looking for survivors to join up with. She sees Bishop still in his medical tent with Rachel and Darrenhoe standing bye. Rebecca passes them and makes her way off to see Hasboro and Rosalia, they will no doubt be looking for her and wanting to know how her Interval went.

Darrenhoe is still standing strong and holding Rachel tight.

His years of training, meditation, and deep breathing exercise allows him to fake it longer than most. Rachel looks up at him and he gives her a reassuring nod. She plays along, she can tell he is still holding his breath. Darrenhoe hasn't passed his Interval, not yet, he is just delaying it. Rachel holds him tighter, and he squeezes back with enough force to calm her a little bit. They are both watching Bishop now and are happy that he has been medicated into a deep and restful coma to try and help his body fight off the dilithium infection. Bishop's lungs give a continual gentle rise and fall showing that he is breathing without his now defunct ROPU. Rachel breathes a sigh of relief and notices Darrenhoe doesn't match her because he is still holding out. Rachel lets him hang on and she hangs on to him for all she's worth. Rachel knows that Rosalia and Hasboro will be coming over later to bring Bishop to their home, his new home. If everything goes according to plan, then this will be the last time she ever sees her teammate and friend; she and Darrenhoe are going to Tranquility Base tomorrow. Overcome by emotion, over her own victorious Interval, the still unanswered fate of her lover, her husband and friends' deaths at their own failed Interval, all of it. It came rushing up all at once and overcame Rachel. She leans forward and gives an uncharacteristically warm and gentle kiss to her teammate's forehead. She knows he will stay here on this planet with Hasboro and Rosalia and won't be going to Tranquility Base. Ordinarily that would be good news, one more extra seat. But with so many dead and dying around her, with so many failing their tests, seat capacity surely wasn't going to be a problem. Plus, if Kitteridge was right, being selected for Tranquility Base might not be such a good thing after all.

With a low audible thud Rachel heard the fate of her lover before she saw it in his eyes. As Darrenhoe finally ran out of air and had to take in a breath Rachel could hear the dilithium crystal spore lodge in his throat. It caught there and immediately choked an already bloody cough out of him. Rachel didn't want to see his eyes; she knew what was happening to him already. Before he can say or do anything, Rachel rips the hose out of his nose and kisses him long and deep as she reaches up to cover his eyes. Darrenhoe kisses her back and then tears his head away as he coughs up more blood. This time it comes out steaming from the dilithium reaction deep inside of him. His strength fades quickly and Rachel cannot hold him upright any longer, so she gently lowers him down to a seated position and lays his head on her lap. She gentle strokes his hair as he takes on the agonizing business of succumbing to dilithium crystal poisoning. In a matter of minutes Rachel had just lost both her husband, her lover, and many of her friends.

Kitteridge arrives in the nick of time and once he finds Rachel and Darrenhoe he begins to work while whistling orders to drone 63 and another drone Kitteridge brought with him. He always travelled with 63, but it was also common to always see Kitteridge with multiple drones. He knows Rachel already passed her Interval but he is here to see if he can save Darrenhoe. "SIT HIM UP!" Kitteridge commands his daughter as he sweeps the man's cape away from him. Kitteridge rips the now defunct and dangling ROPU off Darrenhoe's back and begins to equip him with a new one. At the same time, he reaches into Darrenhoe's vest to get his comms device and hands it to Rachel as he instructs her to follow the prompts. New ROPU secured and hose back in place in Darrenhoe's nose. "Okay, here goes, kiddo," Kitteridge says as he reaches down into his satchel and brings out a Puff tube.

"No, not that, he hates that stuff!" Rachel begs but she knows

362

this is the only way – really what did either of them have to lose? Darrenhoe is already dead. If he should make it back to her somehow then he can be mad at Kitteridge for the rest of his second life, however long that might be. She can't okay it but steps away with a nod and doesn't stop it as Kitteridge jams the Puff tube into the modification slot and presses the trigger release. Just a single hit to get him up and running. A 'first timer' with extra peppercorns would do.

Darrenhoe immediately springs to life and jumps to his feet ready for battle. Rachel looks up from the commotion to see her father helping steady her Darrenhoe on his feet. She is frozen in place, not sure how Darrenhoe is going to react to the Puff resurrection. He is immediately awakened with no apparent side effects other than the fact that his clothes are drenched, and he looks like hell for the first time in his life. But the Puff saved him, or rather brought him back, and he is forever grateful. Darrenhoe embraces Kitteridge and thanks him, as Darrenhoe's new drone companion settles in to keep watch over his new ROPU. Kitteridge takes in the moment but only for a second. He had more ROPUs and drones to distribute. He knew he couldn't save them all, not this Tranquility Base, but he could hopefully save a few.

Hasboro, Rosalia, and Rebecca come running in to help. Kitteridge had sent an army of drones over to their compound with instructions on how they could help save the people of DZ: 23N. They begin to distribute and equip the nearest person that had recently failed their Interval. The picking was easy as people were dead or nearly done dying everywhere. By the end of the evening, with everyone helping their neighbors with their new ROPUs and helper drones many lives were restored. Couples were matched back up and given new hope and life. Kitteridge's discovery and risk that these drones could help more than just him had paid off. But despite their efforts still millions die across the DZs tonight, failed Interval after failed Interval. They can't save everyone, too many like Justin and the interns, were already too far gone. Kitteridge had a plan that would save future generations. Another set is scheduled to arrive shortly, just a few seconds now. Trust me, been doing this a long time.

Scenes like that play out at DZs all across this planet tonight. Ready or not the Interval had arrived. Husbands and wives had become widows, friends and neighbors separated, coworkers and spouses gone, the dilithium ravaged through most all of them. Only a precious few were immune and left to wonder what would happen next. Sure, they all had thought they would make it past their own Interval and even make it to Tranquility Base. The one thing that was certain was only a small fraction of the population was still alive to see Tranquility Base seat assignments tomorrow.

December 17, 2021 Winter Holiday Break Seattle, WA

"Ms. McKitteridge can you come see me after the bell please? The rest of you please have a safe, emphasis on safe, holidays. Don't forget too much of what I taught you though because we still have our social studies midterms to finish when you get back. And no Sophie you don't get extra credit for turning it in early – take a break, play with some toys, you're just barely a teenager. Now everyone, except you please, get out of here and Happy Holidays."

She approached her teacher's desk with her head held high for she knew she had completed the assignment, and went a little overboard maybe, but still she was always looking for extra credit. Everyone liked the drawings she turned in but no points for sketches and watercolors in Mr. H's class.

"Did you write this whole thing all by yourself, Rachel?" he asked her. He was tough but fair and didn't mind jumping right into the heart of the matter.

"Absolutely I did, sir," she quickly but respectfully fires right back.

"But how could you have, I just gave the class this writing assignment two weeks ago?" he wondered out loud.

"Well, I hit a bit of a creative wall filling out my sketchbook, and was between a few books, trying to read a bit ahead and see if any of them got interesting," she explained. "So, about October, after all the fall fishing is done and my dad and I are both looking for a winter hobby, something that could be done indoors," she goes on further.

"Still, Rachel, kiddo, even if you started writing in October that would be at least three or four hours a day if you spaced it out. I mean this thing took me hours to read."

"Wait… you read it all? The whole thing?" she demands to know. "In just a few hours?" Man, it must have really been a page-turner she thinks to herself, or Mr. H just skimmed it over.

But, no she could tell by the seriousness in his voice as he responds with a deadpan, "Absolutely I did, ma'am." He was mocking her phrase and throwing it back at her; says he is preparing her to be the captain of the debate team, or a career litigator. She keeps grinning and he smiles in a way that reveals he did indeed read it all in one sitting.

By this point she is grinning ear-to-ear, and she wants to go in for a big hug. She has been sharing her creative side through her art for years now, but this was different. Something about writing felt more personal, more vulnerable. Would people read what she thought and wrote down and think she was weird or disturbed? The piece was a little dark, she had to admit. Rachel continues the story as she tells him…

"Story? Let's be honest, girl, you wrote a full novel in just a little under three months."

"I didn't set out to do anything major really, just something to do in the dark winter days when the sky outside is nothing but black and the thick clouds below it cut the horizon into thirds. Yeah, rain on the ground and all around you in a little mist."

"What does Rosalia, I mean Mrs. Gonzalez your science teacher, what does she call that again? Cloud pee?"

"I believe the scientific name for it is 'pissing rain', not unlike the Londoners' 'raining cats and dogs' in their country," she recites. "'Rain on the ground, rain in the cloud, and nothing but darkness all day long.'"

"And while we are at it, let's tell the truth, it isn't really all that fun running around outside when it seems to always hover a constant thirty-four degrees!" he tells her, and they both laugh. Yeah, the Pacific NW made for a great novel writing locale no doubt, with its views of the Puget Sound and mountains, when and if they were not hidden behind the clouds. Young Ms. Kitteridge remembers when they moved here all those years ago her dad kept telling them that the view of Mt. Rainier was just something else. But they didn't see even a mountain tip until six months later. He also told her Seattle was good for IPAs, bicycles when it is warm and the summer days are nice and long, and as everyone knows it was great for software engineering. "Great weather for making software!" was a saying passed down from her grandfather about all the rain in Seattle. You needed something to do indoors. But she knows her teacher loves it around here, just like she does.

"So?" she asks, breaking the long silence. He is sitting at his desk and she had pulled up the guest chair to sit sideways a few feet catty-corner from his desk. Her middle-school writing assignment, rather her book he reminds her, is sitting on his lap. He keeps idly flipping through the pages, as if he wants to read her an excerpt. She wants to know if he thinks it is any good but doesn't quite yet have the courage to verbalize it. After all, he reads a lot and not just from her crummy classmates. She had seen for herself the pride they took in their work. If they had spent even half the time over Thanksgiving break writing the assignment that they knew was coming rather than customizing their skins on some insipid Xbox game, they would all be published authors by now. But she didn't fault them, she and her sister had their own electronic vices.

"We all do," Mr. H. agrees; he feels bad taking people's phones away, but they just can't use them during class. Plain and simple. "No, I don't care if your special Mumsie needs a way to call you and make sure you brought your lunch money," he would tell the class on the first day. "You are too grown up now to have to check in with mommy and daddy; you can go a few hours out on your own in this big scary world and nothing permanently scarring is going to happen to you. This is only middle school after all, just wait till high school if you think this is bad."

He hears her unspoken question as it now rattled about loudly in her head. Mr. H. is hesitating, he knows what she is after, she just wants him to give it to her and not have to ask it – she's more than earned it. He comes to and says, "Well, my lady, you have definitely aced this class. And with this alone we should be able to get you high school English credits to help you apply to any college you choose." He grins and gently reminds her that her math skills could use some work, and she might want to wait a little bit and see if she grows any taller because it would be better for her when she tries out for lacrosse in the spring if she wanted to make varsity her freshman year. More than anything Rachel had decided she just wanted someone to read her book all the way through. And her mom didn't count, she *had* to read it. He had read it all right, mission accomplished. But now she understands that deep down she has another need – she wants it to be good. Something you would want to read… maybe not a summer blockbuster in the making, and it wasn't going to be a classic studied in subsequent years at middle-schools like hers across the country, sitting there next to 'Catcher in the Rye'. But did you like reading it? Were you bored in parts? Did you root for anyone? Who did you hate more she wanted to know…

Profant was the worst but that Drew guy went out something awful. "Is Drew an old flame of yours?" he asks and she just giggles. She and her friends had told Mr. H. that they had promised their fathers they wouldn't date until they turned sixteen. He couldn't let her sit there staring at the book in his lap, her life's work at such a tender age, so he breaks the tension and leans back in his comfy chair with the squeaky third wheel.

"In your life you are going to have to face some difficult situations and make some really tough choices once in a while Rache," he confides in her.

"I know that," she replies, "everyone does, that's the way life is."

"Yes, but in your case, kiddo, it is going to be *you* that has to choose. You will need to decide if you will play to your strengths and live the life of an artist or give into your inner author and put down the written word," Mr. H. tells her. "Not many people get to choose their own path and you should know it can be both a blessing and a curse to be gifted. Everyone has their own uninformed opinion of how you should use your talents, but you are better than chasing someone else's lost childhood dreams. And one of life's first big disappointments is that you didn't write a good book, Rachel my dear," he says as he leans in and pulls his chair up a bit closer, no doubt for his famous 'serious talk' look. His dark eyes, a bit larger than their sockets in a way that reminds her of Kitteridge and Hasboro. The dark opals gently assure her, and she knows that he isn't teasing her – the book was great!

"You don't think it was too violent?" she wonders.

"Yeah I didn't want to say anything, but it was pretty intense out there on the Platform!" says Mr. H.

"Well you already see it every night on primetime TV. Come

on, kids! Let's finish up our TV dinners now that Jeopardy is over and see how many people get beheaded on the Simpsons," Rachel replied mockingly.

"Okay, good point," he concedes; why just last week he welcomed the class with a little juicy tidbit of TV sitcom trivia. He had read somewhere that if you added up all the medical bills from all of Homer's accidents and broken bones it would total more than $148 million dollars. Don't quote me on that number he remembers telling the class and had to agree. "...but you didn't have to hang that guy like a meat hook from that pronged ninja weapon. What was that called again?"

"Kusari-gama," she reminds him, "pretty cool if you ask me – good mid-range and up close, a double threat."

"Sounds like you stayed up too late a few nights watching Bruce Lee movies."

"I saw a documentary on the airplane back from Arizona," she admits with a smile as she takes a horse stance and throws a quick jab, cross, hook, uppercut. Quick applause from the man at the desk and she takes her seat again, just at the edge she is very excited. Plus, a book that got people talking, especially overly concerned helicopter moms who had nothing better to do than lobby their local politician, Mr. H. said that might be good for the book. No press is bad press they say. "Trust me, a little scandal sells even better than romance. Been doing this a long time. Trust me." She smirks and knows he recognized the phrase when he read it in the book, another nod to her mentor. "Just think of what all those desperate and complaining housewives did to raise the national attention and recognition of rap as an artful form of expression in the late '80s and early '90s."

"So what's next?" he needs to know, "and how can I help?"

"You're the first to read it actually," she says. "Perhaps you could go on a 'comma hunt' for me? Rephrase, reword, or just help me understand which ones are required and which ones I need to remove. Something tells me this software word processor is lousy with comma suggestions." She knows and tells him after her first draft she found 5,302 commas.

"No worries, I gotchu." And he high fives her. Mr. H. puts the manuscript in his leather satchel. "I'm thinking sequel, Rachel, I need to know more about Tranquility Base. I mean why aren't there more of them if they are so great? Surely an entire galaxy needs more than a single paradise to hope for?"

"Probably. Maybe. I am not sure yet. I keep thinking what the other Intervals and Platforms were like," she laments. "I mean I loved the process of it all, just the act of thinking wild thoughts and imagining characters, their secret thoughts and unmet desires, what would they do and who would they meet? I had to get all these thoughts out of my head, and no one was awake to talk to." She had been getting up around four or five a.m. without an alarm clock lately. "Must be seasonal," she told the teacher, "happens every winter. Go figure, if it is dark outside I am up. But thankfully I have found that writing has become my savior and release. All those people and their crazy antics don't just rattle and make a bunch of infernal racket up in my brain any more. When I get them written down and out on electronic paper that is. And when the fingers touch the keyboard the words just flow."

"As do the commas huh, kiddo?" he grins.

"See? Hunt them down and kill them, will you?" she begs him.

"Will do." He nods in agreement to the plan, and she lobbies back a quick tiny curtsy with her imaginary skirt. "Now, what about that sequel?"

371

"Not sure yet, still mulling it over. I might do something completely different altogether. Something that helps people better balance their work and life. A guide complete with strategies and tips to maximize both your time at work and away. It all starts by making conscious choices about the jobs you take: who you work for, who you work with, and what you work on. You get less and less choice the further you are in your career. And with the added pressures of life and family, many people can't keep up and burn out. When my dad got that persistent insomnia rather than take a year off, he thought a book like that might be something he could turn to for help he tells me." She hesitates but then continues, "My mom got worried when the nightmares started," Rachel told him.

"It got pretty bad there after he fell off the ladder, right?" he whispered to Rachel.

"Well, if by bad you mean he started seeing purple spots everywhere that weren't real."

"Scary stuff and I remember you mentioned that your dad had started hearing people?"

"Yeah I remember you telling me when you came back from that little three-week rest period for your dad. You sure were pretty mature and brave to help take care of him."

"He's much better now, but I can tell when he zones out and stares away that he has the same racing mind as me. And I know I can help him write it all down."

"That's great, Rache, what a fantastic father-daughter project, something to bond over. When you do this together you will create lifelong memories of working together and building something from scratch with the Old Man."

"Dad even has a name for his manuscript, a working title to pitch to the publishers under – Level Down to Level Up."

"Pretty catchy, Ms. McKitteridge, I would read that."

"Well he's hoping a lot of people do, he wants to retire in eleven years and settle down. He keeps telling me this book of ours will be his 'passive income'."

"Listen, sister, writing a whole book in three months doesn't sound very passive to me," Mr. H. says to Rachel.

"My dad says if it could generate even a little residual income that could help smooth things out in their golden years. Not so much make them rich, although that would be nice. But just something to give them more choices."

"Very sound financial planning from your parents, you could learn a thing or two."

"Speaking of titles… you got one for this beauty?" he asks.

"Tranquility Base!"

She's suddenly shy for some reason and he inquires as to why. "You're not just the first person to read it, sir, you're the only person to read it. I shared an excerpt or two, but you're the only one who knows. Only my best friend, my mom, and one other person I know who recently self-published a sci-fi novel know about this project of mine. And now you." She goes on, "All that violence, and there is some cursing in there. I only hinted at anything physical or romantic, as if the camera fades out to a scene of curtains billowing and blowing out the cottage window as the violins play out and the scene fades to black, key-hole lens in the middle and then narrowing down into black nothingness across the screen."

"See, that's the sort of imaginative detail that all your readers, are going to eat up. And surely some of them will dig the violence just as much as your DeathMatch crowds."

"Like I said before, it's nothing you haven't heard on The Simpsons these last twenty odd seasons. You could paint the town crimson with the filth that spews out of Bart's mouth. 'Don't have a cow man' isn't exactly swearing now is it?" she ponders aloud.

"Listen, before you go would you indulge me with a little reading of your own?" he wants to know.

"You want me to read to you? From this thing?" she asks, a little taken aback. She had been made to read out loud in front of the whole class before. But something about just reading to an audience of one felt scarier.

"Exactly! Just think of how much more engrossing it will be."

"Did you have something in mind, a particular chapter? The DeathMatch or screwdriver races? Maybe Darrenhoe's Interval again, that had potential to be heartbreaking."

"No, Rachel, something different for today. You have inspired me, and I want to share with you something that inspires me just as much. You know, the one thing that saddened me the most about your dystopian world was that there was no music. How awful that would be; a life without music would be miserable," he shares with her.

"Worse than no smells? Think of that cinnamon bun."

"Well, I can't argue with that, miss, your book is not to be read on an empty stomach that's for certain. I am leaving here and heading straight to the mall to visit the nearest Cinnabon and get me some bites. And no orange frosting, I agree that is an unholy concoction, an abomination against the Lord almighty."

She giggles but the perma-grin fades a little from her face. "Anyways it is some lyrics your father told me about. From a songwriter named Frank Turner. Your dad confided in me at the last parent teacher conference that this man's music really helped him through his recovery from the two surgeries to put back together his left arm. Promise me two things tonight, Ms.

McKitteridge: one that you will rest and relax this break, we have some American colonists and abolitionists to learn about when you all get back. Two and finally, most importantly, I want you to keep writing. Get to working on that sequel, or the business book with your dad. Whatever it is, keep writing and share them with me. They are great and you have too much potential to let your skills just wither on the vine at such a young and tender age. Take a little risk each day and write something, anything, down. And Rachel, one last thing before you go, a number three if you will. It is a great book, Rachel, really fun to read. Makes me think a Young Adult Reader audience would love it. Maybe you're the next Rick Riordan, or even the next J. R. R. Tolkien if you keep up with this word flow rate. Not an instant classic, but with your permission I would like to assign it as required reading for all the incoming eighth graders next summer."

"Oh absolutely that would be an honor." She blushes and shuffles her feet as the grin gets even wider.

"About that song, are you ready? It's called *I Knew Prufrock Before He Got Famous*."

I am sick and tired of people who are living on the B-list.

They're waiting to be famous and they're wondering why they do this.

And I know I'm not the one who is habitually optimistic,

But I'm the one who's got the microphone here so just remember this:

Life is about love, last minutes, and lost evenings,

About fire in our bellies and furtive little feelings,

And the aching amplitudes that set our needles all a-flickering,

And help us with remembering that the only thing that's left to do is live.

After all the loving and the losing, the heroes and the pioneers,

The only thing that's left to do is get another round in at the bar.

"I am a little too young to meet you at the bar, but I think I get the point." She grins.

"How's that for a little inspiration for you for Christmas? I was going to read it to the class today, but after reading your manuscript I wanted to save it just for you. When you get writer's-block or stumble on a plot twist and the words just don't flow like water, give that guy Frank Turner's album a go, the one called *Songbook,* all the songs are great. Now get out there and let's make some rock and roll!" He's glad she likes it and figures it is time to whip out the classic and give her the good ole signature Midwest knee-slapper 'it-is-a-fixing-to-be-about-darned-tootin-time-we-get-up-and-get-er-going-ma.' She gets the point, she has Aunts and Uncles, and everyone needs a way to get rid of annoying little cousins.

"Was there anything else you wanted? Something about class?" she reminds him. This last part of the conversation, as important and meaningful as it was, stood between these two and their winter holiday break. She grabs her backpack and puts on her jacket and then walks over to the coat rack and pulls out her rainboots from her cubby. She can't help but notice out of the corner of her eye as Mr. H. slings his messenger bag over his shoulder and around his waist, the one with her book in it for the comma hunt over break he promised her he would do, it rests gently and evenly balanced on his waist. She hands him his backpack and notices, probably not for the first time, the big black patch sewn on the front pronouncing he was all about seeking the high that came from a true, authentic Recreational Outdoor Purity Utopia. It is his ROPU she puts it together and she can never recall seeing him without it. The little camelback water hose he is always sipping on from that round Nalgene bottle, well, it looks just sort of like one of the ventilators. Rachel knew she was pulling names from her life for the characters in her book but apparently she was getting inspiration from all around her. Her Keyser Söze and his whiteboard from Skokie, Illinois.

The teacher notices her staring at his backpack and smiles, sees her looking at the bottom right corner of the blackboard behind him and lets her know that he thinks The Usual Suspects is a little too old for her. He rubs her head, pulling off her knit cap, and hands it back to her. "No wonder you slit Drew's throat. Man, I don't wanna see the guy who stands you up for Prom!" Rachel reaches for her umbrella, her constant protector against the mist outside this, and it seems every time of year. He snaps the clasp over his collarbone and secures his cape, just like the fuzzy winter one that Justin wore and reserved only for The Ghost. Yeah, for capes, she thinks and shares that it is the ultimate harsh weather fashion piece for the modern-day gentleman.

"Oh brother," she groans and brings her right hand up to smack her bare forehead. "I can't believe you brought that cane; I don't care if it did belong to James Brown, whoever that is…" she teases him.

"You know darn well who that is. And you know I am serious whenever we are talking 'bout music and the great Godfather of Soul. Show some respect while you're in my damn classroom," he demands in jest. She bows her head and gives him another schoolgirl curtsy with her imaginary uniformed skirt, plaid green and white of course, from Saint Thomas Agnatius Aquanis Arelias Academy for the Gifted and Socially Maladjusted School of Future Artsy and Science Stuff Facility, the private school for any kid that has been expelled from all the other schools in your tax district, that's the school no doubt. He spins around and takes a knee, and she knows what to do – all the boys do this after basketball practice. Mr. H. is the assistant coach, and she rolls her eyes and places the cape over his shoulder like a blanket. "Thank you, thank you very much," he mumbles, more Presley than Brown. There was a reason Mr. H. was everyone's favorite teach.

"Oh shoot! I still have shopping to do and there are nine days left till they close the malls for Christmas," she whines. She reaches out her hand, whoops always the right, her dad insisted, which was annoying because Rachel was left-handed. Rachel reaches out her OTHER hand, her military-left he would joke with her, for a handshake goodbye. She normally just gave him the 'whatz up homie' nod and bolted. But after what she had shared with him she thought it should be more official. He laughs and throws his head back as he pulls her in for a hug that they both needed, it had been a long pandemic and it felt good to be back into the company of other people, in-person and not online through some lagging video chat, exchanging, "You're on mute, Larry, again" and "Can you see my screen? How 'bout now? Whoops, sorry wrong monitor. Must be my new operating system update…" Those days were behind us now thankfully. Not everything was fully back to normal, but things were getting there. Human contact, not six feet apart social distancing nonsense, was back on the table.

Mr. H. opens the classroom door as the last and final bell goes off, the post-class-wrap-it-up-hug-your-sweetheart-no-kissing-and-leave-room-for-Jesus-now-its-a-running-time-boyoif-your-gonna-have-a-chance-of-making-your-bus-before-it-leaves bell. He makes a portside turn. He raises a hand from under his cape and bids her goodbye, yells out, "I will see you after break, kiddo, and don't stop writing!" She waves back and calls out her best Merry Christmas and turns around, but not before she spots Mr. H. peek into his satchel and then tap her book. Seems he didn't want to forget it and her eyes well up with emotion. She can't stop her smile from spreading. I dreamed it, took a risk, wrote it, shared it, he read it, and it was good!

He walks out of the old school building and into some more of that 'pissing rain' he had seen all morning and all day, and would have to tolerate all night, it coated every window in town. He uses the tattered key to unlock the driver's side door, has to actually physically insert it into the lock and turn it just the right way so the cylinder pops out of the Volkswagen Beetle's rusted door, yup that old. "Slug bug," he says out loud, but none of the faculty are around to hear him. The game just wasn't as fun, but his arm was a lot less sore without his twin brother wailing on him. "I think he invented the two-punches for a convertible bit." Mr. H. mumbles to himself. Not just because of his old beat-down jalopy that signaled a kids' pugilist road trip game, but the dedicated parking space reserved just for him was a clear giveaway. "Parking reserved for the coach of the middle-school high-stakes betting line setting and gambling club." It was signed, "CDCG." If that didn't tell you the owner of the designated spot and antiquated mode of transportation, then the custom license plate on the back and front surely did.

"Hasboro."

Fin

Epilogue

He knows by the sound of her approaching that his new bride is coming to check on him and to make sure he took his morning eye drops from Hasboro. Sitting lazily in his rocking chair Bishop is getting a slow start to his evening. He never forgets his pills and always eats a little extra Life[x] to help wash it down. Not so bad, he is alive and lets the warmth of the tea wake him up. Bishop doesn't like the taste of the tea she brews him, but it is the smell that bothers him. As the dilithium lodged inside of him was slowly dissolved by the dandelion tincture drops from Hasboro and Rosalia he began to develop, or rather redevelop, his sense of smell. And nothing on DZ: 23N smelled good to Bishop that's for sure. Bishop is now haunted by the horrible stench of this place. Rebecca lovingly sees to her husband's medical regimen and administration, and she continues to do so every day with care and dedication, making sure he never misses a dose.

Bishop's story continues as he develops and adapts to only four of the five senses. Like most who lose one of their senses, his others are somehow enhanced; his newly developed ear and yes even his sense of smell helps him navigate the world around him. Over time Bishop develops more names and meaning into the countless shades of white he sees. He comes up with more variations than Eskimos have for snow. His new drone buddy and ROPU help, the gentle taps on the shoulder make sure Bishop doesn't run into anything: a little trick Kitteridge had taught him.

Even though Bishop passed his Interval all those seconds back he needs the new modified ROPU to keep the stench of this place from overwhelming him. Even without his enhanced sense of smell Bishop could tell you that the maglev evacuators on this planet haven't been working for a long, long time. Bishop's modified unit is continuously topped off by his personal drone and little micro-doses of Puff are delivered on a regimented schedule. The effect is just enough to keep the olfactory overload of a lifetime of smells rushing in all at once, and Bishop's sanity, at bay.

Rebecca has been watching over him. Not that he could see her but with all his senses and especially his heart he knows she is with him. They both get regular visits from Hasboro and Rosalia. Bishop keeps busy with Rachel, covering shifts for fun they constantly push each other with their own private stats and rankings. They are handlers of their own now but run their own 'open-book betting' gig on the side. People like the novelty of it, nobody gets rich, but no one goes home with a broken nose and penniless either. When he is not coaching, Bishop likes to carve furniture out of compressed dilithium crystals. He is good at it and likes to give the pieces away, his specialty is rocking chairs. Bishop makes regular visits and donations with Kitteridge as he makes his rounds of the DZs checking on the drones and ROPUs he gives out. All the mothers here really appreciate how the gentle motion of the rocking chair gifts from Bishop soothes their infants growing inside. They rock back and forth and sing sweet songs of hope. Songs of Tranquility Base.